The Benghazi Affair

□ □ □ □ □

BOOKS BY STEVEN E. WILSON

Ghosts of Anatolia, An Epic Journey to Forgiveness
Foreword Reviews Book of the Year Gold Award
Fiction (multicultural), 2010

STONE WAVERLY TRILOGY:

Winter in Kandahar
Benjamin Franklin Award Finalist
Best New Voice in Fiction, 2004

Ascent from Darkness
Next Generation Indie Book Award Finalist
Action–Adventure, 2008

The Benghazi Affair

The Benghazi Affair

STEVEN E. WILSON

H-G BOOKS

The Benghazi Affair

Published in the United States by H-G Books.
Website: H-G-Books.com   SAN: 255–2434

First H-G Books Edition: 2018
Library of Congress Control Number: 2016942155
Print ISBN: 978-0-9829707-6-8
eBook ISBN: 978-0-9829707-1-3
Audiobook ISBN: 978-0-9829707-2-0

Editor: Lisa Poisso
Proofreader: Robin J. Samuels
Cover and page design: Janice Phelps Williams
Cover images:
　　Explosion © Ivan Cholakov | Dreamstime
　　Figure © Ostill | Can Stock Photo
　　Helicopter © Mysikrysa | Dreamstime
　　Lilies © Krandaev | iStock

MANUFACTURED IN THE UNITED STATES OF AMERICA

Wilson, Steven E. (Steven Eugene), 1951–

　　The Benghazi Affair / Steven E. Wilson. –
　　Cleveland, Ohio : H-G Books, c2018.
　　　　p. ; cm.
　　　　ISBN: 978–0–9829707–0–6

　　　　1. Libya—History—21st century—Fiction. 2. Action and
　　　　Adventure—Fiction. 3. Historical—General—Fiction. 4. War and
　　　　Military—Fiction.

To question is the essence of knowledge;
reticence is the foundation of ignorance

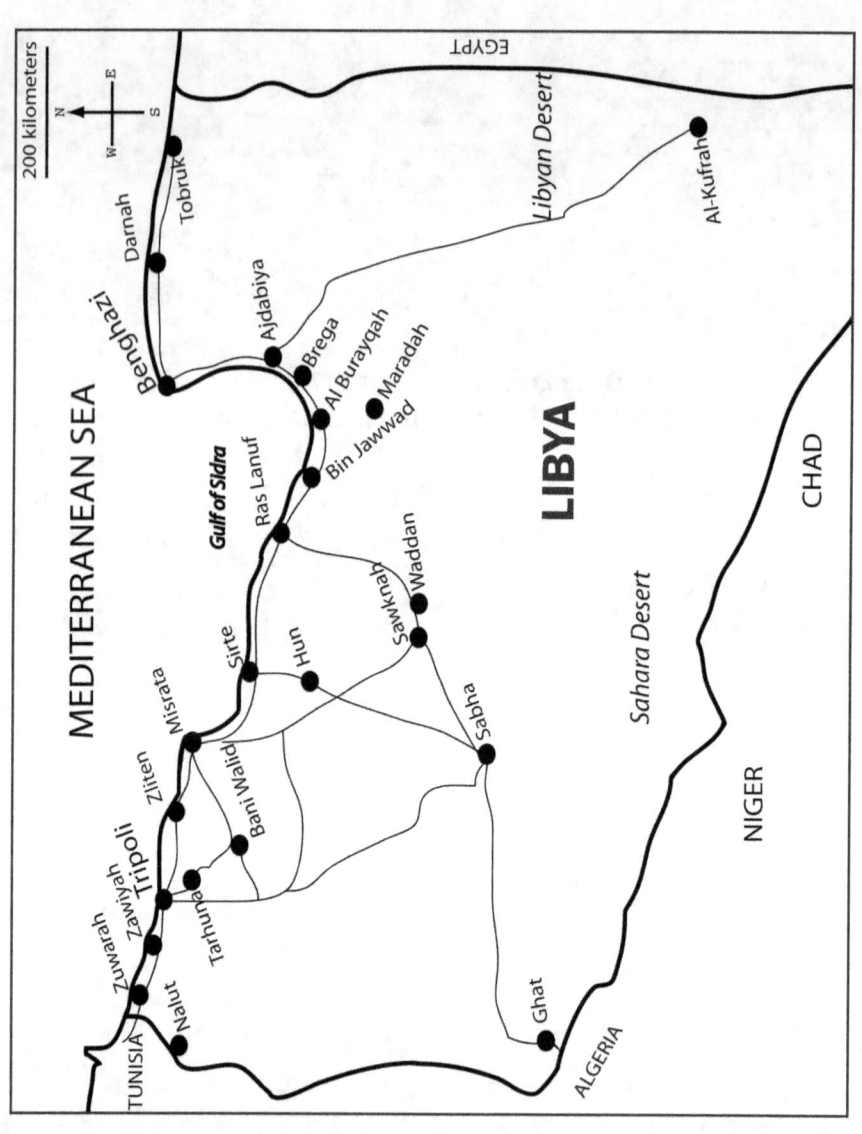

1

Tranquility

Why would someone fly into a building on purpose?" a boy called out from the back of the room. "Did they know they were going to die?"

Waverly sighed and pushed a tuft of hair back from his forehead. He leaned back on the edge of his big metal teacher's desk, and his eyes wandered over the innocent faces staring back attentively. "Well, Tommy, those young Arabs were all religious and very committed to their religion, and some bad men in Afghanistan used the strength of their beliefs to convince them that God wanted them to fly those planes into the World Trade Center and kill all those people. They believed that once they died doing this, they'd go to heaven and be rewarded with a better life there with God."

"Did those Arabs really go to heaven?" Tommy asked skeptically.

"I don't know," Waverly replied thoughtfully. "Nobody knows. What do you think?"

"I don't think they did. In the Bible, it says thou shall not kill, so I think they all went to hell."

A dark-complexioned boy at the side of the room tentatively raised his hand.

Waverly nodded at him. "Yes, Mohammed?"

"My father told me the Quran says that sometimes the killing of bad men can be justified, but never the killing of innocents like all of the people killed by the planes that hit those buildings."

"I think we can all agree on that," Waverly replied with a forlorn smile. "Those young Arab men believed strongly—strongly enough to give up their lives—that what they were doing was right. We don't in any way agree with what they did, but we can admire one thing about them, and that was their commitment to what they believed in. We have young American men and women who give up their lives, so we can have discussions like this without worrying that someone will hear and come to harm us or take us to jail."

He glanced at his watch and took a deep breath. "Well, boys, it's time for lunch. Be back here at twelve forty-five, and we'll watch a film about a real-life American hero, a football player and soldier named Pat Tillman."

The boys shot up from their desks and scrambled noisily out of the room while Waverly scooted into the chair behind his desk and retrieved a bag from a drawer. He unwrapped a sandwich and was lifting it to his mouth when he caught sight of a woman standing in the doorway.

"Marilyn!" He jumped up awkwardly from his seat. "My God, it's so good to see you. How are you?"

"I'm fine, Stone," Marilyn Harrison replied with a warm smile. "How are you?"

Why is she showing up here after all these years? He felt his hands begin to sweat. "Very well, thank you. I've got a great group of boys, and I'm finally feeling up to speed with my teaching."

She chuckled. "That's wonderful. And how are your little ones?"

"Mike and Anne are doing great, but they aren't so little anymore. I hired a strict English nanny to tutor them on their schoolwork and to help me get them to all their activities."

"Let's see, Mike must be a teenager now. Right?"

"That's right, thirteen next month. He's in the other seventh-grade class here at St. Christopher's, and he loves Roman history and playing hockey."

"Somehow that doesn't surprise me. And how's little Anne?"

"She's pretty good, considering. Julie's death hit us all very hard, but it was especially tough on Anne. She's gotten close to our nanny the past six months, and that's been a blessing."

Harrison's expression changed to concern. "Poor little dear. Where does she go to school?"

"She's in the second grade at St. Catherine's."

"Perfect. They'll take good care of her there."

"Please, have a seat," he said, pointing to a chair next to his desk. "Would you like half of my sandwich?"

She slipped into a chair. "No, thank you. I just ate. But please go ahead."

"We've got fresh coffee in the office."

"I just had a cup."

Waverly nodded, took a bite of his sandwich, and chewed for a moment as he regarded the prominent lines in Harrison's forehead and cheeks and around her eyes. "How's everything at the company?"

"Busy. You know, there's a new crisis every day."

"I can imagine. Tunisia, Egypt, Libya, and Syria—it's incredible. I never thought I'd live to see this all happen, this Arab Spring."

She nodded. "Actually, that's why I came to see you."

He took a sip of water from a bottle and stared down at a pile of papers on his desktop. "So, this isn't a social visit?"

"Of course. It's been far too long. Remember when I met you at the airport when you returned home from Syria and Iraq? I never imagined that would be the end of the line for the best specialized skills officer I've ever known."

He wrinkled his nose and crumpled his lunch bag. "Save your flattery. I'm grateful I could make a few contributions, but we both know about those other little untidy details that were expunged from my file—thanks to you, I might add."

She smiled wryly. "I really can't imagine what you're talking about. But the director asked me to come talk to you."

He took another gulp of water and stared steadfastly into her heavy-lidded eyes. "Tell him I said no."

"I know that above all else, you're a true patriot, just like the ones you were telling those young boys about. The only difference between you and Pat Tillman is you're still alive. Still able to serve."

"No."

"I'm not taking no for an answer. The company—"

"No, Marilyn. My kids need me, and for the rest of my life, they'll always come first."

She was undeterred. "And they'll still be first. At the most, your assignment will last six months."

He tossed his lunch bag into a trash can and stared back determinedly. "No. I'm happy here, and I'm not going back there."

"What do you mean, 'there'? I haven't told you where we need—"

"It doesn't matter." His voice cracked. "I mean any there: Afghanistan, Pakistan, Libya, Syria, Iraq, Katmandu—they're all the same. I'm not going back."

"Just hear me out. You lack only twenty-two months to qualify for the retirement benefits at the twenty-five-year level. The director will waive the rest if you serve for only six more months."

He rolled his eyes and chuckled. "You really are desperate."

She leaned over the desk. "Hell yes, we're desperate. With everything that's happened in Iraq, Egypt, Libya, and everywhere else, we ran out of Arabic-speaking operations officers a long time ago. Even the few we have don't have your special skills and experience. Half the Muslim world has plunged into turmoil, and it might well be the critical moment of the twenty-first century. Either that entire region will become a productive member of the international family of peaceful nations, or it will plunge into a churning chaos that will threaten the United States and the rest of the civilized world for the next hundred years."

He sighed deeply. *It's not my responsibility anymore. Stay firm.* "Marilyn—"

"Please just hear me out. Al-Qaeda is on the move in every one of those countries. You know that. Those bastards see what's happening in the Middle East and Africa as their great opportunity to eliminate the secular governments of the Islamic world once and for all and to establish the caliphate they've dreamed of for decades. What kind of world will this become if they're successful? Is that what you want for Mike and Anne's future?"

He glanced out the window for a long moment. "What about Luke Landers? Maybe he'll come out of retirement."

"We already thought of him, but he had a stroke."

His heart raced. "A stroke? When did that happen?"

"Last summer. The entire left side of his body was paralyzed. He's in a wheelchair."

It was hard to believe. Landers had just retired two years ago. Waverly got up from his desk, stepped across to the white board, and erased a list of ancient Roman cities written neatly in blue and red markers. He was doing just fine without full retirement benefits, wasn't he? Teaching had been a tough adjustment, but the boys loved him now. Sure, he was patriotic—Marilyn had that right. But he'd done his time. This wasn't his fight now.

He dropped the eraser cloth on the side table and faced her. "I'm sorry, but I won't go. I'm fifty-eight years old and for over twenty years, I gave everything to this country. I promised Julie just before she died that I'd take care of Mike and Anne, and I won't leave them. Even for six months."

"But you will be taking care of Mike and Anne. You'll be protecting their future here in America, as you were doing before they were even born."

He folded his arms. "Tell the director I won't go."

She stood up. "There's something else. Something critical. I can't discuss it here."

He shook his head. "I'm sorry."

She let out a deep sigh. "My dear friend, I really do understand. I told the director what you'd say, but he wanted me to ask anyway." She reached for his clammy hands. "Still friends?"

He nodded earnestly. "Still friends. You're the best friend I ever had at the company, and I haven't forgotten what you did for me."

The door opened behind her, and a pair of eyes peered at them through the opening.

He glanced up at the clock. It was 12:20. "Just a few more minutes, boys."

The door closed with a click.

She smiled. "Do those boys know what you did before you became their teacher?"

He shook his head and chuckled. "They think I've always been a teacher."

"Aren't you ever tempted to tell them bits and pieces about your service? You know, the unclassified stuff? I'm sure they'd be fascinated."

"I put that all behind me. I've never even told my son. That was my prior life, and I've been reincarnated into this new and happier one."

She nodded. "Goodbye. It's wonderful to see you so happy. Just give me a call if you ever need me to come over and babysit the kids. I'd be delighted to do it."

"Thank you—I just might do that. Don't be a stranger."

She kissed him on the cheek and walked to the door.

Doubt surged through him. "Marilyn?"

"Yes?"

"Where?"

"Where what?"

"Where did the director intend to send me? I mean, just out of curiosity."

She grinned. "It's still in your blood, isn't it?"

"No, it's not. I'm just curious."

"Benghazi."

His mind flashed a memory of a man lying motionless on the sand with a bullet hole in the middle of his forehead. He shuddered. "Libya. I was there once before. For just over a year."

She smiled. "That's a big reason the director thought of you—and the weather is nice there this time of year. You know how to reach me if you decide you want more details. Goodbye, my friend." She opened the door and stepped out into a gaggle of unruly boys.

"Benghazi," he whispered contemplatively.

The image of a large tent guarded by sentries flooded from his memory. Abruptly, the tent door opened, and a man wearing white robes and dark sunglasses ducked outside and strode toward him with several armed guards trailing behind. Beyond them, waves of heat rose from sand that stretched as far as the eye could see.

"Gaddafi," he whispered.

The din of a dozen boys yelling and laughing outside the open door snapped Waverly back to the present. "Come in, boys. Are you ready for the video?"

"Yes!" they cried out in unison, scrambling across the room like the emotions that rushed through his brain.

2

Dilemma

Waverly stuffed his briefcase into the trunk of his car and climbed into the driver's seat. A moment later, the front passenger door opened, and Mike slid his backpack under the dashboard and scooted in beside him.

"Hey, buddy, how was your day?" he asked, roughing the boy's hair.

"Great! I hit a double in PE."

"Give me a fist bump." He smacked Mike's knuckles, backed the car out of the parking space, and inched toward the exit. "Did Mr. Farrell show the Pat Tillman documentary?"

"Yeah, it was awesome! I can't believe another American soldier shot him by accident."

"Unfortunately, it happens sometimes. It's one of those terrible tragedies that occurs in war."

"Mr. Farrell said the military tried to cover it up. Why would they do that?"

"I don't think they tried to cover it up."

"That's what Mr. Farrell told us."

"Well, right after he was killed, there was confusion about what really happened. Those units were in the middle of the tallest mountains in Afghanistan, and I don't think the soldiers themselves were clear about how he died until the investigation was completed. I've got to believe our military leaders just wanted to be absolutely certain before they told his family."

"Well, Mr. Farrell thinks they tried to hide it. He used to be a sergeant in the National Guard, you know. Isn't that really cool?"

"That *is* cool." Waverly accelerated into traffic.

"Didn't you ever want to go into the army or the navy, or even the National Guard?"

"Well, I thought about it when I was younger, but after college I chose to do other things."

"Like what?"

His mouth went dry. "Like what?"

"Yeah. What did you do after you went to college?"

"Well, let's see. First, I thought about being a pastor of a church, but then I worked on a few things in the government to prepare myself to be a better teacher."

"That's *so* lame."

He grinned. "You think so?"

"Yeah, totally boring. I'm joining the Navy SEALs when I'm done with school."

"Oh, really?" Waverly shot him a sidelong glance. *Is he being serious?* "Where did you learn about the Navy SEALs?"

"From Joey Anderson. His brother has a really cool PS3 game called *Call of Duty: Black Ops.* He says the SEALs are the toughest Special Forces fighters, and I want to be a SEAL when I grow up."

"Well, you better get good grades in school and make sure you stay healthy. That's important if you want to be a Navy SEAL."

"I will, don't worry. Oh, I got an A on the algebra test."

"That's great. Keep up the good work."

They turned left past a little strip mall and drove into a neighborhood of older homes lined with maple trees. Waverly's mind chewed again on the conversation with Marilyn.

"Dad, who was that lady who came to meet with you at school today?"

"At school?" he repeated warily.

"During PE Tommy Ventura told me there was a lady talking to you at lunchtime."

"Oh, I guess I did have a visitor. She was just an old friend, someone I've known for a long, long time."

"Did she know Mom?"

"Boy, you're just full of questions. Yes, she knew your mother."

"Are you like dating her now?"

He guffawed. "No, I'm not dating her. Why would you ask that?"

"Tommy said she kissed you, and he told all the boys you have a new girlfriend."

He laughed again and shook his head. "Well, it's none of Tommy's business, but I don't have a girlfriend. Mrs. Harrison kissed me goodbye on the cheek. That's it. I haven't seen her in years before today, and we're certainly not dating."

"Is she going to visit you again?" Mike asked suspiciously.

He glanced at his son. "I don't think so, but if she does, we're just old friends. Okay?"

They drove for several blocks past middle class homes without speaking, each one lost in his own thoughts.

"Dad, do you think you'll ever get a girlfriend?"

Waverly was taken aback by the sincere innocence in his son's question. "I really hadn't thought about it. I don't have any plans to right now, and I haven't dated anyone since your mother died."

"I don't want you to date."

"You don't?"

"No." Mike picked at the sole of one Nike.

"Why not?"

"I just don't want you to. Anne would be upset."

Waverly smiled. "Since when did you start worrying about your sister?"

"She's my sister, isn't she? Now that I'm grown up, I should worry about her, right?"

"You always need to watch out for each other. I'll tell you what, if I ever think about dating, I'll talk to you and Anne about it first. Okay?"

"Okay," Mike muttered. He looked out the window at two boys tossing a baseball. "Hey look, Brad got his cast off. Can I play pickle?"

Waverly eased across the sidewalk and up to their garage door. "Just for a half hour. Then you need to come in and do your homework, okay?"

Mike was out of the car in an instant. "Okay!" He pulled a glove and baseball bat out of a bin by the garage and sprinted across the yard toward the next-door neighbor's house.

Waverly stepped around the car and fetched his briefcase from the trunk. He turned and smiled at Beatrice as she followed Anne up the driveway on her bike. "Hi, Anne."

"Hey, Daddy!" Her bike skidded to a halt inches from his leg. "I rode to Cathy's house all by myself. Beatrice didn't help me at all."

He winked at Beatrice. "Really? All by yourself?"

"Yes, all by myself."

"Excellent," he deadpanned. He squatted and kissed his cherub on her forehead.

"Daddy, can I have a puppy? Cathy down the street got a cockapoo puppy, and she's so cute."

"Well, I don't know about that. Let's discuss it at dinner. Okay?"

"Oh, please! She's so cuddly, and she licked me on the nose and let me dress her in a pink doggie sweater."

"We'll talk about it at dinner."

"Can we go eat breadsticks at Maggiano's for dinner? Please, Daddy?"

"Not tonight. You need to go in and practice your piano. Mrs. Flick will be here for your lesson in a few minutes."

"But I want breadsticks." Anne jumped off her bike and handed it to Beatrice.

"I cooked up a steak and vegetable pie, Mr. Waverly." Beatrice's shrill Cockney accent grated into the silence. "What time will you be taking your dinner, sir?"

"Let's plan to eat right after Anne's piano lesson."

"Right, sir. Will you be taking a spot of tea?"

"No, thank you. I'll be working on bills in my office."

"Great!" she said. "Please don't forget me paycheck. I'm bloody broke, and I'll be going out with me girlfriends Friday night."

"Broke already?" Waverly said. "There might be a need to fast-track that raise in your contract. I'll discuss it with you later." He hurried past the open-mouthed Beatrice and closed the door behind him.

Waverly patted Mike on the shoulder and sat at the head of the table as Beatrice stepped into the dining room carrying a large casserole dish. She set it in front of Waverly and took her seat.

"Where's Anne?" Waverly asked with a hint of irritation.

Beatrice rolled her eyes. "She's in the bathroom."

"Why is it she always seems to go to the bathroom just when dinner is ready?"

"Sorry, sir. She's been having a bit of the runs."

"Again? I thought we were over that."

She shrugged. "Well, we've definitely improved on that front, but from time to time, we've a bit of a crisis."

"Great," he muttered.

Just then, Anne, beaming with cheer, skipped into the dining room and took her seat.

"I trust we've been successful?" Beatrice whispered to her. "Did you wash your hands?"

Anne nodded and raised her index finger to her lips.

Waverly offered a hand to each child and bowed his head. "Dear Heavenly Father, we thank you for this food and the many other blessings you have given us. Forgive us our sins and help us to enjoy this time we have together. Amen."

He grabbed a spoon and dished a large serving onto Mike's plate.

Mike carefully inspected the scoop with his fork. "This doesn't have any kidney, does it?"

"No, it does not," Beatrice replied curtly. "It would've been much better if it did, but I know all too well your irrational opposition to everything British."

"What's this?" Mike held up a small, dark bead with his fork.

"That's a caper," she replied.

"A what?"

"A caper. It's a small vegetable. Try it—it's good."

He ignored her. He set the caper aside and sifted through his plate for any other offensive morsels.

"Did you get all your homework done?" Waverly asked Mike.

"Yes, except I don't understand one of the problems in my math assignment."

Waverly nodded as he swallowed. "Let's look at it together after dinner, and then we'll have quiet reading time."

"Daddy, you promised we'd discuss our new puppy at dinner," Anne said. "I want a cockapoo just like Cathy's. Please, can we?"

Mike groaned. "Yuk, I don't want any cockapoo! Johnny Caruthers has one of those, and all it does is bark and nip at everyone who comes to his house. And it rolls over and pees on itself every time I go over."

Waverly set a brawny hand on Mike's shoulder. "Both of you loved Buddy, right? How about if we get another retriever?"

"No, I want a border collie," Mike said.

"A border collie?" Waverly repeated with surprise. "Why a border collie?"

"Mr. Farrell told us border collies are the smartest dogs of all. They always win the skills contests."

Anne screwed up her face and crossed her arms across her chest. "I want a cockapoo."

Waverly cringed. *No yappy dogs.* "Didn't you love Buddy? I think a bigger dog would be better."

"All Buddy wanted to do was fetch the ball," she said. "I want a puppy to dress up when I play with my dolls."

He glanced at Beatrice. She winked and took a bite from a roll.

"Hey, I've got an idea!" Mike offered excitedly. "How about if we get two puppies? We can get a cockapoo for Anne—"

Waverly could see exactly where this was headed. "We are not getting two dogs. Beatrice and I will be the ones cleaning up after them."

"Please, Daddy!" Anne begged. "Please, please, please! Mike and I will feed them every day and even pick up all the poop. Right, Mike?"

"No way!" Waverly barked. "We are not getting two dogs. That's my final decision."

The table grew uncomfortably quiet, and both children stared at their plates and pushed their food around. Beatrice served each of them peaches, but neither child showed any inclination to consume even a bite more.

"I don't want any more," Mike said flatly. "Can I be excused?"

"Okay, but no snacks at bedtime," Waverly replied.

Mike got up from the table and trudged away into the living room.

"I'll be there in five minutes to help you with that math problem," Waverly called after him, "so don't start any games."

He spun back around. "Dad, I haven't gotten to play all day. Can't I play *Call of Duty*?"

"You know I don't like you spending a lot of time playing war games. Just one game, please—no longer than thirty minutes. I want to help you with that math problem, and then we'll play one game of chess and it'll be quiet reading time. Okay?"

"Okay."

He waited until the boy's footsteps resounded in the room above them. "Ever since he got his braces, he's been eating like a bird. The monitor in the lunchroom told me he only ate about two bites of his lunch today."

"You wouldn't know it from his arse," Beatrice said as she slid bowls of ice cream in front of Anne and Waverly. "It took trips to four different department stores before we found those khakis he's wearing."

He took a spoonful of ice cream. "It's the hockey. But he'll lose that too if he doesn't start eating."

"Dr. Bennett told me we could expect it the first two weeks," she said. "He should be fine by next week."

"Let's hope so," he mused. "How do you like your ice cream, princess?"

"It's really yummy." Anne scraped her bowl to get the last traces. "Can I have another scoop?"

"That's all for tonight," Beatrice said. "It's time for your bath before your daddy tells you a bedtime story."

"Daddy, will you tell us a story about a white cockapoo tonight?"

Waverly laughed. "A white cockapoo, huh? I'll see what I can do."

Half an hour later after he'd finished with the monthly bills, Waverly took the stairs up to Mike's room. He found Mike in his pajamas, lying on his bed with his head propped on his arm. He was staring at a book.

"How'd you do in the game?" Waverly asked him.

"I lost. I got shot in the first five minutes."

"Well, can't win 'em all."

"I haven't won anything since I got these braces on. I think they've short-circuited my brain."

Waverly sat on the edge of the bed. "Oh, really? I thought you got an A on the algebra test."

"I did. But that was easy."

"Let me see that homework problem you're having trouble solving."

"I think I figured it out." He handed over his workbook. "Is this right?"

It was an exponential equation, and Mike had shown in detail the steps to solving it. Waverly handed the book back to Mike. "That's right. Good job."

Mike closed the workbook and stuck it in his backpack. "Dad, can I ask you something?"

"Of course, you can. You can always ask me anything. You know that."

"Well, if I become a Navy SEAL instead of an NHL hockey player, do you think I'd chicken out the first time I went into battle?"

His stomach churned at another mention of the Navy SEALs. "You'd be afraid. Every soldier's afraid the first time he goes into battle. With time, most of them learn to control their fear. But even the mightiest soldier knows fear from time to time. Otherwise, they wouldn't be human."

"Did Mr. Farrell tell you that?"

"I've known a lot of soldiers during my life, including some Navy SEALs."

"Really?" Mike asked as he fluffed his pillow. "Where did you meet SEALs?"

"Oh, various places. When I was taking classes to be a better teacher, some SEALs were also taking classes."

"And they told you they were scared the first time they went into battle?"

"Yes, absolutely. Several of them did."

Mike stared down at his bedspread. "I'm glad. Because I really want to grow up and serve my country, like Mr. Farrell talks about, but I don't want to end up being a big chicken or something." He looked up into his father's eyes. "It's like that football-player-turned-soldier, Pat Tillman, that we saw in the video today."

"What about him?"

"Wasn't he amazing? Mr. Farrell said he was a true American patriot."

Waverly nodded. "He was. He was a great man."

Mike's eyes locked onto Waverly's. "Didn't you ever want to be a patriot?"

Waverly felt the hairs on the back of his neck stand up. "There are many ways to be a patriot, Son, without necessarily being a soldier."

"But al-Qaeda hates us and wants to destroy our country and everyone in it. Mr. Farrell says America needs even more great soldiers to defeat them and protect our way of life. I'd hate it if someone forced Beatrice and Anne to wear those burka things, wouldn't you?"

"Of course."

"Well, that's why I want to be a Navy SEAL. So I can be a patriot too."

Waverly pulled the covers up to Mike's neck, leaned over, and kissed the boy on the forehead. "I'm sure you'll be a great soldier if that's what you really want. Do you want me to say a prayer with you?"

"Not tonight. I'll just say one myself."

He nodded and smiled affectionately. "I love you."

"I love you too."

"Okay, lights out at nine thirty. Good night."

As he walked down the hall, he nearly bumped into Beatrice coming out of Anne's bedroom.

"She's already asleep," she whispered. "She was really tired."

"Okay. Good night, I'll see you in the morning. I just have a few more things to do downstairs."

"Good night, Mr. Waverly. See you in the morning." She walked to the end of the hall and eased her bedroom door shut behind her.

Waverly shuffled down the stairs to his office. He flipped on the light over his desk, sat in the leather chair, and leaned back, staring at the ceiling. A patch of paint had come loose from the ceiling, and he made a mental note to call the handyman the following day.

Abruptly, he sat forward, fished a key chain out of his pocket, and unlocked the side desk drawer. He pulled the drawer open and glanced inside. A CIA Career Commendation Medal sat atop a stack of papers. His thoughts ran back to the windy day in 2004 he'd received it from Director Tenet after his final mission to Syria and Iraq. Pulling the medal out of its velvet-lined wooden box, he cupped it in his hands and ran his index finger across the seal. After holding it for a minute, he slid the medal back in the box and set it on the desk.

His eyes locked onto the yellowed photograph Jalal and Tenya had mailed from Iraq a year after he left. The beaming young parents sat in a bed of daffodils holding their newborn son, Ibrahim. Waverly picked it up and read the note of gratitude they'd scribbled on the back. He sighed and slid the photograph onto the desk.

His eye caught the next item in the drawer, a photo of a young woman holding her horse's reins and squinting happily into the bright noonday sun.

"Faridah," he whispered, as he traced his fingertips across her full, smiling lips. "Dear God, haven't I done enough?" He tugged at the hair on his temples and leaned forward, resting his forehead on the desk.

"Mr. Waverly," Beatrice called from the hallway. She peeked into the office, a glass of water in her hand. She wore a robe, and her long blond hair was curled up in a bun. "Is everything okay, sir?"

He sat back in the chair. "I'm fine. I was just looking through some old photographs, and I'm afraid they've given me a bit of melancholy."

"Can I get you anything? Perhaps a spot of brandy?"

"No, I'll be off to bed soon. Go on to sleep, and I'll see you in the morning."

"Good night, sir."

"Good night—and thank you."

He listened to the creak on the stairs and the distant click of the door, then sat silently pondering for a few more minutes.

Finally, he pulled his cell phone from his pocket. He fetched a small address book from the desk drawer and fingered through the pages until he found the number he was looking for. He punched the number into his phone and leaned across the desk to push the door closed before the call went through. Two rings later, there was an answer.

"Marilyn Harrison," came the woman's voice on the other end.

"Hi, Marilyn. It's Stone. I hope I didn't wake you."

"No, not at all. Truthfully, I half expected your call."

"Oh, you did, huh? Well, I haven't changed my mind. But can I come and talk to you on Saturday, just you and me? I want to hear more about what the director has in mind. Then I'll make my decision. Okay?"

"Of course. Can you meet me at eleven?"

"Are you still on the seventh floor?"

"Same office."

"I'll see you then."

"Good night. I really appreciate your call."

He held the phone to his ear long after she'd hung up. He pursed his lips and blew out a long exhale, followed by a guttural groan. *I'm not really going to do this, am I? Too late now.*

He transferred the medal and photographs back into the desk drawer and locked it.

Here we go again.

3

Tranquility Lost

Waverly turned onto the familiar but somehow different access drive. Every time he passed through this gate after a long absence, something terrible happened to him. He pulled his car to a stop at the guarded entry to CIA headquarters and handed the brawny guard his driver's license.

"I'm here to see Deputy Director Harrison."

The guard took his license inside the post while two others checked the engine and trunk compartments and used mirrors to check underneath. They had Waverly step outside and searched beneath the seats and dash.

After a few minutes, the original guard returned and handed him his license and a badge.

"Welcome back, Mr. Waverly. Please wear this badge and park in one of the visitor's spaces. Ms. Harrison said she'd meet you in the courtyard of the new headquarters building next to the Kryptos sculpture. Do you remember where it is?"

"I think I remember," he replied with a smirk.

He pulled away from the guards and parked his car in one of the designated spaces. Then he made his way past a bed of budding tulips nestled among a cluster of small trees at the side of the building.

Harrison, dressed in a smart business suit, was sitting on a stone ledge beside the sculpture.

She smiled up at him through the morning rays of the sun. "Good morning. I trust you remembered how to get here."

"No problem. I ate in this very spot at least three times a week when I worked here at headquarters. Everything looks about the same." He motioned at the Kryptos sculpture. "Anyone solve K4 yet?"

She smiled. "No—at least not that I know of."

"I remember the day Victor Barnes came running in to tell us he'd solved it. Whatever happened to him?"

"He died from a brain cancer three years ago this summer."

The hair stood up on Waverly's neck. *Dear God, everyone I knew is disabled or dead.* "Really? That's horrible. He was always one of my favorites, probably smarter than all the rest of us put together."

"How about if we go upstairs?"

"Okay, let's go."

They walked around the perimeter of the building to the front entrance.

"Sign in," she said, "and we'll head upstairs."

Waverly gave the security guard his driver's license and visitor's badge and waited for the man to verify his identity on the computer workstation before he performed a retina scan. After a few more moments, the man handed him back the badge.

"You're cleared for the seventh-floor administrative complex, sir. I just need you to step through the metal detector."

Waverly completed his screening, and Harrison led him back through the building to the familiar elevators. They both scanned their badges and underwent retinal verification before the doors opened. They stepped inside, the doors closed, and the car accelerated up to floor seven. Waverly tailed Harrison through a maze of hallways to her office.

Waverly sat in one of the chairs that faced her desk.

"Would you like something to drink?" she asked cordially.

"No, thank you."

She slapped her palms on the desktop. "Okay, let's get right to it. What do you want to know?"

Go time. "What would my mission be?"

"Pretty much the same as it's always been, except with a very important secret mission. Your cover will be a supply officer for the covert operators, but your overall job will really be to assess the situation, oversee our covert team sent to help the rebels, recruit agents to provide critical intelligence, and when the time comes, work with the State Department diplomat who'll be sent to Benghazi to be a liaison to the rebel leaders. That's why you *are* the man for this job. You worked with some of these leaders on your prior mission in Libya."

She settled back into the soft leather executive chair. "You'll also be our moneyman in Libya. You'll provide cash to rebel leaders or anyone else we need to assist or manipulate. It's possible we'll call on you at some point to use your special skills to covertly eliminate some bad guys who stand in the way of our objectives. Basically, you'll do what needs to be done to ensure the Libyan revolution ends in a way that is beneficial to the interests of the United States."

There's something she's not telling me. "Okay, but what's the important secret mission?"

She punched a few keys on her computer and turned the screen so they both could view it. It showed a photograph of a large, rectangular object that looked like a huge backpack with large straps on each end. "Have you ever seen one of these before?"

He stared at the image. "I don't think so."

"This is the only known photograph of a Soviet RA-115 second-generation device, the so-called suitcase nuclear bomb that Russian defector Stanislav Lunev told us about."

"Lunev? I thought his intel was discredited."

"Most of it was. But several sources have confirmed that the RA-115-2 exists. We prefer to call it a nuclear backpack bomb. It weighs fifty kilograms and has a yield of two kilotons of TNT. The Russians upgraded the electronics, so it doesn't require the constant maintenance of the earlier models. Unfortunately, two of these were stolen by the Russian mafia from a nuclear storage site on Kola near Norway two months ago."

He glanced up from the photo. "Oh, shit."

"Exactly—our worst fears realized. One of them was recaptured by the Russians from al-Qaeda operatives two weeks ago after they were transported by truck all the way across Russia to southern Chechnya near the city of Shatoy. The captured operatives were interrogated by the GRU, and one of them confessed that the second RA-115-2 had been trucked to the port on the Black Sea in Anaklia, Georgia, and put on a freighter loaded with hazelnuts. That freighter unloaded its cargo in Tobruk, Libya, two weeks ago. We don't know with certainty who took possession of the backpack bomb, but evidence collected from the captured operatives suggest it was the Libyan Islamic Fighting Group or a splinter group such as the February 17 Martyrs' Brigade. Captured documents suggest they intend to transport it to another country, possibly the United States, and detonate it there. The Libyan revolution provides the perfect environment to hide that backpack bomb for later use."

She leaned forward. "Your primary mission, which will be known only to you, will be to find that RA-115-2 backpack bomb. When you do, a specially trained team will be inserted to remove it and bring it here for analysis."

Waverly felt his stomach churn as a wave of foreboding swept over him. "What a disaster."

"This is top secret, code word Tobruk, SCI information that will only be known to the president, a few higher-ups in the CIA, and the operative who accepts this mission. I shouldn't tell you this before you accept the mission, but I want you to fully appreciate the magnitude of the situation. We picked you because of your prior experience with nuclear weapons—and because we know you can keep your mouth shut. If you accept the mission, I'll forward you a video developed by DS&T that details what we know from Lunev about the design and operation of the RA-115-2."

She paused to give him a chance to comment, but he stared back in silent horror.

"Let me give you a little more background on the revolution." She clicked to another image, and a distinguished gentleman dressed in a smart western suit stared back at them. "Do you recognize this man?"

Waverly nodded. "Absolutely. Nouri Mesmari, Gaddafi's chief of protocol."

"Former chief of protocol. You've met him?"

"Yes, several times during my assignment in Libya. He actually introduced me to Gaddafi."

"Well, he fled to Tunisia with his entire family after Gaddafi publicly slapped his face and humiliated him. Then he defected to Paris in October of last year. He apparently told the French secret service everything he knew about the regime, which was quite a bit. Gaddafi sent his son Moatassim and several other high-ranking Libyan officials to try to convince him to come back. When that didn't work, he tried to have Mesmari arrested and deported. Mesmari put French officials in contact with military officers and activists plotting against Gaddafi in Benghazi, including an air force colonel named Abdallah Gehani."

Waverly's eyes darted about as he fit the pieces together in his head.

"Shortly thereafter, I believe in November, the French sent a wheat-trading contingent to Benghazi to ostensibly sign some juicy contracts. But there were also French special forces in the group, disguised as businessmen, and they met with Gehani and other opposition leaders and gave them money. A few weeks later, the new revolt in Libya began. Incidentally, Abdallah Gehani was arrested in Benghazi by Gaddafi security forces on January 27 and has not been heard from since."

She turned the monitor back around and tapped a few keys. "I'm sure you also remember this delightful gentleman."

The heavy-browed, brooding black eyes of a middle-aged man with a bushy, gray-flecked mustache and beard stared back at him.

"Abdul-Karim al-Rashid."

"Right again. Did you ever meet him?"

Waverly shook his head. "No, but I observed him being interrogated via a video link."

"What do you know about him?"

He flicked at the band on his watch. "Hardcore al-Qaeda, and a close confident of Osama bin Laden. During the mid-nineties, he was a member of the al-Qaeda-linked Libyan Islamic Fighting Group, which carried out guerrilla attacks around Derna and Benghazi. He was captured in Peshawar by Pakistani forces, I believe in 2002 or 2003, and handed over to the CIA. He was interrogated—which is when I observed him—and then imprisoned in Libya."

"Until his release in 2006," she said. "After that, he rejoined LIFG and is reported to have had a falling-out with al-Qaeda's top leadership. We're convinced that was just for show and that he remains in close contact with bin Laden. Anyway, he's now a Libyan rebel leader and a member of the National Council, the opposition leadership committee. We believe he's the most likely custodian of the miniaturized backpack bomb."

He's definitely at the top of my list. "That's a good bet."

"He's freely admitted that some of his opposition fighters are al-Qaeda operatives, calling them, quote, 'just good Muslims.' What we don't know is what proportion of the rebel leadership is also al-Qaeda. Is it one percent or eighty percent? We need to know more about al-Rashid and all the members of the National Transitional Council, including where their true loyalties lie. Part of your assignment will be to help us sort this all out, as well as to recruit other key Libyans to find that backpack bomb and protect our interests in Libya."

She reached for the Mont Blanc pen on her desk blotter, idly turning it over and over in one hand as she continued. "We also want to know where Gaddafi forces have their munitions depots and where large pro-Gaddafi forces are positioned in the country. President Obama signed a secret finding authorizing us to provide arms and other support to the rebel Libyan National Army, but no weapons have been shipped into Libya while administration officials debate the merits and dangers of giving them to the rebel groups. We obviously don't want to arm al-Qaeda with other advanced weapons."

She tapped the blotter with the end of the pen for emphasis. "Already, Idriss Déby Itno, Chad's president, has sent alarming messages that al-Qaeda pillaged military arsenals in the Libyan rebel zone and acquired advanced arms, including surface-to-air missiles. If that's true, we need to destroy those missiles too and make sure they don't get their hands on any other nasty toys they could use to hurt our friends or us in Afghanistan, Iraq, or God knows where. The special American representative to the rebel National Transitional Council I mentioned will also soon arrive to work with the rebels, and we want you to help him develop relationships with the rebels and assist with their finances. We haven't decided yet whether to inform him about the backpack bomb."

She set down the pen. "One thing you will not be doing is in any way directing the military operations of the rebel Libyan National Army. The president wants the British and French operatives in Libya to do that."

Waverly continued to flick at the band on his watch. *I'm not sure I'm prepared for a mission like this.* "Would I go in alone?"

"No, we've had a small team of paramilitary operations officers in place near Benghazi for several weeks now. You would join them, along with a covert team that is being sent in to give them the muscle they need to direct possible American air strikes and to potentially help you eliminate those undesirables who might, how should I say it, misdirect the revolution and likely be guarding the backpack bomb. For al-Qaeda, Libya represents a blank slate where they have the chance to dominate a new government, unlike the revolts in Egypt and Tunisia that seem almost certain to result in at least partially democratic governments. This rebellion is viewed as their last chance to turn Libya into a true Islamic state that they can use to foment turmoil all over the world. We aim to see that doesn't happen, and you would lead those efforts. You will be assigned to SAD during this mission."

Waverly sat back and thoughtfully rubbed the fronts of his thighs. "It doesn't sound like a six-month job to me."

"Probably not. But at least I can trust you to get things off on the right foot. When it's time for you to leave, we'll turn it over to someone else. I'm sure by then, we'll be in a better situation."

She folded her hands on the desk. "There's one more thing we may need your help with."

He raised his eyebrows.

"Gaddafi. At this point, we haven't decided whether it's best to split Libya and leave him in power but seriously weakened in the west or to simply eliminate him. If we decide to eliminate him, it would be best if he just died in his sleep, if you catch my drift. We don't want to be overtly in the dictator assassination business. To accomplish that, you'd need to recruit someone very close to him… Perhaps someone you knew well when you were in Libya."

He held her gaze for several moments. "I see. Okay, how long can you give me to think about all of this?"

She gave him a wry smile. "How about tomorrow morning?"

His heart skipped a beat, and he felt his palms grow moist. "Tomorrow?"

"The covert team is leaving for Frankfurt on a commercial flight from Dulles tomorrow night. At Ramstein Air Base, they'll be outfitted and fly by military transport into N'Djamena and then on to Tobruk Air Base in eastern Libya. That base fell to the rebel forces three weeks ago. From there, they'll helicopter into Benghazi. If you're going, you'll be safer going in with the team. Also, we'd like you to carry some cash to the rebels."

He began to flick at his watchband again and rubbed his sweaty palms on his pants legs. "Do I know any of the operators I'd be working with?"

"I don't think so. Most of them have been with Directorate of Operations for less than five years, but everyone in the group has a lot of military experience."

"Fine. I'll call you tomorrow morning. One other thing. Can I get the director's deal in writing? Directors—and their deals—seem to change around here fairly frequently."

She smiled. "I can't give it to you in writing, but you have my word it will happen."

"And do I have your word that my assignment will end by six months?"

She nodded once. "Absolutely. I promise."

He stood up. "Mike has a baseball game I want to see this afternoon. I'll call you in the morning."

"Thanks." She reached into her desk, pulled out an old-fashioned RAZR phone, and handed it to him. "Use this phone to call me."

He slipped the phone into his pocket and smiled glumly. "If I do this, it's not for the retirement money or the director. Or even you. I'll go only because I love this country, and I want to do everything in my power to keep it safe and free for my children and their children."

She grinned. "That's what I appreciate most about you. You've always been a true American patriot." She stepped around her desk and took his hand. "I'll walk you out. I'm so looking forward to working with you again, and I've got a feeling you'll find this backpack bomb, just like you sniffed out the smallpox plot when you were in

Mosul. You know we wouldn't ask if there were anyone else we thought could get this job done right."

He glanced down at his hands. "And one more thing."

"Yes?"

"If I do this, will you and the director promise you'll never ask me to go on a mission again? Social visits will always be welcome, but no company business. Okay?"

She smiled munificently. "Well, I can't speak for the director or the director after him, but you have my word that I'll never again serve as your recruiter."

He stared at her and then shivered. "Whew."

"What?"

"Déjà vu all over again."

"Me too."

4

A Step Over the Threshold

Waverly slammed the door behind him, slid behind the desk in his home office, and glanced at the mantel clock on the bookshelf. It was a little after six in the morning.

"Dear God," he whispered, "show me what to do."

He sat contemplatively for nearly forty minutes, first convincing himself he needed to stay home for the well-being of Mike and Anne, and then deciding he must accept the mission out of loyalty to the country he loved so dearly. He was also terrified of what al-Qaeda might do with the nuclear backpack bomb, and he needed to ensure his children's futures.

He shook his head, fished his key ring from his pocket, and unlocked the side desk drawer. He pulled out his commendation medal and the stack of photos and letters beneath it, and eyed his Beretta 92 pistol. He weighed it in his hand. It felt strange after not picking it up for eight years. He retracted the slide to make sure there was no bullet in the chamber and set it back in the bottom of the drawer, then shuffled the commendation medal and papers back into the drawer.

One photo fluttered from the bundle to the floor, a faded photograph of him standing on a grassy plateau with a young couple and their toddler boys, squinting into the afternoon sun. The beaming father held a falcon resting on his gloved hand.

Mustafa and Reka, so long ago.

His thoughts drifted back to the relaxed dinners in their apartment, filled with laughter and long conversations about Libya and the Middle East. Grinning, he remembered the afternoons he'd spent with Mustafa and his sons flying their falcons over a long-abandoned quarry, where sheep grazed on the nearby hillside. Their young sons had come to adore him like a family member, taking his hand as they skipped and ran along the edge of the rocky rim of the quarry. What would happen to them and their family members and friends if the jihadists took over Libya?

He stared at the photo for nearly a minute, then slipped it between the other papers and locked the drawer. Fetching Harrison's RAZR phone from his pocket, he dialed and pressed the phone to his ear.

"Up nice and early this fine spring morning?" Harrison said.

"Good morning. To be honest, I didn't sleep a wink."

"I didn't expect you would. I didn't sleep much myself. My dog kept burrowing his way under the covers to get warm."

He glanced at his sleepless red eyes in the mirror behind his desk. "Well, I accept the mission."

"Really? You've made my day."

His emotional momentum was gathering now. "What's the plan?"

"I'll send a car to pick you up at five p.m. Just pack your bag with clothing and toiletries—no weapons, computers, or phones. In the trunk of the car, you'll find a preloaded company computer and phone, both with your start date with the company as the password, along with your airline ticket and ten thousand dollars to use at your discretion. In the zippered side compartment of the computer bag, you'll find a shaving kit with familiar implements in the handle."

"You mean…?"

"It's a microinjector filled with carfentanil that's ten thousand times more potent than morphine. Highly effective, if you manage to recruit a suitable agent."

"To administer to whom?"

"No target at this point—but this way, you'll have it if the need arises. You'll meet up with several members of your covert team, led by a brawny man called Fisherman, at the airport. He'll supply you with weapons once you get to Germany. A courier in Ramstein will also bring you three million US dollars to give to the leader of the NTC in support of the rebels. Any other questions?"

"None right now. I'll email you if I think of any."

"I thank you from the bottom of my heart, and your country thanks you. A tremendous load has been lifted off my shoulders just knowing you'll be in Libya finding that backpack bomb."

"You're welcome. I'll be giving your number to our nanny as an 'old friend' she can call if any problems arise."

"Rest assured I'll be checking on them."

He was already moving toward the door. "Thank you."

"Godspeed, my friend."

Waverly draped his arm over Mike's shoulder, and they walked through a biting wind down the church steps. "Let's get some lunch down the street at Chipotle."

"Great! What about Anne?" he asked, looking around.

"Mrs. Roberts is driving her and Beatrice home. I want to talk to you in private."

Mike glanced up at him with surprise. "In private? What about?"

"Let's get our food, and then we can talk. Okay?"

Mike nodded dubiously, and they ambled down the street. They ordered their food at the counter, and Waverly carried the meal to a table at the back of the bustling restaurant. Waverly set a burrito and a cup of lemonade in front of Mike.

Mike unwrapped his burrito. "Are you going to start dating?" he asked without looking up.

My God, why does he keep bringing up dating? "I'm not dating anyone. I told you that."

"Then what do you want to talk to me about? I'm getting all As and Bs this quarter."

"I know you are. You've done very well in school this year. It's not about school. Mike, I have to go away for the next six months."

Mike's mouth dropped open in surprise. "You're going away? Why?"

He reached across the table and grasped his son's hand. "There's some work I need to do. I can't tell you specifics; it's just something I must do. But I promise you I'll be back in September."

Dumbstruck, Mike stared at him in disbelief.

Oh God, I've totally crushed him. "I know this is completely out of the blue. It's important, or you know I'd never do it. Trust me."

Tears pooled in Mike's eyes. "But what about Paul, and Tommy, and all the other boys in your class at school?"

"Mr. Spears asked Mr. Anderson to come back and take over my class until the end of the school year and then to fill in next year until I get back."

"What about baseball? My first game is in two weeks."

"Don't worry. Beatrice will get you to all of your practices and games."

"But she can't play catch."

"You can play catch with Brad Walters as much as you want. I talked to his dad about it. Take a bite of your burrito."

Mike's face screwed up, and he wiped his eyes on his coat sleeve. "I don't want you to go. Where are you going?"

Waverly patted his hand. "I can't tell you any more about where I'm going or what I'm doing. You need to trust me when I tell you it's important. But if anyone at school asks you, I want you to tell them I had to take care of important family business. No matter who asks, I need you to tell them that. Can you do that for me?"

Mike's eyes bulged. "Are you sick?"

"No, it's just some very important business. I told Beatrice about it too, and I'll tell Anne when we get home."

The tears suddenly gushed from Mike's eyes and he buried his face against his father's chest.

Waverly ran his fingers through Mike's hair. "Don't worry, I'll be fine. I'll be home in six months, and then things will be back to normal. After that, I promise I'll never leave you and Anne again."

"When are you leaving?"

"Tonight."

"Tonight?!"

Two of the teens at the adjacent table glanced over.

Waverly wrapped the foil over the burritos and put them back on the tray. "Come on, we can talk more in the car on the drive home."

They got up from the table and slipped out of the restaurant.

Mike stared silently out the window all the way home. Angry? Upset? It was impossible to tell. Waverly thought he might have more to say once they pulled up to the house, but Mike bolted across the driveway and into the house.

Beatrice met Waverly in the foyer just as a door slammed on the second floor.

"He's terribly hurt," she whispered.

"I expected him to be upset, but I'm sure he and Anne will be fine here with you."

"Yes sir. And don't you worry, I'll take care of Mike and Anne like they're my own children."

"I know you will, and we're lucky to have you. You'll get the twenty percent increase in salary that's in your contract beginning today. I've set things up so you'll get paid every two weeks, and you'll also receive enough money to pay for food and activities for you and the kids. All of our bills will be paid automatically by the bank." He handed her a sheet of paper. "If any problems come up or you need more money, call this number and ask for Mrs. Harrison. She'll see that you get anything you need. Do you understand?"

"Yes, Mr. Waverly. You can count on me."

He smiled appreciatively. "Thank you, Beatrice. Now, I've got a lot to do before the driver picks me up at five. Get Mike and Anne to play a game or watch a movie. I'll come down when I've finished packing. Do you think you can keep them occupied?"

"Of course, sir."

"Another thing. Tomorrow after school, I want you to take the children to Perfect Pets on Broad Street and buy a cockapoo for Anne and another puppy for Mike. Whatever breed he wants, okay?"

"That's smashing, sir! Nothing like a puppy to put a smile on a child's face."

"I'm counting on it. I'll tell them when I come down. Be sure to get females, and have the vet fix them when they're old enough."

Waverly pulled on a leather bombardier jacket over his blue jeans and plaid wool shirt, heaved a duffel bag over his shoulder, and hurried down the stairs into the foyer. Mike and Anne were sitting beside Beatrice on the couch in the family room, intently watching an animated movie.

Waverly leaned his bag against the doorjamb and sat on the end of the couch next to Mike.

Beatrice paused the movie. "All set, Mr. Waverly?"

"I think so. I forgot to tell you to pay Derek's Lawn Service starting next month. The bill will come in the mail."

"Dad, please don't leave," Mike said. "Coach Little needs you to coach third base."

Waverly wrapped his arm around his son's shoulders. "I called Coach Little, and he'll get another coach. He promised to look out for you during the season, and he also told me you're the starter at second base. Congratulations!"

Mike buried his face in his father's side. "I don't want to play any-more."

Anne got up from the couch and grabbed her father's knee. "Daddy, where are you going?"

He wrapped his arms around her and hugged her to his chest. "Daddy needs to take care of some important family business, but he'll be back in six months. Beatrice will be here to take you to school and Girl Scouts until then."

"Are you sick?" she asked gloomily. "Are you going to heaven to be with Mommy?"

"No, no, sweetheart. I'm fine, and I'll be back in six months. I promise." He kissed her on the forehead. "I love you so much. Listen, I've got a surprise for both of you. Beatrice is taking you to the pet shop after school tomorrow, and each of you can pick any puppy you want. What do you think about that?"

"Really?" Anne shrieked. "I can pick a cockapoo?"

A wave of relief swept over his body, even though he knew the excitement would fade with his departure. "Absolutely, but you must take good care of her."

She hugged him. "Oh, thank you, Daddy! I'll take such good care of her."

"What breed of puppy do you want, Mike?" Beatrice asked enthusiastically. "A border collie?"

"I don't want a puppy," Mike muttered.

The sound of car tires splashing through the gutter grew closer and stopped just outside the window.

"There's my driver," Waverly said. "Give me a goodbye kiss, sweetie." He pulled Anne close and kissed her cheek. "I love you so much."

"I love you too, Daddy."

Mike clung to his side, resisting his efforts to stand up from the couch.

"I need to go. Come on, give Dad a hug."

Mike shook his head and buried his face in the cushion.

Waverly leaned over and hugged his back. "I love you. I'll be back in six months…I promise. You're a big boy now, and I want you to watch out for your sister. Okay?"

He waited a moment longer, patted his son on the head, and finally got up from the couch. "I'll miss you and be praying for you all." He hugged Anne one last time and squeezed Beatrice's hand. "I love you, Mike. I'll call you as often as I can."

Mike sobbed uncontrollably, his head still buried in the couch.

"He'll be fine, sir," Beatrice whispered. "I'll help him pick out that puppy."

He nodded, slung the duffel bag over his shoulder, and stepped onto the porch and out into a driving rain. He jogged through the deluge to the black sedan in the driveway.

The driver sprang from the car and opened the rear door, then took the duffel bag from Waverly.

"Dad!" a voice bellowed from the porch. Wearing only a T-shirt and jeans and no shoes, Mike sprinted through the pouring rain.

Waverly stepped around the car and embraced him.

"I love you!" Mike cried out above a clap of thunder. He stared up at his father mournfully.

Waverly clutched him to his chest. "I love you too. You'll always be Daddy's best friend."

"Will you call me?"

"I said I would—whenever I can. Now go inside and dry off before you get sick."

Mike gave him one more hug and jogged back to the covered porch, where he stood beneath the overhang, staring gloomily through the downpour as thunder rumbled in the distance.

Waverly gestured a thumbs-up and ducked into the back seat of the car. The driver backed the sedan out of the driveway and sped away down the street.

A bolt from the sky struck the lightning rod on top of the house on the corner, illuminating the entire tree-lined street as thunder shook the car.

"Holy cow," the driver muttered.

That's nothing compared to a two-kiloton nuclear explosion.

5

A Lingering Moment of Peace

1800H SUNDAY, MARCH 6, 2011
WASHINGTON DULLES INTERNATIONAL AIRPORT, VIRGINIA

Waverly wove his way through the waiting passengers in the crowded departure hall. There they were: three athletic-looking men in their late twenties standing alone next to the windows overlooking the brightly lit runway. All three men sported full beards and shoulder-length hair and wore faded jeans with hooded sweatshirts.

The older man caught sight of him and offered his hand. "Waverly?"

"Yes, good to meet you," Waverly replied as he firmly shook his hand.

"My name is Coleman, but most everyone calls me Fisherman. I'm the team leader." He turned to the younger men. "This is your communications specialist, Patrick O'Brien—but he answers to Redbeard. And this is Brian Winters, your air operations expert, better known as Puckeater."

"Puckeater?" Waverly chuckled, offering his hand. "You play hockey?"

"I used to. I had a chance to play on a junior team after high school, but I chose to join the army instead. Did you play?"

"No way, but my son does. He's a big Capitals fans."

Puckeater grimaced. "He likes that Russki Ovechkin?"

"Actually, Nicklas Backstrom is our favorite."

Puckeater grinned. "Now there's a player—more assists than goals, same as me. What do I call you?"

"Just call me Stone." Waverly replied with an amused twinkle in his eyes.

Redbeard shook his hand next. "But what's your nickname?"

"No nickname."

Redbeard gave a good-natured chortle. "That won't last. I'm sure we'll come up with something, right, Puckeater?"

"No doubt," Puckeater said. "Redbeard here's the master. Don't tell him anything he doesn't need to know, or he'll pin something on you."

"Thanks for the advice." Waverly glanced around the crowded waiting area. "Where are the others?"

"The other three took an earlier flight," Fisherman said. "We'll meet up in Ramstein." He glanced back at the gate and picked up his large duffel bag. "Looks like we're boarding. I'll see you men in Frankfurt."

Waverly boarded behind Redbeard and Puckeater, each of them filing into a different row in business class. He sat next to a young Arabic man with his head pressed against the window. A nervous-looking woman across the aisle glanced at the man and then widened her eyes dramatically at Waverly before returning to her book. He snickered at the thought of someone trying to hijack an airplane carrying half a covert operations team.

The flight departed thirty minutes late. He picked at his dinner and read a bit before falling asleep for the last few hours of the nine-hour flight. Once they arrived at Frankfurt International Airport, their gear was loaded into a plain-looking truck and from there they took a two-hour train to the central station in Kaiserslautern, where a van was waiting for them just outside the terminal. The men piled their duffel bags into the rear and climbed inside.

Forty minutes later, they pulled up to the main gate at bustling Ramstein Air Base on a cloudy Monday morning. The guards at the gate carefully inspected each man's identification before lowering the barrier and allowing them to pass. The van driver skirted the end of a runway and drove to the back of the sprawling base to a windowless Quonset hut with an enormous US flag painted on the side. The van jerked to a stop beside two Jeeps just as a C-130J Super Hercules lifted off the runway and thundered into the overcast sky.

"Great!" Fisherman barked above the roar. "We won't be getting much sleep in this shithole. Good thing we leave tomorrow."

The four men grabbed their bags from the back of the van and headed to the hut. As they turned up the walk, the front door swung open and two scruffy, long-haired men in civilian clothes stepped outside to meet them.

"Welcome to Shangri-La, boys," one of them blurted with a sweep of his hand. He was a muscular man in his early thirties with Persian features. "We managed to rustle up three more cots, but one of you sleeps on the floor."

Fisherman winked at Waverly. "Redbeard loves concrete. Isn't that right, Redbeard?"

"Hell, yes," the ruddy operator bellowed. "I'll sleep on nails. Just buy me a few beers tonight at dinner."

Fisherman helped Waverly with his bag. "Men, this is Stone. He'll oversee our team and be leading efforts to vet the rebels in Benghazi while maintaining a cover as our supply officer. He served several tours in Afghanistan, Iraq, and Syria, and he also spent over a year in Libya back in the late 1990s. Stone, this is Jasper Peterson, our weapons specialist and kick-ass interrogator. We call him Checkmate. This is Doug Brunello, one of our shooters. Everyone calls him Spaceman, for reasons you'll soon appreciate."

"Hey," the young operator said, without bothering to shake Waverly's hand.

"And that's our other shooter, Tommy Waters, just coming out the door."

"I'll be damned!" Deadeye bellowed as he stepped outside. He pushed past the others and drew Waverly into a warm embrace. "Stone Waverly," he said in a heavy East Texas drawl. "I can't believe it! How the hell are you?"

Waverly grinned and thumped Deadeye on the back. "Just fine, Tommy. How've you been?"

"Fair to middling. Maria and I live in Amarillo, Texas, and we have two boys, four and five years old. We're fixin' to have a baby girl." He turned to the others. "Stone here is one of the best damn specialized skills officers there ever was or ever will be. Any of you men ever hear about that smallpox incident that went down in Dohuk, Iraq, in 2003, about a year into Iraqi Freedom? Actually, I guess that ain't happened, right?"

"I don't know what you're talking about," Waverly quipped with a grin.

"Well, anyway, Stone here's a man who mixes it up with the big boys and handles an AK-47 like a pro."

"So, you're still sniping?" Waverly asked him.

"Damn straight. It's great to have you with us. Come on, let's claim your cot before Redbeard nabs it."

"This is our last chance to get some good grub," Fisherman said. "Stow your shit, and we'll secure our weapons before the van picks us up at eighteen thirty hours."

"Great!" Redbeard yelled over his shoulder. "Where we headed?"

"K-Town," Fisherman replied.

"Awesome."

The operators and Waverly ate a quick lunch and headed to a nearby hangar to secure their weapons and other equipment. Just about everything was Russian-made: Kalashnikov AK-47 rifles with folding stocks, SR-1 Gyurza pistols, Kornet antitank missiles, Russian handheld surface-to-air missiles, and even Russian hand grenades, mines, and detonation components. About the only US-made equipment they carried were the communication gear and the handheld laser designators used to paint targets for attack from the air. Russian-made gear offered some level of deniability, since the president had promised the American people there'd be "no boots on the ground" in Libya.

Waverly picked his own AK-47 and SR-1 pistol. Three notches in the pistol barrel were eerie signs the weapon had been used before. He gripped it and sighted down the barrel at the back wall. *It feels so strange holding a pistol after all these years away from the company. I just pray I don't have to use it.*

6

Into the Abyss

Before dawn in the clear, chilly morning, Waverly and the covert operators loaded their weapons and gear. The Lockheed turbo-prop transport plane painted with Libyan Air Force markings would fly them first to the military airbase at N'Djamena International Airport in Chad and then on to Tobruk Air Force Base in rebel-occupied eastern Libya.

Each man checked his AK-47 rifle and Gyurza pistol and then helped the ground personnel stow the Kornet antitank missile systems, the Russian SA-18 surface-to-air missiles, and the hand grenades, mines and detonation components. They loaded two large pallets of ammunition and another pallet of MREs through the rear-loading ramp, then drove six Polaris MV 850 ATVs into the cargo bay. Finally, they stowed the communications gear and handheld laser designators in side cabinets in the forward personnel compartment, where they would spend the flight in side-facing webbed seats.

Waverly was the last one to climb aboard. He lugged a large black suitcase through the door and sat it on the floor across from Fisherman.

"What the hell is that?" Fisherman asked.

"Three million dollars," Waverly replied. "The courier brought it."

"Really?"

"Yeah. I'm taking it to the rebel leaders."

"Maybe we should just retire to Costa Rica."

He chuckled. "Don't tempt me."

A few minutes after six a.m., as the sun hinted its rise to the east, the two pilots assumed their positions and the turboprop engines roared to life. After a discussion between the pilots and navigator, the copilot stuck his head into the cabin.

"You guys comfy?" he bellowed above the engines with a broad grin.

Fisherman nodded and gave him a thumbs-up. "Ready to rock!" He leaned over to Waverly and half-shouted in his ear, "Sometimes these guys rip it up to altitude just to prove to us how tough they are. Hold on."

After a short taxi to the runway and a delay while two fighter jets took off, the transport plane thundered down the runway and, sure enough, seemed to go vertical.

Waverly felt his stomach heave. He stared at the floor as his memory crawled back to that time in a C-2 transport plane over the Arabian Sea near the coast of Pakistan.

"Not again," he moaned.

Fisherman gazed back knowingly, then reached back, pulled a vomit bag from a canister on the fuselage, and handed it to Waverly. "Don't worry about it. It happens to our guys all the time. I'm betting Checkmate will be right behind you."

Waverly buried his face in the bag and retched up his breakfast. As if on cue, two seats to his left, Checkmate leaned over and followed suit.

"Hey, jackass!" Fisherman bellowed at the cockpit. "Curtail your ascent!"

The copilot glanced back through the open cockpit door, grinned, and jabbed the pilot on the shoulder. A moment later, the turboprops slowly wound down, and the plane leveled off.

Waverly took a deep breath, inserted earplugs, leaned back in his seat and closed his eyes. *What'd I get myself into? I'm too old for this crap.*

Just shy of two hours into the five-hour flight, as the plane flew smoothly at twenty thousand feet, Fisherman passed out energy bars and water to the operators and crew members.

Waverly, feeling much better, took a few bites, sipped on his bottle of water, and leaned back in his seat. Redbeard peered out the window at the Mediterranean Sea far below and the first blush of land in the distance. "Aren't we practically flying over Benghazi?" he shouted across the fuselage to Fisherman. "Why not fly directly in?"

Fisherman shrugged. "The pilot told me we'd fly over Tunisia, Algeria, and Niger on the way into Chad, then pick up a fighter escort for the trip from Chad into Libya," he shouted.

"Oh, really?" Spaceman yelled sarcastically. "I guess that *could* come in handy. The Libyans might take offense if we just moseyed into their airspace."

"No shit, Sherlock," Redbeard said. "But why couldn't the fighters just meet up with us here over the Mediterranean? It seems to me even the French or Brit fly-boys could handle some junk Libyan fighters from the twentieth century. What've they got, MiG-23s and Mirage F1s?"

"I don't know what they've got," Fisherman yelled with rising irritation, "but for some reason they want us to go in through the back door. If that's the safest way into Tobruk, then I'm all for it. A Cessna with a bottle rocket could bring this crate down."

Waverly howled with delight, and the rest of the team joined him in a laugh. Even Spaceman grinned and slapped his knee.

The copilot stuck his head through the door. "What's so funny?"

"Nothing," Waverly said, waving his hand. "How much longer to N'Djamena?"

"Two hours and forty-five mikes, give or take ten. We'll land there about eleven hundred hours—same time zone as Ramstein."

"How long on the ground before we head for Tobruk?"

"An hour at the most, just long enough to refuel and take a piss. The fighters should be there waiting for us."

Waverly nodded his understanding. "Okay, keep us posted. And tell your partner up there we expect a smooth descent, or I'll ask Langley to give your commanding officer a call about recklessly jeopardizing this mission."

"No need for that, sir. He was just having a little fun—spicing up an otherwise dreary assignment."

"We'll see how dreary it turns out to be," he shouted back. "But we'd all appreciate it if you just keep it SOP the rest of the way."

"Absolutely, sir. You can take it to the bank. We'll let you know when we're twenty mikes to touchdown."

"Thank you, Captain," he hollered.

The copilot withdrew into the cockpit, and Checkmate raised his hand and high-fived Waverly. "Way to put them in their place."

"Fucking Airedales," Redbeard muttered.

Waverly settled against the bulkhead and wondered what was going on at home. *What were Mike and Anne doing?* He checked his watch. It'd be about four a.m. there. Hopefully, they were sleeping. Had they gotten their new puppies? When would he be able to call them? When would he get to hug them again?

He couldn't believe he'd agreed to this assignment. *Were they happier than the day he left?* His tortured thoughts finally gave way to merciful sleep induced by the monotonous drone of the turboprops.

True to his word, the copilot aroused them as the transport began a gradual descent over the endless flat plains surrounding the military airbase at N'Djamena. Waverly gazed out the window as the city of N'Djamena came slowly into view. A couple of minutes later, he caught sight of a cluster of featureless buildings surrounding a runway several miles outside the city. Several vintage fighter jets were parked haphazardly on a strip of asphalt just off the runway. Nearby, a fuel truck was servicing three identical fighter aircraft with US markings, which he recognized to be F-15 Eagles.

The pilot brought the transport plane into a broad, sweeping descent and taxied under the direction of ground personnel to a spot adjacent to the fighters. He shut down the engines, and the loadmaster opened the hatch. Waverly and the covert operations team shuffled down the ramp into the scorching midday sun.

"Damn," Deadeye groaned, shedding his jacket, "it's hotter than hell here."

"Where's the pisser?" Redbeard called out to the ground personnel.

One of the workers pointed to a line of outhouses next to a single-story shack about fifty feet away. The team members and flight crew made a beeline to the facilities. Waverly stopped for a moment to ask the two men at the fuel truck a few questions about Chad's geography, then followed the others.

Half an hour later, the transport plane was already taxiing down the tarmac as the F-15 fighters took off, one after the other, down the runway.

Once they were airborne, Waverly passed out individual boxed servings of schnitzel and fries.

"Where'd you get this?" Puckeater shouted over the din of the engines as he took a giant bite out of the meat. "It's delicious."

"I asked the cook at Ramstein to hook us up. I figured it might be the last real meal we'll get for a while."

"Brilliant," Puckeater grunted with a full mouth.

"Hey, Captain," Fisherman yelled to the copilot, "what's the plan?"

"Five hours to Tobruk. We hope to land there by seventeen hundred hours. The next two-plus hours, we'll be flying over Chad, and then we'll refuel in the air before proceeding into Libyan airspace."

He disappeared back into the cockpit, and the team members ate their lunches in nervous silence.

Two hours later, the sound of metal-on-metal contact reverberated through the airplane. After the refueling was completed, another clank signaled disengagement. At the copilot's invitation, several team members stepped into the cockpit to watch the enormous air tanker refueling the fighter jets. Waverly thought the view of the tanker and fighter framed by the desert below was one of the most beautiful sights he'd ever seen.

"Welcome to Libya," the copilot yelled.

Everything was quiet for nearly an hour and a half. Then Waverly became aware of increased activity in the cockpit and the heightened crackling of radio transmissions.

"What's going on, Captain?" he yelled up to the cockpit.

The copilot stuck his head out a moment later. "Several bogeys approaching from the west. They're still over a hundred miles out, but we're turning slightly to the east, and the Eagles are getting into position."

"What kind of bogeys?" Checkmate called out.

"We're not sure. Probably MIGs. Two of the Eagles are off to check them out."

"Shit," Checkmate groused. "I wonder how many MIGs they've got?"

"Just relax," Waverly reassured him. "It's nothing these F-15s can't handle."

The team members sat in tense silence until Checkmate could bear it no more. "Hey, Captain, what's happening?"

"The bogeys fled to the west as soon as they saw our Eagles coming their way."

"Have you ever taken fire in this crate?" he asked.

"We try to avoid that."

"Good. Let's keep it that way."

The copilot smiled and ducked back into the cockpit. Checkmate caught Waverly's eye.

"I don't know why," Checkmate yelled over the drone of the turbo-props, "but the thought of getting blown out of the air in one of these crates scares the hell out of me. Helicopter gunships, tanks, RPGs, grenades, rifle fire—no problem. But the idea of taking a missile in this flying coffin makes me crazy."

"I told you to stop playing those video games," Deadeye bellowed.

Checkmate bristled. "Shut up, Deadeye."

Waverly smiled sympathetically. "I know what you mean. I prefer the ground myself."

Despite the tension gripping the team, the transport plane landed without incident on the runway at the abandoned Libyan Air Force base near the eastern rebel-held city of Tobruk. Waverly glanced at his watch when the wheels screeched down—sixteen hundred and fifty hours, the sun low in the western sky.

The pilot pulled the plane to a stop at the end of the runway, under the direction of a dark-skinned Arab with a red wand. A few yards away, a group of two dozen men—mostly other Arabs dressed in civilian work clothes, but also four Westerners with heavy beards—waited patiently. Several goats foraged in a large patch of grass just off the runway.

Fisherman was first down the ramp, and he headed directly for a beaming Hispanic man who had his hand extended. "Chico, my man, how the hell are you?"

Perspiration running down his temples, Chico gripped Fisherman's hand. "Damn good, my friend. What took you boys so long to get here?"

"You know, the age-old story—Nero fiddled while Rome burned. How long have you been here?"

"Two weeks tomorrow."

"How's it been going?"

"Damn crazy, man. The rebels are holding off trained regulars armed with jets, tanks, and howitzers using little more than pea shooters and slingshots."

"Will they listen to you?"

"Some will, but a lot of them are true believers here to establish the next caliphate. You can trust these guys." He pointed to the group behind him that was already starting to unload the supplies from the rear of the transport plane. "They're all regular people just wanting to live a better life."

A fighter jet thundered over at low altitude, and all the workers dived for cover.

"They're ours," Fisherman yelled in Arabic. "Keep unloading." He scrutinized the three camouflage-painted helicopters parked on the other side of the runway. "Where'd you get those pieces of shit?"

Chico laughed. "They don't look like much, but they're mechanically sound. We've been using the Hook since we got here, and it's slow but reliable. The seventeens are newer. They're both armored and carry rockets, bombs, and fifty-caliber machine guns. They'll do the job."

"Who are the pilots?"

"I picked them myself. All three are former Libyan Air Force pilots who defected to the rebels. They're solid."

"Sounds good. Let me introduce y'all to our team leader, Waverly, and the rest of our men."

Fisherman and Chico gathered the Americans together, and the men exchanged greetings and handshakes.

Waverly was the last to leave the transport, lugging the suitcase. He shook Chico's hand.

"So, Waverly," Chico asked, "weren't you in Afghanistan in 2003? Kandahar Air Base?"

Waverly looked at him with surprise. "Yeah, I was there."

"Working with Blake Jensen?"

He nodded. "Yeah."

Chico grinned. "Damn straight, man, I never forget a face. I was with that group of operators who helped you assault the cave complex where we found that Afghan dude you'd been hunting. Remember? One of the Pashtun shot him, and you went freakin' ballistic."

A smile came to Waverly's face. "That was my last day in Afghanistan."

"Well," Chico said with a nod, "it's great to be working with you again." He glanced at his watch. "Let's hump it, men. We need to head back to Benghazi."

It took just short of two hours for the operators and the ground crew to transfer the weapons and supplies from the transport plane to the helicopters. When they were just about finished, Waverly approached the pilot of the transport plane.

"Captain, Fisherman told me you'd offered your satellite phone for the men to call home. Can I take you up on that offer?"

"Absolutely, sir. What's the number you want to call?"

Waverly gave him his home number, and the pilot punched it in and handed him the phone. The phone rang and was answered almost immediately.

"Hello," came Beatrice's cheerful voice.

"Hi, Beatrice, this is Stone Waverly."

"Mr. Waverly!" she gasped. "Where are you?"

"I can't tell you that. How are the kids?"

"They're just fine, sir. They both have the afternoon off for parent-teacher conferences, and they're in the back yard playing with their dogs. Just a minute and I'll get them."

He heard her yelling in the background before Mike came to the phone, out of breath.

"Dad?"

"Hi, Son. How are you?"

"I'm okay. Are you coming home?"

"Let me talk to Daddy," Anne was chirping excitedly in the background.

"Not yet, Son. I'm just getting started. How are your new puppies?"

"They're great! I got a German Shepherd, and Anne got a cockapoo. Mine's named Warrior. He's a little older, like three, and he was a trained police dog, but they retired him because he was kinda shy. He already knows how to fetch a ball."

"Let me tell Daddy! Let me tell Daddy!" Anne demanded in the background.

"Isn't a German Shepherd a little big for our back yard?" he asked.

"No, it's perfect. I throw a tennis ball off the back wall, and Warrior tries to catch it. He loves it!"

"I'm glad to hear you're doing so well. Keep up your grades. I'll probably get a chance to call again in a week or so. I love you."

"I love you too."

"Now let me talk to Anne."

She grabbed the phone instantly. "Daddy?"

"Yes, honey. How are you?"

"I'm good. Daddy, I named my new puppy. Her name is Cece. She's so cute!"

"Cece? Where'd you come up with that?"

"I thought it up all by myself. Are you coming home?"

"Not yet, honey. Are you being good for Beatrice?"

"Yes, and she let Cece and me sleep in her bed last night. It was really fun."

"Okay. Well, I love you. I'll try to call again soon. Let me talk to Beatrice one more time."

"I love you, Daddy," she sang.

Beatrice came back on the line a moment later. "Yes, Mr. Waverly?"

"A German Shepherd?" he asked evenly.

She chuckled. "You said to let him have what he wanted, sir, and he's already house-trained."

Just great, now we've got a giant police dog and a yappy mutt. "Any problems?"

"Well, there was an armed robbery last night at the Millers' house, three doors down. Mr. Miller got shot in the arm."

A sick feeling dropped into the pit of his stomach. "Is he okay?"

"He was really lucky. It was a flesh wound. But they took his wallet and his car."

He took a deep breath and exhaled through pursed lips. "Damn, we've never had trouble like that in our neighborhood before. Be careful. Pull the car all the way into the garage and close the door before you get out. And make sure all the doors are locked all the time—even the patio door."

"I will, sir. Don't worry. Oh, and we had a small leak in the living room ceiling. Mr. Miller next door called a roofer, and he's coming tomorrow."

Waverly shook his head. *Damn, I should be there to make sure that gets fixed the right way. Relax, she's got everything under control.* "Good. Remember, you can call Marilyn Harrison if you need anything."

"Yes sir. I have her number on the refrigerator—but really, I've got everything under control."

"Thank you. I can't tell you how much I appreciate you."

"Take care, sir."

"Goodbye. Give Mike and Anne a good-night kiss for me."

"I will, sir. Goodbye."

He handed back the satellite phone. "Thank you."

The pilot took the phone and glanced up at the sliver of moon on the horizon. "It's tough when you have young children."

Waverly nodded. "Yes, it is." He offered his hand. "Good luck to you. Thank you for your help."

"My pleasure, sir. Take care of yourself. I don't want to hear anything about Americans getting hurt or missing here in Libya."

Waverly watched the pilot walk back to the transport plane. He turned and jogged to the helicopter with his black suitcase.

"Ready?" Fisherman asked above the *whop-whop-whop* of the helicopter rotors.

"Ready." Waverly passed up his gear, jumped into the helicopter, and scooted past Deadeye, who was manning a machine gun.

The *whop-whop-whop* accelerated, and the helicopter lifted off the ground. They banked to the west behind the much larger transport helicopter, the second gunship tailing behind them.

"How long to Benghazi?" Waverly yelled to Fisherman.

"Just under two hours. We're headed to Benina, just to the east of Benghazi."

He nodded and glanced around the wind-whipped fuselage. Deadeye was scanning the terrain below through the open door, and Spaceman was peering out the starboard windows. He glanced up to the cockpit. The pilot was a dark-skinned Arab, and his copilot looked Egyptian, with olive skin, thin lips, and an aquiline nose. Waverly watched them for a while before deciding they knew what they were doing.

The pilot leveled off with the other two helicopters. Deadeye shut the door, and they all settled back in their seats for the last leg of the journey.

Suddenly, an audible whoosh reverberated through the cabin.

Waverly raised an eyebrow at Fisherman.

"The Eagles are shadowing us into Benina," Fisherman shouted.

He nodded and settled back into his seat. He closed his eyes and flicked at his watchband. *I wish Marilyn Harrison would call Fisherman's satellite phone right now to tell me the nuclear backpack bomb's been found, and I can go home. Dear God, I've never wanted anything more.*

7

Arrival

The helicopters descended quickly into the moonless darkness toward an infrared beacon projected from the ground to the pilots wearing night-vision goggles.

"Five seconds," the copilot yelled from the cockpit.

The helicopter bumped down gently, and the pilot shut down the engines. Out of the darkness, a group of men came running to the open door. Fisherman jumped down to the sandy ground, and Waverly followed him.

"Welcome to Benghazi," one of the men said in English. He was white, with a long, bushy beard and mustache and an AK-47 slung over one shoulder.

"Thank you," Fisherman replied.

"I'll take you men to your quarters. Don't worry about your gear. These men will bring it."

Spaceman and the other two team members followed the operator to a small, ramshackle structure, little more than a shed, about twenty yards from a larger cinderblock building where the men were stowing supplies and weapons.

"Here you go, men," the operator said as he opened the door. "It's not much to look at, but it's a lot better than the shack on the other side of that storage building."

Their quarters consisted of a large, single room with another door near the back. Ancient linoleum tiles, many missing, lined the floor. Several naked light bulbs dangled from the ceiling.

"There's a latrine out that back door," the operator said. "Stow your equipment and then join us on the west side of the storage building. Our rebel hosts prepared a feast to welcome you, and three members of the National Transitional Council plan to join us for dinner."

"How many men do you have?" Waverly asked as he set his suitcase against the wall.

"Five, including myself. Not enough to have much impact here— but now at least we have thirteen," he said with a toothy grin.

"How many rebel fighters?"

He gave an approving nod. "I heard you were all business. We'll fill you in at dinner. Get yourself settled."

Waverly laid out his sleeping bag at the very back of the room and set about stowing his weapons, cameras, computer, and other equipment, as did the rest of the operators. The room was strangely quiet as each man concentrated on readying his weapons and equipment for combat that could come at any moment.

A quarter of an hour later, they all made their way across the darkened courtyard past the main building to another single-story shack, Waverly lugging the suitcase along. The temperature had dropped precipitously to nearly 50 degrees Fahrenheit, with a stiff breeze coming out of the south. In the dim light, Waverly could make out several Libyan workers scurrying about, covering the helicopters with camouflage tarps.

On the other side of the barn, Chico and three other Americans stood beneath a cluster of palm trees conversing with three Libyans. They all turned to greet him.

"Stone," Chico said, "let me introduce you to our hosts. This is Mahmoud Jibril, who was just named interim prime minister and chairman of the executive board of the National Transitional Council."

"As-Salaam-Alaikum," the clean-shaven and balding man said, as he shook Waverly's hand with a broad smile.

"Wa-Alaikum-Salaam," Waverly replied.

"Thank you, my friend, for coming to help us. I hope your mission here in Libya is a big success. My countrymen and I welcome you. I also bring greetings from Mustafa Abdul Jalil, the chairman of the National Transitional Council. He wanted to join us tonight, but family issues prevented him from coming." He turned to his colleagues. "I'd like to introduce you to two other members of the National Transitional Council. This is Commander Juma Ibrahim and Abdul-Karim al-Rashid. Commander Ibrahim is one of our military commanders, and Mr. al-Rashid leads our internal security force."

Waverly had recognized al-Rashid before Jibril introduced him. He'd seen his gray-flecked mustache and beard dozens of times before, the last time during Harrison's briefing, along with the long, sinuous scar ranging across his right cheek. But it was the man's eyes he never forgot—heavy-browed and intense, with a look of cold-blooded ruthlessness.

Ibrahim made a point of shaking each of the team members' hands, while al-Rashid merely nodded, finally acquiescing to shaking Redbeard's hand when the operator offered it to him.

Once the introductions were completed, the men sat around a large wooden table, and servants brought them fresh roasted lamb, couscous, and vegetables, along with several loaves of flatbread.

"So, gentlemen," Waverly finally said when there was a lull in the small talk, "how many fighters does the NTC have at its disposal?"

Ibrahim glanced at Jibril, who spoke up after a moment of reflection. "We aren't prepared to discuss specifics about the strength of our forces."

Waverly glanced at Fisherman and Chico. Neither of them responded, so he decided to press on. "Sir, if we are to help you, we need to understand both your strengths and weaknesses."

Al-Rashid clenched his jaw and gave Waverly a contemptuous stare. "We do not need your help. We are fully capable of ridding ourselves of Gaddafi and his henchmen, if you will only give us the weapons we requested."

"Abdul, bite your tongue," Jibril chided. "These are our guests. Mohammed," he called out to one of the servants, "bring coffee and tea for our guests."

Al-Rashid glared menacingly at Jibril for a long moment and then jerked back into his chair.

Waverly openly considered the man's averted gaze. *I'd bet six months' salary this bastard has that backpack bomb.*

"I'm sorry, Mr. Waverly," Jibril continued in an apologetic tone, "but Abdul is passionate about our cause, and as you Americans say, he wears his feelings on his sleeve."

"No problem. If you don't feel comfortable giving us numbers—"

"Twenty-five to thirty thousand fighters," Jibril said. "More men are coming to our side every day, but that's my best estimate."

"What percentage of those have prior military experience?" he asked.

"Five or six percent."

He glanced at Fisherman and Chico again.

"Many of our officers previously served in the Libyan military," Ibrahim said. "All of our pilots were Libyan Air Force officers."

"Do they all have weapons?" Waverly asked.

"Many have rifles, a few have machine guns, and the rest help carry ammunition and supplies."

"How many fighter jets do you have?" Chico asked.

"Operational, ten to twelve. Half Mirage F-1s and the other half MiG-23s obtained mostly by defection."

"How many tanks?" Waverly asked.

"Forty or fifty, most of them old relics abandoned by the army. We do have several hundred technicals, trucks mounted with machine guns. We also have about two hundred Chinese- and Soviet-made antiaircraft guns scattered around Benghazi and our front lines."

This is way worse than I thought it would be. "We'll get you more rifles and other small arms. Where's the fighting now?"

Jibril unrolled a map and placed it in the center of the table. "We are in control of everything east of Ras Lanuf and this string of small cities in the west around Nalut. There was major fighting today three hundred kilometers to the west of us, here in Ras Lanuf. Our forces drove as far west as Bin Jawad but then got pushed back by Gaddafi's tanks. There is also major fighting in the west at Misrata and Zawiyah. What we really need, Mr. Waverly, is American airplanes to shoot down Gaddafi's airplanes. If the fighters and bombers weren't constantly strafing and bombing our men and supplies, we would've already taken over the entire country. When will they come to help us?"

"That's not for me to decide, Mr. Jibril. Our president, the leaders of France and England, and the United Nations will decide that."

"They promised us weeks ago," al-Rashid scoffed. "Meanwhile, our fighters and even our women and children are killed like flies by Gaddafi's airplanes."

"I'm sure more help will soon be on the way," Waverly said reassuringly. "But it takes time to get the men and equipment into position. In the meantime, we'll help train your fighters in military discipline needed to win this war. If American fighter planes do come to help, we will help them identify targets so that your people don't get hurt. Can you bring fifty men here to begin training tomorrow at thirteen hundred hours? We'll equip each of them with an AK-47 and provide three days of training."

"I'll make sure they're here," Jibril said with a nod.

Waverly pointed to the suitcase behind him. "Mr. Jibril, that suitcase contains funds to support the rebel cause. There will be more once I establish your specific needs."

"And what will you expect in return for this help?" al-Rashid asked. "Oil at a cheap price?"

He stared into al-Rashid's piercing black eyes. "Anything else?"

"Yes. When we triumph, Libya will remain a Sunni Muslim state but will be governed by Sharia law. Are we in agreement?"

"Mr. al-Rashid," Waverly replied testily, "you're asking political questions I can't answer. I suggest that the NTC take this up with political representatives from the United States and the other countries trying to help you. It's my understanding that a representative of the United States is on the way to Benghazi to confer with you on these matters."

He waited for one of the Libyans to respond, but none of them did. "Let me ask you, Mr. Jibril, where are British and French soldiers' headquarters?"

"There are about fifty Frenchmen and forty or so Englishmen."

"Where are they based?" he repeated.

"The Englishmen are on the other side of the airport, about two kilometers from here. The French are just outside of Benghazi, ten miles to the west, but twenty to thirty French soldiers are fighting with us in Ras Lanuf and Misrata."

He nodded. "Okay, I'd like to meet the English leaders in the morning. Can you spare us a guide?"

Jibril glanced toward the tent. "Jalal bin Koussa!" he shouted.

An Arabic teen ran into the room a moment later. He had fine features and a short-cropped beard and mustache.

Jibril placed his hand on the young man's arm. "Mr. Waverly, this is Jalal bin Koussa. Jalal is one of my most trusted lieutenants. I've known him since he was five years old, and he's worked with me since the Khamis Brigade killed his father and brother after the protests began in February. He'll stay with you and do whatever you require of him."

Waverly shook Jalal's hand. "Thank you, sir. We'll take good care of him."

"I'll be there in my tent any time you need me, Mr. Waverly," Jalal said helpfully.

"Thank you, Jalal. We'll be good friends. You can call me Stone. You remind me of a good friend I had during the time I worked in Iraq. Jalal was his name too—Jalal Rashid."

"Was he brave?" Jalal asked.

"Very brave. One of the bravest men I ever knew."

"Then he truly was like me."

Several of the team chuckled behind him, and Jalal spun around and glared them into silence.

"Was your friend Arab?" Jalal asked Waverly.

"No, he's Kurdish. He and his family live near Kirkuk in Iraq."

"I would like to meet this Jalal someday."

"It'd be my pleasure to introduce you. We'll be starting very early tomorrow, so we should all get some sleep."

"Yes, and we have quite a drive back to Benghazi," Jibril said with a nod as he leaned over and picked up the heavy suitcase. "We'll see you gentlemen tomorrow afternoon."

Ibrahim made a point of shaking each American's hand. "Thank you for coming to help us," he said to each one in turn. "May Allah protect you," he added after he shook Fisherman's hand.

"Good night, my friends," Jibril said. "Jalal, please carry those maps to the vehicle."

Fisherman, Chico, and Waverly looked after the Libyans as they returned to their old Toyota Land Cruiser.

"What a piece of work al-Rashid is," Fisherman muttered, shaking his head. "No telling what that bastard's capable of."

"Anything," Chico said. "He's the one we should be going after, and the others like him, not Gaddafi."

Waverly didn't respond. He stared up at the star-studded sky. "Look, there's Orion. I've never seen it so bright. When you see it like that, you can understand why the ancient Egyptians were so fond of this constellation. They associated it with their sun-god of rebirth and the afterlife, Osiris."

A rustling behind them caught them off guard, and all three men wheeled around. A stooped old man dressed in a dirty tattered *thobe* with a torn *shemagh* on his head shuffled out of the darkness between the buildings on crutches, dangling one leg that was amputated below the knee. He muttered unintelligibly.

"Who are you?" Fisherman demanded.

The man let loose a guttural moan and continued shuffling toward the three Americans with his head tucked against his chest.

Fisherman yanked his pistol from its holster. "Stop! Not another step!"

Waverly also drew his weapon.

The man stopped, swaying to one side and then the other, using his crutches to keep from toppling over.

"What do you want?" Waverly said, then turned to the others. "Watch out, he may be wearing an explosive vest."

"I want meat or cheese," the man whispered in Arabic.

"How did you get in here?" Chico demanded as he circled to the man's right.

The old man cleared his throat. "I come with a message from Gaddafi."

Fisherman raised his pistol. "Get down, down on your knees."

The old man let his crutches fall to the sand, stooped on his one good leg, and fell onto his side with a loud grunt.

"What's the message?" Waverly aimed his pistol at the man's chest.

The man looked up from the ground and wiped his cheek with his *shemagh*. "I was told to only speak to the leader."

"I'm the leader," Waverly said in Arabic. "What's the message?"

"Spaceman," the man whispered.

Waverly glanced quizzically at Fisherman. "What about Space-man?"

The man didn't respond. He only stared at Waverly.

"What about him?"

The man looked down at the sand. He cleared his throat, looked back up at Waverly, and muttered something barely audible.

"What?" Waverly demanded in Arabic. "What did you say?"

"Spaceman is the best clandestine operator in the Special Operations Group," the Arab said in perfect English.

Dumbstruck, Waverly's mouth gaped. "What did you say?"

"Spaceman—he's the best."

"What the—?" Fisherman blurted, stepping forward. "Spaceman? Is that you?"

Spaceman laughed and pulled the *shemagh* off his head. "Of course it's me. Who else?"

Chico dropped his gun barrel. "You're a flaming idiot. I almost shot your ass."

Spaceman grinned up at Chico. He reached beneath his *thobe*, untied a ligature holding his flexed leg, and extended it in front of him. "Ah, that feels better."

This blockhead is crazy as a loon. "What the hell are you doing?" Waverly demanded. "Have you lost your mind?"

Spaceman pushed himself up from the sand. "Proving a point."

"What point?" Waverly demanded.

"That I can make myself up to be a damn authentic Arab beggar."

"Okay, I'll give you that, but why?"

"I did a lot of research before we left the States. Gaddafi spends a lot of his time in his compound in Sirte. I could be inserted there posing as a poor Arab beggar. When I catch sight of him, I'll paint him with a laser—and boom, it's over."

Waverly's nerves melted into a chuckle. "You're crazy as a loon. They'd spot you in a heartbeat."

"*You* didn't."

"Here in the dark, no. In the middle of the day, that's another story."

"Okay, I'll show you tomorrow. I bet I can completely fool the Libyan cooks—and if I do, you approve the mission. My grandfather was half Arab, for God's sake."

"No way," Waverly said. "We're here to support the rebels and find dangerous weapons. Killing Gaddafi isn't part of our mission."

"Come on. Think out of the box."

Was this guy serious? He bristled. "That's bullshit. We're here to support the rebels, not send you off on some ill-conceived treasure hunt in Sirte." He scooped up the *shemagh* and handed it to Fisherman. "Where'd you get this?"

Spaceman grinned. "I bought it back home along with this *thobe*, and I stowed it with my gear."

Waverly shook his head and rolled his eyes. "You planned this before you left the States?"

"Well, not completely, but I came prepared."

"You're a moron," Fisherman muttered dismissively. "Get that crap off and go get some rest. I don't want to hear another word about this, or I'll have you shipped out of here. You got it?"

Spaceman reached out and jerked the *shemagh* from Fisherman's hand. "Whatever." He disappeared into the darkness between the buildings.

Fisherman shook his head. "Do you believe that crap?"

"It just might work," Waverly said with a stiff smile. "Sometimes the craziest ideas work the best. But that impromptu performance worries me. How long have you known Spaceman?"

"About a year," Fisherman replied. "He'll be all right. He's quirky, but he's a top-notch operator and sniper, and he'll do whatever it takes to accomplish our objectives. The three of us just need to keep him focused on our objectives."

Note to self: this guy could be trouble.

"I'll keep an eye on him," he said. *This guy could submarine the entire mission.* "Meanwhile, let's head over to meet the Brits first thing in the morning. Then we'll sit down and plan our first mission. While we do plan to support the rebels in their fight against Gaddafi's forces, our priority is going to be to hunt down surface-to-air missiles and other advanced weapons that are a future threat to the US and our allies. That includes Gaddafi's weapons and weapons captured and squirreled away by jihadist groups for future use."

Fisherman nodded. "That sounds like a plan."

A yawn broke through his composure. "Oh boy, I need some sleep. I'll see you in the morning."

As he rounded the barracks on the way to his sleeping bag, Waverly's thoughts continued to fret over Spaceman. *He reminds me of that whack-job operator, Dudley Trueblood, from my unit back in Kandahar. That's the last thing we need here in Libya—another operator flipping out.*

8

Cat and Mouse

First thing the next morning, Waverly, Fisherman, and Chico went to visit the British Special Air Service headquarters on the other side of the airport, while the other operators prepared for the first contingent of rebel fighters due to arrive for training that afternoon.

Waverly and Fisherman, riding an ATV, followed Chico's ATV up to the guarded entrance of a sprawling enclosure with several one- and two-story buildings arrayed in the center. They pulled to a stop just shy of two soldiers in a bunker who were dressed in desert camouflage and armed with machine guns.

"Who goes there?" one of the soldiers shouted.

"Harper's boys," Chico replied, using the prearranged code.

"Major Collin is expecting you." The soldier lowered the barrier. "You'll find him in that building with the flagpole, mate."

Chico gave the soldiers a mock salute and parked his ATV in front of the indicated building. Flanked by the two covert operators, AK-47s at their sides, Waverly walked through the open front door manned by a sentry, who paid them little attention.

The major was seated behind a desk. He was sipping from a teacup and pointing at a map as two other soldiers looked on.

"Major Collin," Chico said. "Harper's boys here."

The major sprang up from his desk with a broad smile and thrust out his hand. "Good morning! I expected you two days ago. Where the devil have you been?"

"Leading from behind, sir?" Chico replied with a grin.

"Bloody hell, what load of cack are you—"

"It's an Obama saying, sir," Fisherman said.

"That's what happens when you elect a leader without a shred of military experience. Gone quite barmy, if you ask me," Collin said.

"I couldn't agree with you more, sir," Fisherman said. "Four of us flew in a few days ago, but the others just arrived last night. Our orders were to await the full team before linking up with you. Sir, this is our team leader, Stone Waverly."

"Nice to meet you, Mr. Waverly," the major said, shaking his hand. "Very well, then. Better late than never, I always say. We've been having a smashing good time doing our best to bollocks up Libyan communications and interdict their supply and petrol deliveries. Now that you men are here, we can divide and conquer."

He motioned to the map. "Most of my men are stationed here around Misrata and Tripoli, but I got word this morning that the Libyan army has begun a new thrust toward Ras Lanuf from the west, led by thirty to forty tanks. I'm guessing from Ras Lanuf, they aim to continue up the Mediterranean coast to Brega, Ajdabiya, and finally on to Benghazi. No way the rebels can stop them without our help. Perhaps you gentlemen could slow them down a bit by banging a few tanks and petrol tankers?"

"I think we could manage that," Waverly replied with a grin at Fisherman. "What we really need are some fighter jets of our own."

"Don't hold your breath," the major said. "Be sure to take SAMs with you. The Libyan fighter and helicopter pilots aren't very skilled, but if they show up, they could still ruin your day. If you take a couple of them down, the rest tend to bugger off like jackrabbits."

Waverly glanced through the office doorway at several soldiers manning communication equipment. "Nice camp you have here, Major."

"Quite adequate, I must say."

"Are your men training rebel soldiers?" he asked.

"We've attempted it. Mostly a sorry lot with no military experience—and most of them are chavs."

"Chavs, sir?" Chico asked.

"Teenagers. Mostly blooming idiots."

"We'll try our hand at training some too," Waverly said, "and we brought small arms to equip them. What are the French doing?"

"Your guess is as good as mine. We tried to coordinate with them when we first arrived, but they have their own agenda. You could run into some of them stationed with the rebels up near Ras Lanuf, but most of them are bumming near Tripoli and Benghazi and trying to influence the rebel leaders, I presume."

"Well," Fisherman chuckled, "you never know. The rebels may need the Frenchies to show them how to surrender."

"Ha!" The major guffawed and slapped his leg. "Isn't that the queen's truth? Well, jolly good, you better get on with it. Oh, my communications specialist is next door. Link up with him on your way out so we can stay in touch."

Waverly flicked at his watchband. "Major, there's a favor I'd like to ask you."

"Name it."

"If your men discover any weapons caches belonging to any of the al-Qaeda-aligned groups such as LIFG, the Libyan Islamic Movement, or the February 17 Martyrs' Brigade, could you allow me to personally inspect them before you blow them up?"

"Absolutely. May I ask what you're looking for?"

"My superiors ordered me to keep careful records on advanced weapons systems such as surface-to-air missiles that were obtained by jihadists."

He nodded crisply. "I'll alert my men, and I'll also alert the leader of the French special forces when I meet with him tomorrow."

"I'd appreciate that, sir," Waverly said. "I'd also like to meet with the French. What's the leader's name?"

"Colonel David Assouline. I'll let him know you'd like to chat."

"Thank you, sir. It was a pleasure meeting you."

Waverly pulled his ATV past the guards at the gate of the American compound and eased to a stop near a bench where Deadeye and Puckeater sat deep in conversation over a cup of tea. Fisherman pulled up beside him.

"Welcome back," Deadeye greeted. "How goes it with the Brits?"

"Smashing!" Fisherman replied with a big grin. "Got their arses frightfully tickety-boo—and Bob's your uncle."

"I'm afraid I don't speak English," Deadeye said with a rueful laugh.

"'They've got their butts running like a well-oiled machine, and from here, it's all child's play,'" Fisherman said. "I learned a bit of British slang when I was stationed in Mildenhall."

"How many men do they have?"

"Forty to fifty," Waverly replied. "There are a few MI6 guys here too. Let's get the men together for a little powwow before we fly over to Ras Lanuf to help the rebels. Apparently, they're getting their butts kicked by loyalist tanks and jets."

"Sounds good," Deadeye replied. "Puckeater and I had a long talk with Jalal bin Koussa while you were gone. He's been working with Jibril and several other members of the executive board of the NTC. Of the sixty members of the NTC, he believes there are three with ties to the Libyan Islamic Fighting Group and possibly al-Qaeda. We need to watch out for the February 17 Martyrs' Brigade that provides internal security for the rebels. It's made up of hundreds of civilians who joined the rebellion and Jalal estimated thirty percent of them, including many of their leaders, are Libyan Islamic Fighting Group members. Twenty or so are jihadists who fought against US forces in Iraq and came here to join this fight. Abdul-Karim al-Rashid, our cheery friend from last night, leads that February 17 Martyrs' Brigade."

"We can't trust that bastard any further than we can throw him," Waverly said with a glance at the servants gathered near the service tent. "I'll bet my new boots some of those guys report directly to al-Rashid."

Deadeye nodded. "Jalal confirmed three of them worked for al-Rashid or other leaders of the February 17 Martyrs' Brigade in the past. We should demand that Jibril reassign those three."

"I'll do that tonight," Waverly said. He glanced at his watch. "Let's get the helo loaded. Deadeye, tell Jalal bin Koussa to join us and plan on heading out at twelve hundred hours."

"You got it."

It took an hour for the operators and their Libyan helpers to load four of the ATVs, Kornet antitank missiles, SA-18 surface-to-air missiles, and other equipment and supplies into one of the Mi-17 helicopters. Waverly pored over the maps and directed the pilot to fly southwest to a point just south of Ras Lanuf. They hugged the ground to avoid detection by the loyalist jet fighters and gunship helicopters they saw attacking along the main highway from Bin Jawad to Ras Lanuf.

The pilot landed in a depression in the desert plain, and Waverly and the operators jumped down from the helicopter. The din of tank, machine gun, and rifle fire rumbled from the distance.

"Fisherman," Waverly ordered, "deploy the weapons."

Fisherman and Spaceman quickly readied the SA-18 surface-to-air missiles, while Checkmate and Deadeye mounted the Kornet antitank missile launcher on one of the ATVs.

"Okay," he yelled when the weapons were armed and ready. "Checkmate and Redbeard, you stay here with the helo and monitor Libyan radio traffic. If they detect us, we'll return for extraction."

The team secured their weapons on the ATVs and headed due north toward the raging battle. Waverly sat behind Deadeye on one ATV, and Jalal sat behind Spaceman on another. They raced across the desert to within two kilometers of the front lines before they pulled the vehicles to a stop behind a small ridge. Lying on their bellies at the crest of the ridge, they scanned the battle through binoculars. Several Libyan tanks were speeding east ahead of loyalist infantry and firing on a disorganized mob of rebels retreating toward the city. One truck flying the rebel red, black, and green flag exploded into a fireball. A moment later, two pockets of rebels evaporated in fiery explosions.

A jet swept in from behind the rebels, and two bombs tumbled out of its belly. They exploded in the center of the panicked line.

"Shit," Checkmate muttered as another pickup truck exploded into a fireball. "They're getting a royal butt-kicking."

If those jets spot us we're toast, too. "Fisherman," Waverly said, "stand ready with the SA-18 missiles. Puckeater, bring the Kornet up here behind the crest."

Puckeater ran to the ATV with the mounted launcher and eased it up the incline until the vehicle was just behind the crest. He loaded a missile tube and then tracked the lead tank through the optical sight.

"Jalal," Waverly ordered, pointing, "get down in that ravine!" He waited a moment for the boy to scamper down the ravine in front of them. "Okay, fire!"

Puckeater fired. The missile launched with a *bam-whoosh*.

The operators watched through their binoculars as the missile raced across the desert just above the ground and hit the side of the first tank. It exploded into a ball of fire.

"Here comes the cavalry!" Puckeater yelled. "That second tank is saying, what the fuck was that?"

He loaded a second tube, sighted on the side of the nearest tank, and fired another missile. The second tank exploded a moment later. The flanking tanks ground to a halt and reversed course back through the tailing infantrymen.

Puckeater loaded another missile tube and locked onto the only tank standing its ground. He fired, and the Kornet streaked across the desert and obliterated the tank.

Waverly scanned the action through his binoculars as the remaining tanks accelerated back toward the line of infantrymen in headlong retreat. "Get that tanker truck too."

Puckeater turned slightly to his left, sighted on the tanker, and launched a fourth missile. The tanker exploded in a huge fireball.

Two fighter jets swooped down across the battlefield and banked toward the American position.

Waverly felt the blood drain from his face. "They know we're here!" he shouted. "Fisherman, fire!"

Fisherman, glanced behind to make sure back blast area was clear, dropped to one knee, braced the SA-18 firing tube against his shoulder, peered through the sight, and fired. The missile streaked skyward, and one of the jets erupted into a ball of fire. He stepped to his right to get another missile but plunged waist-deep into a sinkhole.

"Shit! Oh God, help!"

Waverly dived to the sand and crawled to him. He grabbed Fisherman's arm and worked him free of the sinkhole.

Fisherman rolled onto his back and clenched his leg. "Damn, I broke my ankle."

"Give me the tube," Waverly yelled. He loaded another SA-18 missile, sighted, and fired. The missile whooshed into the air and blew the second jet out of the sky.

Jalal bin Koussa leaped to his feet and jumped up and down, waving his arms. "You guys good!"

Waverly rolled his eyes amusedly. He double-checked through his binoculars. The Libyan tanks and infantry were in full retreat to the west. A commander on the turret of one of the tanks was trying to rally the others, frantically waving his arms as his tank raced back and forth behind the retreating line. Two of the tanks ground to a stop.

"Puckeater, get that tank with the commander in the turret," Waverly ordered.

Puckeater eased up the incline and fired. The missile darted across the sand and blew the turret off the tank. The tanks that had stopped reaccelerated in panicked retreat. One rumbled over a cluster of infantrymen and sped to the west, trailing a cloud of dust.

Half a dozen rebel pickup trucks, their mounted machine guns blazing, raced across the desert after the retreating tanks.

"Damn, the rebels are all teenagers," Waverly muttered beneath his breath. He dropped the binoculars to his chest. "Okay, Puckeater, help Fisherman onto your ATV. Let's get the hell out of here."

Spaceman reached up and secured an AK-47 rifle that had slipped out of its overhead rack. He slumped back in his seat and glanced at Jalal bin Koussa. *Was I that immature fifteen years ago?*

The teen couldn't stop gushing about the carnage he'd witnessed. These Americans were incredible. On and on, with his hands mimicking explosions, he rattled on above the rotors about the destruction of the tanks and fighter jets.

"I wouldn't believe it if I hadn't seen it with my own eyes. Now I finally believe in my heart, *Inshallah*, that Gaddafi the monster will soon be gone."

His chest was bursting with joy for the first time in months. *I've prayed for this moment for months. Allahu Akbar.*

"Why do you hate Gaddafi so much?" Spaceman yelled.

His elation came tumbling down. Tears welled in his eyes. "His men killed my father, my brother, and two of my friends. The evil one ordered them slaughtered like dogs. They weren't even part of the protests in Benghazi. They only watched, but Gaddafi's policemen shot them like dogs and tossed them into the back of a truck. My cousin saw it." He buried his head in his hands.

Spaceman reached out and patted his shoulder. "I'm sorry for your loss, my friend. You and I, we have more in common than you'll ever know. I, too, hate the murderer Gaddafi with all my heart."

He looked up through his tears at the unexpected tone in the soldier's voice. *This American is very different from the others.* "Why would you hate him?"

Spaceman gazed at him evenly. "He's a monster. I hate him for the evil shit he did to people inside and outside of Libya over the past thirty-five years. One day, he'll die like a rat. On that day, you and I will celebrate."

Shocked by the vehemence of the man's hatred, he nodded. "That will truly be a magnificent day, *Inshallah.*" And every day he spent with these Americans, that day drew a little closer.

Waverly helped Fisherman to the makeshift infirmary, wrapped his ankle with an Ace bandage, and helped him hobble back to the dinner table to join the other operators. *We're not off to a very good start here.*

"How's your ankle, buddy?" Checkmate asked.

"Just sprained it. It feels a lot better with this bandage."

Waverly nodded. "Other than your injury, I think we made a good showing out there today and gave Gaddafi's legions something to think about. One thing's certain: there's no way the rebels will survive without air support."

"You think they'll approve it?" Chico asked.

"Your guess is as good as mine. If it happens, I'm betting it'll be the French and British who carry out the air strikes." He tore off a piece of flatbread and stuffed it into his mouth. "Hey Chico, did Jibril reassign those three tent-boy spies today?"

Chico set his coffee mug down on the table. "Yeah, they packed up and left before the training session was over. They weren't happy about it either. They all glared at me from the back of their pickup truck as they drove off, and one of them shouted something about seeing me soon."

"You can bet he wasn't kidding," Waverly said. "We've got to be on guard here. I'll ask Jalal bin Koussa to find us three replacements he knows. The more everyday Libyans we have working with us, the better."

"Damn straight." Fisherman snipped off the end of a cigar. "You guys want to share this Cohiba I bought at the BX back in Ramstein? Who knows how long it will before we'll get another one."

"Why not?" Chico glanced back over his shoulder at a truck that had pulled up to the entry gate. He watched the guards check the engine and cargo compartments and wave the truck through, then grabbed the cigar from Fisherman and took several puffs. "Damn good." He blew out a cloud of smoke.

Waverly took a puff, handed the cigar back to Fisherman, and looked up at the star-studded sky, wishing he felt as peaceful as the sky above. *I've got to figure out where LIFG is storing its advanced weapons— that could include the nuclear backpack bomb. I think I can trust Jalal bin Koussa. I'll ask him tomorrow to ask around discreetly about any weapons caches hidden around Benghazi or out in the desert.*

He got up from the table. "Well, I need to answer some emails. I'll see you men in the morning." And he had a lot more thinking and planning to do.

9

Slaughter Alley

For the next eight days, Waverly and the covert operators launched daily raids on the loyalist front lines. They destroyed scores of Libyan tanks, personnel vehicles, and tankers, as well as five more fighter jets. Despite their daily efforts, loyalist armor, artillery, and warplanes pushed further into rebel territory, and Ras Lanuf fell to government troops on March 11. Pressing further east, Gaddafi forces drove into Brega on March 15 and Ajdabiya two days later.

Meanwhile, despite the best efforts of British and French special forces, government forces also retook Zuwarah, surrounded Misrata, and attacked Zintan and Nalut further west. It seemed likely that all the rebel cities in western Libya would once again fall under Gaddafi domination.

Then on March 17, as the disorderly rebel forces fled in headlong retreat and appeared on the verge of total collapse, the United Nations Security Council voted to authorize military action in Libya to protect the civilian population. Gaddafi responded the following day by announcing an immediate cease-fire, even as his ground forces launched a final assault on Benghazi. Libyan infantry, backed by dozens of tanks, bypassed Ajdabiya along coastal roads and pressed near to the western and southern gates of Benghazi, the erstwhile rebel stronghold.

During that week, Waverly and the operators found a small LIFG weapon cache hidden in an abandoned factory in Benghazi that Jalal bin Koussa had learned about from an old friend of his father. They blew up seven Russian-made Grinch SA-24 shoulder-launched surface-to-air missiles and twenty kilograms of C-4 plastic explosive.

Waverly searched the facility and grounds with the handheld detection unit shipped to him by Marilyn Harrison, but he found no sign of the backpack bomb.

"What the hell are you looking for with that scanner?" Fisherman had asked him.

He kept his head down and tried to look noncommittal as he swept the search head across the ground in the bunker. "Artillery shells that might contain chemicals or biologicals."

"What kind of biological weapons?"

"Anthrax, most likely."

"Shit," Fisherman muttered, "we don't have any hazmat suits."

"It's a long shot, but they want me to be thorough."

"Well, if you find anything suspicious, let's get some of those rebel trainees to dig them up."

Waverly chuckled, pleased to see the subject avoided. "That sounds like a plan."

He was awakened the next day before dawn by a call from the British commander. In coordination with the French special forces, Major Collin was requesting every available American fighter to join his men in blocking the advance of Gaddafi's forces on Benghazi. The two teams agreed to rendezvous at 0600 hours at the American base and helicopter from there to a point just south of the western gate of Benghazi.

Both American Mi-17 helicopters were loaded and ready to go before a pair of British helicopters landed nearby. Carrying his AK-47 and the handheld detector, Waverly jogged to meet the major first before sprinting back and jumping into the lead helicopter.

Jalal bin Koussa ran to the open door.

"Can I come?" he yelled over the whipping rotors.

"Absolutely," Waverly bellowed. "Get in."

Jalal climbed into the fuselage, and Waverly guided him into a seat beside Deadeye before stowing the detector in a compartment in the rear. The helicopters lifted off and flew due east before landing a quarter mile off the road that connected Suluq to Benghazi.

The teams offloaded their equipment and headed north toward the city by parallel routes as the sun began to rise above the desert to the east. Thirty minutes later, as they drew near the rally point, the heavy rumble of artillery rolled over them from the northwest.

"That's it," Waverly yelled at the men. "That's the southern gate there in the distance. Spaceman, you and Deadeye take the point."

The two operators hustled off with rifles and disappeared over a sandy ridge.

"Fisherman and Redbeard, follow them in the ATVs and set up your Kornets where you can best cover the southern gate. Jalal, you stay here with me."

Fisherman and Redbeard trudged forward through calf-deep sand toward the city looming in the distance and dropped to their bellies in a deep ravine.

Chico pressed a radio against his ear and then twisted toward the others. "Spaceman spotted more than two dozen enemy tanks converging on the southern gate from the west. They're setting up the Kornets. We should move to the west to cover their flank."

"Okay, let's move," Waverly said.

Moving stealthily through the bottom of the sandy ravine, the tailing group moved several hundred yards to the west toward the roar of engines and screech of tank treads.

Just after they pulled to a stop, the roar of tank fire rolled in from the distance. Chico scaled the wall of the ravine and slithered on his belly to the crest.

Waverly scurried up beside him as the attacking tank formation came into view.

"Jalal, keep your head down," he ordered. "Damn, where are the rebels?"

"It looks like they've fallen back inside the walls. Let's give them something to cheer about."

As if on cue, a *bam-whoosh* burst from their right, and a missile streaked along the desert floor. A tank on the right of the formation went up in flames. A second later, another missile slammed into the side of the lead tank.

Puckeater pumped his fist in the air. "Take that, you sons of bitches!"

The tanks ground to a stop. Then the entire formation veered off and sped away from the walls, throwing a cloud of sand high into the air. Waverly watched with increasing frustration as the line of tanks accelerated to the east toward a line of sand dunes and a wide ravine.

"Oh my God, they're headed straight for Fisherman and Redbeard," he yelled. "Puckeater, get on that radio and raise air command. Tell them we need air cover now!"

Another *bam-whoosh* rose above the din, and a missile darted across the desert and slammed into the tank nearest to Fisherman's group. The remaining tanks bypassed the burning hulks and lumbered forward across the sand.

"There's no more cover available," Puckeater called out. "They're on their own."

Waverly grabbed the radio from Chico. "Fisherman, get the hell out of there! Circle back!"

Several tanks pulled up and fired. A line of flashes threw smoke and sand high in the air.

Damn it. He tried to raise Fisherman on the radio but got no reply. "Spaceman, what's your position?"

"To the northeast of the tanks by 300 yards," came the radioed reply.

"Do you have a visual on Fisherman and Redbeard?"

"Negative. But they're near that ravine the tanks just shelled."

Damn, I've gotten them killed. Chico stared back in stunned silence.

"Fisherman, can you hear me?" Waverly yelled into the radio.

Only a crackle came in reply.

He glanced at Jalal. The boy's eyes were as big as saucers, and his lips were trembling. He took a deep breath and wiped his brow with his forearm.

"Jalal," Waverly called out, "are you okay?"

Jalal nodded, but his wide-eyed stare betrayed his terror. As a line of artillery shells exploded a few hundred yards to the east of their position, he dived headfirst into the sand.

"Fall back," Waverly bellowed. He got to his feet and scurried down the ravine with Chico, Checkmate, and Puckeater behind him. He tripped and fell to his knees on the embankment. He looked back over his shoulder as he arose. Jalal was frozen with his face buried in the sand.

He glanced over his other shoulder at the tanks rumbling toward them. "Jalal, let's go!"

Jalal remained stretched in the sand.

He scrambled to his feet, clawed his way up the embankment, and grabbed Jalal's shirt. "Come on, Jalal! We've got to move!"

Jalal stared at him with a look of sheer panic. "You go. I stay."

Waverly yanked at the boy's shirt. "Get up!"

He didn't move.

Waverly grabbed Jalal's arm and rolled him onto his back. Then he grasped the boy's ankles and dragged him down the sandy slope to the bottom of the ravine.

Chico trudged back to them, sinking calf deep in the sand, his forehead streaked with perspiration. "What the hell's wrong with him?"

Waverly gasped for air. "Shell shock."

Chico rolled his eyes. "We've got to go. The tanks!"

"I'm not leaving him."

Chico grabbed Waverly's arm. "Leave him."

"You go on," he yelled above the rumble of the approaching tanks. "I'm not leaving him."

Chico trudged a few steps, then whirled around and clomped back. "Help me pull him up."

"I'll carry him," Waverly said. "Just help me get him up."

Chico pulled the young man to his feet and onto Waverly's back. They trudged down the ravine after Checkmate and Puckeater. When they caught up, Chico stopped for a moment to transfer Jalal onto Checkmate's back and slogged on. The ravine made a sweeping turn to the south, and the group clomped for over a hundred more yards before the whine of engines rose ahead them. Checkmate dropped Jalal to the sand, and the three operators dived and aimed their rifles up the ravine.

Two ATVs driven by Fisherman and Redbeard barreled around a turn ahead of them. Both vehicles hurtled down the sandy incline and skidded to a stop beside Checkmate.

Thank God. "Why didn't you respond to my radio call?"

"I dropped the damn radio, and I sure as hell wasn't going back to get it." Fisherman motioned at Jalal. "What's wrong with him?"

"He's scared shitless," Chico said. "Checkmate, put him on the back of the ATV." He glanced down at two streaks of blood running down Redbeard's arm from a deep gash just below his elbow. "What the hell happened to your arm?"

"Shrapnel," Redbeard said. "That first tank barrage hit less than forty yards in front of us."

Waverly glanced behind them at the empty ravine. "Well, let's not wait around for them. Did you see the Brits?"

"Yeah, they split to the east as soon as the tanks headed our direction."

"Okay, we'll meet up with Spaceman and Deadeye at the rally point half a mile from here. Let's move."

They made it several hundred yards before a series of explosions boomed across the desert behind them. Three jet fighters streaked overhead.

"Take cover," Waverly yelled, and everyone dived for the sand.

Puckeater rolled to his knees. "They're French! It's the freakin' French!"

Sure enough, Waverly spotted the circular red, white, and blue insignia of the French Air Force on two of the jets. He scurried up the embankment and gazed out over the crest toward Benghazi. Two dozen tanks bellowing black smoke were scattered across the desert, with another group sprinting west in retreat. Waverly beamed at Fisherman as another formation of French fighters bore down from the east, launching missiles that decimated half a dozen more tanks and armored personnel carriers.

"I'll never mock the French again," he yelled.

"I wonder where our own fighter jets are?" Redbeard said.

Chico spit on the sand. "Probably back in Norfolk. Come on, let's get the hell out of here."

Waverly and the others linked up with Spaceman and Deadeye, and the team headed back to the base. Behind them in the distance, the pounding of Gaddafi loyalist forces continued for nearly two hours before tapering off just before they made camp.

The men cleaned and stowed their weapons, and then Waverly tended to Jalal. He got the jittery youth to drink some water, convinced him to take a Valium tablet, and covered him with a blanket. He ducked out of the tent and around the side of the barn, where he found the other operators eating around a billowing fire in the pit.

"Grab yourself some grub," Fisherman said between mouthfuls.

"Thanks." Waverly stepped over to the serving table, where the attendants served him chicken, rice, and flatbread.

A grinning old Arab piled his plate high with meat. "You great man of Allah," the stooped man said in broken English. "Allah will protect you and your family."

"This man's the idiot who almost got us all killed," Chico barked derisively from the fire.

Waverly took a deep breath and suppressed the urge to lash back. He took his plate of food and a cup of coffee and stomped around the side of the mess tent to where Spaceman was sitting by himself beneath a cluster of palm trees, gazing at the darkened sky.

"Did you get something to eat?" he asked Spaceman.

"I'll eat later."

"You mind if I sit down?"

The young operator shook his head. "Puckeater told me what you did out there today. You're an honorable man, sir."

"Please, call me Stone," he replied. "Anyone else would've done the same."

"No, they wouldn't. I wouldn't have."

"You weren't there. You would've done the same thing."

Spaceman stared at him for several moments and then gazed back up at the sky. "Deadeye told me you saved his butt once back in Iraq."

"That was a long time ago. And he saved my butt there a few times too." Waverly tore off a piece of bread and scooped up a bite of chicken and rice.

The two men sat in silence while Waverly ate.

Spaceman never took his eyes off the stars.

"Do you believe in God?" he finally asked.

Waverly nodded and rocked back from his plate. "I'm a Christian."

"Catholic?"

"Lutheran."

"I used to be Catholic."

"Used to be?"

"Yeah, before my parents died, I went to Mass with them every Sunday."

"What happened?"

"After they died, I just stopped going."

"No, I meant what happened to your parents?"

Spaceman broke his gaze on the stars. "They were killed in a plane crash when I was younger. It tore me apart and ruined my sisters' lives."

This kid's been through hell. "Sorry to hear it."

Spaceman scooped up a handful of sand. "It's hard to believe in God when shit like that happens. Or like the crap that happened today. How many men do you think were killed out there?"

"I don't know. I try not to think about it."

"Do you have any kids?"

"A boy and a girl."

"What are their names?"

"Mike and Anne." Just saying their names lifted his spirits.

Spaceman nodded. "I bet you're a great father."

"I try to be."

Spaceman pushed his beard back with his palms. "I miss my dad so much. I mean, I miss my mom too, but my dad was flat-out amazing." He sighed. "Sometimes you don't realize things like that when you're a kid. Then something terrible happens, and you can never stop thinking about it."

"Yeah, I know what you mean. My wife died of cancer a year ago."

"Who's taking care of your kids?"

"We have a nanny."

Spaceman jerked his head around. "What are you doing here? You should be home with them."

A wave of apprehension swept over him. *I've got to call them tomorrow.* "I was. I was retired—and then the Arab Spring happened. The company asked me to help them out for six months."

"Well, then, stop trying to be a hero. For their sake."

He frowned. He wasn't going to retread that territory with this young pup. "I wasn't being a hero, I only—"

"Promise me. Promise me you'll think of your kids before you do something like that again. Better yet"—Spaceman reached into his pocket and pulled out a small pistol—"I'll give you a flesh wound on your arm, and you can be on your way back to the States and your kids by the morning."

Waverly shook his head with frustration. He scooped up a handful of sand and pounded it on the ground. "I am helping my kids, Spaceman, and I'm helping my friends."

"How are you helping your kids and friends? This I gotta hear."

He dusted off his hands on his pants. "What do you think will happen to Libya if the rebels find a way to win and jihadists like Abdul-Karim al-Rashid come to power?"

"It'll go down the shitter."

"That's exactly right. And after working here in 1998 and 1999, I've got a lot of friends here in Libya—good, simple people with families—and I don't want that to happen to them. If the jihadists take over, the next thing you know, they'll be launching 9/11-style attacks on the US. I don't want my kids living their lives wondering when and where the next attack is going to come or even end up victims themselves." He pulled up short. *This kid doesn't have a clue what I'm talking about.* "Did you know anyone who was killed in the 9/11 attack?"

"No."

"Well, I did. John O'Neill, the head of security at the World Trade Center, was a good friend of mine. He died in the attacks. He worked at the FBI before he took the position at the World Trade Center. We worked together for nearly a year on the al-Qaeda bombings in Kenya and Tanzania just before I came here on my first Libyan assignment in 1998. He was a wonderful man, and I don't want any other John O'Neills killed back home. So that's why I took this assignment, to help my kids and my friends. Do you understand?"

Spaceman continued to stare up at the stars.

"Do you understand?" he repeated.

Spaceman finally met his gaze. Was it a trick of the starlight, or were those tears in his eyes? "I understand."

He bent over to fidget with his shoe, and Waverly lost sight of his face.

Waverly looked out across the blackened desert as a gust of wind whipped over them. None of what he'd just said would matter unless he could fulfill his mission. *Where the hell is that backpack bomb? I've lost my focus amid all this fighting between the rebels and Gaddafi's forces. I need to get the team looking for jihadist caches first thing tomorrow—before that backpack bomb ends up on some freighter cruising up Chesapeake Bay.*

10

The Worm Turns

A*s-Salaam-Alaikum,*" Interim Prime Minister Jibril said with a broad smile and a gleam in his eyes as he offered his hand to Waverly. "Welcome, my friends, to free Benghazi on this blessed day."

Waverly took his hand. "*Wa-Alaikum-Salaam*, Your Excellency. It is indeed a blessed day. Congratulations on your great victory."

"We know this would never have been possible without the help of our good friends. We are forever indebted to you and your country. Please convey my personal thanks to President Obama."

"I will, Your Excellency." Waverly finally ended the prolonged handshake and turned toward Spaceman. "You remember Mr. Brunello."

"Of course," Jibril replied as he shook Spaceman's hand, "one of America's great warriors. Thank you for all you and your honored friends did to help us survive the onslaught of Gaddafi's forces."

"It was an honor to help you, sir," Spaceman replied graciously.

"My colleagues are waiting in the conference room," Jibril finally said. "Let me take you to them."

Jibril led them to the second floor of the Tibesti Hotel and into a worn conference room where a dozen men chatted loudly around a large table. The group fell silent as soon as the door opened. Waverly spotted the brooding, black-haired Abdul-Karim al-Rashid at the end of the table. He also recognized General Abdul Fattah Younes and General Omar El-Hariri, two of the top rebel military commanders, and several men he'd worked with during his last mission in Libya. The rest of the men were strangers.

Jibril motioned to the head of the table. "Please," he said as he pulled out chairs for Waverly and Spaceman.

An attendant scurried in and poured each man a cup of tea and set a plate of thin pastry squares on the table between them.

"My friends," Jibril said with pomp, "let me introduce you to our good American friends, Mr. Waverly and Mr. Brunello."

"As-Salaam-Alaikum!" several men shouted. The group clapped politely—all except al-Rashid, who glowered at the two Americans.

"Wa-Alaikum-Salaam," Waverly replied with a slight bow of his head.

"Mr. Waverly," Jibril said, "perhaps you'd say a few words."

Waverly stood up and cleared his throat. "Thank you, my friends, for such a warm welcome. It gives us all enormous pleasure to see the people of the great city of Benghazi in such a festive mood. As representatives of America, we salute you on your great victory and hope that it won't be long before all of Libya can enjoy the peace and happiness that have come to this city that led the rebellion against tyranny and injustice in Libya."

"Thank you, my friends," Jibril replied with a toothy smile. "Now some of my colleagues from the National Transitional Council would like to ask you a few questions."

The hand of a balding, rather slender man with a clean-shaven face shot up.

Jibril acknowledged him with a nod. "General Omar El-Hariri."

El-Hariri stood up from the table. "Mr. Waverly, it is a pleasure to see you again here in Libya."

"The pleasure is mine, General."

"We thank you for America's support, but when will America provide us with the fighter jets we need to defend ourselves from the scoundrel Gaddafi and his henchmen? We need modern tanks and artillery too."

Do I need to answer this question every time we meet? Waverly cleared his throat. "I understand you have many needs, sir, but I am only here today to give greetings from the American government and to announce that in two short weeks, a representative of President Obama will arrive here in Benghazi. Once he arrives, you are welcome to address this question directly—"

"We also need money," El-Hariri said. "Many of our fighters haven't been paid since the rebellion started."

Waverly nodded and glanced questioningly at Jibril.

"I told my colleagues about the contribution you provided when you arrived," Jibril said, "but of course it only scratched the surface of our needs."

"I understand. My superiors in America authorized another larger payment, and I will see that you get it by the end of the week."

"Thank you, Mr. Waverly. May I ask who this representative is? Is he familiar with Libya and its people?"

Waverly nodded. "Honestly, I don't know who President Obama is sending, but I'm sure it will be someone with suitable qualifications." *And hopefully with answers to your endless questions.*

Another man dressed in a suit stood up at the opposite end of the table, and Jibril acknowledged him with a nod.

"Mr. Waverly, I am Mustafa Honi, vice chairman of the National Transitional Council. It is a pleasure to meet you, sir. I want to reinforce my friend General El-Hariri's request. We desperately need modern tanks and artillery. Air support alone will not be enough. We'd appreciate if you could get that message back to President Obama as soon as possible. Two weeks is a very long time in our present situation."

Waverly glanced at Spaceman. "Sir, I promise to do my best to get word back to my superiors. I know the situation here is desperate, and I will make it clear to my leaders what you are facing. As many of you know, I have many good friends in Libya, especially here in the east, and I give you my solemn vow to do everything in my power to support you both militarily and financially."

The NTC's al-Rashid stood up and rested his hands on the table, waiting patiently for the murmurs among the other members to subside. Waverly sensed abhorrence in the man's penetrating black eyes, which glared from beneath bushy eyebrows. *The feeling is mutual, you bastard.*

"Yes, Mr. al-Rashid," Jibril said with a nod.

"Mr. Waverly, I also want to express my personal thanks for both the ground and air support our fighters received yesterday. I only wish the air support could have come a month earlier so many more men could have been saved, but it finally came, thanks be to God."

"Thank you, sir. I think I also speak for operator Brunello when I say we too wish the air support could have come earlier. Our forces, including operator Brunello and my other American associates, have been supporting the rebel forces for nearly two weeks now, and I believe they made critical contributions to the rebel cause during many battles leading up to yesterday's major battle in Benghazi. I know you are aware of this."

Al-Rashid nodded. "Yes, of course. My question, however, is how soon operator Brunello and the other American fighters will leave Libya once the dog Gaddafi and his henchmen are routed?"

A broad-shouldered Libyan dressed in military uniform jerked up from the table to face the Islamist, his teeth clenched in rage. "How dare you insult these men, who risked their lives to stop Gaddafi's tanks when they drove on our city gates? Where were you, al-Rashid, when the tanks pushed through the west gate? Hiding somewhere far away, I am certain. Such rudeness directed at our guests will not be tolerated."

Another man seated beside al-Rashid leaped to his feet. "You are one to talk, Younes. Where were you when Gaddafi's henchmen slaughtered my brother and his sons two years ago in Ajdabiya? Where were you when dozens of my fellow Zuwaya tribe members were executed later that year? Oh, of course—you were minister of the interior in Gaddafi's government and the leader of Gaddafi's security service."

Younes's face grew red with anger. "Sit down, Mohammed Zuwaya. Do you accuse me of murdering your brother and tribe members?"

Jibril held up his hands in a conciliatory manner. "Gentlemen, calm yourselves," he said sternly. "I'm certain Abdul meant no harm. Mohammed, General Younes is now our military chief, so you will keep your theories about who's responsible for your brother's death to yourself. I'm confident Mr. Waverly understands that we are all eager to see the soldiers from the many countries helping us leave once the tyrant is defeated and Libya is stabilized. Please don't be offended by our bickering. We are truly grateful for your help."

"We take no offense," Waverly responded evenly. He turned to al-Rashid. *You ungrateful bastard.* He gave a stiff smile. "I can answer Mr. al-Rashid's question. As soon as the situation here in Libya is stabilized and Muammar Gaddafi is no longer a threat to you and your families, I'm certain my president will order us all to leave. In the meantime, we only aim to assist the freedom-loving people of Libya in bringing this revolution to a timely and satisfactory conclusion."

Jibril nodded just as the divider in the rear of the room was pulled aside to reveal a dozen tables set for lunch. "Thank you, Mr. Waverly. Now I hope you and Mr. Brunello will join us for a celebratory lunch. We can continue our conversation over several Libyan delicacies prepared by our chef."

"We'd be delighted," Waverly said, with a nod at Spaceman. "Any chance *fil fil mahshi* is on the menu? I told operator Brunello he must try it."

Jibril smiled. "Your wish is our command. *Fil fil mahshi* is one of my personal favorites, and I asked the chef to make sure to prepare this dish."

Waverly returned the smile easily, relief rippling across his shoulder muscles. *Thank God that's over. At least most of these leaders seem appreciative of what we've done for them. As for al-Rashid, screw him.*

The men moved into the adjoining room and sat down in groups at the tables—all except Abdul-Karim al-Rashid and Mohammed Zuwaya. They stepped out through a side entrance, and al-Rashid slammed the door behind them.

Waverly took his place at the table as the others settled around them. *What a piece of work. The man can't even stay for a celebratory lunch after we saved them from defeat. I'm more certain than ever he's got that backpack bomb.*

He smoothed his napkin across his lap. *We're coming for you, you bastard.*

11

Old Friends, New Friends

Waverly, his palm shading his eyes, stared across the tranquil waters of Benghazi Harbor past a pair of anchored tugboats at the northern approach to the harbor from the Mediterranean Sea. He glanced over his shoulder at the curve in the road beyond the wharf and caught a glimpse of Fisherman and Chico standing near a group of Libyan dockworkers who were preparing breakfast over an open fire pit that billowed white smoke. He scanned back along the shore toward the High Court Building but failed to spot the other covert operators he knew had positioned themselves discreetly along the waterfront from the Breakwater Building to the Berenice Hotel.

"I still don't see any sign of them," he said into his radio. "And the tugboats haven't moved."

"Spaceman sees something beyond the bridge," came Fisherman's reply. "Look, the tugboats are headed out now."

Fifteen minutes later, the upper decks of a freighter flying the Greek blue-and-white cross and stripes appeared beyond the breakwater. Guided slowly by the tugboats, the freighter turned into the harbor entrance and headed straight for the wharf. Paralleling the outer breakwater for nearly a kilometer, the tugboats slowed the freighter and gracefully turned the ship one hundred and eighty degrees just beyond the end of the wharf.

Fisherman came up behind Waverly and patted him on the shoulder. "Quiet so far."

Waverly used his binoculars to scan the faces of a group of Westerners gathered on the deck of the freighter. He locked onto a neatly groomed man dressed in a coat and tie. "I'll be damned!"

Fisherman shaded his eyes from the blazing morning sun. "What?"

"It's him, all right!" He trotted to the end of the wharf, where a group of dockworkers struggled to draw in the lines and ease the ship against the dock.

"Gus!" he called out to the man in the middle of the starboard deck.

The man beamed and held up a victory sign with his fingers.

As soon as the workers positioned the gangway, the new arrival leaped onto the pier, grinning from ear to ear with youthful air. A dozen other men dressed in civilian clothing followed behind him.

"Stone!" he called out excitedly. "You're the last person I expected to find here."

"Gus Morgan! My God, I'm speechless."

The two men embraced warmly, laughing like schoolboys who'd just won the junior high baseball championship.

"Where'd you come from?" Waverly finally asked.

"Malta. We left there yesterday afternoon. Hey, Thad Bartley told me you retired."

"I did, for seven years."

Morgan's blue eyes sparkled with delight, "Ha, but you couldn't stay away, could you?"

Waverly grinned. "As they say, the director made me an offer I couldn't refuse."

Morgan pushed a lock of brown hair sprinkled with gray back from his forehead. "Damn, I was just thinking about you a couple of days ago. How long has it been?"

"Well, I left Cairo in late 1995, so…seventeen years. Can you believe it?"

Morgan shook his head. "God, where did the time go? Those were the best times of my life."

"Yeah, for me too. Remember that time we drank too much bourbon and you backed your Hyundai into the ambassador's new armored BMW?"

"Ugh! Don't remind me. I thought my diplomatic career was over before it even started."

"Did you ever marry?"

"Hell no—who would have me? Did you?"

"I finally did. Her name was Julie. She passed two years ago, but I have a thirteen-year-old son and a seven-year-old daughter, Mike and Anne."

Morgan smiled warmly and grasped his arm. "I want to hear all about them when we get settled. Who's this with you?"

"This is Fisherman. He's the team leader of the muscle boys I brought with me to Libya."

Morgan shook the operative's hand. "Good to meet you. I heard about the heroics you and your men pulled off to hold back Gaddafi's forces. Great work."

"Good to meet you too, sir. We're happy to do our part."

Morgan turned to the group behind him. "Let me introduce you to rest of my team. This is Political Officer Bert Hanson and Special Agent in Charge Roger Mead. We also brought seven security agents. Listen, we've got two armored cars and several crates of communications equipment to offload, but first we need to find a place to set up shop. Any suggestions?"

"How about the Benghazi Cathedral?" Waverly said. "It's under renovation but vacant at the moment."

Morgan shook his head. "Too much symbolism. I want something where the real people of Benghazi live and work."

"You could stay at our base while you look," Fisherman offered. "It's in Benina."

"No, thank you, I want to be here in Benghazi. I'll tell you what—if necessary, we can stay on board the ship tonight while we look for a perfect spot."

"Well, first things first," Waverly said. "We need to head over to Freedom Square. Mahmoud Jibril and Mustafa Honi are waiting up at the street to take us there. Do you know them?"

"Absolutely. They're old friends."

Hmm, why would they have known who was arriving before I did? "Did they know you were coming?"

"It's possible. We sent the British representative a message last night."

"Major Collin?"

"No, a man named Winston Clark. I've never met him. I was told he arrived the day before yesterday."

"I haven't met him either. And if Jibril and Honi knew, they didn't let on—of course, they wouldn't have known we knew each other, since we weren't here in Libya at the same time." Waverly smiled brightly to cover his consternation. "We'd better head over. The entire city is waiting to thank us. Several of Fisherman's men walked over there to provide security after your ship docked."

"Super," Morgan replied happily as he glanced back toward the ship. "Roger, ask them to unload the cars into that secured lot over there while I go see Jibril and Honi. Tell the captain we'll be back in an hour and we'll likely stay on board tonight." He turned back to Waverly. "Roger and I are heading out to the olive orchards west of the city around six this evening for a run. Why don't you join us and tell me what you know about what's going on?"

"No way! I stopped jogging five years ago, but how about dinner later? There's a great little seafood restaurant only a few blocks from here."

"You mean Mata'am al-Arabi?"

"You know it?" Waverly asked with surprise.

"Of course, it's one of my favorites. It opened about a year before I left—early 2009, as I recall. Then after dinner, I've got a stash of bourbon we can break out. Okay?"

Waverly grinned. "Fantastic, as long as you're not driving."

"Don't worry, I'll get Roger to drive," Morgan said. "Why don't you ask the ops guys to get you over there, and we'll take you back? I'll meet you at seven thirty tonight—casual."

"You're on. I'll ask the guys to make sure those orchards are swept for IEDs before your run. I'd be miffed if I had to miss out on that bourbon."

Morgan laughed. "I appreciate it."

The driver inched around the rear of Atiq Mosque and parked the Toyota Land Cruiser just outside the south entrance to Freedom Square. As soon as they got out, Mahmoud Jibril greeted them effusively, then took Morgan's hand on one side and Waverly's on the other and led them between the buildings through a break that emptied into an expansive square teeming with people.

The crowd erupted into cheers and rhythmic chants the moment they were spotted. Libyans hoisted British, French, Qatari, and American flags next to the large red, black, and green banner of the rebel movement. Scattered across the square were people of every social level. There were businessmen in suits, young men in casual clothes, and old men in traditional Arabic attire. Women carried children and pushed babies in strollers, and many of the children in the front of the throng waved small rebel flags.

The Americans stepped into the square, and several young boys ran up and scattered flowers beneath their feet.

"It's incredible!" Morgan yelled to Jibril above the din. "Thank you."

"Thank you!" Jibril yelled back. "Thank you both and the American people for making this day possible. After forty-one long years, we are free at last."

Morgan's face broke into a broad, toothy smile. "It's great to be back," he shouted. He scanned the delighted faces pressing forward to greet him. "This is where I belong."

For more than an hour, with six diplomatic security agents clustered around them, Waverly and Morgan meandered back and forth across the square shaking every hand that was offered. A chant of "U-S-A, U-S-A, U-S-A!" began quietly, building to a frenzied crescendo that drowned out the crackling of rifle fire and thud of bombs in the distance that reminded everyone that the revolution was far from won.

Morgan raised his arms and acknowledged the crowd with a jovial smile and the word *shukran* on his lips.

They were nearly across the square when Waverly spotted a brooding figure staring down at him from a terrace. Abdul-Karim al-Rashid. He tapped Morgan on the arm and motioned toward the terrace. Morgan looked up and nodded at al-Rashid, but he didn't acknowledge it.

Jibril paused behind Waverly and leaned forward, speaking just loudly enough for Waverly to hear above the din. "Don't worry about al-Rashid. We have him under control."

He glanced back at Jibril and nodded.

When he looked back at the terrace, al-Rashid was gone.

12

Liaison

Waverly could just make out the dimly lit sign of Mata'am al-Arabi in the gathering darkness. Fisherman bumped the car over a low curb and into a parking lot lit with a string of naked light bulbs hung from the facade.

Spaceman jumped out the passenger-side door and checked a dozen cars parked against the building. "Clear!"

Fisherman raced the car across the parking lot and squealed to a stop beside a pair of DSS agents posted at the door.

Waverly leaned forward in the back seat. "Why so tense?"

"Mustafa Honi came to meet me today. He and General Younes think the February 17 Martyrs' Brigade is planning something big."

"Like what?"

"Like an attack on the NTC designed to tear the rebel coalition apart so they can seize control of the new Libya."

He jumped at the sound of a machine-gun burst in the distance. "That was close."

"It sounds like it's coming from the western gate," Fisherman said. "Don't worry, our entire team is here backing you up."

He nodded. "Does he think someone specific is being targeted, or is this a generic caution?"

"He thinks they want to get you or Morgan, or even both of you... kidnap you if they can or kill you if they can't. We intend to make sure that doesn't happen."

He sighed. "You really know how to boost a guy's appetite."

Fisherman turned back in his seat. "Sorry, but we need to be prepared."

"You could've at least waited until after dinner."

"You need to alert Morgan too."

"He doesn't know?"

"There was no time."

"Great dinner conversation. 'Hey, Gus, my old friend, it's so good to see you. Oh, by the way, the February 17 Martyrs' Brigade is planning to assassinate us.'"

"Wait until dessert," Fisherman said with a grin. "Our team got here earlier, and they'll make sure you're not disturbed. Don't worry. We have everything under control."

"Thanks." He pushed the rear door open and ducked out of the car.

"Good evening, Mr. Waverly," one of the American DSS agents said as he pulled the restaurant door open. "Mr. Morgan is in the private room in the back."

"Thank you."

Two Arabs attired in western suits waited for him in the foyer. The smaller, squat man stepped forward and took his hand. "Welcome to Mata'am al-Arabi," he said with formal aplomb.

"I'll be joining Mr. Morgan," he replied.

"Yes, of course, sir. Right this way." The man pushed aside a curtain and led him into the main restaurant.

About a dozen tables were set, but only one near the window was occupied. The young man there looked away from his companion, momentarily catching Waverly's eye. For a fleeting moment, Waverly thought he recognized the man. He was gaunt with a long, bushy beard and dark-rimmed glasses that framed heavy-lidded eyes. He looked as if he might get to his feet, but then he leaned back into his chair and whispered something to his companion, who glanced at Waverly too.

"Right this way, sir," the maître d' said. He opened a side door and ushered Waverly into a dimly lit room where Gus Morgan sat alone at a table set for four.

Morgan sprang to his feet. "You made it! I was beginning to worry."

"Sorry I'm late. I had to wait for the car."

"No worries. I took the liberty of ordering a bottle of French Champagne. I remembered your favorite—Louis Roederer Cristal."

"*Whooo-eeey,*" Waverly exclaimed. He glanced at the open bottle in an urn overflowing with ice.

Morgan laughed. "But unfortunately, we'll have to settle for Alfred Basely. Only the Old Ripy bourbon I brought with me is top shelf."

"After being here for a month, any champagne will do just fine."

Morgan filled two glasses and handed one to Waverly. "Here's to a successful mission in Libya and bringing peace and prosperity to these deserving people." He clinked his glass to Waverly's.

"And to renewing a great old friendship." Another staccato of rifle fire resounded from the distance. "You know, I can't begin to tell you how relieved I am that they've sent someone with the same feelings about the common people of Libya that I have. Someone like me who has so many friends here in Libya."

"I know how you feel. I felt the same way as soon as I spotted you on the dock. Have you visited any old friends since you arrived?"

"No, I've been reluctant to. I feel like I'm being watched, and I don't want to increase the dangers these friends already face. My dream is that we can return Libya to a time you and I knew, back when we could visit our friends here in Benghazi without worrying about retribution—and without Gaddafi, of course."

"Let's drink to that," Morgan said, lifting his glass.

The two men clinked their glasses and sipped. Conversation turned to small talk about Morgan's jog in the olive orchards.

Finally, Morgan spread his napkin across his lap. "Well, tell me what's been going on here the past month."

Waverly let out a long sigh of frustration. "What's going on here can best be described as a royal standoff. All along the coast from Ajdabiya to Brega to Ras Lanuf and even as far west as Sirte, there've been continuous battles. One side pushes the other out, only to be repulsed a few days later. Without the air power of the coalition forces and the support provided by the American, British, and French soldiers, the rebels wouldn't have a chance. One thing you should know, if you don't already, is that a coalition fighter jet killed thirteen rebels on the highway between Brega and Ajdabiya on Friday night after the rebels fired on them with antiaircraft guns."

Morgan shook his head. "I know. We sent apologies and condolences for our unfortunate mistake, although you and I both know those rebels need to be damn sure about who they're trying to shoot down. I got briefings about the assistance the team was providing to the rebels before I left Washington, but what I really want to know more about is the rebel leaders—the makeup of the National Transitional Council and the other political groups, what tribes they represent, and where you see opportunities and potential difficulties."

Waverly felt a wave of relief flow through his body. *It's so great to be working with someone who knows what they're doing.* "First, let me tell you what I've discovered so far about the leadership of the NTC. Over the past month, I've come to believe that Mahmoud Jibril and Mustafa Honi are capable leaders who actually have the interests of most Libyans in mind."

Morgan set his bread down and nodded. "I know both of them well. They're men of character and integrity. One of our priorities must be to see that they retain their leadership. Do you know who represents the Muslim Brotherhood and the other Islamic extremist groups?"

"Four I know of from a document that was seized in one of our raids near Al Marj. Mohammed Zuwaya, Alamin Belhaj, Abdel Hakim

Ghashir, and Khalid Qnan are Muslim Brotherhood. There are likely more clandestine supporters we don't know about, but those are definite." He shifted uncomfortably in his chair. "Then there's that bastard Abdul-Karim al-Rashid."

"Al-Rashid," Morgan repeated with a sneer. "A true believer if there ever was one."

Waverly picked up some nuts from a tray and popped them into his mouth. "Many people are happy with the direction things are going here in Libya, but he's not one of them. I see him as the main threat to a peaceful transition once Gaddafi's gone."

"You're right about that," Morgan said. He stabbed his fork into the salmon appetizer. "He's supposedly in a power struggle with al-Qaeda's top leadership, but I'm betting that's a ruse to make them seem less threatening to us, as well as to their countrymen."

Good, I'm glad we're on the same page. "That's my gut feeling—and my superiors' too. Al-Rashid is ruthless, and he'll do everything he can to turn Libya into a base for the Sunni Islamist movement governed by Sharia law. The one thing we must never lose sight of is the importance of the tribes and clans here in Libya. I've met with many of the leaders of the major tribes over the last two weeks. They are the people who will ultimately determine the outcome of this revolt."

"But don't you think Gaddafi will—"

"Gus, this whole revolution began based on Gaddafi losing control of many of the tribes he once dominated through bribe or intimidation. The role of the Obeidat tribe in the rebellion is a key. This began when Major General Suleiman Mahmud al-Obeidi, commander of the Tobruk military region, defected in February to join the anti-Gaddafi rebels. Staff Major General Younes al-Obeidi, an old friend of Gaddafi's and the former interior minister, announced his defection to the rebels on Al Arabiya television just a few weeks later. Those were heavy blows to Gaddafi."

Morgan took another sip of Champagne. "I heard one of the prominent Obeidat women got assaulted by loyalist troops."

"That would be Iman al-Obeidi, a young law student. She stood up at a restaurant at the Rixos Hotel in Tripoli and told some members of the international press corps she'd been gang-raped by Gaddafi's soldiers after they arrested her on the Tripoli-to-Tajura road." He raised one eyebrow. "Some believe this was direct retaliation for the recent defections."

Morgan jumped at the crash of a breaking glass in the other room, then leaned forward. "So, you think Suleiman Mahmud al-Obeidi and Younes al-Obeidi defected with the blessings of their tribal leaders?"

"Absolutely. I think it's likely both of them were under pressure from the tribe when they made the decision to defect and that they received assurances that their past sins would be forgiven. That's a big deal for Younes, considering he was Gaddafi's interior minister and likely complicit in many of the acts committed by Gaddafi and his henchmen."

"So, he's just playing it safe?" Morgan asked in disgust.

"No, not at all. I'm convinced he finally had enough of Gaddafi's treachery and joined the rebels out of principle, despite great personal risk from both sides. One thing's certain: the February 17 Martyrs' Brigade will never forgive him. Many of their leaders were members of the Libyan Islamic Fighting Group, and they all remember that Younes was instrumental in crushing LIFG as minister of the interior in Gaddafi's government."

Morgan folded his arms across his chest. "I'm sure he's got a lot of information on these February 17 Martyrs' Brigade characters. I know him well from my first mission here in Libya. I'll talk to him about it."

"Take a bottle of bourbon," Waverly said with a wry smile. "He loves it. Better yet, let's meet with him together. He's a hoot." He took a bite of naan. "All these defections helped create rifts among the senior officers loyal to Gaddafi, and his power began to crumble. The defections also served to support rebel claims for assistance from the NATO powers."

"Gaddafi's henchmen will do everything they can to suppress this dissent. They've already killed hundreds of dissidents in the villages around Tripoli…maybe thousands."

"Yes, and unfortunately that's unavoidable. But the execution of dissident soldiers from the Ferjan tribe likely turned that entire tribe against him. Two loyal tribes now dominate the security forces: the Qadhadhfa, Gaddafi's own tribe, will stick with him to the bitter end, and the Megharha. Two other tribes that have traditionally been close to the regime appear to be splitting off completely: the Warfalla, the biggest tribe in the country with something close to a million members, and the Tarhona."

"So…"

"So, the key issue now is whether Gaddafi can maintain their loyalty —and that's something we need to exploit if we want to bring Gaddafi down." Waverly looked Morgan straight in the eye. "We do want that, don't we?"

Morgan smiled. "I'm not sure, at this point. Some in Washington feel that the best outcome here would be a standoff with no clear winner—perhaps a split country into east and west."

Waverly sighed. "I sense growing support for that outcome too, but that would be a disaster for the Libyan people. It would lead to death and destruction for years to come."

"The possibility keeps me awake at night. Anyway, starting tomorrow, my political officer, Bert Hanson, and I are going to make a point of meeting with all the members of the National Transitional Council. But before that, I want to host a dinner party for all the members of the NTC. I'd like you to be there."

That'll be a clusterfuck if there ever was one. "No problem, just let me know when and where."

Morgan glanced back at the door. "One more thing before they bring in the food. I was briefed about the stolen RA-115-2 just before I left. You and I are the only ones here in Libya to know about it for now, but the president wants us to step up the search."

Thank God, I can finally discuss the search for the backpack nuclear bomb with someone else. Waverly flicked at his watch and nodded. "I've been trying to do just that. But we've only found one jihadist weapon cache, and it wasn't there."

"We need to press the search by all the allies under the guise of searching for surface-to-air missiles."

"I'll get Fisherman—" He stopped in mid-sentence as the waiters pushed through the door with small platters of meat, fish, and vegetables. They would have to finish these details later.

Over dinner, they discussed less sensitive issues and strategies for close to two hours before the waiters brought in dessert and coffee.

Waverly set his coffee cup down. "Gus, when you were here in 2009, did you ever dream an uprising like this could happen in Libya?"

"Never. Gaddafi and his secret police were in complete control. Even a hint of protest was crushed with overwhelming force. But then again, it's hard to imagine a lot of what's happened throughout the Middle East and North Africa since 9/11. That success gave jihadi groups the confidence that anything was possible if they were willing to sacrifice. And here we are now, dealing with al-Qaeda in Libya."

"Fisherman told me intel from an informant suggests that al-Rashid and the February 17 Martyrs' Brigade are planning to kidnap or kill both of us."

Morgan's eyes widened, but he waited for Waverly to go on.

"I also believe al-Rashid's the most likely person to be hiding the backpack bomb."

Morgan nervously drummed his fingers on the table. "I'm certain that al-Rashid had it in his mind to cut my throat since the first time I was posted here in Libya. I've never given him the opportunity."

As likable as he was, Morgan was sometimes insufferably cocky—and those jogs through the olive groves could get him killed. "You've got to be more careful with those runs in the groves and your efforts to shake the hand of each and every Libyan."

Morgan grinned. "Don't worry. I have plenty of friends here looking out for me. I'm not going to let al-Rashid and others like him change how I interact with my Libyan friends. We both know what they need. How about if we make a pact here and now to work together to see that they get it, even if it's not exactly what Washington wants?"

"You know nothing would satisfy me more. But finding that nuclear backpack bomb takes even more precedence now."

Morgan pursed his lips in consideration. "Let me ask you a hypothetical question. If despite all our efforts al-Qaeda somehow manages to transport the backpack bomb up Chesapeake Bay and detonate it, how much damage would it do?"

Waverly exhaled long and slow. "Well, I guess that depends where it was detonated. This bomb is about one-tenth the power of the bomb dropped on Nagasaki in World War II. If they somehow managed to truck it to the parking lot near the Raven's stadium during a football game…"

The two men stared into each other's eyes for a long moment, each with the image of a mushroom cloud in his mind.

13

Settling In

The covert team's helicopter set down in the compound a little after noon on a blistering hot afternoon, and Waverly was the last one to jump down to the sand. Looking up, he caught sight of Morgan and Hanson sitting in the open tail of a Toyota Land Cruiser, staring at a computer screen.

Jalal bin Koussa dashed to the helicopter, and Waverly handed him his backpack.

"Any battles today, Mr. Waverly?" Jalal asked.

"No battles. Just trying to locate Gaddafi's tanks."

"Did you find them?"

He shook his head. "They're in hiding now that the air strikes have started, but they could come back at any moment."

"Mr. Fisherman told me I can't come with you to fight anymore. Can you help me? I can never restore my honor unless I'm given another chance to fight."

Poor kid. "I'm sorry. Mr. Fisherman looks out for the safety of the soldiers on his team, and he's worried about your safety too."

Jalal stared down at his feet. "Could you make one more chance for me? Please, just one more chance?"

Waverly patted him on the shoulder. "I'll talk to him, but I can't promise anything."

Jalal bowed. "I am grateful for your kindness, sir. Perhaps Mr. Fisherman will respect me more if you teach me how to shoot the Russian rifle."

He couldn't help but smile. "That's a good idea—but in a few minutes. I need to talk to Mr. Morgan."

Morgan got up when he saw him coming.

"Afternoon," Morgan called. "Find anything?"

Waverly sank gratefully into a chair. "We found the weapons bunker near Ajdabiya, but there were only a few AKs, some small arms ammunition, and three surface-to-air missiles inside. Then we headed over to Brega to check out the rebel tanks that the coalition fighter jets hit last night. They lost two tanks and four men before the fly-boys realized their mistake."

"Damn, that's the second time this week. I'm surprised I haven't heard from Jibril."

He gave a weary sigh. "He was at the site when we got there. Apparently, one of the men killed was the son of a council member."

"Oh, shit. Which one?"

"Ahmed Dirssi's son Mohammed."

Morgan frowned at Hanson and then closed his eyes. "We *just* met with him yesterday, and he thanked us for everything America has done. What a tragedy."

Waverly reached into his shirt pocket. "Jibril had one of his couriers bring me this note."

Morgan unfolded the small paper and read out loud. "Dear Mr. Waverly, my son would not want his death to hinder our cause but would want America to redouble its attacks on our enemy in his memory. May Allah bless you and your men. Ahmed Dirssi."

Morgan took a deep breath, shook his head, and stuffed the note in his shirt pocket. "I'll make sure he gets what he needs for his son's wife and children. At least we have an office now to do that from. We found office space in the Tibesti Hotel."

"Oh, really?" Waverly said wistfully. An office in a place like that would be sweet. Heck, he could call home every day if he wanted. "That's perfect. I hope you got the office with a view of the sea."

"I'm afraid not—but the hotel does offer easy access to the city. Join us for dinner tomorrow. I'll show you around."

"Great. Think I could call my kids while I'm there? Tomorrow's Saturday, and they should be home."

"Absolutely. Should we come get you?"

"I'll ask the team to drop me off."

"Actually, why don't you come in the morning? We can pay our respects at Mohammad Dirssi's funeral first."

He gave a decisive nod. "Perfect. I'd like to be there with you. See you tomorrow."

Jalal approached again as soon as Waverly turned.

"Are you ready now, Mr. Waverly?" he asked eagerly.

A sense of déjà vu swept over him. *That sounded like Mike asking to play catch.* "Sure thing. Let me get my AK."

They fetched several discarded soft drink bottles from the trash and set them up at the perimeter of the base behind the helicopter landing pad.

"Never point the rifle at anyone you don't intend to shoot. Take the rifle like this and insert the magazine like this. Okay, you do it."

Jalal repeated the maneuver.

"This is the safety. If it's here, the rifle won't fire, but if it's here, it will. Leave the safety on until you're ready to shoot. Then always check to see if the magazine is full of bullets and whether a bullet is in the chamber. See these bullets? This magazine is loaded and ready to go. Now, to check if the chamber is loaded, you pull this slide back. If there's one in the chamber, it will fall out. There's no bullet in this chamber. Okay, you do that."

Jalal repeated the maneuver twice. A quick study.

Waverly set the rifle down and removed several bullets. "Here's how you unload the magazine, and here is how you load the magazine." He handed the magazine to Jalal. "Okay, you do it."

Jalal repeated the unloading and loading perfectly. The kid was good.

Waverly picked up the rifle. "The safety is on. Hook the magazine like this and snap it into position. Okay, you do it."

Jalal again repeated the maneuver.

Waverly stepped back and put his hands on his hips. "You've done this before."

"My father taught me when I was ten years old. It's all coming back to me."

"Aha, you're a sandbagger," he said with a chuckle. "But let's make sure you do it the right way. To fire the rifle, you push this safety to the off position, pull back on this slide, and release it. Now you're ready to fire. I'm going to fire first. Only a short burst, because the gun barrel will try to climb as the rifle fires. Like this." He aimed at one of the plastic bottles thirty yards away. "Make sure the stock is tight against your shoulder, or it'll knock you on your butt. Now I'm going to fire one bullet at a time." He aimed and fired three shots a couple of seconds apart, then put the safety on and handed the rifle to Jalal. "Your turn. One shot at a time."

Jalal took the rifle, slid the safety off, aimed, and fired. His bullet sent the second plastic bottle soaring.

"I did it!"

"You're a natural. Three more times, each a second apart."

Jalal aimed and fired three more bullets. The first two hit to the side of the third bottle, but the third was on mark.

Waverly's heart swelled. "Great! Now put the safety on and hand me the rifle. No! Always pointing away from people. I'm going to show you burst fire, shooting three to five bullets in each burst. Hold the rifle down at your waist with your right arm like this and your left hand holding the stock like this. Turn the safety off and fire a burst of no more than five bullets by pulling and holding the trigger like this."

He aimed toward the bottles and fired a burst, pulverizing two plastic bottles. He flipped on the safety and handed the rifle to Jalal. "Turn the safety off, hold the rifle firmly, and fire."

Jalal fired. The rifle barrel jerked upward out of control.

Waverly knocked the barrel down.

"Oh," Jalal said. "Sorry."

"That's okay. It always happens the first time. Put the safety on, and keep the rifle pointed away. Now, position it like this across your body, and hold it firmly. Try to fire only a burst of three. Try it again."

Jalal took up the position, turned off the safety, and fired one burst that kicked up sand to the side of the remaining bottles, then another that blew them away. "I did it! I'm a mujahideen."

Waverly laughed. "Well, not quite, but we'll keep practicing. Fire up the rest of the magazine, and then that's it for today."

Jalal fired several bursts at brush near the perimeter fence until the rifle was empty. He put the safety on and handed the rifle to Waverly. "Can we do it again tomorrow?"

If only it were this simple to guide every Libyan toward responsibility and a hunger for a better future. "Not tomorrow, because I'll be away. But definitely later this week."

Jalal beamed. "Thank you, Mr. Waverly. You are a master teacher. May Allah bless you."

Waverly stood beside Morgan the next day watching the morning sun rise over Freedom Square. Several American security agents were arrayed around them, eyeing the more than a thousand men and boys waiting for the funeral to begin. Many in the crowd were chanting loudly and shouting the names of the fallen rebels. The square where

Waverly and Morgan had been saluted a few days earlier had become the focus of a mass funeral to honor the victims of the recent friendly fire, including Mohammed Dirssi.

Waverly wiped his brow with a handkerchief as a shout arose from the assembled multitude. Four wooden coffins were being carried around the side of Atiq Mosque and into the center of the square. Ahmed Dirssi was among the men carrying the first coffin, his eyes swollen with sadness as he helped carry his son's coffin to a waiting truck. Hundreds of men reached out to touch Dirssi and mutter their condolences. Finally, the boisterous throng loaded all four coffins into a truck, then climbed onto the running boards and into the bed as the driver pulled in behind a line of pickup trucks headed to the cemetery.

The Americans followed the procession of vehicles bearing the red, black, and green flags of the rebel movement as it wound through the city past hundreds of mourners and out of the city walls to the Hawari Cemetery. As they exited the city, many of the fighters in the horde fired their guns into the air and let out mournful shouts that echoed across the neglected, sandy graveyard, where weeds and thistle grew among the stone markers. The acrid smell of gunpowder filled the air, burning Waverly's nostrils.

The lead vehicle pulled to a stop near a line of freshly prepared graves just thirty paces outside the city walls. The angry mob pulled the coffins from the truck and trudged across the sandy ground behind an imam holding up the Koran as he shouted in Arabic.

Waverly and Morgan abandoned their security detail and followed a short distance behind the coffins.

"Killers!" a young rebel shouted at them before an older man pulled him away.

Waverly watched solemnly as the bodies, wrapped in white burial shrouds, were removed from the coffins and lowered into the ground. The imam said a prayer, and the bodies were covered with the sandy red dirt.

Waverly bowed his head and said a short prayer. He looked up to find Ahmed Dirssi and three other men walking toward them.

"Thank you for coming," Dirssi said to Waverly and Morgan as he drew near.

"I want to express my personal sorrow for your great loss," Waverly said. "I can't begin to grasp the pain you must feel over the loss of your son."

"Thank you, sir. I believe it was another American diplomat who said the tree of liberty must be refreshed from time to time with the blood of patriots and tyrants."

"When it is your own flesh and blood, I think somehow that truth holds less meaning."

Dirssi acknowledged the sentiment by inclining his head. "Mohammad was an idealistic young man who knew he could be killed in battle against our better-armed opponents, but I doubt he imagined being bombed by the airplanes we all saw as our salvation. Did you receive my note, Mr. Waverly?"

He stepped closer. "Yes, I did."

"Please honor my son by stepping up your attacks. Crush Gaddafi's forces. Restore dignity and honor to Libyans."

"I will do my best to see that happens, sir."

"I know you will. Thank you again for coming, Mr. Waverly. Mr. Morgan."

Waverly's extended hand fell uselessly back to his side as Dirssi shuffled back to his son's grave, his hands pressed over his face. He knelt in the soft sand, threw back his head, and let out a mournful wail.

14

Double Cross

The camouflage-painted Russian Mi-17 helicopter settled onto the bull's-eye of the helipad outside the Tibesti Hotel. Fisherman jumped down and ran to where Waverly was sitting along with Morgan.

"Are you ready?" he yelled above the clamor of the rotors as the backwash whipped his long hair and beard.

Waverly stood and nodded at Morgan. "Let's go."

The three men ran to the helicopter and ducked inside the open door. Puckeater, Deadeye, Redbeard, Checkmate, and Chico were strapped into seats with AKs in hand.

Chico motioned at the space across from him, and Waverly and Morgan strapped themselves into adjacent seats.

Once Waverly was secure, he craned to look back at Spaceman, sitting next to Jalal bin Koussa in the rear. He caught Jalal's eye, and the boy beamed back at him with satisfaction. Waverly gave him a thumbs-up.

The engines revved, and the helicopter lifted off the ground.

The bird flew along 23rd July Road and banked over March 28 Stadium headed southwest. Crossing over the eastern shore of the Gulf of Sidra, they were joined by a pair of French fighter jets that repeatedly flew west and back again to cover them against a Libyan aircraft ambush. They penetrated inland over Sabkhat Ghuzayyil, the lowest point in Libya.

I wonder what Gaddafi wants? The undulating desert plains unspooled below them, and the pilots began to parallel a broken and potholed road that was in many stretches completely obscured by sand. *Maybe he found out about the RA-115-2 and is afraid the rebels will use it on him. Maybe he's ready to leave Libya.*

"That's the El Agheila to Maradah Road," the navigator yelled back to them. "It's no longer used."

"Really?" Waverly yelled. "How do people get out here?"

"Helicopter or camel."

They paralleled the road another ten minutes until a palmed oasis arose seemingly from nowhere. Flying over the shantytown, they spotted a pair of helicopters parked across from a small one-story building.

"That's it," the pilot called back to them. "Maradah Clinic."

"Circle it," Waverly yelled.

The pilot banked around the perimeter of the building in a series of decreasing circles. On the fifth pass, a man in a suit appeared outside the front of the clinic and gave them a full-arm wave.

"Okay," Waverly bellowed. "Land a kilometer down the road to the west. And make sure those fighter jets stay close by. There's something fishy about this."

The pilot nodded and banked to the west along the road. The operators readied their gear.

"We'll drive in on the ATVs," Waverly told Morgan just before the helicopter set down on a smooth patch in the road.

The team jumped from the helicopter and fanned out around the perimeter. Fisherman sprinted back to the helicopter a few moments later. "All secure," he shouted to Waverly. He jogged to the tail of the helicopter and lowered the ramp cargo door to the pavement. Then he climbed inside the cargo bay, untied the lines from the nearest ATV, and rolled it down the ramp as the two French jets thundered past above them. Fisherman started the ATV and gunned it several times.

Chico jogged back around the side of the helicopter. "There's a Toyota Cruiser headed this way," he bellowed over the powerful Mi-17 rotors.

Waverly nodded curtly. "Good. Maybe we won't even have to leave the chopper. Get the other ATV, just in case."

Chico rolled out the other vehicle, secured his rifle, and started the engine. Just as he mounted it, Jalal ran around the side of the helicopter.

"Mr. Chico, please, let me ride with you."

Chico shook his head. "Not this time." He gunned the engine and pulled away.

The boy's shoulders slumped.

"Jalal!" Waverly yelled. "Stay here with Mr. Morgan and me. We need your help."

Jalal's face brightened. "How can I help, sir?"

"Here." Waverly held out a pair of binoculars. "Keep an eye out for any other vehicles headed this way while we're meeting." He pointed to an elevation about fifty yards away. "I want you to take up a position on that mound over there where you can see in all directions."

Jalal took the binoculars, looked through them toward Maradah for a moment, and then grinned happily. "Don't worry, sir. I will watch carefully." He ran off to his perch.

"Good work," Morgan said with a chuckle.

Waverly winked. "I've had a lot of experience keeping boys busy."

Chico and Fisherman sped off toward the town, throwing up a cloud of sand behind them. They disappeared over a ridge as Spaceman jogged back to the helicopter, talking into the radio microphone attached to his chest.

"Did you reach your kids last night?" Morgan asked Waverly.

"Yes, thanks. I'm afraid I ran up your phone bill talking to all of them."

"No problem. How are they doing?"

"Just fine. The nanny keeps them busy, and they're taking their dogs to obedience classes. I think I'm missing them a lot more than they're missing me."

Morgan grinned. "I'd like to meet them someday."

He wouldn't mind being able to hug them all right now himself. "We'll have you over for dinner when we get home."

"I'd like that."

One of the ATVs roared back over the ridge, followed by the black Toyota Land Cruiser. The vehicle pulled slowly to a stop a few car lengths from the helicopter, and a clean-shaven Arab of medium height wearing a western sports coat with an open collar climbed out of the rear, followed by two aides. The man removed his sunglasses to reveal piercing, dark-ringed eyes. His enormous mouth dominated a stern expression.

"Good afternoon, gentleman," he began without offering his hand. "I'm Abdullah al-Senussi, and I bring greetings from Brother Leader Gaddafi."

"Please give him our regards," Morgan said. "I'm Gus Morgan, and this is my associate Stone Waverly. Mr. Waverly also represents the American government."

"It's my pleasure to meet you both," al-Senussi said with a nod. "I think we'd be more comfortable meeting at the Maradah Medical Clinic. We've prepared a banquet of fruit, lamb stew, and fresh-baked bread. There's a home next door where Rommel is said to have spent the night during his advance across Libya in 1941. It would be my pleasure to show you around."

Waverly kept his face a mask of calm. *You bastard. Do you think we're stupid enough to let you isolate us from our security?* "Thank you for your gracious hospitality, but our time is short, and I think we should get right to our discussion. What can we do for you?"

"Very well," al-Senussi said as he replaced his sunglasses. "The Brother Leader and I are puzzled as to why you're helping al-Qaeda destroy Libya."

"We aren't supporting al-Qaeda in any way, shape, or form," Waverly responded bluntly.

"You are supporting the same men who killed thousands of people in America on 9/11," al-Senussi said.

Waverly glanced at Morgan for support. "No. We categorically deny supporting anyone affiliated with al-Qaeda or any other terrorist group."

Al-Senussi remained placid. "Surely you must know that Abdul-Karim al-Rashid is a member of the terrorist Libyan Islamic Fighting Group. He's also a commander in the rebel Libyan National Army. We have evidence that he has met with Osama bin Laden himself on several occasions. So, you are supporting terrorists, and—"

Waverly widened his stance. "I can assure you, sir, we are fully aware of the complexities of the rebel leadership and forces."

"Who do you think will take over Libya if the government is destroyed?"

"The National Transitional Council will make sure—"

"Bullshit." Al-Senussi whipped off his sunglasses. "LIFG and other murderous scum will take over the entire country. You alone will be responsible for the thousands of men, women, and children they'll kill to impose their laws on the Libyan people if the Brother Leader is not here to stop them."

Waverly raised an eyebrow. "Is there anything else you want to discuss?"

Al-Senussi replaced his sunglasses. "We demand you stop violating international and American law by trying to assassinate Colonel Gaddafi and other Libyan leaders."

Waverly let a long beat pass to give the man a chance to regain some sense. "We aren't trying to assassinate anyone."

"You clearly are."

"No, we're not. We're only targeting military assets that attack the rebels."

"Then why have so many leaders' homes been destroyed by rockets and bombs in Tripoli and other cities in the east over the past—"

Morgan stepped forward. "I don't believe we have anything more to discuss. Mr. al-Senussi, thank you for your time."

Al-Senussi stood motionless for several moments with the bright sun gleaming off his sunglasses. "I remember you, Mr. Waverly. What year did you visit Colonel Gaddafi?"

Where was he headed with this? Waverly kept his face carefully neutral. "Nineteen ninety-nine."

"Over ten years ago," al-Senussi mused. "What name did you use during that visit?"

"The same one I use now."

"Really? I thought for sure I recalled another. I'll check my files."

Waverly raised an eyebrow. "My recommendation is that you destroy those files. Otherwise, we'll be reading them soon."

Al-Senussi stared at Waverly. "Good afternoon," he finally said gruffly before walking back to the Toyota Cruiser with his aides behind him. The Toyota accelerated back down the road toward Maradah.

"Self-righteous bastard," Morgan muttered. "How many thousands of innocent people do you think that scum killed?"

"More like tens of thousands," Waverly replied. "There's no doubt whatsoever that he was directly responsible for the massacre at the Abu Salim jail in 1996. He should be hung."

Morgan sighed and shook his head. "Come on. Let's get out of here."

Waverly called Jalal down from his sandy perch and was signaling the operators they were ready to leave when Fisherman came speeding his ATV over the top of the hill. He sped down the embankment and skidded to a stop at the helicopter cargo door. He yelled a command at Chico, and they ran their ATVs into the helicopter.

"Get on the chopper!" Puckeater shouted. "A dozen bogeys headed this way!"

Waverly grabbed Jalal by the arm and helped him into the helicopter. "Get your seatbelt fastened." Morgan climbed inside behind them.

Within a minute, the team boarded the Mi-17.

"Launch!" Fisherman yelled at the pilot. The rotors accelerated, and the helicopter lifted off the ground as one of the French fighters screamed over them headed due west.

The helicopter banked to the northeast just as a fireball erupted in the distance. A moment passed, and another fireball exploded in the same direction.

"What the hell?" Waverly exclaimed above the roar of the engine. He locked eyes with Fisherman. "What's happening?"

"A damn dogfight!" the copilot screamed. "And we're right in the middle of it!"

The helicopter dived and banked in the opposite direction but was still pitched sideways by a nearby explosion. Waverly was thrown against his seatbelt, and he grabbed the gun rack behind him to steady himself. Morgan stared back in terror and clutched his seat with both hands.

The helicopter banked back to the east. Ten seconds later, a fourth, more distant explosion resounded through the fuselage.

The copilot ducked into the rear cabin. "It's over. The Frenchies shot three of them down, and the rest are buggin' out. That missile missed us by less than fifty feet."

Redbeard crossed himself. "That was damn close."

The Mi-17 set a course to the northeast.

Fifteen uneventful minutes passed before Waverly leaned over toward Morgan. "Al-Senussi just tried to kill us," he said just loud enough for Morgan to hear.

Morgan nodded. "That means Gaddafi just tried to kill us."

The two men blinked at one another in the silence.

Waverly let out a long breath. "Maybe it's time to reassess our targets."

15

Payback

My God," Waverly muttered beneath his breath. He read the email again. *"Muammar Gaddafi is now deemed a legitimate target. All assets are authorized to terminate same with extreme prejudice."* There it was at the top of the memo: the validation code he'd been given when he left Langley.

He caught bits of the operators' boisterous conversation before he rounded the corner of the barracks. He stepped over a row of ammunition boxes and tripped over a tent stake before catching sight of the men arrayed around the dinner table.

"Hey, Stone," Fisherman called out to him. "Grab some grub. We got a change in orders."

He ladled stew into his bowl haphazardly, his mind already elsewhere. "Gaddafi?"

"Terminate with extreme prejudice."

He nodded and slid into a seat. "I read the email just a minute ago. They plan to target the Bab al-Azizia compound in Tripoli tonight."

Fisherman looked up from his computer. "We've just been ordered to observe missiles that'll be fired at Gaddafi's offices tonight. They want us to determine whether the attack is on target."

Waverly's heart jumped. "We're flying helos into Tripoli?"

"Hell no. It'd be suicide to take our helos anywhere near Tripoli. We're flying to the aircraft carrier Kearsarge stationed off the coast and transferring to some newfangled covert Black Hawk that'll take us to An Nasr Forest, a few blocks away from the compound. Spaceman agreed to mosey over to the compound in his Ali Baba suit for a look-see. When we're done, the Black Hawk will transport us back to the Kearsarge, and we'll return here in the Mi-17."

"Sounds like a real bash. The whole team is going?"

"It's just the five of us: Chico, Spaceman, Deadeye, you, and me. The others will be hitting a company of tanks at Brega."

"When are we leaving?"

Fisherman glanced at his watch. "Twenty mikes."

"I'll fetch my weapons and gear."

Waverly handed his gear up to Puckeater in the fuselage of the Mi-17 and was about to step up when Jalal bin Koussa called out.

"Mr. Waverly! Mr. Waverly!" the boy yelled as he sprinted toward the helicopter. "Sir, please, can I come?"

"Not this time, Jalal. It's too dangerous."

Jalal clasped his hands in front of his chest. "Please."

"I'm sorry. But you can go with me to Benghazi tomorrow."

Jalal trudged away with slumped shoulders.

Waverly watched him for a moment, then jumped into the seat beside Spaceman and buckled his harness just as the bird lifted off the ground. He caught sight of Jalal standing in the blast of sand thrown up by the rotors. The boy shielded his eyes, following the ascent of the helicopter, then kicked at the ground and staggered back to the buildings.

The helicopter bumped and twisted in a choppy wind for fifteen minutes before the ride finally smoothed over open water. Deadeye and Redbeard fell asleep in their seats while Fisherman and Chico pored over maps of Tripoli.

Spaceman was staring at his boots and mumbling unintelligibly. He'd been sick with a fever the previous night, and Waverly wondered if he was well enough to be here today. *He looks like he's about to vomit.*

He gave Spaceman a backhanded slap to the shoulder. "Are you okay?"

"I'm fine," Spaceman answered gruffly, without diverting his gaze from his boots.

"Nobody here will give it a second thought if you decide to stay on the Kearsarge," he shouted just loud enough to be heard above the roar of the engines. "We all know you've been sick."

Spaceman returned an unreadable expression. "I've trained for over twenty years for precisely this moment. I'm going."

"Either the missile kills him, or it doesn't. We'll all find out soon enough."

Spaceman leaned close enough that Waverly could feel his breath on his face. "I want to see that son of a bitch get what's coming to him— to see the missile blow him to fucking pieces with my own two eyes."

Waverly recoiled from the intensity of the hatred in his words. He sat back. "Relax, my friend. You're taking this far too personally. It'll get you killed."

Spaceman banged his fists on the seat between his knees. "Bastard has it coming. He needs to burn for all the evil shit he's done for forty years."

Waverly glanced across the cabin at Deadeye. "You need to talk him down."

Fisherman and Chico looked up from their maps.

Deadeye shrugged. "He's a big boy. I gave up trying to understand him a long time ago."

Spaceman had gone back to staring at his boots and chanting beneath his breath. Waverly watched him for several minutes before pushing an errant strand of hair back with his fingertips and closing his eyes. *My God, he's about to lose it.*

The Mi-17 touched down thirty minutes later on the deck of the aircraft carrier Kearsarge. Through the window, Waverly spotted a Black Hawk on the deck beside them being swarmed by green- and yellow-shirted deckhands. The craft looked like something out of a Jules Verne novel, with its rounded surfaces and odd rotors.

"Behold, the gilded chariot," he whispered.

The flight deck crew took less than ten minutes to transfer their gear and load the team. Waverly glanced at his watch when the helo lifted off the deck: straight up 2300 hours.

The Black Hawk was a much quieter ride, but nobody slept on this leg. Each man sat alone with his own thoughts as the bird flew back over the Libyan coast and headed undetected over an isolated beach, seventy-five miles to the east of Tripoli. Soon they were headed west across the desert directly toward the darkened capital city.

"Ten mikes to touchdown," the copilot yelled back.

Waverly took a deep breath and leaned his head back against the seat. Eight years ago, he'd choppered into the mountains north of Kandahar in a Chinook helicopter with another Special Ops team in search of a Tajik fighter with a biological weapon. *Hope this turns out better than that FUBAR.*

His memories were broken by the buzzing of another aircraft off the port side of the Black Hawk. He glanced at Fisherman and Chico, but they apparently hadn't heard anything.

"Take it easy," he muttered, settling back into the warmth of his seat.

"Touchdown thirty seconds," the copilot yelled back.

The helicopter banked into a gradual descent and then quickly swooped to the ground in a small clearing. Within moments of settling to the ground, the engines fell silent.

The clearing was surrounded by fragrant eucalyptus trees and low-lying undergrowth that effectively blocked the helicopter from view in all directions. Deadeye, Redbeard, and Puckeater grabbed SA-18 sur-face-to-air missiles, scrambled out the open door, and quickly disappeared from sight. Fisherman and Chico, AKs at the ready, jumped down after them and ran in opposite directions to the edges of the clearing.

Spaceman fished the worn Arabic garments from the bottom of his pack and gestured at Waverly. "Once I get this monkey suit on, you can help me tie my leg back."

He checked the magazine on his GSh-18 pistol and slid it back into the holster, then drew the soiled *thobe* over his head and smoothed it down to cover the gun. He pressed the *shemagh* down on his head, pulled off his boots, and slipped on tattered shoes. Finally, he tossed a pair of rickety wooden crutches down from the helicopter, hopped down after them, and leaned forward against the side of the Black Hawk. "Okay, use this ligature to tie my leg back."

Waverly jumped down, set his AK on the ground, and pulled up the back of Spaceman's *thobe*. Spaceman flexed his knee, and Waverly tied the leg into place.

"Grab the end and pull to release it," he said.

"That works. Cover me with dirt."

He helped Spaceman cover the *thobe* with dirt and then soiled his face and neck.

"Put some on my back," Spaceman said.

Fisherman came jogging back across the clearing. "You look like shit, dude. The road is fifty yards through the trees. Once you get there, Bab al-Azizia compound is a half mile to the west." He glanced at his watch. "The attack is planned for just over an hour from now. You got your sidearm?"

Spaceman patted the weapon beneath his garment.

"And the GPS?"

"Sewn into the sleeve." He lifted his arm.

"When we signal, you're to beat it back here no matter what. You got it?"

"Got it."

"Okay, then, let's get you down to the road."

Waverly headed into the trees. Spaceman hobbled off behind him, with Fisherman and Chico bringing up the rear. At First Ring Road, Spaceman crutched away from the others, down the shoulder into the darkness toward Gaddafi's compound.

Over an hour later, Waverly, Fisherman, and Chico were still huddled just inside the tree line along the road.

"What's that?" Fisherman whispered.

"I don't hear a thing," Chico whispered.

Fisherman raised his finger to his lips and pointed the muzzle of his AK-47 up the road. A moment later, two soldiers on motorcycles armed with machine guns rode past, headed away from Bab al-Azizia compound.

Fisherman glanced at his watch. "They must've canceled the strike. That's long enough. Give him the signal."

Waverly sighed impatiently. "Everything's fine. Give it five more minutes."

Fisherman checked his watch again. "Five, and that's it. It'll take him at least—"

A bright flash illuminated the entire road, followed by a tremendous explosion from the west. Several seconds later, two even louder flash-booms shook the ground beneath their feet.

"Kaboom," Chico muttered. The red light on the communicator he was holding lit up. "Bull's-eye."

"It doesn't mean they got Gaddafi," Waverly whispered.

"No, but it means they hit his compound. Even if they didn't get the SOB, if he's anywhere nearby, he just shit his pants."

Another anxious hour passed as dozens of vehicles raced past their position headed toward Bab al-Azizia. Waverly counted more than a dozen ambulances along with scores of troop transports, military vehicles, and a pair of fire trucks. Many of the ambulances sped back in the opposite direction a short time later. Several helicopters flew by in the distance headed east.

Then, for nearly twenty minutes, there was a lull where only a single vehicle passed their position. Fisherman crept onto the road several times but returned each time without saying a word. His frustrated expression told Waverly all he needed to know.

"How long should we wait?" Chico finally asked.

Fisherman bristled. "All freakin' night."

"Shh," Waverly hissed. "What's that?" He lowered the barrel of his AK to listen to a rhythmic patter. "Someone's running this way."

Both operators dropped to the ground and aimed their rifles up the road. Waverly knelt beside them, ready to fire.

Spaceman sprinted off the road and up the embankment holding the *shemagh* and ligature in one hand. "They spotted me. Let's get out of here!"

Waverly wheeled back up the hill toward the helicopter with the three operators right on his heels. At the last bend in the trail, he ran straight into an overhanging tree branch. He dropped his AK-47 and fell to his knees, clutching his forehead.

Fisherman crouched beside him. "Are you okay?"

"Yeah, just give me a second." He staggered to his feet, groped for his rifle, and jogged the last thirty yards into the clearing.

Deadeye, Redbeard, and Puckeater rose out of the brush with their rifles.

"Helicopter," Waverly whispered, motioning.

The rotors on the Black Hawk were already beginning to turn as the team clambered on board. They lifted off in a whirl of dust and fragrant green leaves.

Waverly waited until they were well out over the water before leaning forward in his seat. "So, what happened?"

Spaceman stared at him glumly. "I don't think they got him."

"Why?"

"That's my gut feeling. They were too damn organized after the missiles hit. We definitely got Gaddafi's offices, but I think he's too smart to set foot in there at this point." He reached up and cupped his ear. "I can't hear squat out of this ear. The explosions must've blown my eardrum."

"Well, somebody got blown to shit," Fisherman said. "Did you see all the ambulances?"

Spaceman nodded. "Yeah, twenty or thirty of them. But we missed Gaddafi. I sense it."

"Who spotted you?" Waverly demanded.

"I managed to get to the roof of the building across the street from the complex, and a guy in uniform saw me when I exited the staircase on the way out. But he kept on running toward his vehicle, so I think he thought I lived there. It was a primo recon spot. I recorded the coordinates of other target buildings, including what appeared to be command and control centers and maybe even Gaddafi's sons' homes. Our mission brief noted that they live in the compound, so the homes I saw must be theirs. I'll forward them to CENTCOM when we get back to base."

Waverly grabbed his arm. "Don't pass on coordinates for Gaddafi's sons' homes."

Spaceman tugged free. "Why the hell not?"

"Because they all have young children. Those kids can't help who their grandfather happens to be, and we don't need to kill innocent children."

"So they can grow up to be tyrants and murderers?" Spaceman countered.

Waverly narrowed his eyes at Spaceman. "I'm asking you not to pass on the coordinates of the private residences. Our orders are to avoid civilian casualties, right?"

Spaceman stared back. Finally, he sighed loudly and pounded the back of his seat. "Okay, damn it, I won't upload the residences."

"Thank you." He sat back and folded his arms across his chest. "Good job."

Fisherman yawned and stretched. "If we didn't get Gaddafi tonight, then I'll tell them their best bet is to wait a few days until he gets good and comfortable, then hit every target in Bab al-Azizia, including the mosque, about ten minutes before sunset prayer begins."

Spaceman nodded excitedly. "Exactly. And I'll go back in again to monitor the attack."

"No way in hell," Fisherman said.

"Why not? We got critical information tonight."

"That's right—you got the information we needed, and there's no reason to go back again. You may have some kind of death wish, but the rest of us have families back home."

Spaceman shifted in his seat. "Come on, I'll know exactly where to go next time. They can drop me off, and I'll stay put until I spot Gaddafi going into one of the buildings. Then I'll signal his exact coordinates. After they toast him, I'll signal them to come back to pick me up. It'll be a piece of cake."

Fisherman glanced at Waverly and rolled his eyes. "Crazy as a loon."

Waverly gave an even gaze to Spaceman. "You did an amazing job tonight, but there's no reason to take that risk again. You need to chill out." *Before you get us all killed.*

Waverly rubbed his tender forehead and wondered in frustration how bad the inevitable headache would be. *We've been on this mission the entire night without spending even a minute looking for that damn backpack bomb. I don't have a clue where it might be.*

Spaceman massaged the leg that had been tied up for a moment before looking up at Waverly. "I'll chill out—later. For now, I've got business to take care of. I'll relax when we vaporize that SOB."

16

Closing In

1700H SATURDAY, APRIL 30, 2011
NEAR BENGHAZI, LIBYA

Spaceman looked up from the parts of his disassembled AK-47 arranged on a blanket in front of him as Waverly marched around the corner of the building, headed directly for him.

"Stone," Fisherman called out, "we got new targeting intelligence I'd like—"

"Not now." Waverly made a beeline to Spaceman. "You promised you wouldn't upload the coordinates to the residences."

"I didn't promise—"

Waverly grabbed his shirt. "You promised me you wouldn't upload them!"

Spaceman shoved Waverly's hand away. "I let CENTCOM make their own determination. It's not our—"

"You sick fucking bastard!" Waverly bellowed. "You killed three kids."

"What are you talking about?"

"They launched on Saif al-Arab Gaddafi's home in Bab al-Azizia and slaughtered three of Gaddafi's grandchildren."

A sick hope leaped in the pit of Spaceman's belly. "Did they get Gaddafi?"

"Hell no. Only his son, Saif, and three of his kids. And now you have to live with that on your conscience—if you even have one."

Waverly stormed back across the courtyard to the barracks.

Sensing multiple sets of eyes staring at him, Spaceman looked up at his fellow operators at the adjacent table. "What?"

"You told him you wouldn't upload the residences," Chico said flatly.

Spaceman shoved the magazine into his AK-47. "So what? I changed my mind. I decided the residences were the best chance to get Gaddafi, and that trumps everything else. What is this shit? Have you all gone soft?"

He got up from the table and stomped away toward the helicopter landing pad, where Jalal was sitting cross-legged in the sand just off the tarmac. The teen hastily wiped tears from his eyes.

Spaceman squatted beside him. "What's wrong, man?"

"I just found out my mother died. Now I'm all alone."

"What happened?" He dropped one knee to the ground to get more comfortable.

The teen pushed his hair back with his fingers. "She's been sick since my father and brother were killed, and she died of a broken heart during the night last night. I'm the only one left."

Spaceman patted him on the shoulder. "I know how much it hurts. I lost my parents and sisters many years ago, too, and I've been alone ever since. I'm sorry, man. Do you need some money to take care of things?"

Jalal sniffed hard and wiped his nose on the back of his hand. "No, thank you. Our neighbors buried her this afternoon."

"Well, if you need any help or just need to talk, you come to me."

Jalal nodded. "Thank you, Mr. Spaceman."

"Howdy," Deadeye called out from behind him.

Spaceman twisted around as he stood. "What's up?"

"Nothing. I just thought you might want some company."

"Nah. I'm fine."

"You both look like the cheese just fell off your cracker. Whatever. Jalal, I need to talk to Spaceman. Go get yourself some dinner."

Without speaking, the teen got to his feet and jogged off to the mess tent.

Deadeye stepped closer. "What's got you all bowed up, bro?"

He raised his chin. "It would've been helpful if you'd backed me up with Waverly."

"It's not my fight." Deadeye sat on the other end of the bench.

"It's more than that. You two are thick as frickin' thieves."

"Listen, Waverly and I go way back to Iraq. He's a good man, brave as the first man that ate an oyster. And I agree with him about the residences. There was no reason to give those to CENTCOM. There are plenty of other places to take out Gaddafi."

"But we haven't. That bastard needs to die, and we're the ones who've got to kill him." *And I'm going to see to it that scum dies the most painful death possible.*

"He will die. It's only a matter of time before we catch up to him."

"Maybe. Maybe not." Spaceman straddled the bench facing Deadeye. "You know what's bothered me ever since I joined this unit? I'm a sniper. You're a sniper. We're supposed to be a team."

"We are a team. But sometimes I hear you clucking, and I can't find your nest."

A sniper who couldn't shoot a simple conversation straight. He snorted. "What the hell does that mean?"

"You're crazy as a loon sometimes. I mean, you've got a fucking death wish. I've got a beautiful wife and two kids I adore, and I want to make it home from this place in one piece."

Spaceman stood up and took a few steps toward the helicopter pad. He looked up at the stars exploding across the sky. "I envy you, Deadeye. You know, I've never even had a girlfriend. I was too focused on becoming a SEAL and then joining the CIA. My life is invested in this mission and seeing that Gaddafi gets what's coming to him."

"So, what's your freakin' preoccupation with Gaddafi? If that's your measure of whether this mission is successful, you may find yourself seriously disappointed. I mean, the way this war is going, the politicians might eventually decide to leave him in power—at least, in western Iraq."

He spun around. "That would be flat-out unacceptable. I'm here to kill that fucker, no matter what it takes."

Deadeye stood up. "Whatever. But if you want to stay here, I suggest you make peace with Waverly, or you might find yourself on the next air transport headed back to Camp Peary."

He spit in the sand. "You've got to be kidding. Would he do that?"

"He might if he decides you're a liability to this team. But he's got a big heart. A simple apology would go a long way with him. Make it less about you and more about the team. What's best for the team to accomplish its mission here? That needs to be your tune going forward."

He considered the idea and filed it away. "Thanks, man."

"Don't mention it. Now I've got to get some shut-eye."

Spaceman watched him leave around the side of the infirmary. He turned and looked across the landing pad at the helicopters draped in camouflage and the fence topped with razor wire fence beyond them. *Things were getting tighter…getting harder to control. Get a handle on yourself, man, before you lose your chance to pull this off. Be cool. Be smart.*

17

One Step Forward, Two Steps Back

0330H MONDAY, MAY 2, 2011
NEAR BENGHAZI, LIBYA

Waverly awakened to boisterous voices. He peered through the darkness at Fisherman and Chico, standing in the open doorway. Chico had Fisherman by the shoulders and was shaking him excitedly.

"What's up?" he said, rubbing sleep from his eyes.

Fisherman flipped on the light. "We got bin Laden!"

He bolted upright in his cot. "Osama bin Laden? Really? Where?"

"Abbottabad, Pakistan."

"When?"

"Just over two hours ago. SEAL Team Six raided his secret compound."

"They captured him?"

"No, they blew his head off," Chico said. He crushed his can of beer in his hand and stomped it beneath his boot. "Killed his son and a courier too."

Waverly swung his legs over the side of his cot and rose. *I can't believe they finally got him after all these years.* "Are you sure?"

"Positive," Fisherman replied. "We got a coded message, and it's already all over the internet. The president is making an announcement in about twenty minutes. Morgan's on his way over here."

"Unbelievable. We finally got him."

"Meet us at the mess," Fisherman said. He and Chico disappeared outside into the darkness.

"Amazing." Waverly slipped on his shoes, thrust his pistol into its holster, and hurried out the door.

Morgan leaned against the car, twisted the cork from a bottle of Old Ripy bourbon, and poured two glasses. In the distance, a hint of the morning sun glimmered red on the featureless horizon. He passed Waverly a glass with his trademark grin, and they clinked the two glasses together. "To a night we'll long remember."

"Hear, hear!" Sweet tang flooded Waverly's mouth and senses. He closed his eyes and sighed. "That's nice…really nice."

"Major Collin gave me this bottle the first day we arrived in Benghazi. I've been saving it for a fitting occasion."

He smiled. "I must say, you can always depend on the Brits for suitable libation."

Morgan topped off both glasses and set the bottle down on the hood of his car. "I'd bet the rest of this bottle the Brits are sharing a drink together too."

"Unquestionably." He took another sip as the reality began to sink in. "It's a great victory, but it's not going to change a thing. It might have eight years ago, but not anymore." *And I'm not a centimeter closer to finding that nuclear backpack bomb or getting home to my kids. What the hell can I do differently to successfully accomplish this mission?*

"But the SOB had it coming," Morgan said. "I can't wait to hear the details on how they ran him down. Now the agency can scratch him off the list and go on to the next target."

"Ayman al-Zawahiri?"

"He's now first on the list. That scum had more to do with 9/11 than bin Laden."

He nodded. "And after all these years, he's finally made it to the top of the shit pile. It wouldn't surprise me to discover al-Zawahiri outed bin Laden to get him out of the way. Damn ruthless douchebag, that one."

"Maybe they'll find intelligence at bin Laden's compound that leads them to al-Zawahiri."

"Here's to it becoming a reality."

They clinked their glasses and sipped again.

Waverly's gaze meandered over the sand. *I should be happy about this, but it just makes me feel like more of a failure. For God's sake, I've scanned half this country and found nothing—not even a blip on the monitor.*

Several bursts of automatic gunfire erupted in the distance, punctuating his misery.

"The Brits celebrating?" Morgan asked.

"More likely one of the rebel groups settling an old feud."

Morgan listened to another staccato burst and nodded. "You're probably right."

Waverly set his glass down. *Just more machine-gun fire and bombs exploding in the distance, night after night and month after month. I'm tired as hell of this.* "How much longer do you think it will take to get the job done here in Libya?"

Morgan took a sip. "Your guess is as good as mine on that one, buddy."

"Everything's ground to a screeching halt. Both sides are dug in deep. It seems like the only way to end this now is to kill Gaddafi."

Morgan nodded. "Good luck with that. He'll be in deep hiding now that his family got hit."

Waverly rubbed at his suddenly throbbing temples. "Just like when Reagan was president. But look what's happening in Misrata and the other cities in the west. It's now purely for revenge—not just taking over the city. Each side tries to inflict as much pain as possible on the other side. There's no way we can reconcile the opposing tribes now."

"You're right about that. Getting rid of Gaddafi is the only way to bring about an acceptable end to this mess. With Gaddafi gone, at least there's a chance the tribes can work out a deal to form a new government."

Waverly splayed his hands on the hood of the car in frustration. "But there's just as much chance he'll get replaced by someone even worse. We could end up with some jihadist like Abdul-Karim al-Rashid or Ahmed Abu Khattala in control of Libya."

"That's certainly possible." Morgan lifted his glass and took another sip. "But it's our job to see that doesn't happen."

Waverly leaned back against the car and let out a long despondent sigh as a pair of bombs exploded in the distance. "I've really had it with this crap."

Morgan thumped him on the shoulder. "Why so cynical tonight? I've never seen you this gloomy."

He gazed up at the sun rising above a distant sand dune. "I guess it was the call to my kids last night. Anne whimpered the whole time, and Mike hardly talked at all. It feels like I've already been away two years, and it's only been two months. I don't know how I'll make it another four. Last night, I asked Marilyn Harrison if she could find an early replacement."

Morgan's head shot up. "Really? What'd she say?"

"No chance in hell."

Morgan patted Waverly's arm. "It's got to be torture when you have young kids—especially when you're their only parent. But I guess it depends on your perspective. Me, I love it here. I feel like we're making a difference for the people of Libya. I want to help them build a stable country where they can raise and educate their children and grandchildren. I relish getting out in Benghazi every day to meet these people. I love it when I sit down to sip a cup of coffee with Mohammad at the café or sample some dates with Ali down at the market. They're family now."

You had to admire the man's dedication to the cause. Waverly reached across the table and patted Morgan's slender arm. "They feel the same way about you."

"Most of them," Morgan said with a smile. "This is where I want to be now, not back in Washington. But I understand your priorities are different."

Several loud booms echoed across the desert.

Morgan grinned. "How about if I send a message to the agency detailing how you've suddenly started talking to yourself and acting erratically? A little bit of acting on your part, and you'll be home in no time."

Waverly chuckled. "They'd probably commit me to some lunatic hospital. I'll just finish out my six months."

"Suit yourself." Morgan kicked at the sand. "You know what I think?"

"What?"

"I think you should get away from the covert guys and your search for the backpack bomb for a few days. You haven't even found a Stinger missile this past week. How about we have lunch in Benghazi on Wednesday? There's a new Lebanese restaurant that opened near the farmer's market, and I heard it's fantastic. After that, I'll take you to meet some of my Libyan friends, and you can stay at our place a couple of nights. It'll make you feel like a new man."

Why not? "I'll tell you what—I'll stay one night."

"That's a start. But you need to get away from that base on a regular basis." Morgan downed the last of his bourbon. "Well, I'd better get to work. I'm sure there's a boatload of email waiting for me."

The two men pushed themselves up from the sand and climbed into the front seat of Morgan's Toyota Land Cruiser. As Morgan wove through a sandy stretch of road, Waverly peered out the passenger window at the sun, seemingly balanced on top of a sedimentary rock formation in the distance. *I've got to change course. Somehow, I've got to recruit an agent in al-Rashid's inner circle.*

But who?

18

The Evil Men Do

Waverly peeked through the door to Morgan's office. The diplomat was staring at his laptop screen, clicking from one document to another.

He stepped into the doorway. "Hungry?"

Morgan glanced up and grinned. "Almost done. Just one more email to review."

Waverly slid comfortably into a leather side chair.

Morgan's fingers stopped tapping keys. "So, one of our security contractors got stabbed in the back yesterday."

"Damn it. Where was he?"

"Just around the corner from the hotel. Picking up supplies."

"How bad?"

Mogan swiped a hand across scruffy cheeks. "Bad enough. He's on his way home. It might have been worse if his partner hadn't shot the attacker."

"Damn. I hope you'll be more careful."

"Always—and I asked my boss to send more security. But I'm not going to let fear keep me from doing my job." Morgan stared blankly at his screen for another few seconds, then began tapping the keys once more.

"Are we still on for lunch?" Waverly asked.

"Absolutely. General Younes plans to join us." Morgan hit the save key with a flourish and closed his computer. "Okay, let's go."

They walked down the hall and rounded a corner to find the larger-than-life general and his bodyguards standing outside the hotel staff offices.

"Mr. Waverly, my good friend!" Younes called out boisterously. His broad smile and sparkling eyes exuded genuine affection. "It's so good to see you again." He took Waverly's hand. "How've you been?"

"Just fine, Commander. It's a pleasure to see you too."

"I'm happy to hear this, and even happier to be sharing lunch in Benghazi with you and Mr. Morgan. Listen, let's hold our business until later, but don't let me forget to ask you a little favor before we part. It's a little something I think the soldiers you work with can easily pull off that will be a big help to my forces fighting in Misrata."

"I'll try not to forget," he replied with a chuckle.

Commander Younes grasped Morgan's arm next. "Shall we go, Mr. Morgan? My mouth has watered for two days since you told me about the Lebanese lamb meatballs and rice at Mustafa's restaurant. You can clearly see I love all food, but I'm especially fond of Lebanese cuisine."

Morgan smiled. "I'm ready. Hanson!" He passed the political officer an envelope. "Make sure this gets sent right away."

"No problem, sir."

"Thanks. We'll be back in a couple of hours. And now, gentlemen," he added with a broad sweep of his arm, "without further ado."

Morgan led his two lunch mates out into the bright noonday sun. They walked down the hotel driveway and across the parking lot, one bodyguard ahead and one behind, bantering good-naturedly about where the best Lebanese food in the world was to be found. A pair of seagulls glided effortlessly above them.

"In my opinion," Morgan confided to Younes, "nothing beats a little Lebanese restaurant in Paris called Yara. I agree the food in

Lebanon is hard to beat, but the chef-owner of Yara, a man named Charbel, has taken culinary art to another level. Next time you're there, you really must try his tabouleh. It's unbelievable."

"Very well," Younes said, "I know your taste in food is impeccable, so if you say it is the best, I really must try it the next time I'm there. But you must agree to try Falafel Freiha the next time you're in Lebanon. Just tell Abdel, the maître d', that General Younes sent you. He'll take good care of you."

"Deal." Morgan gave a firm nod. "Maybe we can all go together when this is all over."

"It would be a pleasure."

They walked several more blocks down ancient streets lined with residential balconies and small shops and restaurants. Morgan greeted nearly every owner he saw by name, engaging them in banter filled with humor and warmth. One after the other, the citizens of Benghazi pushed past the bodyguards toward him, seeking his endearing presence. Morgan introduced each friend to Waverly and the great General Younes until they finally reached Al Kabeer and ducked inside.

The restaurant owner, obsequious to the point of embarrassment, showed them to a table of honor adorned with flowers and laden with an enormous platter of appetizers. The bodyguards took up positions outside the main door of the restaurant as the men dived into the food. The conversation ranged across everything imaginable—food, horses, beaches, olives, beautiful women—until the main course was served.

"This truly is delicious," a full-mouthed Younes exclaimed to the owner. "The meat is so tender and seasoned to perfection. It's possible it's even better than my favorite restaurant in Beirut."

"I'm pleased, General," the proprietor gushed. "Wait until you try my family baklava."

"You truly tempt me now." Younes turned and spooned additional helpings of several dishes onto Waverly's plate. "Stone, you eat like a bird."

Waverly winked at Morgan. "Thank you, General. So, tell me, how do you think things are going in Misrata?"

Younes wiped his mouth. "This is what I wanted to speak with you about. It's going very well, but it would go even better with more support from the allied air force. Instead of dozens of strikes a day, we need hundreds, especially around Misrata."

Waverly glanced at Morgan. "We both understand this, Commander, and we're working to convince our leaders that—"

"I hope I don't sound ungrateful." Younes was no longer chewing or smiling. "It's just that many of my men die every day, and I want this fight to be over sooner rather than later."

"We couldn't agree more, General," Waverly said. "Mr. Morgan and I press constantly for more air strikes and equipment for your men. We've begun to see better coordinated strikes in each of the contested areas, and we just got word last night that a freighter filled with weapons and ammunition will arrive in two to three days' time."

Younes took a massive bite of lamb and chewed exuberantly for several moments before washing it down with a gulp of apple juice. "Excellent! I can't begin to tell you how happy this makes me." He picked up a spoon. "Let me serve you more of this truly exquisite lamb."

"No, please," Waverly pleaded. "I'm stuffed."

"I insist. Have some of this wonderful flatbread, too." He proceeded to fill what little space remained on Waverly's plate. "You know, if I hadn't become a general, I'm sure I would have become a chef. When I was a young officer, my commanding general would often ask me to oversee special dinners and parties, and I'd spend hours designing the menu and preparing ornate dishes. General Haftar once told me he planned to make me his personal aide, but then he discovered I was even better at military strategy, and that was the end of that."

"Commander," one of the bodyguards called from the entryway, "Mahmoud Jibril has sent his car to fetch you. He says it's urgent."

"Ah," Younes moaned, "it's always urgent. I shouldn't have told them I was coming here." He stood up from the table. "Duty calls, my friends. I'll leave my bodyguards here with you. We must have lunch again soon. I'll make all arrangements next time."

Waverly and Morgan stood up and shook the big man's hand.

"Our pleasure," Morgan replied. "We look forward to our next meeting."

"General!" The proprietor hustled through the kitchen door with a large plate of baklava. "You must take dessert with you, sir."

"You're a wonderful host, Mohammed. May Allah bless you and yours."

The general disappeared out the door. Waverly and Morgan waited a moment, half expecting the burly Libyan to reappear with more words of enlightenment. Finally, the two Americans looked at each other and simultaneously broke out in laughter.

"You must have some more lamb," Waverly deadpanned.

Morgan groaned. "Not even a sliver more."

Waverly and Morgan continued their conversation over a cup of espresso and a bite of baklava. When Waverly was certain he would burst if he consumed another molecule, they thanked Mohammed and made their way out of the restaurant.

"We'll be back soon," Waverly called back as he stepped out into the street.

Across the street, a woman with tears flowing from red, puffy eyes caught his attention. Was that...? *My God, my old friend Reka. What could have happened? Where are Mustafa and her sons?*

He rushed across the street behind a horse-drawn cart. "Reka, what's wrong?"

"Mr. Waverly!" she whispered hoarsely. "I'm sorry to bother you, but my cousin—my cousin owns the shoe repair down the street—he told me you were here. Please help me!"

Her voice broke and she began sobbing hysterically.

One of the guards reached for her, but Waverly waved him back and took her hands. "No trouble at all, Reka. Tell me what's wrong."

She dabbed at her eyes with the ends of her scarf. "Mustafa. Mustafa is dead."

Waverly's mouth gaped. "What? How?"

"He took our sons to the desert yesterday to train Bashir's falcon. Gunmen attacked, and Mustafa was shot." Tears welled in her eyes once again. "The men forced Bashir and Omar to leave with them in trucks."

Waverly gripped his forehead in shock. "Who told you this?"

"A nearby sheepherder tending his flock. Please help me!" She burst again into tears and fell helplessly into Waverly's arms.

"I'll do everything I can." He glanced at Morgan and shook his head. "How old are Bashir and Omar now?"

"Sixteen and fourteen."

He steered her to the curb. "Sit down here. I need to ask you some questions. Do you know where this happened?"

She sank down. "At the old quarry, just outside the southern gate."

"Where does the sheepherder live? I want to talk to him."

"Just north of the quarry. His name is Ismail."

"And do you have any photographs of Bashir and Omar I could take?"

She nodded and reached into her bag. "These are school photos taken last year."

He stared at the photographs, committing their faces to memory. "Are you living at the same place?"

She nodded.

He squatted beside her. "Okay, this is what I want you to do. Stay at home but let me know immediately if anyone contacts you about your sons, even if they tell you not to speak to anyone. The American Mr. Hanson at the Tibesti Hotel can get any message to me. Do you understand?"

"Yes."

"They may come to you for ransom. I'll have my men check on you in the morning, and I'll come to your house as soon as we know something, okay?"

"Thank you, Mr. Waverly." She reached for his hand and kissed it. "You are a good and honorable man. I knew you would help."

"You and Mustafa are wonderful friends, and I treasured our time together when I was last here in Libya. I've wanted to come to visit you ever since I returned to Libya, but I hope you understand that my absence was out of concern for your safety. There are many troublemakers around Benghazi now." He gestured at Morgan. "This is American representative Mr. Morgan, and we'll do everything we can to help you. Where was Mustafa buried?"

"In our family plot outside the western gate."

"Okay. I must go now. I want to find the sheepherder." He motioned to one of the bodyguards. "This man will see that you get home safely."

He led Morgan briskly up the street. "Reka and Mustafa worked for me for almost a year the last time I came to Libya. They're among the kindest people I've ever known. Her sons were just this tall when I first met them." He held his hand only two feet above the ground. "I want to do everything possible for them."

Morgan nodded grimly.

"The covert guys are at the base today sorting new supplies," Waverly said. "I'll call Fisherman and have them fly here immediately."

"Here, use my satellite phone," Morgan said.

Less than forty-five minutes later, the helicopter landed in the parking lot next to the hotel. Waverly and Morgan, now dressed in jeans, T-shirts, and boots, jogged out to meet them as the rotors decelerated to a stop.

Fisherman's sunglasses gleamed in the midday sun. "Where to, sir?"

Waverly gave him a curt nod. "Thanks for coming. I want to talk to a sheepherder who works near the quarry by the southern gate."

"No problem, sir. Are you ready?"

"Let's go."

They climbed into the Mi-17, and the pilot lifted off over the hotel and across the old city neighborhood. After ten minutes, they swept past the southern gate and circled their quarry before landing about a hundred yards from a small flock of sheep.

Waverly was the first one out of the helicopter. Morgan and the others jogged after him toward a crusty old man fearlessly standing his ground.

"As-Salaam-Alaikum," Waverly said when he was a few yards away.

"As-Salaam-Alaikum," the old man replied. "My name is Ismail."

"I wish you peace, Ismail. We need your help. I've heard you were here yesterday when my friend Mustafa was shot by gunman."

"Yes, they are dogs, these men."

"You've seen them before?"

"Many times. They come here often to shoot guns. It terrifies my sheep."

"Do you know their names?" *Come on, old man. Come through for Reka.*

"One of them, the tallest, named Nasser Ali, once threatened me when I demanded they stop shooting guns. They are with Abdul-Karim al-Rashid."

Waverly glanced at Morgan. "Do you know where they are?"

"I'm not sure, but another herder told me they stay in the canyon on the other side of the date groves." He pointed at an island of green just visible beyond the quarry to the east.

Waverly scowled. *Al-Rashid again! That worthless bastard.* "Thank you for your help. And, sir, please don't tell them we've spoken."

The man spat on the ground. "I do not speak to these scoundrels." He glanced past Waverly at the covert operators and raised his eyebrows. "But there are many in the canyon. You must be careful."

"We'll be careful. Thank you."

"It is nothing. Mustafa was a friend. For thirty years, he came here—even before his sons were born—to fly his beautiful falcons. They are truly a wonder to behold. Mustafa did nothing to deserve what they did to him. I think the evil ones wanted his falcon—and his sons."

Waverly frowned. "What will they do with his sons?"

"They will be slaves, perhaps in a deviant way, and then they will be sold. There were two other boys they took some years ago. I never saw them again."

Waverly cringed. *We've got to move fast.* "You said one of these men was named Nasser Ali?"

The man nodded. "He's the one who shot Mustafa."

"He shot Mustafa?"

"I am certain."

Waverly's hand drifted to rest on his pistol. "Thank you. These soldiers and I will find these men, and we will punish them."

"Thanks be to Allah." The old man bowed and trudged back to his sheep.

Waverly turned to Fisherman. "So, can we take them?"

Fisherman was already nodding. "On our terms. Tonight, we'll land outside the canyon and go in with night vision. Right now, I suggest we circle around and make a single pass over the canyon from the west to take high-resolution photographs. We can use those to develop a firm plan."

"Excellent. Perhaps we'll catch a shot of the boys and find out where they're being kept. We should also be looking for any advanced weaponry they might be hiding."

Fisherman clenched his fists emphatically. "Let's do it."

The men jogged back to the helicopter and they lifted off again, circling to the east to fly at cruising altitude toward the date grove. As they neared the trees, Fisherman directed the pilot to fly over a box canyon less than a quarter mile to the east, while Redbeard manned a high-speed, high-resolution camera mounted outside the fuselage.

"Fly due west," Fisherman shouted to the pilot. "Stay at this altitude."

Waverly looked out the door as they passed over the canyon wall. Several groups of men came into view far below them. Some of them carried weapons, and a few scurried for a cluster of tents when they spotted the helicopter. One man lifted a sand-covered door near the back of the camp and disappeared into a bunker. Waverly made a mental note. *We've got to search that.*

Within moments, the helicopter had completed its pass. It flew over the opposite canyon wall and disappeared to the west.

19

Rescue

Waverly peered over Fisherman's shoulder at a series of images mounted on a viewing box. "What do you see?"

Fisherman turned on a projector and put up one of the images at high magnification on a screen on the wall. He pointed to a cluster of men holding AK-47 rifles and grenade launchers. "These are definitely al-Rashid's fighters. I recognize their distinctive garments." He advanced to another frame showing armed men. "These are likely some of the leaders." He advanced to a third frame showing a cluster of tents. "These two are women, and one of them is holding a baby. I didn't see the boys, but they may be in the tents."

"Or maybe they've already been sold," Redbeard added.

"Maybe," Fisherman said. "In all, I counted twenty-seven men, four women, and three children. There may be more in the tents." He changed frames again. "There's also a bunker here in the back of this base. They probably store weapons there. So, here's my plan." He pointed to a spot on a wide-angle photograph. "We'll land on the eastern side of the canyon, about here. We'll leave Puckeater to guard the helo. Using night vision, the rest of us will make our way to the mouth of the canyon and neutralize the lookouts." He turned to Waverly. "Do we plan to terminate all these people?"

"Not if we don't have to. I just want to retrieve the boys, detain Nasser Ali if we can identify him, and search that bunker."

Fisherman folded his arms. "What if they shoot at us?"

"Then we shoot back," Waverly said. "I'll sedate the lookouts, and we can make our way inside the canyon to the tents, incapacitating as many adults as necessary until we find the boys. Here are photos of the boys." He passed around the copies of the photos Reka had given him.

"How will we identify Nasser Ali?" Redbeard asked.

"We'll coerce some of them into telling us where he is before we sedate them. We think this is what he looks like." He clicked forward to a photograph of a scrawny, narrow-eyed Arab with a long scar ranging across his forehead.

"Where'd you get that?" Puckeater asked in amazement.

"I've been surreptitiously photographing members of al-Rashid's group and others I suspect of being jihadists. This was at one of the shindigs the National Transitional Council held a month back. I'm not certain, but this may be our guy."

Puckeater nodded admiringly. "Nice work."

"Once we have the boys and Nasser Ali, we'll search that bunker, make our way back to the helos, and fly away."

"What will we do with Ali?" Spaceman asked.

"First, we'll see what we can find out about al-Rashid's group and any advanced weapons. Then we'll turn him over to the National Transitional Council and prosecute him for murder and kidnapping. The boys can serve as witnesses."

"What if we don't find them boys?" Deadeye drawled.

Waverly felt his face flush with anger. "If we don't find them, then someone in that camp is going to tell us where they are, and he better pray they're alive. Once we find them, I'll personally take them back to their mother. I don't want anyone seeing our helicopter anywhere near her home. Any questions?"

The operators shook their heads.

"Okay," Waverly said, "let's get the helo loaded."

Waverly rolled his shoulders and stretched as the team members scattered to take care of business. *This could be our big break. If al-Rashid has the backpack bomb, this canyon would be the perfect place to store it. Could this assignment be on the cusp of completion? Surely Harrison would call him home if he found the nuke.*

Two boys and a nuke. It had the potential to be a good night. He hoped.

The Mi-17 lifted off from the base a few minutes after two in the morning under clouds that obscured the three-quarter moon looming above the horizon. A stiff wind gusted through the partially open door.

Waverly pulled his pistol from its holster and advanced a bullet into the chamber. "Have you been out with operators before?" he yelled to Morgan above the din of the rotors.

"Once before, but not on a mission."

"They'll take good care of us."

Morgan nodded.

"No problem if you want to stay with the helicopter," Waverly yelled.

"No, I want to come along."

Waverly nodded, then reached beneath his feet and rummaged through a black bag. One after the other, he held up cartridges, examined them, and placed them carefully back into the bag. He loaded the last cartridge into a small gun-like device and placed it into a holster on his belt.

"What's that?" Morgan asked.

"A fast-acting sedative." He set the bag down, checked his AK, and changed the battery on the handheld detection unit he would use to scan for the backpack bomb. "The operators think this is a metal detector," he whispered. "Let them think that." Finally satisfied, he leaned the rifle against the seat, leaned back, and closed his eyes.

The helicopter settled to the ground nearly a kilometer to the east of the box canyon. Three operators jumped down to the sand and fanned out to secure the area before the helo rotors whipped to a stop. After a few minutes, they jogged back to the helicopter.

"Everything's clear to the north," Spaceman said.

"South as well," Redbeard said.

"Clear to the west," Checkmate called out.

"Okay, Puckeater, you stay here," Fisherman ordered. "We should be back in an hour. Let's go."

Waverly set off on foot with Morgan beside him, and the covert operators fanned out around them. The sand whooshed under foot as they hastened through the darkness across the barren, undulating plain until they were within a hundred yards of the canyon mouth.

Fisherman donned his night-vision goggles. "Hand signals only from this point forward. I'll signal where I want you to stay, Mr. Morgan, while the rest of us secure the canyon entrance. I'll send Spaceman back to get you when it's clear. If you hear gunfire, hotfoot it directly back to the helo. Understand?"

Morgan nodded.

Fisherman shouldered his black bag and trudged off across the sand with the others. After walking a few hundred meters, he pointed to a cluster of sandstone boulders, and Morgan sat down to wait.

Waverly and the operators headed off due east, silently making their way up the hill that guarded the canyon entrance.

At the sound of laughter and Arabic conversation floating on the breeze, Fisherman signaled the others to stop. The moon broke through the clouds. Fisherman pointed at it and held up five fingers—five more minutes.

Redbeard was monitoring the empty winding road that meandered into the canyon. He glanced at the opposite hill, likely the location of other sentries, and pointed. Fisherman nodded.

Finally, once they were shrouded again in darkness, the team advanced stealthily toward the voices now barely audible above the stiffening breeze.

Waverly handed the radiation detection unit to Deadeye and signaled Fisherman to follow him. Sedation gun at the ready, he crawled forward over the rise. Two men were sharing a cigarette just below the crest. He slithered forward and plunged the sedation gun into the nearest man's neck. The gun hissed, and the man collapsed on his side as Fisherman locked the other in a choke hold.

Waverly pointed his pistol at the man's forehead, and Fisherman released him.

Waverly interrogated the young man in Arabic while Fisherman went back for the others. As the team came over the rise, they saw Waverly jab the man with the barrel of his pistol.

The man stared with wide-eyed fear at the goggled covert operators arrayed around him.

"Nasser Ali is in the camp, and the boys are with him," Waverly whispered. "He's in the large tent in the rear, and there may be another man with them. Abdul here says there are two guards on the other hill and twenty-nine men and ten women in the camp. Anything else we need to know?"

After no reply, he pressed the sedation gun to the Arab's neck. "Good night, Abdul."

The gun hissed, and the man dropped to the sand.

"Checkmate," he said, "go back and get Morgan. You other guys stay here while Fisherman and I neutralize the other sentries. We'll be back in ten mikes."

A deathly silence hung over the canyon as the group crept across a clearing to a cluster of tents nestled in the back of the canyon. Waverly stopped in front of the first tent, signaled for the others to wait, and handed his rifle to Deadeye. Sedation gun in hand, he slipped through the tent flap with Fisherman. Four men on cots. He slipped back out and held up four fingers.

They progressed from tent to tent, repeating the same maneuver, until only the large tent in the back remained.

"Twenty-seven," he whispered. "That leaves two men and the boys in the last tent."

He ducked inside quickly with Fisherman and Redbeard right behind him.

In the darkness, he couldn't make out a thing. He shone his flashlight across the floor, illuminating a man sleeping naked next to a slender boy, with another boy on a blanket behind them. The man awoke with a start and reached for his rifle, but Fisherman jammed his boot onto the man's hand. Both boys scurried to the back of the tent and covered themselves with the blanket.

Redbeard rushed the second man and put him in a choke hold.

"What do you want?" the man grunted.

Fisherman jerked him to his feet and shoved his arm up behind his back.

"Ah!"

"What do you think we want, Ali?" Waverly said in Arabic. "You murdered my friend Mustafa and dishonored his sons."

Ali struggled anew, and Fisherman forced his arm higher behind his back, bound him with zip ties, and held him upright.

Waverly couldn't help the wave of revulsion as he looked Ali over. *You fucking pervert.* He stepped nearer and belted Ali in the mouth. Ali bent over at the waist, his lip spurting blood.

"That's for Mustafa," Waverly said with a growl.

He jerked his sedation gun from its holster and pressed it to the other man's neck. The gun whooshed, and the man crumpled to the floor.

Paralyzed with fear, the two naked boys cowered together against the side of the tent.

Waverly stepped over to them. "Bashir. Omar. Do you remember me? I'm Stone Waverly, your father's American friend. These are American soldiers. Get your clothes on, and I'll take you back to your mother. Ali will be charged with your father's murder and your kidnapping, but nothing will ever be said about what happened to you in this place."

Stunned speechless, the boys obediently set about finding their clothes on the cluttered floor. They sat beside each other and slowly pulled on their pants and shirts.

Bashir strapped on his shoes and got quietly to his feet. Without warning, he lunged forward at Ali.

"For my father!" he bellowed.

The man shrieked and crumpled to the floor. Clutching a bloody knife, Bashir stumbled toward the other man, who lay unconscious on the floor, and kicked him squarely in the face. The blow landed with a sickening thud, smashing the man's nose.

"For my brother!"

Waverly pulled the knife from Ali's chest and tossed it aside, then drew Bashir to him even as the boy began to sob uncontrollably. "It's okay, son. You're safe now."

He looked at Fisherman. "Is he dead?"

Fisherman checked Ali's pulse. "Yeah, he's finished."

"Bring the other one," Waverly ordered Redbeard. "We'll interrogate him at the base and then deliver him to the NTC for trial. Fisherman and Deadeye, you come help me search the bunker. Here, give me that detector."

Waverly led the other two operators to the back of the base, where he searched for a few moments before finding a recessed pull handle hidden in the sand. Deadeye pulled the door vertical, and Waverly shone his flashlight down into a small room crammed with boxes. He handed the detection unit to Deadeye. "Hand this back to me when I get down there."

Once below, he tore the tops off two boxes. "AK ammunition. You two check all these other boxes while I scan the room." He skimmed the detector along the floor around the edges of the boxes stacked in the middle of the bunker.

"What are you looking for, anyway?" Fisherman asked, looking up from an open box of hand grenades.

"Any metal hidden beneath the floor. They might have buried some surface-to-air missiles." *Damn it, not a damn peep. Maybe there's another one of these hidden bunkers somewhere else in the camp.*

Deadeye looked up from a box of new AK-47s. "All we've found is AKs, ammunition, hand grenades, and mortar shells. There aren't any ground-to-air missiles in here."

Waverly frowned. "I want to scan around the rest of the base. Then we'll get out of here."

He set about systematically scanning the sand from one end of the canyon to the other.

Fifteen minutes later, he trudged toward the others at the mouth of the canyon, still scanning as he walked.

"Find anything?" Fisherman called.

"Not a damn thing." He drew his pistol and, with a look of frustration, pressed it to the prisoner's ear. "Where's the other hidden bunker?" he demanded in Arabic.

The man gawked with wide-eyed fear. "There's only the one! There's no other."

He slid the pistol around to the man's forehead. "This is your last chance."

"There is no other," the man whimpered. "Allah is my witness."

Waverly sighed and holstered his pistol. "Let's get him back to the helo."

This is hopeless. Totally hopeless.

20

Unlikely Reunion

Waverly glanced out the window at the three grizzled old men sitting beneath a torn awning and smoking a hookah pipe. Redbeard whistled several bars from the old Black Sabbath song "Paranoid" as he steered the Toyota Cruiser around a vendor pulling a food cart down the narrow mixed residential and commercial street.

"Turn left at the next intersection," Waverly called from the back seat.

In the second seat, on either side of the vehicle with rifles at the ready, Spaceman and Deadeye scanned the street and upper-level balconies. Bashir and Omar sat silently in the rear beside Waverly.

"Everything will be fine," he assured them with a warm smile.

The older boy nodded and clutched his brother's arm.

"Okay, it's that door on the right."

Redbeard pulled the Toyota Land Cruiser to a squealing stop at the curb. Deadeye opened the rear door into the searing heat, and Waverly helped the boys out of the vehicle.

The apartment door banged open and Reka bolted from the house.

"My sons!" She gathered them to her sides and kissed them both on the foreheads. "God is great! Thank you, thank you, thank you, Mr. Waverly. I can never repay this debt."

"No debt owed," he said. "Seeing them back here safely with you is all the reward we need." *Finally, something I got right. This makes my mission a success no matter what else happens.*

"How did you find them?" She wiped tears of joy on her sleeve.

"Ismail told us where the men who murdered Mustafa and took them would be found."

She bowed her head in thanks. "I will always be grateful. May Allah bless you all."

"Our pleasure, ma'am," Deadeye said.

Omar buried his face in his mother's shoulder. "The man Ali killed Father."

"I know, my son. We buried him beside his father."

"And they sold our falcons," Bashir added.

"We will get others." She kissed him again on the forehead, but he pulled back.

"I killed him."

She took him by both shoulders. "You killed him?"

He nodded. "I stabbed him with a knife."

She looked to Waverly, and he nodded. "Well, my son, sometimes killing is justified." She drew him close and looked over his shoulder at Waverly. "Please, let me prepare tea and something to eat."

"Thank you, Reka, but these men must return to their base. Could you and I go inside? I must speak with you."

"Of course. Please come in."

He followed the grief-stricken family into their small apartment while the covert operators took up positions in the street.

The front room was cluttered with worn furniture and a hutch with two rows of framed photos. The sweet smell of incense wafted through the room, and a vase of week-old flowers drooped on a table.

"Please, make yourself comfortable," Reka said, pointing to a chair covered with a drop cloth. She pulled her sons to a worn sofa across from him.

"I have something important to discuss with you," he began.

She took each of her sons' hands. "Yes?"

"The place where we found Bashir and Omar... It's a terrorist camp. You and your sons won't be safe here anymore. Bashir killed one man, and we took another man for trial. The terrorists will likely seek revenge."

Her nostrils flared in panic, but she sat steady between her sons. "But where will we go?"

"I've made arrangements for you to enter an American immigrant relocation program. You'll be resettled in America."

Her mouth dropped open. "America? But we can't—our family has lived in this place for generations."

He leaned forward in his chair. "You won't be safe here, Reka. I'm certain Mustafa would want you and the boys to do this."

She glanced around the room. "But our things..."

"You'll get new things in America—and a new life. Bashir and Omar will attend school, and you'll be supported by the US government until you can support yourselves."

She drew a breath. "How long before we'd go?"

"I'm sorry... We need to go now. I'll give you a few minutes to gather some clothes and a few valued belongings."

She rocked back on the sofa and pulled the boys closer. "But what about my sister and her family? Her husband was killed at the beginning of the uprising."

"Where are they?"

"Near Tobruk. They live on a farm outside the city."

"They'll be safe there. You can return, if you want, after everything is settled here in Libya."

She glanced at her youngest. He stared back with eyes as big as saucers.

"Okay," she said softly. "We need a few minutes."

"I'll wait outside. Try to keep what you bring to the absolute minimum."

She stood up, all business. "Bashir, Omar, go pack your best clothes in your backpacks. Then come help me load the suitcases."

Waverly joined the soldiers outside, and they waited patiently for nearly half an hour before the door opened and Reka rolled out a large suitcase. The boys stepped outside behind her carrying overstuffed backpacks and a small suitcase.

"Okay," she said as she locked the apartment door. "We're ready."

Deadeye heaved the suitcases into the rear of the Toyota Land Cruiser as Waverly helped Reka and the boys into the rear seat. As Redbeard restarted the engine and pulled forward, Reka glanced back at the apartment one last time.

Waverly sensed her abject sorrow. *She's doing everything possible to keep her family together. I would too, in her place. But I wonder if there will be anything worth coming back to?*

21

Treachery Arising

Morgan shut the door to his office inside the Tibesti Hotel, walked back around the desk, and handed Waverly a sheet of paper from a dossier. "Look at this." He stepped across the small, cluttered office to a water pitcher half-filled with lemon slices and poured himself a glass. "Do you want a glass?"

Waverly glanced up from the document, shook his head, and continued scanning the page: "Approval for another ninety days of NATO military operations." *Well, that'll take me to the end of my commitment.* "It's hard to believe I've only been here three months."

"If it makes you feel any better, I'm really glad you're here. I planned to come out to your base yesterday, but I got hung up meeting with Mustafa Abdul Jalil."

"What's up with him?"

"Same old thing. The National Transitional Council wants more heavy weapons and air strikes, blah, blah, blah. As if one hundred and fifty sorties a day by the NATO bombers aren't enough."

"Maybe he'll be a little happier when I take him the five million dollars I received yesterday to disburse to them."

"At least for a few minutes," Morgan said with a laugh. "Can I ask you a favor? Can I refer him to you the next time he asks for a meeting?"

Waverly chuckled. "Absolutely. I'll tell him he's gotten all he's going to get—and more than he deserves—and make it clear they'd better rally their forces and finish this revolution in the next three months, or they'll miss their chance."

"Maybe that's what they need to hear. Anyway, I want to see less of them and more of you these next three months. Why don't you move in here?"

Waverly tossed the paper back onto Morgan's desk. "Believe me, it's tempting, but I need to be with the covert operators. I've gotten great intel the last few nights, and they need me there to help maintain their focus and to search for you know what."

"What've you all been up to?" Morgan swept up the document, stuffed it back into the dossier, and commenced to search for the most logical top-heavy pile on which to stash it.

"We go out on a mission almost every night. Mainly, we supported rebel forces near Misrata and Sirte, and lately we've gone as far east as the outskirts of Tripoli. Night before last, we blew up a rebel ammo depot near Brega after I searched it and found three Grinch surface-to-air missiles."

"But not the backpack bomb," Morgan deadpanned, bumping a stack of loose files and sending papers cascading to the floor. "Damn."

Damn, indeed. As if he needed another reminder of his failure. "No, but these raids give me valuable opportunities to recruit high-level agents among Gaddafi's forces. Last week during a night raid in Sirte, we captured an Iraqi colonel. I recruited him to provide ongoing information about troop movements and the comings and goings of senior members of Gaddafi's inner circle—and it's already paid off with information about the location of General Abdul Zayid's command outpost in Souk Talat. We raided it and took out Zayid."

Morgan straightened up with the errant papers in hand. "Has Gaddafi been seen there?"

"Not that we know of, but that damn fool Spaceman nearly got himself killed when he rushed a compound where Gaddafi was supposedly holed up. It turned out to be a few low-level officers, but Spaceman took a bullet in the chest charging their hideout."

"Ouch! Is he okay?"

"Amazingly enough, he's fine. His body armor saved him. Redbeard told him he needed to fix his rectal-cranial inversion."

"Ha!" Morgan laughed and shook his head. "I still say you should send him home."

"I discussed it with Fisherman, actually, but we need all the operators we can get right now, and there are no replacements available."

Morgan slapped the papers onto his desk and closed his computer. "Well, now we know how he earned his nickname. So how are your kids?"

"They're doing well. I called yesterday, and they're both excited about going to summer camp next week. Hey, I also heard from Reka and her sons."

"Oh?"

"I got an email message from Reka forwarded to me yesterday. They've settled in the southwest and they're safe and happy. Bashir and Omar are stars on their travel soccer team."

Morgan smiled with satisfaction. "Great job, buddy."

"It turns out we got them out just in time. Some scum firebombed their apartment two days after they left, and the entire building burned to the ground. Four people in the adjacent apartment were killed."

"Bastards. February 17 Martyrs' Brigade out for revenge?"

"Undoubtedly. But it may backfire on them. The interrogators got a lot of useful intel from the arsonist that was captured after he threw the firebomb." He sat back and stretched. "Brew us some coffee and I'll brief you on it."

"Great. I got some new Turkish coffee from a shopkeeper friend of mine we can try." Morgan got up from his chair and started toward the door.

A tremendous blast blew in the window, ripped Waverly from his chair and flung him across the room. Ceiling tiles and shards of glass cascaded down on top of him.

He struggled to his knees from beneath the debris in complete darkness. Something pricked his scalp, and he reached up. His hair was covered in glass. *Why is everything so dark? It was broad daylight outside.*

He turned toward where he'd last seen Morgan to find nothing but utter blackness in every direction. "Oh my God, I can't see. I'm blind!"

Somebody bolted in from the adjoining offices, and someone else burst in from the hall and shone a powerful flashlight beam in his face. Waverly barely saw a flicker of the light.

A trickle of blood ran down his left cheek. He wiped it away impatiently as someone pushed aside furniture to get to him. His eyes and face ached deeply. *Oh my God, I can't see anyone in the room.*

"Dear God!" came Morgan's voice. "Your left eye's bleeding. Can you see me?"

He covered one eye with his hand and then the other. "No… No! I see shadows with my right eye but nothing with my left."

"Get a stretcher," Morgan called to someone behind him. "Stone, don't move. Stay where you are. Here, take my hands."

Someone else rushed into the room.

"What the hell was that?" Morgan asked.

"A bomb exploded in the parking lot, sir. It destroyed the cars and Toyota Cruisers. You must leave immediately. This side of the building is unstable."

Gentle hands dabbed blood from Waverly's forehead with something soft and then grasped his arms. "Stone, sit here on the desk."

He struggled to his feet, and Morgan guided him to the edge of the desk.

"Stay right there, and we'll get you to the hospital. Can I use your phone to call the team?"

He groped for the phone attached to his belt and handed it to Morgan. "Code 2502, then speed dial 1."

He sat staring into nothingness listening to the call click and beep through the connection.

"Fisherman, this is Morgan. Some bastard just bombed the hotel and Waverly's hurt bad.... Okay, we'll be at the front entrance." The phone beeped again. "They'll be here in fifteen minutes."

Several new arrivals bustled into the room, and then Morgan was guiding him onto his back onto a stretcher. He was lifted and carried through the halls. He inhaled acrid fumes as they drew closer to the entrance. *My mission is over. Life as I once knew it is over. How will I even teach school now?*

It must have been twenty minutes or so before he heard Fisherman's voice. "The parking lot is clear. Mr. Morgan, your arm is bleeding."

"It's nothing," Morgan said. "We've got to rush Stone to the Benghazi Medical Center. He's been blinded."

"Use the hotel van," another voice said. "I'll pull it up."

A minute later, Waverly heard a vehicle screech to a stop outside.

"Roger," Morgan said in a low voice, "I'm going with him. Secure all the computers and files. Then find a new office for us, somewhere with a protected perimeter."

"Yes sir," the man replied.

Morgan moved ahead of them then, opening doors and helping guide the stretcher into the back of the van. He jumped inside and took Waverly's hand. Waverly accepted it gratefully, completely disoriented by the movement.

He turned his head slowly from side to side. "Gus? I can't even see shadows anymore. Everything is completely black."

"I'm right here, buddy." Morgan rolled down the window. "Bert, call ahead to the hospital and tell them we need the best eye surgeon in the city. Get him, whatever it takes."

"Yes sir."

The rear doors slammed, and someone jumped into the driver's seat. Waverly heard someone else insert a magazine into a gun.

"Hold on tight!" Redbeard bellowed.

The van lurched down the driveway and swung onto the wide boulevard that ran along the harbor, then wove its way through the throng of people and vehicles descending on the smoldering hotel to Benghazi Municipal Hospital a few blocks down the road. A clank and blast of hot air told Waverly someone had reopened the back doors.

Morgan leaped out. "I'm Gus Morgan," he said to the men in Arabic, "the American liaison to the National Transitional Council."

"Good to meet you again, sir," someone replied in English. "I'm Dr. Khalid Muhammed, medical director of the Benghazi Municipal Hospital, and these are my two emergency room colleagues, Dr. Ali and Dr. Waled. You are hurt too, sir."

"It's nothing—but my friend in the back has terrible eye injuries."

"Get him inside," Dr. Muhammed commanded.

The stretcher was pulled from the van and loaded onto a gurney, and Waverly felt himself being wheeled away.

"Did you find an eye surgeon?" Morgan asked from behind him.

"Yes, a Mr. Bert Hanson called ahead. Upon his direction, we called for an experienced ophthalmologist from the al-Jala Hospital. He's also bringing a visiting doctor. They should be here shortly."

"Thank you, sir. I appreciate your help. I'd like to wait with my friend for the specialists to arrive."

"I'll tell the staff to let you stay."

They clattered into a small room, where the gurney was jostled between scurrying staff members as they took his blood pressure and started an intravenous line. Even though he couldn't see anything, Waverly closed his eyes and tried to steel his jangling nerves against the assault. *This ache in my eye and head is terrible. Could I die from this?*

Morgan's hand closed around his again. "Stone, it's Gus. A top ophthalmologist is on the way. Are you hurting?"

"My right eye's killing me, and I can't see anything now."

"Can you give him something?" Morgan asked.

"We'll give him some morphine as soon as the IV is running."

Morgan's voice zoomed in as he leaned close to Waverly. "Hold on, buddy. They'll give you some pain medicine in a moment."

"Thank you." *Please hurry.*

Another voice came closer. "Mr. Waverly, I need to protect your eyes, so no further damage is done before Dr. Ahmed arrives. Will you allow me to tape shields over them?"

He nodded. Gentle hands taped a protective shield over each eye. "Please don't touch them."

Waverly felt someone tape IV tubing to his arm and someone else handled the port. Suddenly, something stung his arm.

"That's morphine," a male voice said. "It should take away your pain in a few moments. If not, we'll give you more."

There was a commotion at the door.

"Mr. Waverly," Dr. Muhammed said, "Dr. Ahmed, our ophthalmologist, is here."

"Thank God," he muttered.

"Thank you for coming, Dr. Ahmed," Morgan said.

"My pleasure. This is my colleague, Dr. Arturo Gomez, visiting from Barcelona. If you'll excuse us, I'd like to take your friend to the eye examination room."

There was a brief silence.

"Can I speak to you for a moment?" Morgan said.

"Of course," Dr. Ahmed replied.

Another awkward silence. *What was Gus up to?*

"Yes, Mr. Morgan?" Dr. Ahmed finally asked.

"Uh, well, I mean no offense, but you look so young," Morgan stammered.

The doctors chuckled, but Waverly was appalled.

"Hey, Gus, leave the doctors alone," he called out.

"I understand," Dr. Ahmed replied calmly, "but I can assure you I'm fully competent. After medical school at Cairo University School of Medicine, I did my residency in ophthalmology at Beirut Eye Specialist Hospital and then a three-year fellowship at the Barraquer Ophthalmology Centre in Colombia. I returned to Benghazi three years ago and unfortunately, because of the war, I've attended countless eye trauma cases. If I need help, my friend Dr. Gomez here is an attending surgeon at Vissum Instituto Oftalmológico in Alicante, Spain. I promise Mr. Waverly is in good hands."

"Okay, sorry, I'm just a bit anxious," Morgan said with palpable relief. "Spare nothing to help him. The US government will pay any expenses."

"I understand. We must go now."

The gurney began moving again. Waverly couldn't keep track of what was happening.

"Mr. Waverly, I need to move you to a chair at the slit lamp microscope." A firm grip guided Waverly from the gurney and into a large chair. "Careful. There you go."

He felt the doctor's smooth hands tease the tape from his forehead and pull the shields gently from his eyes.

"I need you to lean forward against this band and stay there while I examine each eye. That's it."

Dr. Ahmed examined each eye in turn with the slit lamp microscope, gently lifting each lid with his finger to expose his eyes. Then he leaned Waverly back in the reclining chair and examined each eye again with an ophthalmoscope. "There's no view into the posterior pole of either eye," he told someone else in the room.

"Whuzzat mean?" Waverly asked.

"It only means we can't see the retina in either eye. We'll get a good look in the operating room. Your right eye has a fragment of glass embedded in the center of the cornea. It's superficial, and I'll be able to remove it without the need for sutures. I expect you to regain full vision in that eye in a few days, once the skin heals back over the cornea."

"Thank God," he muttered.

"I'm afraid the left eye is much more serious," the doctor said. "A piece of glass perforated the central cornea, and the lens was severely damaged. Also, some of the vitreous jelly from the back of the eye is protruding through the cornea, and the eye is filled with blood from a laceration to the iris. In the operating room, we will remove the glass, vitreous, and blood from the eye, repair the iris as best we can, and suture the corneal laceration. The glass fragment appears to be confined to the front of the eye, so I hope your retina is fine. If that's the case, then at some point down the road—like maybe six months from now—I think there's a good chance you can have a plastic lens sutured inside the eye and a corneal transplant to restore at least some vision to this left eye."

"Oh, Stone," Morgan said behind him.

"Thank you, doctor," Waverly said.

"We need to take you right to the operating room now. Mr. Morgan, the nurse will take you to the OR waiting room, and I'll come find you there when we're done."

"Thank you, doctor," Morgan said. "America thanks you."

"This is what I do, and I'm glad I can help. Are you able to get word to his family?"

"I'll make sure they know he's safe and coming home soon."

"Mr. Waverly, what's your line of work?" Dr. Ahmed asked.

Waverly tried to focus. *What should I say to this man in this situation?* "My work? Ah, well, I help coordinate assistance from the US government to the National Transitional Council."

"Do you do anything where binocular vision is critical? You know, work that requires good depth perception?"

Waverly blinked to try to see the doctor's face, but it was no use. "Well, my vision is important, that's for sure."

"We'll do everything possible to get you back to normal. I'll talk with you after surgery about your recovery. Let's get you back on this gurney and into the OR."

I feel very comfortable with this doctor, Waverly thought as the surgeon helped him onto his back on the gurney. And that was the last thing he remembered.

22

Angel in White

A bright young voice broke the silence in Waverly's room. "Good morning, Mr. Waverly, my name is Sofia. I'll be your nurse today. How are you feeling this morning?"

Should I tell her how I really feel? "Okay, I guess. Sofia? Where are you from?"

"Benghazi. I've lived here all my life, but my family's Italian. Are you having any pain?"

Waverly pressed his palm gently to the bandage on his right eye. "This eye is killing me."

"I'm sorry. Let me just take your vital signs, and I'll get you another dose of pain medicine."

He felt the head of the bed elevate a few degrees, and then the diaphragm of a stethoscope pressed against his chest through a gap in his hospital gown. "Okay, take a deep breath. And another one. Good, thank you."

Waverly felt a warm, soft hand feel for the pulse in his wrist.

"I need to take your temperature. Open your mouth a bit. That's it, excellent. Now raise your arm so I can take your blood pressure."

Her hands pushed up his sleeve and wrapped the blood pressure cuff around his arm.

She puffed up the cuff and pressed the stethoscope against his forearm for a few moments. "Okay, all done. I'll go get your pain medicine. Would you like some oatmeal and orange juice? Your doctor said you could have a light breakfast."

"I'll try, thank you."

"You're welcome," she sang cheerfully. "I'll be right back."

In the absence of her sunny presence, he realized he could now perceive a hint of light coming through the bandages on his eyes. He wondered how Mike and Anne would take the news of his injury.

The door flew open and something rolled into the room.

"I'm back," Sofia said. "Can you scoot to your left a bit, so I can sit on the edge of the bed and help you? First, I'll put the morphine in your IV."

She lifted his arm. Waverly smelled the bitter tang of alcohol and then felt the warmth of the bolus running into his vein, which flooded his entire body within moments.

"There you go. You should feel a lot better soon."

He heard her fiddling with the dishes and cellophane on the tray and then felt her weight on the bed beside him.

"How about a sip of juice?" A glass was pressed to his lips.

He took a drink and swallowed. "It's good, thank you."

"They make it fresh here in the kitchen every morning. Here's a spoonful of oatmeal. I added brown sugar, butter, and whole milk, so I hope you like it."

The spoon slid into his mouth and the warm, sweet oatmeal coated his mouth. "It's delicious. Thank you."

"You're welcome. How long have you been in Libya, if you don't mind my asking?"

"About three months. But I lived here before for a year, from 1998 to 1999."

"Open wide for another bite. Where does your family live?"

He swallowed. "In Virginia, in the United States."

"Oh, really? Near Washington, DC?"

"Not far. Have you been there?"

"No, but my father has always wanted to visit there. I'd love to see the cherry blossoms someday. Is your family there?"

"I'm widowed." He opened for another bite.

"I'm sorry. Any children?"

"A thirteen-year old son, Mike, and a seven-year old daughter, Anne."

"Open wide again. There you go." She dabbed at his mouth with a napkin. "They're young. Who's taking care of them? Open."

"Our nanny." He opened.

"Do they know you got hurt?"

"I think so. My colleague promised to call and let them know."

"They must be horrified. You really must call them yourself, so they hear your voice. Do you have a credit card? We can make arrangements with the operator."

"My colleague said he'd be in this evening, and I can use his phone."

"Good, it's important for them to know you're okay. Open wide, last bite." She wiped his mouth one last time, and he felt her stand up from the bed. "I need to give my other patient his medications, but I'll be back in a while. Just push this button on the bed controller if you need anything." She took his hand and guided it to the button.

So soft. So gentle.

"Thank you."

"You're very welcome. I'll be back."

The tray rolled back across the room and out the door.

Some endless length of time later, the door opened again. "I'm back, Mr. Waverly. How's your pain?"

He smiled. "It's fine."

"Are you sleepy? If you like, Head Nurse Fatima said I could read for you. The ward is only half full, and she's taking care of my other patient."

That sounded heavenly. "I'd like that."

"I love to read," she said conspiratorially. "My father bought me an e-reader for Christmas. It's the best thing ever. What do you like to read?"

"I'm afraid I don't get to do much pleasure reading anymore. I read some stories to my kids, though, especially my daughter. She loves *Grimm's Fairy Tales.* I've probably read them to her a dozen times."

"Oh, those are wonderful. What would you like to hear?"

What wouldn't he want to hear from this angel of mercy? "Oh, anything. What would you like to read?"

He could hear her finger tapping and swiping across her Kindle. "How about *The Great Gatsby*? It's one of my favorites, but it's been years since I read it."

"That sounds wonderful."

She fiddled with the Kindle for a few moments. "Can I sit here on the edge of the bed?"

"Of course."

He felt her weight on the bed beside him.

She cleared her throat. "'In my younger and more vulnerable years, my father gave me some advice I've been turning over in my mind ever since…'"

Her soothing voice and mesmerizing cadence took his mind off the grinding pain in his eye. He found himself as much captivated by her warmth of expression as the literary masterpiece itself. Occasionally, she shifted her weight on the bed or offered him a sip of water. After a couple of hours, they broke for lunch and she fed him a delicious corn chowder.

"I need to get your medicines and complete my report. I'll be back."

"Thank you, Sofia. It's a wonderful story."

"It's my favorite Fitzgerald novel. I like *Tender is the Night* too, but this one is more entertaining, and I love reading about the Roaring

Twenties. Sometimes I feel like that's when I should have lived, with all its fashion and energetic music. I'll be back in a half hour or so."

She hadn't been gone long before Waverly began listening for the sound of the door heralding her return. Just as he began to fear she had been reassigned or taken away by an emergency, the door creaked open.

"I'm back. Here's your antibiotic." She slipped a pill into his mouth and pressed a glass of water to his lips. "I was helping another nurse admit a new patient. Are you ready to finish the book?"

"I'd love to. Are you sure it's not a bother?"

"No bother at all. I only get to do this once in a while."

Interrupted only once by the head nurse, she read the enthralling tale to the end, stopping only to readjust her weight on the bed, give him a sip of water, or dab his forehead with a wet washcloth.

"'Gatsby believed in the green light, the orgastic future that year by year recedes before us. It eluded us then, but that's no matter— tomorrow we will run faster, stretch out our arms farther.... And one fine morning— So we beat on, boats against the current, borne back ceaselessly into the past.'" She sat quietly, letting the climax sink in. "Did you like it?"

"It was wonderful," he replied. "Thank you so much."

"You're entirely welcome." Her weight left the bed. "Oh, my goodness, it's time for report. I'll be leaving for the evening after my report, but I'll see you again in the morning. The evening nurse, Imelda, is a friend of mine. She'll take good care of you. I'll ask her to bring your dinner and some more pain medication after my report."

"Good night, Sofia," he called out.

"You be sure to call your children. That's an order, mister."

He chuckled. "I will, thank you."

"Good night."

The door creaked, and Waverly found himself again in silence, nothing but the repetitive hum of the intravenous pump to keep him company. *What a special person.*

ood morning." Sofia's voice rang out as she pushed through the door. "How was your evening, Mr. Waverly?"

"Fine, thank you—but please, call me Stone."

"Stone. I must take your vital signs, and then I'll feed you breakfast. What did Dr. Ahmed say about your eyes?"

"He said they were healing nicely, especially the right one. He thinks I can get the bandages off tomorrow."

"Wonderful! Are you having any pain?"

"Not really."

"Let me know if you do. Dr. Ahmed changed you to pills, and I can give you one any time you feel you need it." She pressed a stethoscope to his chest.

"That's cold," Waverly protested. "Could you—"

"Shh," she scolded. After listening for a few moments, she lifted the stethoscope away. "Sorry, I was listening. What'd you say?"

"It's cold."

"Oh, sorry." She warmed the diaphragm with her hand. "Let me listen to your respirations." She pressed it again to his chest. "Better?"

He smiled. "It's fine."

"Deep breath. Now another. Perfect, thank you."

"You smell nice this morning."

"Thank you. It's my favorite perfume, L'Ambre des Merveilles from Hermès. Are you ready for breakfast? I can offer you couscous with honey and milk or boiled eggs and, of course, orange juice."

He wanted all of it. "Can I have both? I'm really hungry this morning."

"Of course. I'll be right back." The door creaked open, and a few moments later, back came the sound of the tray with a squeaky wheel.

"So, did you call your children?" she asked.

He nodded. "My colleague came to visit last night, and I used his satellite phone to speak to them for almost half an hour."

"How are they?"

"They're just fine. The school year is almost over, and both of them are excited about summer camp and having more time to play with their new dogs."

"That's wonderful. I'm glad they're happy and safe." She sat on the edge of the bed, and he heard crinkling plastic wrap. "I love dogs, although I've never had a pet myself. What breed?"

"A cockapoo puppy and a three-year old German Shepherd. Quite a combination, huh?"

"What's a cockapoo? I've never heard of that breed."

"It's a cross between a cocker spaniel and a poodle. They're quite popular in America, especially with little girls."

"How cute. Open up—this is couscous with honey and milk."

He accepted the spoon into his mouth. "Wow, that's delicious."

"It's a very popular breakfast in Libya. It's a little too sweet for me, but I occasionally enjoy it." She fed him a couple more bites and set the bowl back on the tray. "Would you like some orange juice?"

"Yes, please."

She pressed the glass to his lips and he took a long drink. Then she tapped the boiled egg on the tray and began peeling away the shell.

If only he could see this mysterious angel. "Are you married, Sofia?"

She laughed. "I've never even had a boyfriend."

So young! Perhaps he ought to back off. "How old are you?"

"Thirty-one. But you're never supposed to ask a woman her age."

He grimaced. "I'm sorry. I was surprised."

"That's fine. It's not that I avoided marriage. It's just that there aren't many opportunities here in Benghazi to meet eligible Catholic men, especially when you live with a very traditional father." She placed a warm orb in his hand.

"Here's your egg."

He took a bite. "And your mother? Is she traditional too?"

"She was very traditional but also so loving and sweet. She died five years ago."

"I'm sorry."

"No more questions. You finish your egg and I'll go get your medication, and then I can read for you, if you like."

He nodded enthusiastically.

"I'm scheduled to admit a new patient this afternoon, so it needs to be shorter. Any requests?"

He shook his head.

"How about *The Old Man and the Sea* by Earnest Hemingway? I downloaded it almost a year ago after I read *The Sun Also Rises*, but I never got around to reading more than the first chapter."

He cleared his throat. "I've only read *For Whom the Bell Tolls*, so that sounds great to me."

She went and fetched his medicine, pressed the pills into his mouth and held a glass of water to his lips. Finally, she pushed the tray away from the bed and fetched her E-book reader from her coat pocket. "'He was an old man who fished alone in a skiff in the Gulf Stream and he had gone eighty-four days now without taking a fish…'"

Waverly spent a restless night but was sound asleep when Sofia awakened him for his vitals the next morning. She cheerfully gave him his antibiotic, fed him his breakfast, and read him a few news stories from a month-old copy of the International Herald Tribune.

The head nurse ducked her head through the door. "Dr. Ahmed called. He's in surgery and won't come by until sometime around lunch. Your patient in room twelve is asking for help with her bath."

"Please tell her I'll be right there," Sofia replied. She set the newspaper on the foot of the bed. "You seem tired today, Stone. Why don't you take a nap, and I'll bring your lunch in later?"

"Sounds good. Thank you for feeding me and reading the news."

"You're welcome. I'll be back later."

He was awakened two hours later by a gentle pat on the arm and Sofia's voice.

"Wake up, Stone. Dr. Ahmed's here."

"Mr. Waverly, how are you feeling today?" the surgeon asked.

"Fine, really."

"Good news. We can take the bandages off now. Are you ready?"

"Absolutely," he replied happily. *Please, God, let me see.*

Dr. Ahmed's steady hands teased the tape up over Waverly's right eye. The doctor gently pulled off the bandage, dabbed at his lids with gauze, and helped him pull the lids apart.

Light flooded into his vision. He squinted in an exquisite combination of pain and joy. "I can see! It's a little blurry, but I can see you."

"Let's try the other eye. I don't expect you to see much at all from this eye until you have the corneal transplant and intraocular lens, so don't be disappointed."

"I know—ouch." He winced as the doctor tugged something free from his lid.

"This eye has a lot more dried discharge." Dr. Ahmed dabbed at his eyelids and then pried them open with his fingers.

Dr. Ahmed asked him to tip his head back and put a drop from a bottle in each of his eyes. Then he checked the left eye with a blue penlight. "It looks great. The skin has healed on both corneas."

Waverly covered his right eye. Nothing appreciable changed. "You're right about my vision in this left eye. I barely saw that light."

"It'll get better after restorative surgery." Dr. Ahmed gathered the bandages and stepped away to the trash bin. Waverly almost gasped at the sight of the nurse standing behind him.

"Sofia?"

She smiled sweetly. "It's me."

He laughed with delight. "You're a brunette! Somehow I had it in my mind you were blond." He reached out his hands, and she took them in hers. "Thank you for taking such good care of me."

"You're welcome. It was my pleasure, and I'm so happy you can see. I've got to get back to my other patients, but I'll be back with your lunch in a bit." She bustled from the room.

"What a beauty," he murmured, then glanced up at the doctor. "I mean inside and out."

Dr. Ahmed smiled. "Mr. Waverly, you're ready to be discharged. I need to see you in the clinic in a week, if you're still in Benghazi. Otherwise, you'll need to see another ophthalmologist. I'll leave some steroid drops for you to use in the left eye twice a day for two weeks and antibiotic pills to take once a day for ten days. Do you need a ride anywhere?"

"No, thank you. I'll call my colleague to pick me up."

Dr. Ahmed stepped to the door. "Take care of yourself, and don't lift anything over twenty pounds for another week."

"I will. Have a good afternoon."

An hour later, an orderly wheeled Waverly out the front door of the hospital and into the searing heat and sunshine. He relished the warmth on his forehead, grateful that he needed to squint into the glare.

"Stone," Hanson called from the crosswalk to the parking garage. "How are you doing?"

"I'm feeling great, and the vision in my right eye is almost back to normal."

"That's wonderful. Well, you just wait right here, and I'll bring the Toyota Cruiser around." He hustled back toward the parking garage.

Waverly took a deep breath and exhaled. "What a beautiful day," he said over his shoulder to the orderly behind him. "What a beautiful day, indeed."

23

Return to the Hunt

Waverly jostled against Fisherman as the behemoth Russian BTR-60 armored personnel carrier pulled to a stop outside the gate at the dilapidated, single-story restaurant that over the previous three weeks had been transformed into the new American diplomatic compound. Marine guards checked each vehicle, then raised the gate to admit the pickup trucks past a sandbag bunker protecting a mounted machine gun. The armored personnel carrier was too large to negotiate the zigzagging path between massive concrete barriers, so they parked outside the fence.

The pickup trucks parked next to the building alongside a pair of old Toyota Land Cruisers. Waverly climbed out ahead of Fisherman and Chico and trudged to the entrance.

Morgan rushed outside before he reached the door. He grasped Waverly's hand. "Stone, how are you?"

"Much better," he said with a grin. "I can't see diddly-squat out of this eye, but my right eye is back to normal."

"Completely normal? Better than when Bert picked you up at the hospital?" Morgan asked dubiously.

No way was he letting Morgan slow him down. "Completely normal, I swear."

Morgan wrapped an arm around his shoulders. "I'm so glad. We're just sitting down to lunch. Please, join us."

Waverly turned back to the operators. "Fisherman, tell Redbeard to come eat."

Morgan peered through the chain-link fence at the truck parked outside. "What's with the armor?"

"It's a present," Chico sniggered. "A squad of Libyan soldiers defected in it yesterday, and we thought you might use it until your replacement vehicles arrive. It's loud as hell and rides like a freakin' tank, but otherwise it's in good shape."

Morgan chuckled. "We'll take it. We've used those Toyota Cruisers we bought from a used car dealer since the attack, but one of them threw a rod yesterday. It's toast."

Chico took an unlit cigar out of his mouth and spit on the ground. "That BTR-60 might throw a rod too—but until then, it'll provide protection if some a-hole attacks you again."

"Much appreciated. Now let's eat before it gets cold."

Waverly and the operators joined Morgan and his aides around a pair of tables. Attendants brought platters and bowls of lamb with vegetables and rice dishes.

Morgan passed Waverly a basket of naan. "Did you give your beautiful nurse a thank-you kiss before you left the hospital?" he asked with a grin. "Hanson told me she was quite a looker, right, Bert?"

Hanson grinned. "Indeed."

You can't even imagine. He took the basket. "I didn't kiss her. But I met her father."

"You did?" Morgan said with surprise. "How did that happen?"

"He came to pick her up from work after Hanson went to get the car."

"Really? Did you ask him if you could come visit?"

He shrugged. "I didn't ask."

"Why not? Even Hanson said she was clearly fond of you."

"Sure, I'll ask a distinguished Libyan-Italian Catholic gentleman if I, a one-eyed American protestant twenty-five years Sofia's senior, can come court his daughter."

Morgan chortled loudly, and the other men erupted in laughter. Redbeard guffawed so hard he snorted.

"But she was beautiful," Waverly said. "Imagine that face being the first thing you see when the bandages are taken off your eyes."

"Maybe you should thank that bomber," Morgan said.

"Oh, I'd like to thank him all right. With my boot."

Spaceman looked up from his plate. "What are Italians doing living in Benghazi?"

Waverly dabbed his mouth. "The Italians conquered Benghazi in 1911 and ruled this area for thirty years until they were defeated by General Montgomery and the British Army during the second World War. That's why you see so much Italian architecture throughout the city. It's also why soccer is all the rage here. I read somewhere that before World War II, over one-third of the population here in Benghazi was Italian. Only a handful of them still live here. I forgot to ask Sofia why she and her father are still here."

Morgan passed a massive, sweaty pitcher of cold orange juice. "She can't have many suitors to choose from in Benghazi. Her father might be delighted if you showed interest."

Waverly shook his head and passed the pitcher onward. "He did invite me to come join them for dinner sometime."

Morgan's eyes widened. "Oh, really?"

He smiled coyly. "And we exchanged phone numbers."

Morgan glanced at the other men. "Are you going?"

"Probably. When I get time."

"Are you crazy? You better make time."

"We'll see how things go." He flapped a piece of naan in the air. "Here, try some of this. It's delicious."

The conversation turned to the ongoing struggle between Gaddafi's forces and the rebels. Fisherman detailed intel about battles that raged in hotspots throughout the country and described how the seesaw fighting had been especially intense around the coastal city of Misrata. Meanwhile, NATO air strikes had decimated loyalist forces and shot down any of Gaddafi's aircraft that dared take to the skies.

Waverly took a bite out of an apple and contemplated while he chewed. "And you haven't found any rebel or loyalist advanced weapon systems for over two weeks—not even a single Grinch missile?"

Morgan shook his head.

"But the British and French began helicopter attacks last night," Waverly continued. "They'll be covertly going after jihadist groups that have been deemed a threat to the NTC. I've asked them to alert me when they find weapon systems, so I can assess them."

"How's that different from what they've been doing?" Morgan asked.

"Over the past two weeks, they've attacked Gaddafi's communications and control facilities until they ran out of targets. Then they concentrated on pockets of loyalist forces near the eastern cities of Ras Lanuf, Bin Jawad, and Maradah, but they couldn't get the rebels to occupy the areas they liberated, so the loyalists always moved back in the next day."

Morgan sighed. "Somehow, we've got to get the rebel forces better organized, or this war will go on forever."

"That's going to be tough," Fisherman said. "They fight among themselves as much as they fight Gaddafi's forces."

"That's for sure," Morgan agreed. "That reminds me—Stone, do you remember my Libyan aide, Mohammad?"

"The one who asked if he could buy my old boots?"

"That's him. He lost an arm in the hotel bombing. We didn't find him for two hours after the blast."

He shuddered. "That's terrible."

"They're still not sure he'll make it. Anyway, I went to visit him in the hospital, and he fingered our kitchen worker, Hassan, as an informant to Abdul-Karim al-Rashid. Conveniently, Hassan called off sick the day of the bombing."

Waverly leaned back from the table and clenched his jaw. "I knew that bastard had something to do with the bombing."

"Yeah, well, we've got plans for him," Fisherman said. "While you were in the hospital, we paid Jalal bin Koussa fifty bucks to find out where al-Rashid and his men moved their base."

Waverly looked up with surprise. "Jalal?"

Fisherman nodded. "And it only took him four hours to find out. It's actually been a training site for the jihadists for years."

I knew that kid would turn out to be an asset. "Where?"

"In the desert two klicks east of Brega. And we just got the okay from Langley to target him. We're going to take al-Rashid out when we're certain he's there."

Waverly nodded. "Good—and the sooner the better, before he kills us or any NTC members."

"We plan to hit them tonight," Fisherman said. "We'll drop in a klick from their desert base and hoof it over there. If we spot al-Rashid, we'll light him up."

"I'm going with you."

"No, you're not," Morgan exclaimed. "You're not allowed on this mission. That's an order from the CIA director himself. He forbade you taking part in direct combat until further notice. I'll show you the memo."

"That's ridiculous," Waverly said with a huff. "I'm fine, and I want to be there." He caught Morgan's eye. "There's a good chance they've moved any advanced weapons systems they have to the new base. I've got to be there myself to search that base. You can just leave my name out of your report."

"I'm not doing that," Morgan said. "If you get hurt again, it'll be my ass in a sling."

Waverly put down his fork. "Gus, I'm going on this mission. If I get hurt, everyone at this table can attest that I went against the director's orders and your best judgment, but I'm going."

Morgan didn't respond.

"Gus, please. I want to go."

Morgan white-knuckled the arms of his chair. "Okay."

Relief and elation surged through Waverly. "Thank you." *This could be it. This is where I would hide the backpack bomb, if I were in his shoes—far enough from Benghazi to escape notice but close enough to a major port when time comes to transport it. I've got a good feeling about this.*

24

A Target Too Many

The two helicopters set down in a depression in the desert floor lit only by a waxing moon. Several of the operators fanned out from the aircraft and up a sandy incline with their weapons at the ready. The pilots cut the engines, and the whirl of the rotors decelerated to an eerie silence punctuated by a stiff breeze.

"Checkmate and Puckeater," Waverly half-whispered. "You stay with the helo unless we call for backup." He patted Fisherman on the shoulder. "Let's go get that bastard."

Lugging his AK-47 and the radiation detector through ankle-deep sand, he tailed Fisherman for over two hundred yards before stumbling over sandstone to his knees.

"Are you all right?" Fisherman whispered.

"I'm fine. Just give me a couple of seconds." He got to his feet and adjusted the detector sling over his shoulder. "Okay, let's go."

Fisherman jogged up an incline to a plateau overlooking a dark, featureless valley. He grabbed binoculars from his belt and knelt. "I see a couple of lights. Let's get closer."

Waverly jogged down the other side of the embankment with Spaceman, Deadeye, and Redbeard right behind him.

They trotted down a series of switchbacks into the valley and then up another sedimentary rock formation to a ridge. When the camp below them came into view, Fisherman signaled for everyone to get down.

Waverly dived to the ground and pulled his night-vision goggles from their case on his belt. He looked through them at two men smoking cigarettes outside the nearest tent.

"That's not him," he whispered to Fisherman.

"Agreed." Fisherman panned his own binoculars across the encampment of more than two dozen tents arrayed haphazardly across the rocky plateau. "Another Haji in a long nightshirt just came out of the large tent in the back. That might be al-Rashid."

Waverly zoomed in on the man's heavy beard and angular nose. "That's him!"

Al-Rashid lit a cigarette and took a few puffs before snuffing it out on the ground. He slipped his lighter into his pocket and ducked back into the tent.

"It was him, all right," Spaceman whispered. "If it wasn't, it was his twin brother."

Fisherman reached for the communications gear Redbeard was carrying, put on the earphones, and raised the mouthpiece to his lips. "Foxtrot, this is Tango, do you hear me?" A few seconds passed before he nodded at the others. "I've got you loud and clear. We've sighted Pontiac and will paint him in ten seconds. Tango out."

Spaceman retrieved the laser designator from Deadeye. Looking through the sights, he put the laser beam on the center of the large tent and held it steady. Time for the planes to do their work. He glanced up at the sky but neither saw nor heard anything.

Waverly felt every muscle in his body tense as Spaceman began counting, "One, two, three, four, five, six, seven—"

A pair of tremendous explosions and huge fireballs erupted near the back of the camp. Dozens of fighters and a few women and children scurried from the remaining tents. Screaming in terror, they fled *en masse* up a nearby slope away from the camp as the fire raged behind them.

"Take that, you son of a bitch," Deadeye muttered.

Spaceman beamed. "It hit on seven, my lucky number. Only thing better would've been a napalm inferno."

Waverly couldn't tear his eyes away from the families running from the carnage. "Nobody said anything about women and children being here."

"The intel was wrong," Fisherman said. "There were only supposed to be fighters in this camp. I'll note the failure in my report. Come on, let's search the base for advanced weapons."

They jogged down into the camp. Deadeye and Spaceman set a perimeter on the side of the camp where the rebels had fled while Waverly and Fisherman raced for the targeted tent.

They found nothing—no sign of the occupants.

"My God," Waverly said. "Nothing's left but shards of the tent poles."

He set up his radiation detector and scanned the area. "Nothing. You and Redbeard search the other tents while I scan the rest of the camp."

It took just over thirty minutes to search the camp. They found mortars and shells, a dozen crated AK-47 rifles, and what Waverly estimated to be two tons of rifle ammunition, but no surface-to-air missiles or other advanced weaponry. And no backpack bomb.

Rifles in hand, the team jogged over an incline and back to the helicopters. Waverly slogged along at the rear. *I was so convinced we'd find the backpack bomb here. At least we got al-Rashid. Maybe he's hidden the backpack bomb in some cave, and nobody else knows where it is.* He laughed bitterly at himself. *Dream on, fantasy man.*

Checkmate was sitting in the helicopter door, boots dangling above the sand. "Did you get him?"

"Yeah, we got him," Waverly replied with a nod. "Along with a bunch of women and kids."

"What?" Puckeater said. "There were women and kids in the camp?"

"Yeah, and we didn't see them until the bombs hit. The intel was wrong."

Spaceman shrugged and pushed past Waverly to climb up into the helo. "That's war. Embrace the suck."

Waverly stopped in his tracks. "You embrace the suck!" He swung up into the helicopter and got up in Spaceman's face. "It's fucking unacceptable. You don't have an empathetic bone in your body, and I'd think you would have after what you've been through yourself. These women and children were innocents. Do you hear me? Innocents."

Spaceman stared back impassively.

Waverly suppressed the urge to punch Spaceman in the mouth. "You're a pathetic excuse for a human."

"There's zero we could've done differently," Fisherman said from below. "They were asleep in the freakin' tents. We're not even sure if any of the women and children were in the tent we hit."

Waverly slammed the scanner case down. "There's a lot we could've done better. We could've scouted them longer, even for several days, until we were sure there were no innocents in that tent. From now on, I want to be absolutely certain we aren't hitting innocent people."

Fisherman shook his head in frustration. "Stone... Man. Come on, let's get the helo in the air."

Morgan and Waverly headed up the sidewalk to the main entrance of the Tibesti Hotel.

Waverly glanced up at the freshly repaired and painted upper floors of the building that had been damaged by the bomb explosion. "It looks like they've made a lot of progress on the repairs."

"To the facade, yes," Morgan replied, "but our space is still a complete disaster. It'll take them a year to get those repairs finished. But our new spot offers better protection, anyway."

Inside the hotel lobby, Mahmoud Jibril and Mustafa Abdul Jalil were deep in conversation on a couch outside the entrance to the ballroom. When Jibril caught sight of the Americans, he patted Jalil on the arm, and the two men stood to greet them.

Jibril hailed them cheerfully. "Mr. Waverly, Mr. Morgan. Thank you for joining our little soirée."

"Mr. Prime Minister, Mr. Chairman." Morgan shook each man's hand. "It's indeed our pleasure."

Jibril took Waverly by the elbow. "Mr. Waverly, how are your eyes, if you don't mind my asking?"

"Better every day, Prime Minister, thank you."

"Please, you must call me Mahmoud. I'm pleased to hear this. We've all been terribly worried." He turned at the sound of the door opening behind them, and a waiter scurried across the lobby to the front desk. "Gentleman, I must warn you that Abdul-Karim al-Rashid is also here, and he's in a truly foul mood. His nephew and niece and their children were killed by a bombing at their camp a few nights back."

Damn, we missed him. That's the last time I rely on anything I don't see with my own two eyes—well, at least one eye. He grimaced. "I'm sorry to hear that. Another car bomb?"

"No, an air strike on their camp. According to Abdul-Karim, it was a precision air strike. I must advise you, he's barely in control of his emotions."

"That's horrible," Waverly replied glumly.

"Shall we join the others?" Jibril guided Waverly and Morgan to the double doors at the rear of the lobby. "It was his favorite nephew, so please understand he's not himself at this moment."

Jalil opened the doors on the ballroom, where two dozen men gathered around tables adorned with impressive flower arrangements, silver, and fine china. Bunting in the colors of the rebel flag was draped over the serving tables and podium.

"Cowards!" al-Rashid bellowed as he caught sight of them. He rushed toward the Americans, his piercing black eyes wide with anger. "I know it was you! This was a precision bombing, not one of Gaddafi's incompetent pilots. Mustafa Mohammed had just finished his degree in engineering, and his oldest son was only nine. Why would you do this? I'll have my revenge."

General Younes stepped away from another group to convey his condolences.

"Fuck you too, Younes," al-Rashid shouted and stormed for the door. "You're with them." He disappeared through the door, slamming it behind him.

Younes approached the Americans. "Good evening, gentlemen. You must forgive my colleague. He's stricken with grief."

"Completely understandable," Waverly said. "I can't imagine the pain he must be feeling."

"How's your eye coming along?"

"It's better, thank you. I need another surgery on my left eye, but the pain is gone."

"I'm happy to hear this. Whoever bombed this hotel needs to pay for it, but my sources tell me it wasn't al-Rashid or anyone from the February 17 Martyrs' Brigade."

Waverly looked up with a start.

"No?" Morgan remained cool. "How do you know?"

Younes smiled coyly. "I have my sources. And those sources tell me it was a splinter group called the Knights of Allah. We arrested four men involved in the hotel bombing the day before yesterday, and two of them confessed."

Waverly felt queasy. He stared at his feet. *It's my fault. If I hadn't been so hell-bent on getting al-Rashid, this wouldn't have happened. Lord Jesus, forgive me.*

Younes sipped his orange juice and broadened his smile. "Whoever carried out this attack on the February 17 Martyrs' Brigade should hold off on retaliatory attacks until we get to the bottom of what really happened."

"I agree with you, General," Waverly replied solemnly. "It won't happen again. You have my word on that."

A waiter in the back of the room opened the doors to the dining room and tolled a large bell.

"Please, gentlemen," General Younes said. "After you."

25

Wheels Spinning

Waverly accepted the paper plate of pinto beans and a slice of cornbread with a nod, grabbed a bottle of water from the cooler, and made his way to the tables where the covert operators were bantering about the Major League Baseball season.

"Puckeater," Redbeard said, "you're living in a dream world. The Pirates have about as much chance of winning their division as Army has of winning Army-Navy. The team to beat's the Atlanta Braves. Mark my words."

"I second that," Fisherman said. "They have some great young talent on that team."

"Young talent," Deadeye scoffed. "Let's see how they do against Josh Hamilton and the rest of the Rangers crew. My boys are winning the World Series, no doubt about it."

"Baseball?" Checkmate said. "How can you stand to watch that stupid game? It bores me to freakin' tears." He turned his attention back to his beans.

"Oh, and I suppose you think soccer is exciting as hell?" Puckeater said.

"To handle and pass a ball with only your feet is truly skillful," Checkmate responded. "Very few men master it."

Puckeater swung with an imaginary bat. "Listen, buddy, there's nothing harder than hitting a curve ball or a ninety-seven-mile-an-hour inside fastball. I'll tell you what—when we get back to the States, I'll take you to a batting cage that blasts baseballs at ninety miles an hour, and we'll see how you do."

Checkmate shrugged. "Okay. And then we'll go out to the soccer field, and you can try to take the ball away from me. Fifty bucks says you can't even get close."

"Shit, why would I want to?"

"Have a good time, boys," Redbeard said, "but when I get back to the States, if it's not wearing a skirt, I'm not interested."

Puckeater punched Redbeard in the shoulder. "Tell us something we don't know."

"Stone," Fisherman said after a gulp of beer, "who are you picking to win the World Series this year?"

"The Nationals."

All the operators erupted in boisterous laughter.

"The Nationals," Checkmate repeated incredulously. "You're picking the Nationals? Didn't you hear their manager resigned over a contract dispute? You're drinking the Kool-Aid, my friend."

"We'll see," Waverly replied confidently. "But if they bring up Bryce Harper and he doesn't get hurt, they've got as good a shot as anyone."

"No way. There's no way they can beat the Phillies."

One of the staff slung a fresh pan of cornbread onto the center of the table. "More beans?" Nobody replied, so he grabbed the pot and headed back to the kitchen tent.

"Stone," Fisherman said, "I noticed your left eye is redder today."

"It feels fine," Waverly replied. "It just looks like hell."

"Can you see out of it?" Deadeye asked.

"Not much. The doctor said I need a corneal transplant to get the vision back in that eye."

"Why the hell don't you go home and get it fixed?"

"Because I've been ordered to stay. And besides, I want to see this assignment through. I've got a lot of friends in eastern Libya, and I want this conflict settled for their sakes. I'm staying six months."

Deadeye smirked. "Friends like that hottie nurse Hanson told us about?"

Waverly smiled indulgently. "All the families I worked with in Benghazi the last time I lived here."

"Well, I've seen men go home for a lot less," Fisherman said.

Waverly bristled. "I'm not an operator, but there's still a lot I can do to help bring this mission to a successful conclusion."

"Nobody here doubts that, Stone." Fisherman got up from the table and raised his voice. "Spaceman, what the hell are you doing over there?"

Spaceman looked up from where he was sitting alone next to an electric lantern. "I'm reading a download from *Time* magazine. There's a story here about Gaddafi hiding in Sirte. Why aren't we running missions there?"

"Like *Time* magazine really knows," Fisherman scoffed. "He's just as likely to be in Tripoli—or anywhere else his troops control. If I were him, I'd sleep in a different city every night."

"Whatever," Spaceman muttered dismissively. He looked back down at the magazine. "But we need to do a lot more to get this shit done."

"You mean like the friendly fire air strike you brought down on that rebel column in Ajdabiya last week?"

"That was on them," Spaceman retorted. "How should I know they were suddenly fielding a column of tanks?"

Fisherman took a swig of water from a bottle and wiped his mouth on his sleeve. "General Younes claims he informed us. Anyway, for the next few days, we're concentrating our efforts around Brega. But we need to make sure we don't target any more rebel tanks."

"Maybe they should paint them pink?" Redbeard said.

"With Mickey Mouse ears on the sides," Puckeater added.

Fisherman chuckled. "I have a conference call scheduled with the general later this afternoon. I'll suggest it."

"Suggest what?" Chico walked out of the darkness toward the others.

"Puckeater wants the rebels to paint Mickey Mouse ears on their tanks," Fisherman replied.

"I'd love to see that—a whole column of them," Chico said. "Anyway, the helos will be ready in thirty mikes. Waverly, do you have our targets?"

"Yep, a command and control center in Brega."

"Again," Chico muttered. "I thought we destroyed that the night before last."

"Apparently not," Waverly said. "And they also want us to try to find what's left of that MQ-8 drone that got shot down three days ago. And I want to check out the satellite intel pinpointing a large new rebel weapons depot near Derna that Mahmoud Jibril and Mustafa Abdul Jalil claim to know nothing about."

Chico kicked at the sand. "I'm getting sick of this crap."

A few minutes of silence passed. Deadeye got up and slid in next to Waverly. "Called your kids lately?"

He nodded. "This morning, in fact."

"How are they?"

"Just fine."

"Glad to hear it. What are they up to?"

Waverly grinned. "The usual routine. Mike had two singles in a Little League game yesterday, and Anne's decided she wants to learn to ice skate. Apparently, her best friend from school just started lessons."

Deadeye groaned. "That'll cost you a bundle. I dated a girl in high school whose family had to take a loan out on their house just to pay for her skates and four or five coaches. Her dad lost his job, and they ended up losing their home."

"I'll keep that in mind. My sister was an ice skater, so I know the drill."

"What's the weather like in DC?"

"Stifling. Several days a couple of weeks ago were over a hundred degrees. Our nanny said they expected more high temperatures and humidity over the next week."

"So, same as here," Deadeye said with a sigh. "That's comforting."

"Tomorrow it's expected to be one hundred and two in the shade," Fisherman said.

"Damn," Checkmate said. "We need to start wearing shorts like the Brits did in World War II."

"The hell with that," Redbeard scoffed. "Not after I saw that viper last week."

"No snake's going to bite your legs, dude," Checkmate said. "They look too much like trees."

"Trees covered with hair," Chico added with a snicker.

"You should talk. Didn't they teach you to have respect for your elders at Fairleigh Dickinson?"

"Only those deserving of respect." Chico paused and looked around. "There's the pilot. Let's go."

"I'll be right there," Waverly said. "I need fresh batteries for my metal detector." He creaked wearily to his feet, dumped his trash into the nearest garbage bin, and trudged for the supply bunker. *I don't know how much more of this futile searching for the backpack bomb I can take. It's the same damn thing night after night, week after week, no end in sight. I'm so tired of it all.*

26

Stalemate in Brega

The morning sun glinted through the binoculars as Waverly scanned a column of tanks two thousand meters away. "Take out the commander in the first tank."

"What if they're rebels?" Deadeye muttered as he tracked a soldier wearing a helmet and goggles through the scope on his Lobaev sniper rifle.

"They're definitely loyalists."

"Keep your head down, Stone," Fisherman said. "You even being here goes against my better judgment."

Waverly shot Fisherman a glare. "I'm fine, and I'm free to resume full activity. Do you want to see the email?"

"Just take it easy."

"Ten days in a row hitting targets in Brega," Deadeye grumbled. "How about if we go to Gharyan tomorrow? Anywhere else is fine. I just need a change of scenery."

"Fire," Waverly commanded.

Deadeye let out a breath and fired. The bullet struck the tank commander in the chest. "Bullseye. Now I'll get Ali Baba the sheik climbing down the last tank." He took a shallow breath, exhaled, and fired again. The man clutched his chest, dropped to his knees, and face-planted in the sand.

"How'd you know he's a sheik?" Fisherman asked.

"He looked like one."

He tracked another Libyan soldier running from tank to tank shouting encouragement, and dropped him with a single shot.

"Okay, that'll slow them down," Waverly said. "Let's go."

The three men clambered down the sandy incline to their ATVs and sped down a dry riverbed, Waverly holding on for his life every time Fisherman went airborne over a bump. They sped east for nearly a mile before pulling into a small oasis where Redbeard, Puckeater, and Spaceman waited with their ATVs. Fisherman signaled as they continued through, and the others fell in line behind them. Less than ten minutes later, they pulled up beside the Mi-17.

"How'd it go?" Chico called.

"Hat trick!" Deadeye shouted over the drone of the rotors. "We lit up the commander of a column of loyalist tanks and two of his lieutenants. How'd you do?"

"Blew the crap out of them. Spaceman was amazing. He took out a dozen of the bastards after a bomb vaporized their command center. Then before we left, he took out a Toyota Cruiser with a single shot. It must've been filled with explosives, because it blew like a mother."

Fisherman patted Spaceman's back. "Good work."

Spaceman nodded. "It was awesome. It's been long time since I shot that well."

A burst of automatic rifle fire erupted from the distance, and bullets tore through a scrub tree behind them. They dived behind an embankment.

"Do you see him?" Waverly gasped.

Deadeye peered through the sight on his rifle. "Behind the burned-out truck near that stand of palms."

"Redbeard," Fisherman said, "flank him on the left."

Redbeard dashed behind a sandy berm as another burst of rifle fire erupted.

Several minutes passed as Waverly, Fisherman, and Deadeye lay beside each other.

Waverly stowed his binoculars and peered through the sight on his AK. "I don't see anything."

"He's there," Fisherman replied. "Keep watching."

Waverly jumped as a single shot rang out from Deadeye's rifle.

"Got him." Deadeye rolled onto his side and wiped sweat from his brow.

Waverly looked through his binoculars. "Are you sure?"

"Hell yes. I hit him right between the eyes."

Waverly spotted Redbeard behind the stand of palm trees, running with his rifle aimed at the vehicle. Redbeard caught his eye and signaled all clear.

They jogged across the clearing to his position. The bearded sniper lay on his back spread-eagled, a bullet hole in the top of his forehead.

"You missed high," Fisherman said.

"So I did," Deadeye replied.

Waverly stooped to grab the sniper's rifle and slung the strap over his shoulder. "Let's get back to the base."

Waverly heaped rice and several slices of lamb on his plate before making his way to the team at the table.

"And that was the last time I saw her," Puckeater was saying. "A few years later, I found out she married the preacher's son. I guess she knew I wouldn't be around much."

"I'd say you got lucky," Redbeard said. "A babe like that would've spent every dime you earned and then some." He glanced at Waverly. "How about you, Stone?"

Waverly slid his plate onto the table and sat. "What?"

"Did your woman ever leave you for another man?"

He took a spoonful of rice and stuffed it into his mouth. "Yes, for a few months."

Redbeard, suddenly interested, sat up in his chair. "She came back?"

"No, I came back—after I'd been away for a year."

"Where were you?"

"On a mission in Iraq and Syria."

"Did you forgive her?"

Waverly set his spoon on his plate. He took a deep breath and stared at the waning moon on the horizon. "I forgave her."

"And you lived happily ever after?"

He shook his head. "She died."

Redbeard winced. "Sorry. What happened?"

"She got cancer and died just over a year ago."

"That really sucks, man."

Fisherman tossed his empty Coke can into the trash. "We're not making any real progress here, so why don't you get the hell back home to your kids?"

When would everyone quit harping on him to go home? "That's not true. We've made a lot of progress. It's slow but steady, especially the last few weeks."

"What progress have we made?" Redbeard demanded. "We shot up those loyalist troops in Brega today, and they still routed the rebels two hours later."

"Think about it. Benghazi and everything to the east of it is now firmly in the rebels' hands. We've stopped the air attacks, destroyed scores of tanks and artillery, and pushed the loyalist forces back beyond Brega. We've also confiscated more than fifty surface-to-air missiles from rebel jihadist groups. I'd say that's pretty good progress for a few days shy of four months."

Fisherman slid back into his seat and leaned forward on the table with both forearms. "That's BS. We're bogged down here with no end in sight, and the rebel troops are no better organized than they were three months ago."

"Maybe, maybe not," Waverly replied, "but I sense things are changing for the better. We haven't seen a Gaddafi helicopter in two weeks, and most of the troops we're fighting have lost their morale. The number of loyalist tanks we see on the battlefield isn't ten percent of what it used to be. We've got Gaddafi holed up somewhere in a bunker, and al-Rashid and the February 17 Martyrs' Brigade have disappeared."

"Don't get complacent," Fisherman said. "They're around, and that bastard al-Rashid won't stop until he gets his revenge."

"All the more reason to keep searching for him. This country will be better off if he's dead when we leave."

"Some other jihadist currently training in Iraq will just replace him. They'll still be fighting this battle when you and I are six feet under, buddy." He stood and stretched. "I'm getting a couple hours of shut-eye before we head out tonight. I suggest you boneheads do the same." He walked away toward the barracks.

"Think about what I said about al-Rashid," Waverly called after him. "We've got to find him and his brigade."

Fisherman waved an arm in reply and disappeared around the corner of the mess tent.

Redbeard and the others had already turned their conversation back to the cheating ways of their women. Waverly took a deep breath. *I really don't make a very good cheerleader, especially when even I don't believe there's been significant progress. It's the backpack bomb, stupid—forget about everything else.*

27

Doubt Takes Flight

Waverly glanced back at the angry honk from a black sedan whose path up the driveway of the Tibesti Hotel was blocked by their massive Russian armored personnel carrier. Spaceman slipped out of the vehicle, his rifle shouldered, and jogged ahead up the driveway and into the main entrance.

By the time Waverly and Morgan made it into the lobby, Spaceman was coordinating with NTC leaders Mustafa Abdul Jalil and Mahmoud Jibril. Behind them, more than a dozen AK-47-armed rebel fighters were observing their conversation from across the lobby. The unit leader leaned over and whispered to the fighter to his right.

"Mr. Jalil, Mr. Jibril." Waverly shook each man's hand and peered beyond them at the rebel fighters, several of whom appeared to be inserting magazines. *What is this, some kind of ambush?*

Jalil's face was drawn with angst. "Thank you for agreeing to meet with us on short notice. Mr. Spaceman says you'd prefer to meet here in the lobby."

Waverly nodded. "Right here is fine."

"As you wish," Jalil replied, "but I assure you we'll be safe here." He motioned to a cluster of chairs at the far corner of the lobby. "How about over there?"

"That's perfect." He and Morgan walked across the room with the two NTC leaders, while Fisherman, Chico, and Spaceman took up positions flanking the rebel fighters.

Waverly took a seat. "Well, what can we do for you?"

Jalil glanced at Jibril. "Mr. Waverly, Mr. Morgan, it is our sad duty to inform you that General Younes has been assassinated."

Waverly bolted upright in his chair. "What? When?"

"Yesterday evening," Jalil said. "It's a terrible tragedy for the rebel cause and me personally."

Waverly bowed his head in respectful acknowledgment. "Who...?"

"Abdul-Karim al-Rashid."

"Al-Rashid? Are you sure?"

Jalil nodded. "We are certain. The NTC summoned General Younes to Benghazi. We intended to speak to him about the mistakes made at the front lines over the past two weeks. Al-Rashid murdered him as he traveled from Zuwetina to Benghazi."

"Mistakes made. What mistakes are you referring to?" Waverly asked.

"More than seventy-five rebel fighters were killed and nearly two hundred wounded in an ill-conceived advance on loyalist forces in Brega."

Waverly cleared his throat. "So, you summoned General Younes because he pressed the battle for Brega that'd been stalemated for nearly two months?"

"Mr. Waverly," Jalil responded heatedly, "it's our prerogative to question decisions made by our military leaders, as your own presidents have been known to do, dating back to the administrations of Washington and Lincoln."

Morgan sat forward in his chair. "We'll concede that point. But why did you send al-Rashid with your summons?"

Jibril bristled. "We did not send al-Rashid! I sent the summons with my lieutenant, Tarik Huwaidi, but al-Rashid intercepted him and took my summons to General Younes at the command center in Zuwetina without my knowledge or consent."

Waverly felt a wave of foreboding sweep over him. He flicked at his watchband and took a deep breath. *Al-Rashid again. The rebellion is finished.* "Have you spoken to al-Rashid?"

"Nobody's seen him since then," Jalil replied. "I sent Commander Ibrahim and a dozen men to bring him to Benghazi, but we haven't heard back from them since they left last evening."

Waverly glanced at Morgan. "What a mess."

"We find ourselves in a most challenging situation," said Jalil.

Waverly jumped as Deadeye advanced a shell in his AK. "I'd say that's the understatement of the year."

"I want to assure you the NTC had nothing to do with the murder of General Younes," Jalil said.

An uncomfortable silence fell over the group.

"Who'll take over military command of the rebel army?" Waverly finally asked.

"General Younes's top deputy and relative, General Suleiman Mahmud, has been named commander of the National Liberation Army," Jalil replied. "I hope you support this choice."

Waverly nodded. "He's a good man. I am compelled to inform you that President Obama will have serious concerns about this assassination and its effects on the morale of the men fighting the loyalist forces."

A bead of perspiration trickled down Jalil's forehead. "Tell President Obama we share his concern. Last night, the leaders of the Obeidat tribe claimed publicly that the NTC conspired with Islamic extremists to kill General Younes. If we lose their support, the rebellion will collapse."

"Can you blame them?" Waverly asked. "Their most famous son gets shamefully murdered by a thug linked to the NTC."

Jalil wiped his brow with a handkerchief. "I understand how they feel, but I assure you, we had nothing to do with this dishonorable killing. They refuse to even meet with us to discuss it. We're hoping you might approach them on our behalf."

Unbelievable. "You want us to try to smooth things over?"

The two NTC leaders stared back in silence.

Waverly pondered for a moment and then sighed loudly. "Ibrahim Said al-Obeidi has been a good friend for many years. I'll try to reach him." He stood up and Morgan followed his lead. "I'll call you tomorrow."

Pull up in front of the bunker," Waverly called out from the rear compartment.

Deadeye pulled the armored personnel carrier to a stop at a fortified gate outside a high-walled compound. He stepped from the vehicle and approached the heavily armed guards gazing at them from behind a four-foot sandbag bunker. A menacing machine-gun muzzle poked out through a port in the center.

"We've brought representatives Stone Waverly and Gus Morgan of the United States to meet Ibrahim Said al-Obeidi," Deadeye called out in Arabic.

"He's expecting them," a young guard yelled back. "Mr. Waverly is welcome to enter. One of you may accompany him but leave your weapons behind."

Waverly and Morgan climbed down from the transport. Sunglasses gleaming in the afternoon sun, they walked slowly to the gate with their open palms before them. A pair of guards emerged to pat the two men down and guide them into the compound. Once inside the twelve-foot concrete walls, the guards led them to a small hut. As they neared the door, it opened and a middle-aged Arab rushed out to greet them.

"Stone!" The man seized Waverly by the shoulders. "It's so good to see you again." He grinned, then gathered him into a full embrace. "How long has it been, my friend?"

"Over ten years. Far too long."

"I meant to come see you when I heard you were here, but it's been chaotic. Please forgive my discourtesy."

"I understand. Ibrahim, allow me to introduce Gus Morgan, American representative to the NTC."

Al-Obeidi took Morgan's hand. "I heard wonderful stories about you from my cousin, Abdul. He was very fond of you, sir."

"And I of him," Morgan said. "We're devastated by this terrible loss for all the people of Libya."

"He was a great leader and an even better friend," al-Obeidi said mournfully. "It's impossible to grasp this senseless murder at the hands of those he risked his life to help. I just had dinner with Abdul and his son three nights ago. He was so confident about the course of the battle. And now he's gone." He sighed. "Please come inside and have a cup of tea."

The single-roomed command center was lined with screens monitoring every inch of the compound walls. Al-Obeidi stepped across the room and poured tea from a steaming pot. He handed cups to each of the Americans. "Goat's milk?"

"No, thank you," Waverly replied. "This is fine."

"Please, let's be comfortable." Al-Obeidi led them to chairs. "How can I help you?"

Waverly sipped the tea and set his cup on the coffee table. "Ibrahim, let me be frank. We've come to appeal for your help in keeping the rebellion from fracturing over the murder of General Younes."

Al-Obeidi nodded. "I see. As you Americans are fond of saying, this will be a tall order. I attended a meeting of the Obeidat tribal elders last evening, and little sentiment remains to back the NTC. The elders will likely decide to withdraw support for the National Liberation Army and order my cousin, Suleiman Mahmoud, to resign his position leading the rebel forces."

"Oh God, no," Waverly said. *This could be the end.*

"Will they shift their support back to Gaddafi?" Morgan rubbed his hands up and down his thighs.

"No, I don't think so, at least not yet," al-Obeidi replied. "I think they aim to be neutral."

Waverly blew out through pursed lips. "You know, Ibrahim, as well as I do, this isn't possible. There can be no neutrality in this war—either they support the revolution, or they support Gaddafi."

"They'll never again support the NTC," al-Obeidi said firmly. "Several NTC members are complicit in the murder, and the murderer himself, Abdul-Karim al-Rashid, is a close ally to these scoundrels. Al-Rashid must die."

"Would the elders be placated if al-Rashid were eliminated?" Waverly asked.

The two men stared into each other's eyes for several moments.

"Perhaps," al-Obeidi finally replied. "I can't promise, but I believe this would be an important step—especially if his allies were also removed from the NTC."

"Let's begin with al-Rashid," Waverly said. "We promise to redouble our efforts to eliminate al-Rashid. In return, we ask the Obeidat elders to allow Suleiman Mahmoud to command the National Liberation Army and to withhold judgment on pulling their support for the NTC. Is it a deal?"

"Does President Obama agree to this deal?" al-Obeidi asked Morgan.

"Yes," Morgan affirmed. "It cannot be stated publicly, but you can relay our promise to the elders."

Al-Obeidi nodded. "I will speak to the elders about your proposal. Give me twenty-four hours to reply."

Waverly stood. "Thank you, Ibrahim. You're a true friend."

A new undercurrent of urgency energized Waverly's steps as al-Obeidi walked them back to the door. *We've got to eliminate al-Rashid within a week. But first we need to find him.*

tay with me, no matter what happens," Waverly yelled above the cacophony of the helicopter rotors, "and keep your rifle on safety unless you plan to fire. Do you understand?"

"Yes, Mr. Waverly," Jalal shouted. "I will obey you."

Waverly patted him on the knee and gave him a thumbs-up.

Fisherman gave a shout and motioned for Waverly to join him at the front of the fuselage where the operators were poring over detailed maps.

"I'll be right back," Waverly said to Jalal. He stumbled forward and pulled himself into a seat beside Fisherman. "What's up?"

"Al-Rashid, that's what. We just got confirmation that al-Rashid is commanding elements of the February 17 Martyrs' Brigade near Zliten. Rebel army forces just entered the city, and we're headed there to lend support and kill that son of a bitch."

"Where the hell's Zliten?" Spaceman yelled from behind him.

"Along the coast, almost equidistant between Misrata and Tripoli," Fisherman hollered.

Waverly thumped his fists against his knees in triumph. *I thought we'd never find that bastard.* "We've got to make sure he's eliminated. Otherwise, we won't be able to hold the rebels together."

Fisherman nodded. "Getting him is the top priority. You should stay at the beach with the kid."

He shook his head adamantly. "I want to be there. He'll be fine."

"No, I need my men focused on tracking down al-Rashid, not on making sure Jalal is safe."

He sighed. "Okay. No problem."

"Thanks."

The Mi-17 flew low over the inland hills and streaked across the western edge of Zliten to the empty beach. As soon as it jolted down on the sand, the operators scattered to secure the perimeter. Fisherman and Chico jogged back a few moments later.

"Al-Rashid and his men were spotted in a neighborhood near the teaching hospital. All the loyalist forces are on the east side of the city."

Fisherman handed Waverly a radio. "You and the kid stay here while we hunt down al-Rashid. If anything threatens you, we can be back here in ten mikes, okay?"

"Good hunting."

The operators climbed back aboard the helicopter, and it sped inland. Waverly and Jalal watched until it disappeared, and then Waverly smiled at the boy. "Are you disappointed?"

Jalal nodded. "I want to fight al-Rashid myself, but Mr. Fisherman always leaves me behind whenever the soldiers go fight. How can I ever reclaim my honor if I'm never given another chance?"

Waverly smiled and patted Jalal's back. "Mr. Fisherman wants you to be safe."

"No, he's afraid I will—how do you say—frost up again."

"Your time will come, son. You've got your entire life ahead of you, and you shoot that rifle better than I do now."

Jalal picked up a rock and hurled it into the sea. He took off his shoes, slung his AK-47 over his shoulder, and meandered into a breaking wave.

Waverly checked his radio to make sure it was on. *What the hell is happening? Have they found al-Rashid or not?*

Jalal fetched another stone and skipped it across the water. "My father loved the sea," he called to Waverly.

"Me too. It always reminds me of when I was a young boy and my family vacationed at a small cottage my uncle owned in Florida."

"Where's Florida?"

"The southeastern coast of America, where there are many beautiful beaches."

"More beautiful than this?"

"Some of them," Waverly replied.

"I'd like to see them someday."

Waverly smiled. "I hope you do. What did your father do for work?"

"He was an engineer. He and my brother both got engineering degrees at the University of Tripoli, and they worked for the government. They planned for me to begin my training in engineering at the university this summer, but then they were killed, and this war began. Now that'll never happen."

"Nonsense. This war won't last forever, and you can resume your studies when it ends."

Jalal tossed another stone as far as he could up the beach. "Who'll pay my expenses and support my sisters?"

Good question. "Don't ever give up on your dreams. If you pursue your goals with passion, anything can happen. Perhaps the new government will have programs for students. I'd be happy to send a letter of recommendation for you."

Jalal spun around. "You'd do this for me?" His eyes grew wider and wider.

"Of course. When I leave, I'll make sure you have my contact—"

"Mr. Waverly!" Jalal pointed. "Tanks!"

"Oh my God." A pair of armored personnel carriers was headed their way along the shore.

He grabbed Jalal's arm, and they ran up the beach to a stand of palm trees. He grabbed the radio from his belt. "Foxtrot, this is Blue Marlin, do you hear me?" No reply. He repeated his call.

The radio crackled to life with what sounded like rifle and mortar fire in the background. "This is Foxtrot. I've got you."

"We have APCs headed our way up the beach from the east. Not sure if they're loyalists or rebels."

The radio went silent for nearly a minute. Waverly and Jalal stared up the beach at the vehicles, which had closed to within three hundred yards.

"Get ready to fire," Waverly whispered.

The radio crackled. "Foxtrot to Blue Marlin, do you read me?"

"We read you."

"We're on our way. Hold them off."

"Roger," Waverly replied. "Over and out."

Waverly shouldered his rifle and fired a burst, kicking up sand a dozen yards in front of the lead truck. More than a dozen uniformed soldiers poured out of the vehicles and spread out across the beach.

"Shit," Waverly moaned, "they *are* loyalists." He patted Jalal on the back. "Get ready to fire."

"I'm not afraid," Jalal said. He glanced determinedly at Waverly and then peered up the beach as a volley of rifle fire resounded from the distance and sand kicked up two yards to their left.

"That was close," Waverly muttered. "Fire on that first truck!"

Waverly fired a burst that blew out the windshield of the first truck. Jalal fired, dropping two soldiers running from the second truck.

"Good shot," Waverly yelled. "Move to the road. Go!"

He sprinted between two palm trees toward a large sand dune, with Jalal right behind him. Another volley from the rifles ripped out just as they made the dune.

"Ah!" Jalal screamed. "My arm!" He fell face-first to the sand with his rifle beneath him.

Waverly rolled him over. A gush of blood ran down his sleeve and across his hand.

"They shot me!" Jalal gasped. "I can't move my elbow."

Waverly tore away Jalal's upper sleeve, exposing a bloody wound above the elbow. He pulled a handkerchief from his back pocket and pressed it Jalal's arm. "Hold this tight. Don't let go."

Jalal grimaced. "I'm not afraid. I'm not afraid."

Waverly grunted. "Well, I am." He rolled over on his stomach, aimed at two soldiers running up the beach toward them, and fired. Both men dived to the sand. He peppered the beach with rifle fire as the soldiers rose and worked their way closer. "We need to run."

Jalal, his head beaded with perspiration, nodded.

"When I fire, you sprint to those palm trees on the other side of the road. Don't stop until you get there. Understand?"

Jalal nodded, adjusted the blood-soaked handkerchief wrapped around his arm, and struggled to his knees behind a palm tree.

Waverly was aiming at the dune where a group of soldiers was hiding about fifty yards away when the beat of rotors broke his concentration. "Wait, Jalal!"

The Mi-17 streaked over their position, machine guns peppering the personnel carriers with bullets. The nearest truck burst into flames.

Several soldiers broke away from the beach and ran for their lives. Two others tossed their rifles to the sand, sprinted across the highway, and disappeared into a palm grove.

The Mi-17 swooped down and landed. Waverly tugged Jalal from the sand, and they ran to the open door. Spaceman pulled them inside.

"Did you get al-Rashid?" he gasped as he eased Jalal into a seat and pulled the soaked handkerchief off the boy's arm.

Spaceman shook his head. "We lit up some squirters, but al-Rashid wasn't one of them. We had him flanked and were about to attack, but then we had to split."

"Damn!" Waverly slammed a fist into the flooring. *I totally screwed things up yet again.*

"It's not your fault that patrol showed up," Fisherman yelled. "I'm just glad we made it back in time."

Waverly pushed to his feet, slumped into a seat, and buried his head in his hands. *There was al-Rashid on a silver platter—and we lost him because I had to bring Jalal on the mission. When am I going to learn that the mission trumps everything else?*

He looked miserably over at Deadeye tending to Jalal. "How's he doing?"

"He'll be fine. Missed the bone and went straight through."

"Jalal," Waverly called out. The boy looked over, and Waverly gave him a thumbs-up. "You did good—really good."

Jalal smiled and nodded contentedly.

Waverly dropped his head back against the side of the helo and closed his eyes. *That boy may have metamorphosed into a warrior, but al-Rashid escaped again because of my stupidity. I'm just too old for this shit. I've lost my edge.*

28

Déjà Vu

Waverly dumped his backpack on Morgan's desk and slumped into the chair across from him.

"Okay, I guess that's it," Morgan was saying into the phone. "I'll get back to you Tuesday with a progress report. Goodbye." Shaking his head, he set the phone receiver back in its cradle. "Hardy," he informed Waverly. "I barely hear from him for four months, and suddenly he wants a report every two days. He thinks we should be doing a better job finding the backpack bomb."

Waverly shook his head. *Damned desk jockey.* "That's a laugh. All I think about on every mission is where that damn backpack bomb might be. I think I've scanned half the real estate in Libya by now."

Morgan laughed. "It's got to be somewhere. Unless they already loaded it onto a ship."

"Don't say that. But I don't think that's happened yet. NSA intercepted a cell phone conversation two days ago. One agent was identified by MYSTIC as a man named Mohammed Zuwaya, and the caller as a confidante of Ayman al-Zawahiri named Ustad Ahmad Farooq, calling from Lahore, Pakistan. Zuwaya reassured Farooq that—and I quote—'the bomb is hidden in a safe place no one would suspect.'"

"Holy shit." Morgan swiped a hand across his face. "That's our first solid lead."

"Exactly."

"Wasn't al-Rashid's sidekick at that NTC soirée named Zuwaya?"

"Bingo." Waverly held out his phone. "Here's his photograph."

Morgan tugged at the cord on his computer. "Oh yeah, I remember him now. A real charmer. I love the elevated, jagged scar across his cheek."

"Well, Zuwaya or whoever was using his phone took that call in Zliten."

"Where Jalal got shot?"

"That's right. The covert operators and I flew there this morning. It's completely under rebel control, so I started scanning everywhere no one would suspect. I started by checking the entire Al-Asmarya University and then the mausoleum and mosque of Sidi Abd As-Salam Al-Asmar."

"And?"

He shook his head.

"Didn't think so. What'd you tell the operators?"

"I told them we were looking for the mother of all surface-to-air missile hoards. But they're getting suspicious. Spaceman asked me what we were really looking for."

"Maybe we need to tell them. You know, in confidence."

Waverly pushed a strand of hair back from his forehead. "No. Not yet, anyway. A lot of them have families along the east coast back home, and I don't want anyone lying awake at night like I do worrying about their families."

"I see your point. So, what's your plan?"

"I'm going to search every square inch of Zliten and the surrounding desert. In the morning, we're headed to the boys' school, the girls' school, and the hospital. The city itself isn't that big. I should be able to scan all the public buildings by the end of the week, and then we'll start on the homes and apartments."

"Have Marilyn Harrison send another radiation detector. We can divide and conquer."

Waverly flicked nervously at the band on his watch. "That's a good idea. I'll email her tonight."

"What about al-Rashid?"

"Nothing. No sign of him whatsoever since that first day in Zliten. He's just disappeared into thin air."

"He'll show up somewhere soon. When do you think the rebels will move on Tripoli?"

"Well, they took Bir al-Ghanam this morning."

Morgan's eyes opened wide. "Really?"

"And Sirte is surrounded. I see them pushing on to Tripoli in the next two to three weeks. Things really picked up after I told Mahmoud Jibril the US would contribute twenty million more dollars to the NTC when the attack on Tripoli began in earnest."

"Wow. Things are suddenly on the move."

Waverly leaned back in his chair and gently rubbed his eyes with his fingertips. "I think we're finally headed in the right direction. Fisherman and I met with General Suleiman Mahmoud two days ago. I really like him. He's planning some sort of an uprising in Tripoli."

Morgan stepped over to the wet bar in the corner of his office and pulled down a bottle of bourbon from the cabinet. "Would you like a drink? I've had nothing but orange and pineapple juice since the last time we had dinner."

Waverly glanced at his watch. "Sure."

A phone rang, and Waverly reached for his belt. "It's my cell. Hello." He listened for a moment, and his eyes crinkled with his smile. "Mr. Pellegrini! It's a pleasure to hear from you, sir. I hope you're well.... My eyes are fine, thank you." He glanced at Morgan and shifted the phone to his other ear. "Tomorrow night? What time?" He held his phone away. "Hand me a pen and paper," he whispered to Morgan, then went back to the phone. "I'm honored, sir. What's your address?" Morgan handed him the implements, and he scribbled a note. "I'll be there. Thank you. Goodbye."

He put the phone back in its holster on his belt. "That was Roberto Pellegrini."

Morgan raised an eyebrow and handed him the glass of bourbon. "Who?"

"Sofia's father."

"Sofia?"

"My nurse in the hospital."

Morgan's eyes lit up. "Oh, *Sofia*."

I'm not actually going to blush right here, am I? "Her father Roberto invited me to have dinner with him tomorrow night."

"Fantastic! So, you're going?"

He took a sip of bourbon. "Why not?"

Morgan was positively beaming. "Where do they live?"

"Across from Martyrs' Square on Omar Al Mukhtar Road."

"Oh yes, I know that area well. You'll need security. We've got a good team now, including four American contractors who were Special Forces operators."

"I'll talk to Fisherman tomorrow morning and let you know if I need a ride." He lifted his glass. "To victory."

Morgan clinked Waverly's glass. "Hear, hear." He took a sip. "And to romance in exotic Benghazi."

He snorted. "No way. I'm having dinner with Roberto, not Sofia."

Morgan winked and grinned. "We shall see, my friend. We shall see."

29

Father and Daughter

Waverly nervously flicked at his watch and then smoothed his hair back with his fingertips. *Relax. She's probably at work.*

Redbeard turned the hulking armored personnel carrier onto Omar Al Mukhtar Road and drove down to a busy intersection across from Martyrs' Square. He parked along the street beside a white-and-yellow-trimmed three-story building that faced the square. A group of children with their parents, feeding dozens of swarming pigeons, turned to gawk at the noisy vehicle.

"This is it," Redbeard said.

Spaceman leaned his AK-47 against the side panel, checked his pistol, and opened the door. "There's an entrance over there next to the flower shop."

Waverly stepped down into the waning afternoon sunlight. "Thanks. I won't be more than a couple of hours." He motioned across the street. "Why don't you guys hang out at that café?"

"We'll be around," Redbeard replied. "Ask her if she's got any sisters or cousins."

He grinned. "Sure thing."

He stopped to buy a small bouquet of pink lilies from a sidewalk vendor before ascending the staircase to the second floor. He checked all the numbers down one corridor before realizing their flat was directly opposite the stairs. He knocked.

The door opened to reveal a smiling, gray-haired gentleman dressed impeccably in a sports coat and tie.

"Stone!" he exclaimed joyfully, offering his hand. "I'm so glad you came."

Waverly shook his hand. "Thank you, Mr. Pellegrini. The pleasure is mine, sir."

"Please, call me Roberto. Welcome to our home." He peered past Waverly into the foyer. "Where are your associates?"

"They're with the vehicle."

"They're welcome to join us."

"They're planning to eat at the café. But thank you."

Roberto shrugged. "As you wish. Sofia! Stone's here."

Sofia emerged from a doorway in the back, adorned in a white ankle-length dress with Arabic embroidery. Her brown hair was gathered on top of her head with twin curls cascading over her ears, and a teardrop emerald pendant necklace and matching earrings framed her angelic face. But it was her tastefully shadowed almond-shaped eyes and full red lips that drew Waverly's attention.

"Hello, Stone," she said. "I'm happy to see you again."

He was taken aback by her elegance. "You look...beautiful." He cleared his throat and extended the bouquet. "I'm happy to see you too. I brought you flowers."

"Pink lilies—my favorites. Thank you." Her eyes crinkled. "Do I look that different without my hospital uniform?"

He felt the heat rise to his face. "That's an understatement."

Roberto grinned. "Sofia hasn't had an opportunity to dress up since before the revolution. I guess the last time was Frederico Verdi's wedding over a year ago, hmm?"

She leaned in so close he could feel her breath on his cheek. "Your eyes look *very* good. How do they feel?"

He shifted his feet, as if to move back onto more solid ground, and flicked furiously at his watchband. "The right one is back to normal, but the left one will need surgery when I get back to the States."

"Are you still taking medicine?"

"No, my doctor stopped them a month ago."

She smiled. "I'm so happy you're better."

Roberto turned to a young Asian woman who had followed Sofia in. "Riza, tell Malaya we'll have dinner in twenty minutes."

"Yes sir," she replied with a slight bow.

"Can I offer you an aperitif?" Roberto asked. "Brandy, whiskey, vodka—you name it."

"Whiskey sounds great, thank you."

"Lemonade?" Roberto asked Sofia.

"Yes, *Babbo*."

"Let's take it in the living room," Roberto said. "Right this way." He led Waverly through a doorway into an expansive, beautifully adorned living room with high ceilings. Heavy drapes framed the arched windows, and fine high-backed couches and chairs surrounded a massive coffee table in the center of the room. Waverly sat on one of the couches, and Sofia took an adjacent chair. Roberto prepared the drinks at a side bar.

"*Prosit!*" he toasted.

"*Cin cin!*" Sofia replied.

"To new friends," Waverly offered, clinking both their glasses. Waverly took a sip. *Wow, this is so smooth.* "This is superb."

"It's Bowmore twenty-five-year-old single malt whisky." Roberto settled beside Waverly on the couch. "One of Scotland's finest. I save it for special occasions."

"It's fabulous." Waverly smiled nervously at Sofia and then nodded at a pair of old oil portraits on the nearest wall. "Your home is beautiful. I love your art."

"Thank you," Roberto replied. "That is my father, Roberto senior, and my mother, Elena. My father was the architect of this building. He designed this block in 1935 at the apex of what was called Italian Libya. At one time, Father rented flats to more than two hundred Italian families, but over time, we sold one apartment after another. When Gaddafi came to power in 1970, the rest were taken from us. Now only Arabs live here, except for Sofia and me."

Waverly shifted nervously in his seat. *I'm shocked they live here alone like this.* "Why didn't your family leave with the other Italians?"

"Gaddafi greatly valued my father's talents, as did King Idris of Libya and the occupying British before him, and he was well paid. I too was a government architect until I retired five years ago. Actually, there are still a few thousand of us Italians living in Libya, mostly in Benghazi."

Waverly glanced at Sofia, and she smiled cheerfully. He returned her smile and turned back to Roberto. "Would you ever consider leaving Libya?"

"Where would we go? My family has lived here for almost a hundred years." He affectionately patted a cushion in his daughter's direction. "Of course, now that it's just Sofia and me, I do from time to time wish for a better future for her."

Unsure how to reply to that, Waverly stared at his glass and took another sip.

"My wife died of amoebic dysentery five years ago," Roberto said. "It was a shock to us all. How about you, Stone? Are you married?"

"I was, but my wife died of cancer a year and a half ago."

"I'm sorry," he said. "Do you have children?"

"I have a thirteen-year-old son named Mike and a seven-year-old daughter named Anne. They're at home with our nanny while I work here in Libya."

"And he lives in Virginia," Sofia added.

Waverly nodded. "Yes, in Richmond, about two hours' drive from Washington, DC."

"A beautiful city, Washington," Roberto commented.

"You've visited there?" Waverly asked.

"No, but I've seen pictures, and I've always dreamed of visiting the Lincoln Memorial. I always thought he was America's greatest president."

"Many Americans agree with you." As he lifted his glass, he sloshed what was left of his glass of whiskey on his shirt. "Oh, forgive me."

Roberto stepped to the bar and returned with a wet hand towel. "Here you go."

"Thank you," Waverly said with a laugh as he dabbed at his chest. "I just bought this shirt today."

"Let me wash it for you," Sofia offered.

"Oh no, it's fine," Waverly demurred.

Roberto settled back onto the couch. "Anyway, I've dreamed of visiting Washington someday."

"And I've always dreamed of visiting New York City," Sofia added.

"Well, you both have a standing invitation to come and stay with us whenever you want. I'll be your guide in both Washington and New York."

"Really?" Sofia glanced at her father. "I would truly love this."

Waverly beamed. "I mean it. Any time you like."

"We'll hold you to this promise," she said.

Roberto rolled his glass between his hands. "Stone, what is it you do here in Libya?"

"Well, I help coordinate assistance from the United States government to the rebel leaders."

"Assistance? What kind of assistance?"

"I supply them with whatever they need to do their job."

"Weapons?" Roberto persisted.

Waverly glanced nervously at Sofia, who smiled brightly. "Sometimes. In addition to medical supplies, vehicles, and food."

"I see," Roberto said.

An older Filipino woman walked into the room and bowed. "Dinner is ready, sir."

Roberto stood up from the couch. "Thank you, Malaya. Stone, please join us."

The dining room was furnished with an exquisite glass-topped mahogany table and high-backed chairs, along with a matching china cabinet. The massive table seated eight, but one end was set for three.

Waverly pulled out a chair. "Sofia."

She smiled. "You are such a gentleman. I noticed that first thing at the hospital."

He grinned. "My mother taught me my manners—along with the nuns at Notre Dame Elementary School in Chardon, Ohio."

"Chardon, Ohio?" Roberto asked as he pulled out a chair for Waverly opposite Sofia and then sat at the head of the table between them.

"That's where I grew up. I moved to Virginia after college."

"So, you're Catholic?"

"I'm Lutheran. But there weren't any Lutheran schools where we lived, and my parents wanted us to attend parochial school."

Roberto nodded. "Please, Stone, enjoy this fabulous Serralunga d'Alba Barolo from the Piedmont region. Unfortunately, I have only six bottles left from the ten cases I brought back to Benghazi fifteen years ago. It's a treasure—and Sofia's favorite."

Waverly took a sip and nodded at Sofia.

"It is, as they say, truly the king of wines and the wine of kings," she said.

Waverly tasted the aromatic, earthy red and relished its bold finish. "It's amazing," he said, allowing the wine to dance on his tongue. "Really remarkable."

The Filipino women swept into the room with a tomato, cucumber, olive, and crab apple salad. She served it onto salad plates.

Waverly took a bite. "This is delicious. I love crab apples."

"Sofia insisted on making this herself," Roberto said proudly.

"Really?"

"It's my mother's original recipe."

"Sofia's truly a chef in her own right," Roberto said with a smile. "I think in many ways, she's better than her mother. She's certainly more daring. You really must come to dinner again soon and try her sausage and wild mushroom risotto." He kissed his fingertips. *"Magnifico!"*

"That sounds delicious," Waverly said. "I love risotto."

Roberto took another bite of salad. "Richmond, Virginia. Isn't that where the CIA is located?"

Waverly stuck his fork in a crab apple. "The CIA?"

"The Central Intelligence Agency of America."

He kept his attention on his plate. "No, the CIA is in Langley, two hours from Richmond."

"Have you been there?" Roberto asked.

"I had a tour there when I was a senior in college at Georgetown University. It's a fascinating place."

"I'll bet it is. Would it be possible for us to tour the CIA headquarters and the Lincoln Memorial when I come to visit you?"

"I'll make it happen," Waverly replied confidently. "That's a promise."

A stimulating discussion about Libyan politics punctuated their main course of chicken parmigiana and tiramisu for dessert.

Sofia perked up over dessert, talking animatedly about the novel she'd recently read, *The Girl with the Dragon Tattoo* by Stieg Larsson. "You know, it wasn't published until after Larsson died, but it went on to become a worldwide best seller. I read in the *International Herald Tribune* that the original title was *Men Who Hate Women*, which I found unfortunate."

"Do you read fiction?" Roberto asked Waverly.

"Not much anymore." He smiled at Sofia. "I hadn't read a novel in years until Sofia read to me in the hospital while I couldn't see. I must say, that rekindled my interest in fiction. But I have no time to read right now."

"I really have no patience for fiction," Roberto said. "I prefer biographies. I read one about Mussolini last month. What a bastard he was."

Waverly glanced at his watch and scooted his chair back from the table. "Oh my, where has the time gone? It's been a wonderful evening, but I must be leaving. I told my escorts I'd only be two hours."

Roberto stood up. "Nonsense! It would be uncivilized to leave without espresso and an after-dinner drink. Malaya," he called, "we'll take espresso in the living room."

"I really can't," he protested. "It's a long drive to—"

"Twenty minutes. You really must try my homemade *limoncello*. I'll take down a tray of food for your men to enjoy." He stood up and headed to the kitchen.

Waverly looked after him helplessly, then turned to Sofia. "I guess we're having *limoncello*."

She grinned. "Forgive my father. He can't help himself, but he means well. Let's see if we can spot your friends from the balcony." She led Waverly into the living room, opened a set of glass doors behind the couches, and showed him outside onto a large balcony overlooking Martyrs' Square.

The darkened square was busier than it had been earlier. Many large groups of Arabic men bantered over cigarettes and coffee. Spaceman stood beside the truck with a dozen Arabs, laughing as Redbeard tried to ride a skateboard.

"Redbeard, Spaceman," Waverly called down. "Twenty minutes."

"No problem," Redbeard called back. "I've almost mastered this."

"Mr. Pellegrini is bringing you dinner."

"Great!" He lost his balance and fell hard on his backside. "Any sisters?"

"No sisters," Waverly called back with a grin.

"Cousins?"

"No cousins."

Mr. Pellegrini stepped out onto the balcony with a tray filled with chicken parmigiana, bread, and tiramisu. "It looks like they're having a fine time. I'll take this down."

"I'll go," Waverly offered.

"No, you and Sofia enjoy the espresso. I'll be right back."

They followed him back inside and sat on one of the couches in front of two espressos.

"Only a sip," Waverly said, sitting beside her. "Espresso totally wires me, and I need to sleep tonight. I've got a long day ahead of me tomorrow."

Sofia handed him his cup. "I missed you."

"I missed you too," he replied awkwardly.

Riza set a tray of glasses on the coffee table and retreated to the kitchen.

"You can kiss me good night if you like," Sofia whispered.

"Sofia, I can't. I like you very much, but I'm old enough to be your father."

"I've always preferred older men."

He put one hand on top of hers. "I can't do this. I do like you, but I can't." *What am I doing holding her hand? I really can't help myself, can I?*

After what seemed like an eternity, she pulled her hand away. "Was your wife prettier than me?"

"It's not that. You're beautiful, and a very intelligent and decent woman, and I'm honored to call you my friend. But I won't be here much longer."

"Oh? When will you leave?"

"I don't know… Maybe a couple of months from now."

She took his hand and smiled. "Then promise you'll come again. Very soon."

He smiled. "I'll try."

"Promise me."

"Okay."

She waited.

"I promise."

"Thursday?"

"I'll need to check."

"Friday?"

"I need to check my schedule."

"Then Thursday or Friday, whichever is best for you."

"Okay."

She leaned close and put her hand on his shoulder. "I want a little goodbye kiss on the cheek before my father comes."

He leaned over and pecked her cheek just as the sound of the door opening in the foyer jerked her upright.

Roberto walked into the living room, grinning. "Your friend Spaceman is *pazzoide*."

"Pazzoide?"

"Crazy in the head." Roberto pointed to his forehead. "But Redbeard makes me laugh. He insists on meeting Riza next time."

Waverly laughed. "That's not happening."

"Why not?" Roberto asked. "She's single, and he says he loves Filipino women."

"He loves *all* women."

"Stone agreed to come next Thursday or Friday for dinner," Sofia announced.

Did I really agree to that? He flicked at his watchband.

Roberto spread his arms wide. "Excellent! You must stay longer next time. Do you play chess?"

He nodded. "Mike and I play quite often back home."

"Do you have talent?"

The man goes right for the jugular, doesn't he? "I'm okay, I guess. I won the annual chess tournament at Georgetown my junior year."

Roberto picked up the *limoncello* bottle and poured three small glasses. "You must play Sofia. I'm afraid I'm no longer much competition for her."

He grinned at Sofia with delight. "You play chess?"

She smirked. "A bit."

"You must be careful, Stone," Roberto cautioned. "My daughter is a very cunning opponent." He handed glasses to Waverly and Sofia. "*Salude*. To a wonderful evening."

Waverly smiled and clinked both their glasses. "*Salude*."

Sofia sat down at the piano and began to forcefully play Beethoven's "Für Elise." *I think he likes me. So then why wouldn't he kiss me? Maybe he's just really shy? Or maybe there's someone else back home he cares about?*

Roberto came up behind her and rested his hands on her shoulders. "Well?"

"Well what?"

"Do you like him?"

She stopped playing and turned to her father. "I do. But the next time he comes, could you put away the guns in the case? At least the rifles that are visible? He kept looking over there, and I think he was uncomfortable."

"That's nonsense. Something tells me he's very comfortable with guns."

"Would you please do it for me? You can put them back after he leaves."

"I would do anything for you, my princess. And will you do me a favor?"

She smiled up at him.

"When he comes back, finalize plans for a visit to the States later this year. How about December? Wouldn't you love to visit New York during the Christmas holidays?"

"That sounds wonderful. The two of us?"

"You know I must stay here in Benghazi. But Riza can go with you. And who knows? Maybe you'll decide to stay."

"Not without you, *Babbo*."

"Listen to me." He took her hands and drew her up from the piano bench. "If you come to love him and he comes to love you, then I want you to go live in America. I want you to be happy—but most of all, I want you to be safe. Who knows when this war will end? And when it does, who knows how it will end? The future here is so uncertain, and you may never have another chance to leave." He pointed to his head. "Be smart, my princess."

"*Babbo*, if a romance develops between Stone and me, it will be because I admire what a good person he is, how he's always thinking of the feelings of others, and how he speaks to me warmly and respectfully. It won't be because of some concern for my personal safety. I've lived here in Benghazi for thirty years, and I can live here another thirty if that's the hand God deals me." She squeezed his hands. "Do you understand me?"

"Yes, my princess."

But Sofia saw the glimmer of admiration on his face fade to trepidation.

30

What Are Friends For?

Waverly sat propped up on his bunk with his laptop balanced on his chest, adding X marks to a map of Zliten to indicate the buildings he'd searched that morning. Several dozen marks were scattered over the map. *We should be able to finish the public buildings in two more days. God, I hope the backpack bomb's in one of these locations. I don't want to have to start searching people's homes.*

Morgan ducked through the door.

"Hey, I went out for a run in the palm groves and decided to take a road trip in my new Toyota Cruiser."

Waverly closed his laptop. "They finally arrived, huh?"

Morgan nodded. "Yeah, along with a shipment of weapons and supplies and a new team of guards. What've you been up to?"

"Well, I've scanned ninety-five percent of the public buildings in Zliten now, and I haven't found a trace of the RA-115-2."

"That sucks. You'll probably find it in the last building you search. Where are the covert guys now?"

"They went to pick up supplies from a ship that arrived in Benghazi early this morning."

Morgan settled on the edge of the cot with a widening grin. "So how was dinner at Sofia's?"

Waverly hid his expression by getting up to stash the laptop on top of his duffel bag. "Interesting. I'm invited to dinner again tomorrow night."

Morgan's eyes lit up. "*Really?* Are you going?"

He pulled on a light jacket. "Probably. But there's a problem."

"Oh?"

"Let's get some coffee and I'll tell you all about it. I could use some advice."

The mess tent was deserted at that hour. Waverly pulled a chair beneath a palm tree, and they chatted until their coffee arrived about a heated argument Morgan had witnessed among three prominent NTC leaders.

"So, what's this problem?" Morgan finally asked.

Waverly wrapped both hands around the steaming cup. "Well, it appears my dinner with Sofia and her father was intended to be more than just a social visit."

"What do you mean?"

"She likes me."

Morgan grinned from ear to ear. "That's a problem?"

"Yeah. It's a big problem. I like her too—in fact, I can't stop thinking about her. But I also keep thinking about what happened to Faridah."

"But Faridah was Muslim, and that was an honor killing."

"It doesn't matter. I'm really worried what al-Rashid and the February 17 Martyrs' Brigade might do to the Pellegrinis if they spot me with her. I should nip this in the bud—but I can't. I can't stop thinking about how kind she was to me in the hospital and the sweetness of her disposition. There's a real fondness in her eyes when she looks at me. It's all I've thought about the last two days." He set his coffee too roughly on the table. The hot liquid burned the back of his hand, and he rubbed it along one pants leg. "I'm a basket case."

"I see," Morgan replied. "Perhaps, as their friend, it's time for you to warn the Pellegrinis about the unpredictable consequences of the rebels winning this rebellion? I certainly wouldn't want anybody I cared about to be here during the power struggle that's about to flare."

"That's what I plan to do at dinner tomorrow. I thought about just telling them something came up and I can't come, but she's so sweet… I just can't bring myself to do it."

"Well, then you've got to go see her and whatever happens, happens."

Waverly ran his fingers through his hair. "You're right."

Morgan patted him on the shoulder. "Things will work out."

I wish it were that easy. I know damn well nothing will keep me from seeing Sofia again. I'm so moonstruck.

"But you're right to worry about their safety. The key is to walk softly and leave a small footprint. Don't go out with them in public and slip in and out with discretion. I assume the operators took you over there Monday?"

He nodded. "Spaceman and Redbeard."

"I wouldn't do that again. It draws too much attention. I've got an important dinner tomorrow, but Hanson could drop you off and come back to pick you up afterwards. What time's your dinner?"

"They asked me to come around 1700 hours. We're playing chess before dinner."

"Really? You and Roberto?" Morgan chuckled.

"Me and Sofia. Apparently, she's very good."

"That should be interesting. You'll have to let me know if you can manage to keep up." Morgan pushed back from the table and crossed one leg over the other. "Oh, by the way, Hardy is coming next week."

"Your boss?"

"Yes. He says he wants to see what's happening with his own eyes. I'm setting up meetings with NTC leaders, but I have a hunch he's really coming to review your efforts to find the backpack bomb. Will you meet with him?"

"Sure, just let me know when and where." He flicked at his watchband.

"Thanks." Morgan smiled. "He'll probably ask you how I'm doing too."

"If he does, I'll tell him you're the greatest. And I'll mean it."

"Thanks, buddy. I—"

Morgan's satellite telephone rang. He pulled the phone from his belt clip. "Hello." He listened for a few moments. "He's with me right now. Just a second."

He handed the phone to Waverly.

Waverly took it with a slight frown. "Hello.... Beatrice? How did you get this number?" He listened for a moment. "No, I'm glad you called Mrs. Harrison. What's wrong? ... Oh my God! Did you confront him about it? ... You did the right thing. Just flush it down the toilet without saying a word about it.... No, I'm fine. I'll call you back tomorrow. Thank you, Beatrice. Goodbye."

This never would have happened if I were home right now. He handed the phone back to Morgan.

"What?" Morgan demanded.

"Beatrice was cleaning Mike's closet while he was at school. She picked up his baseball glove, and a plastic bag fell out of it. It was marijuana. My God, he's only thirteen years old."

Morgan patted his arm. "You've got to go home. Mike needs you." He reached for his phone again. "Here, call Marilyn—"

Waverly pulled away. "Not yet. I want to think it over first. Please, let's keep this between us two."

Morgan sat back and tucked the phone away. "You can count on me. You're right. No reason to rush home for something like this. Everything's going to be fine."

"But you just told me I had to go home." *Damn it all. I never should have left.*

"Listen, I smoked some dope when I was in middle school too. I even took some downers. It was just curiosity. Everything turned out. Mike will be fine."

"Maybe. But I'm sure this happened because I was gone. You were right the first time—I've got to get home." He stood up. "But I need to think things over. Thanks for helping me think things through."

Morgan gave him a hug. "Let me know if there's anything I can do to help."

Waverly walked Morgan to the Toyota Land Cruiser, its hood gleaming in the setting sun. "What a beautiful sunset. It makes me want to be out on a boat on Chesapeake Bay fishing for striped bass as the sun goes down. I can feel that cool breeze in my face right now. One thing I won't miss at all about this place is this stifling heat." He wiped the sweat from his brow.

Morgan paused with his hand on the door handle. "So, I'll have Hanson come get you tomorrow evening, right?"

I should leave tonight if I can—but then I'll never find that damn backpack bomb. God help me. What should I do? "Listen, there may be a change of plans. I'll call you tomorrow morning and let you know for sure."

"No problem. Take care of yourself."

Waverly stood watching the Toyota Land Cruiser as it pulled away to the security gate.

"What the hell am I going to do now?" He kicked listlessly at a few rocks beneath his feet. *Mike needs me—but so does my country, and the RA-115-2 is still nowhere to be found. And how can I leave Sofia here in the middle of this quagmire that's only going to get worse?*

He glanced at the last flicker of the sun as it slipped behind a sandstone rock formation. Deep in thought, he headed back to the barracks.

31

Forbidden Fruit

Waverly climbed into the back seat of the shiny white Toyota Land Cruiser. "Thanks for the ride. "

"No problem," Hanson replied. "Morgan told me you might be leaving for home."

His stomach clenched. "There's no way to get me home until the next air cargo comes in from the States in another five to seven days. I could leave tomorrow on a freighter to Malta, but that could end up taking even longer. I'll wait for the cargo jet."

"That makes sense. Stone, this is Larry Birch, one of our new MSGs. We call him Lax since his sport in high school was lacrosse."

"Nice to meet you, Lax. Where're you from?"

The blue-eyed MSG turned in his seat. "Originally Houston, sir," he said with a thick Texas accent. "But I just arrived from Marine Corps Embassy Support Group at Quantico three days ago."

Waverly smiled. "Fresh out of training?"

"Yes sir."

"Ever been stationed overseas?"

"Yes sir. I served a seven-month tour with the 2nd battalion 6th marines at Camp Leatherneck in Helmand Province, Afghanistan, during 2010."

He nodded with approval. "That's a tough assignment."

"Yes sir. Have you ever been there, sir?"

"I spent two years in Panjshir Valley on my very first assignment from 1985 to 1986 and a few months at a base near Kandahar in 2003."

The young marine's eyes lit up. "Wow, Panjshir Valley. Did you meet Commander Ahmad Massoud, the Lion of Panjshir?"

Waverly nodded. "Many times. We played chess a couple of times a week for the last six months I was there."

"Really? Hear that, Hanson? Stone knew Commander Massoud."

As he turned back in his seat, Waverly spotted a young Arab standing along the shoulder of the road beside a motorcycle, waving for them to stop.

"Veer left," Lax shouted. "IED!"

Hanson swerved into the opposite lane and accelerated.

"But it looks like he broke down," Waverly said as they passed the frantic boy.

"Sorry, sir," Lax said. "You never know."

Hanson drove for nearly an hour before turning onto Omar Al Mukhtar Road and following Waverly's directions to the Pellegrinis' building.

"Give me a call a little before you're ready to leave," Hanson said. "We'll be at headquarters twenty minutes away."

"Thanks, buddy." Waverly climbed out and headed upstairs.

Roberto opened the door. "Welcome, Stone. How are you, my friend?"

"It's been a hectic day, but I made it. Thank you for inviting me to dinner."

"It's our pleasure." Roberto led him to the living room, where a chess table was set up on a small table near the window.

"*Buon pomeriggio*, Stone." Sofia swept in wearing a long-sleeved, calf-length, deep-blue dress. Her long hair reached to her waist, fastened back with a sapphire-and-diamond barrette on one side.

"Good evening. You look fabulous."

She drew Waverly to the chess table immediately, squeezing his hand. "We missed you, right, *Babbo*?"

Roberto winked at Waverly. "We could hardly sleep last night."

Waverly settled into a chair and picked up a rook. "What a remarkable chess set."

Roberto nodded. "It was my father's. Vasari bronze, with gold and silver trim. He once beat the Italian grand master Mario Monticelli with this very set."

He held the piece up to the sunlight. "Superb artistry."

"Well, no time like the present, as father was fond of saying. I'll read in the study while you two play."

"You're not going to watch?" he asked with surprise.

"I can't stand to watch a grown man cry," Roberto called over his shoulder as he disappeared through the doorway.

Waverly turned back in his seat. "I feel like a lamb being led to slaughter. Have mercy, kind maiden."

Sofia smiled. "One hundred dollars a game?"

His mouth dropped open.

"Just teasing. You go first."

Waverly smiled and advanced his king's pawn two spaces.

Sofia returned his smile and advanced her king's pawn as well.

After only ten moves, Waverly had lost his queen and was in deep trouble. "I'm out of my league here."

She pouted playfully. "You lost your queen on purpose."

"No, I assure you, I didn't. And I resign."

"Another game?" She had the smirk of an assassin.

"Maybe later." He grinned.

She reset the pieces, handed him a glass of water from the wet bar, and curled up beside him on the couch.

"What happened here?" she asked, gently touching a bruise on his temple.

"I'm afraid I'm not very good at soccer either."

"Football? Where do you play football?"

"There's a young assistant at my base who likes to play." He set his water on the coffee table and inched away from her.

She pouted and took his hand. "Where are you going?"

He thought he heard a door open and pulled his hand away. "I like you. I like you a lot. But there's a time and a place, and this isn't a good time for me."

The smile faded from her lips. She took her glass to the sink. "I'm sorry if I've been too, how do you say, forward?"

He joined her at the sink. *Here goes nothing.* "I need to tell you about something that happened to me."

"I'm listening."

He shifted his weight uncomfortably. "In Syria, when I worked there eight years ago, I fell in love with a Syrian woman after my wife left me for another man."

"Did you love this woman?"

He nodded. "Very much. We planned to marry. But then an evil man killed her and her brother when he found out about our relationship. Losing her nearly destroyed me."

"I'm sorry." She gently touched his arm. "But I don't understand. When did your wife die?"

"Julie died a year and a half ago. We got back together after I returned from Syria and Iraq."

She considered what he'd said. "So, you're afraid I could die too?"

"Or that something horrible could happen to you and your father if the wrong people here in Libya found out we're friends."

"This makes no sense," she protested. "Why?"

"Please, Sofia, I can't tell you anything more—and I beg you not to tell your father. This is between us, okay?"

She looked into his eyes. "But we *can* be friends?"

"Of course—but only friends." He shuffled his feet again. *Damn, I'm such a rube at this.* "There's another reason too."

She waited expectantly.

"Something's happened back home, and I'll be leaving Libya in about a week."

Her hand flew to her mouth. "What happened? Are your children okay?"

"They're fine, but I need to go home and help my son through a difficult situation."

She bowed her head and licked her lips nervously.

He patted her hand. "I'm sorry, really sorry. Would it be easier if I left?"

"No!" She took his hand. "We will be friends, okay?"

Warm relief flooded across his chest. "I'd like that very much. And let's keep it 'secret friends' for you and your father's safety, okay?"

"If it must be, then it must be." She squeezed his hand. "I'll ask Malaya to serve dinner now."

Waverly looked after her as she left the room, savoring every last moment of her presence. *I must be nuts.*

Dinner was seafood risotto and breaded veal cutlets prepared by the Pellegrinis' Filipino chef, and homemade pistachio gelato and Sambuca with espresso capped an evening of intriguing conversation punctuated with laughter. Roberto was truly in rare form.

Waverly glanced regretfully at his watch. "Thank you both for another wonderful evening. You've spoiled me."

"It's been delightful," Roberto said. "One last game of chess?"

"I can't. It's getting very late, and I must call my ride. We have a long drive ahead of us."

Roberto stood up. "A neighbor got us a copy of the new movie *Avatar*. Have you seen it?"

"Not yet, but I've heard it's great."

"How about we watch it together the day after tomorrow? Sunday evening? I'll ask Malaya to prepare her famous sausage soup with tortellini. It's my absolute favorite dish—and that special day is also Sofia's birthday."

Waverly smiled. *Roberto makes this impossible.* "Your birthday? How could I possibly decline an invitation for a special occasion like that?"

"Fantastic!" Roberto exclaimed. "Let's plan on dinner at six so we have plenty of time for the movie."

"It'll be an honor to share your special day," he said earnestly to Sofia. "Thank you both for your friendship."

"Sofia will show you out while I help Riza and Malaya," Roberto said as he shook Waverly's hand. "Until next time, my friend." He hurried away to the kitchen.

"Thank you for your tolerance," Sofia said. "He means well."

"He loves his daughter."

He dialed his cell phone. "Ready…. Great, coming down now." He hung up.

"They're five minutes away." He took her hand. "Thank you for a wonderful evening."

"I'll look forward to my birthday." She stood on her tiptoes and kissed him on the cheek. "Good night."

"Good night."

He stepped into the hall and bounded down the stairs to the entry door. *She's wonderful. How can I possibly keep up this pretense of just wanting to be friends? How will I ever leave her behind?*

Five minutes felt like fifty as he struggled with his conscience while waiting for the car. Finally, the white Toyota Land Cruiser pulled to the curb, and he darted out from the building. The passenger door opened, and he climbed in beside Lax.

"Thanks, guys."

He had a lot to think about on the ride back.

Sofia rearranged the pillows on the couch and took the glasses to the sink as she passed Roberto carrying his rifles to their cabinet. She stood for a long moment gazing sightlessly at her reflection in the mirror. *He can't go. Not now, please, God.*

Three loud knocks in rapid succession issued from the front door.

Her heart leaped. *Stone must have forgotten something.*

"Coming," she called. She hurried to the foyer and opened the door.

A hand thrust through the doorway, brandishing a knife blade inches from her face.

She spun and ran for the living room, but her soft evening slippers caught on the carpet. She stumbled to her knees with an ear-piercing scream.

Her father was still standing at the open gun cabinet with two rifles in his hands. He dropped one on the floor and charged the foyer.

"Basta! Per carità!" he bellowed and fired three shots into the surprised intruder.

The man crumpled to the floor.

Her father grabbed her arm and dragged her behind him, then aimed his rifle at the man now lying motionless, bleeding from his chest and abdomen. He kicked the knife away from the intruder.

"Who are you?" he demanded.

Malaya and Riza gaped from the dining room doorway.

The man didn't move.

"Sofia," her father ordered, "call the police."

32

Tripoli Falls

Waverly darted in front of the Fadeel Hotel doorman to open the rear door of the Toyota Land Cruiser for Hardy and Morgan.

"Good morning, sir," he said to Hardy. "Are you ready to meet Haftar?"

"Ready as I'll ever be."

Assistant Secretary of State for Near Eastern Affairs Joshua L. Hardy had been in Libya on a fact-finding mission for four days now. So far, he'd met with more than a dozen members of the National Transitional Council, several senior rebel military leaders, and a few business leaders.

This next meeting would be even more challenging, since it was with a figure Waverly knew well and found to be difficult, Lieutenant General Khalifa Haftar.

Waverly flicked at his watchband. *I just hope I can keep them from coming to blows. All I need to do is get Hardy through this last meeting.*

Haftar had run afoul of Gaddafi more than two decades ago and had been living in the US ever since, until the rebellion enticed him to return. There were rumors he'd received training from the CIA, which

Waverly knew to be true. In 1993, Haftar was convicted in absentia of crimes against the Libyan government and sentenced to death.

He returned to Libya in 2011 to join the rebel Libyan National Army, and in March 2011, a military spokesman announced he'd been appointed commander. But then the National Transitional Council named Abdul Fatah Younes to the position instead, relegating Haftar to the third most senior position as the commander of ground forces. Haftar was furious about this demotion and had been a thorn in the side of General Younes right up to the day he was assassinated.

Immediately after Younes's assassination, Haftar had lobbied to become the new head of the rebel army, but the NTC promoted General Younes's top deputy and cousin, Suleiman Mahmoud. Haftar was livid about what he saw as another betrayal. When the US government lent its support to the NTC decision, Haftar became even more enraged, calling Hardy a "two-bit bureaucrat."

Hardy paused just inside the hotel entrance. "Gus told me what happened to your agents last night. Are they okay?"

He'd been trying to put what had happened to Sofia and her father out of his mind. "They're shocked and terrified. The guy who attacked them was a February 17 Martyrs' Brigade fighter. Roberto Pellegrini killed him. If he hadn't been moving his guns into a cabinet, there would have been a tragedy."

"I understand from Morgan that the Pellegrinis have been very helpful providing intel about Gaddafi's inner circle."

Waverly glanced at Morgan, who smiled sheepishly. *Thanks for the cover, buddy.* "Pellegrini's daughter is a nurse at Benghazi Municipal Hospital, and she's taken care of three of Gaddafi's officers over the years."

"Where is the family now?"

"They're still at home, with guards posted at the door and on the street outside."

Hardy put a hand on his shoulder. "Let me know if they need political asylum and I'll expedite it."

"Thank you, sir. I know they'll appreciate your help."

Several armed guards were arrayed throughout the lobby, where a young aide was waiting patiently for them to finish their conversation.

"Mr. Hardy, Mr. Waverly, Mr. Morgan." The aide cheerfully offered his hand to each man in succession. "I am Lieutenant Hussein, General Haftar's assistant. It is wonderful that we have such a beautiful day."

Hardy stretched his cheeks in a rote smile that never reached his eyes. "I'm just happy the rain finally stopped and the sun is out."

The aide's smile faltered almost imperceptibly. "Right this way, gentlemen. General Haftar is waiting for you in the conference room." He led them down a hall off the lobby and through an open door.

General Haftar was dressed in military fatigues and stylish wire-rim glasses. His receding hair was totally gray, but his bushy brows and mustache remained jet black. He sprang to his feet.

"Jeff!" he greeted Hardy boisterously, kissing him on both cheeks. "How long has it been?"

Hardy shot a furtive smile at Morgan. "I was trying to figure that out on the drive over. At least five years."

"If I remember correctly, it was at a benefit dinner at the Smithsonian. Am I right?"

"I think so. I vaguely remember it being a reception in the space travel exhibit, but I don't recall the specifics."

Haftar smiled expansively. "Well, welcome to Benghazi. When did you arrive, Mr. Morgan?"

"Just over four months ago, although it seems like a year," Morgan said.

"Yes, this has been six months I never thought I'd live to see—especially the tragic murder of General Younes," Haftar said. "What a pity."

"His death was heartbreaking. Do you know our colleague Stone Waverly?"

The laser of Haftar's gaze swung Waverly's way. "Of course. We've known each other for years. Nice to see you again, Stone."

"And you, General."

A waiter entered the conference room with a tray of tea and pastries.

"Thank you, Yousef," Haftar said. "Please tell the guards we're not to be disturbed."

"Yes, General." The waiter bowed and closed the door behind himself.

Haftar lifted his cup and took a sip. "The NTC has asked me to update you on the upcoming battle for Tripoli. We could never have come to this point without your help and the help of the French and the English. For that, we'll always be grateful."

"We've all made enormous sacrifices to come to this moment," Hardy said appreciatively. "I have the pleasure of informing you that President Obama is planning to announce the opening of the new American Embassy here in Benghazi."

Haftar's eyes widened with surprise. "That's very good news."

"When will the rebel forces begin their push on Tripoli?" Hardy asked. "President Obama is concerned about the pace and expense of this war."

"Very soon, my friends. The battle for Tripoli will begin in the Souq al-Jumaa neighborhood. Then other neighborhoods will rise up with weapons that have been smuggled into the city. Finally, after the people of Tripoli have claimed the revolution as their own, rebel forces will advance on Tripoli from the east."

Hardy leaned forward. "When will this happen?"

"It is imminent."

Waverly sipped his tea. *The same old runaround.* "What do you mean by 'imminent'?"

"Very soon," Haftar assured him.

"We've heard that before," Morgan said softly. He glanced at Waverly and sat back in his chair.

Haftar looked from one face to the next. "The revolt will begin tonight," he finally said.

Waverly set down his cup harder than he'd planned. "Tonight?"

"At 2100 hours local time."

He lifted his cup again in a toast. "In that case, may victory soon be ours."

Haftar extended his own cup. "Inshallah."

The meeting was more productive than Waverly had dared to hope. Afterwards, Hardy privately asked Waverly and Morgan about the search for the RA-115-2. Waverly described his failed search of the entire city of Zliten based on the intercepted phone call. NSA had tagged no subsequent phone calls by Mohammed Zuwaya or Ustad Ahmad Farooq, Hardy noted, but he confirmed they would report any future conversations intercepted from either jihadist.

"Press on," Hardy said. "The president orders you to make this your top priority."

Waverly smiled grimly. *If only you knew.* "It's been my top priority for four months," he assured Hardy.

The flight over choppy seas to the USS Kearsarge was bumpy but otherwise uneventful. It was the first leg of their trip to Tripoli to observe the revolt firsthand. Waverly spent the entire flight thinking about Hardy's instruction to focus his efforts on finding the backpack bomb. He worried about leaving Jalal behind at the base after the teen pleaded to come along. *He's really been indispensable helping me gather intel. I must make an effort to include him in some other mission later this week.*

The helicopter bumped down on the Kearsarge late in the afternoon. Waverly and the covert operators transferred their gear to the stealth helo within the hour and set out for Tripoli just before sundown, with an ETA to An Nasr Forest of 2100 hours.

The Black Hawk landed gently in a clearing surrounded by towering eucalyptus trees. Small arms fire crackled in the far distance.

"It's a couple of minutes past 2100 hours—but that just sounds like someone taking target practice," Waverly said.

Fisherman checked Redbeard's display. "It seems to be coming from the center of the city."

"If that's a battle then I'm Derek Jeter," Puckeater said.

Waverly checked the safety on his rifle. "Give it a few more mikes. They're on island time here in Libya." His stomach was churning. *Damn it, Haftar better be right about the timing of this revolt.*

Another ten minutes passed. The operators wandered away from the helicopter and sat in a circle on the ground arguing over who was tougher, Army Delta Force operators or Navy SEALs.

"Why do you think they picked the SEALs to go after bin Laden?" Puckeater said. "Because they're the best."

"Sheee-it, bin Laden was a pussy," Redbeard said. "He didn't even grab a weapon when the SEALs busted into his house. When Delta Force took down Pablo Escobar in Colombia, he and his bodyguard put up a ferocious—"

Boom, boom, boom resounded from the distance, followed by another *boom, boom, boom, boom* that brought the operators to their feet.

"Those are antiaircraft guns," Fisherman said, "and they're firing directly south of here."

The antiaircraft guns maintained their pace as small arms fire joined in, soon punctuated by the familiar staccato of heavy machine guns. A few minutes later, intense gunfire also erupted to the northeast of their position.

"That sounds like it's coming from Fashloom or Ben Ashur," Waverly said as he craned over Fisherman's shoulder at a map.

Spaceman pumped his fist. "Yeah! It's on! We're coming for you, Gaddafi!"

Redbeard held up his hand to quiet the others as he listened to the tactical headset connected to his radio. He jerked off the headset. "NATO aircraft are headed this way for strikes on Gaddafi's Bab al-Azizia compound, the port, and Mitiga Airport. They want us to stay put for now."

Within minutes, the scream of fighters heralded the concussions of dozens of bombs hitting Bab al-Azizia a few blocks to the west of An Nasr Forest. Dozens of white antiaircraft tracers darted into the sky.

"Fucking A!" Spaceman yelled. "It's Iraq all over again!"

Waverly crouched on one knee. *Dear God, protect the innocents beneath that inferno. This revolt is truly nearly over, but please limit injury and death of the innocents.*

Three squadrons of unseen aircraft made runs on Gaddafi's compound as rapid-fire explosions and a blitz of antiaircraft tracers lit up the sky beyond anything Waverly had ever seen. Finally, the bombing ended, and the antiaircraft fire tapered off.

Redbeard jogged over to Fisherman and handed him a headset. "Major Collin wants to speak to you."

Fisherman slipped on the headset. "Fisherman. Yes, we're hunkered down in An Nasr Forest with a stealth Black Hawk." He listened intently for a moment, then glanced at Waverly. "We can land there in fifteen mikes. Good luck."

Fisherman handed the headset back to Redbeard. "The British want us to support their assault on Mitiga Airport. They're east of the airport, taking heavy fire. The plan is for us to land south of the main runway and flank the loyalist forces, so they can be driven from the airport. Let's load up."

Minutes later, the Black Hawk lifted off and climbed into a far different world than before they'd landed. To the west, multiple structures inside Gaddafi's Bab al-Azizia compound were engulfed in flames. To the north and east, thousands of short-lived green, red, and white tracers crisscrossed the otherwise black metropolis, punctuated by the explosions of tank, mortar, and artillery shells.

"Activate electronic countermeasures," Waverly heard the pilot say over the intercom. The helicopter banked to the northwest and darted low across the flat terrain. With Deadeye and Spaceman manning M240H machine guns on either side of the aircraft, they flew the five miles to Mitiga Airport in less than two minutes via an indirect route along the Second Ring Road and over Souk al-Jama, where an epic firefight raged below them along 11th June Road.

Waverly closed his eyes and prayed that none of the fighters on either side would blindly aim their machine guns skyward and pulverize the helicopter they neither saw nor heard. Antiaircraft guns blinded by the electronic countermeasures were firing tracer rounds haphazardly for miles around them.

They were within two hundred yards of the runway when the *boom, boom, boom* of an antiaircraft gun directly below them yielded a stream of tracer bullets that streaked just yards from the port door.

Waverly exchanged a look of alarm with Fisherman.

The pilot banked directly down the main runway from west to east, launching Hellfire missiles at two tanks firing their guns at the Weryama neighborhood. Both tanks exploded into fireballs as Spaceman raked the loyalist infantry on the taxiway.

Waverly recoiled from the door of the helicopter as rifle bullets pinged off the ceiling. "Hot damn, that was close!" *I'm going to get my head blown off.* Smoke blew through the open door, engulfing them in the mingled smells of burning flesh, tanks, and diesel fuel.

"Five seconds to touchdown," the copilot announced over the intercom.

Waverly checked his magazine, leaped from his seat, and jumped to the ground behind Chico and Redbeard. As he dropped to the ground, Waverly grunted from a blow to his chest that felt like a whack from a baseball bat. He gathered himself, and the three of them laid down a barrage of AK-47 automatic fire on a squad of soldiers crouching in the darkness behind a pair of burned-out Mirage F1 fighter jets. Tracer bullets ricocheted off the fuselages of both jets. Three men crumpled to the ground, and the others dropped their rifles and dived headlong into the waist-high grass.

Fisherman crouched beside Waverly. "Nice shooting." He grinned. "Are you trying to win a jockstrap medal?"

"Look at this," Waverly replied. He yanked his shirt open to reveal a bullet slug embedded in his body armor. "It nearly knocked me down." *I'm one lucky bastard.*

Fisherman frowned. "If you get hurt out here, it'll be my ass. Get back to the helo."

"Hell no. I'm more likely to get shot standing there." He shouldered his AK and fired another burst.

To their right, Spaceman, Checkmate, and Puckeater took out another squad of loyalists who'd snuck forward behind one of the tanks that was billowing smoke. Several bursts of rifle fire took down half the group, and the others retreated into the surrounding brush.

Waverly, Chico, and Deadeye advanced to the west end of the main runway to take out an armored personnel carrier racing toward them from an aircraft hangar. It got within forty yards of them, mounted gun blazing, before Deadeye took out the driver with his sniper rifle. The vehicle rolled and burst into flames. Chico and Deadeye sprinted to the aircraft hangar.

Waverly spotted the pair of Libyan soldiers squatting behind the burning APC at the same moment they spotted him. One of them fired a burst that kicked up sand just to Waverly's left. He rolled behind a mound of sand and peered with his good eye down his rifle sight as the soldiers broke for a stand of brush. He fired, and one of the soldiers went down. The other man jerked a grenade from his vest, pulled the pin, and tossed it.

Waverly buried his face in the sand a second before the grenade exploded twenty feet in front of him.

"Shit, that was close," he yelped.

The soldier was now running directly at him, screaming and firing bursts from his rifle. He aimed and calmly pulled the trigger, but the AK-47 jammed. With bullets kicking up sand behind him, he drew his SR-1 pistol and fired. The man clutched his chest and fell face-first into the sand.

He sprang to his feet, snatched the soldier's AK, and tossed it behind him. Then he knelt in the sand and rolled the soldier over. The man's frozen stare told him he was dead.

Across the way, Chico and Deadeye ran from the hangar. Waverly grabbed the soldier's AK-47 and ran after them.

Several more skirmishes between the operators and Gaddafi troops trying to hold the airport yielded dozens of dead or severely wounded Libyans. The remainder melted into the surrounding desert.

Fisherman jogged to the asphalt in front of the burning APC. "Everyone all right?"

Spaceman, Checkmate, and Puckeater walked out to meet him. "We're okay," Spaceman yelled. "Yeah, what a rush!"

Waverly, Chico, and Deadeye came running around the side of the hangar.

"Did you see Waverly take out those two soldiers?" Deadeye yelled. "What a fight."

Waverly held out his sleeve. "Look at this bullet hole in my jacket. He came that close to shooting me."

The others gathered closer to celebrate their victory until a group of British Special Forces jogged over from the east end the runway.

"Thanks for the backup, men," Major Collin said with a broad smile.

"It's the least we could do after you saved our butts in Brega," Fisherman said.

As the two groups mingled, Waverly wandered back to the helicopter. The reality of what had just happened had begun to sink in.

He fetched his cell phone from his pocket and called Morgan.

"It's over," he said giddily. "The rebels have taken Tripoli. Bab al-Azizia is in flames, and the Libyan army is finished. I've got to go. The operators are loading up, and we're heading back to the Kearsarge. I'll call you when I get back to Benghazi."

He buoyantly punched the end call button before Morgan could say anything at all. *We've done it! The rebels have taken Tripoli. Another month, and this war will be over.*

His shoulders slumped.

But where's that damn backpack bomb, and how the hell am I going to find it?

Waverly thumped Jalal bin Koussa on the back and jogged out to meet Morgan, Hanson, and Lax. Beaming with satisfaction, he climbed inside the Toyota Land Cruiser and slammed the door.

"Fisherman just talked to Mahmoud Jibril. The rebels finally overran Green Square and Gaddafi's Bab al-Azizia compound."

"Hallelujah!" Morgan exclaimed. "Did they get Gaddafi?"

"No word yet, but at least ninety percent of the city is in rebel hands."

Morgan held up a bottle of Old Ripy bourbon. "This is my last bottle. How about a little toast?"

"Don't you think we should wait until it's really over?"

"This is for you, buddy. I just got a call from Washington. They're sending five military transport planes that'll be here tomorrow. You'll be on your way home the day after tomorrow."

Waverly sank onto a bench. He looked up and tried to speak, but all he could manage was a shake of his head. *I can't go now, not with Sofia in danger.*

Morgan patted his back. "It's all right, buddy."

He shook his head again. "Libya's disintegrating into chaos. I can't leave here until Sofia and Roberto get political asylum."

Morgan gave him a long look, then glanced at his watch. "Hardy doesn't land in Washington for six more hours. I'll call him first thing in the morning and ask him to expedite their asylum."

Waverly stared at his feet. *What in hell am I doing? I'm letting my personal feelings get in the way of going home to help Mike and even my performance here in the field. I'm nothing but a damn shirker.*

Morgan spoke softly. "I know you're thinking about the backpack bomb. Don't worry. I'll make it my top priority, and the CIA will assign another top operative to finish the job. There's nothing you can do about it anyway without more intel."

He looked up. "Thanks, Gus. You're a true friend."

But the little voice inside him kept going. *Am I really going to leave now? Am I going to leave without finishing the job that brought me here?*

Nothing but a damn shirker.

33

Evil's Ugly Head

Waverly grabbed the overhead handle as the Toyota Land Cruiser bumped over a rut in the highway. Hanson veered to the left to avoid an even bigger pothole.

"They must've been maneuvering tanks on this road," Waverly said. "It's falling apart."

"Every road in eastern Libya is like this now," Hanson said. "Say, did you see the Benghazi update this morning? It had photos of Gaddafi's sons' and daughters' homes in Bab al-Azizia. Boy, were they living large."

"We already knew that," Waverly replied. "I read a briefing just before you picked me up that said rebel fighters chased five armored Mercedes sedans to the Algerian border at Gradates last night. Our man in Algeria confirmed the cars carried Gaddafi family member Safia Farkash, her daughter, Ayesha, and her sons, Muhammad and Hannibal. Neither Gaddafi nor his sons were with them, but they found a fortune in gold, US dollars, and Euros in the cars."

"The rats are abandoning the sinking ship," the guard, Garcia, called out from the front passenger seat.

"Exactly. I wonder how Gaddafi escaped Tripoli?"

"He probably left before the uprising," Hanson said. "God only knows where he is now."

Waverly flicked at his watchband. "There's already fighting between rebel factions over the land and possessions that loyalists left behind in Tripoli. This will quickly get out of hand after the governmental forces are defeated and the jihadi groups they tyrannized, like the February 17 Martyrs' Brigade, start seeking their revenge—hey, stop at that flower stand?"

Hanson pulled over to a roadside vendor selling nuts, dates, vegetables, and flowers. Waverly jumped out and bought a bouquet of pink and white lilies. On his way back to the Toyota Land Cruiser, he spotted an old lady selling jewelry from an open valise and picked out a pair of gold hoop earrings to go with the flowers.

He jumped back into the car. "Thanks. It's Sofia's birthday."

Hanson chuckled. "I knew you were a romantic the first time I met you."

He laughed. "I feel sorry that she's lived alone with her father all those years."

Hanson grinned at him in the rearview mirror. "Uh-huh, sure you do."

He smiled back and stared out the window. *I wonder whether Sofia even feels like celebrating her birthday after nearly being murdered. Damn jihadists...*

Fifteen minutes later, Hanson pulled up to Pellegrinis' building, and Garcia jumped out to open the rear passenger door. Two men Waverly recognized as trusted NTC guards stood on the sidewalk at the entrance door.

"Thanks. Plan to pick me up in about five hours, but I'll call you." He glanced at his watch. "Let's say about nine thirty."

"Sounds good," Hanson replied. "Have a good time."

Waverly greeted the guards as he passed and bounded up the stairs. The American guard, Lax, was posted outside the Pellegrinis' door. An assault rifle leaned against the wall beside him.

"Hey, Lax, how's it going?"

"Hey, Mr. Waverly. It's been quiet."

"Keep it that way. Just knock if you need anything."

"I will, sir."

A tired-looking Roberto opened the door a moment later. Sofia stood behind him wearing a simple dress and her hair gathered in a bun on top of her head.

"Hello, Stone," Roberto said solemnly. "We're glad you could come."

"I'm glad to be here. Happy birthday, Sofia." He handed her the flowers.

"Thank you. They're beautiful."

"I'll pour you a drink," Roberto said. "Bowmore whiskey?"

"I think I'll pass tonight," Waverly replied. "Just water, thank you."

Roberto nodded. "Suit yourself, but I need a stiff one. *Salude.*" He clinked Waverly's water glass and took a sip of his whiskey.

"So how did the terrorist get in?" Waverly asked.

"Sofia opened the door for him. She thought it was you because you'd just walked out a minute earlier. Thank God I was putting my rifles back in the case. But enough of that. Are you still interested in watching *Avatar*?"

"I am," Sofia said emphatically. "I need the diversion."

Roberto opened a large armoire across from the couch and started *Avatar* on a flat-screen TV. They snacked on cheese and dates, stopping in the middle of the movie to refill their drinks. After the movie, they ate Malaya's sausage soup with tortellini and a delightful tiramisu before retiring to the living room for espresso.

Waverly set his cup on the coffee table and fished the earrings out of his breast pocket. "I'm sorry they're not wrapped, but happy birthday."

"Thank you—they're so beautiful!" She took off her studs and put on the hoops, then admired them in the mirror. "I'll always treasure them."

"They look lovely on you." He glanced at his watch. "Before I go, I have something important to discuss with both of you."

She sat on the couch beside him. "Yes?"

"I've been recalled to the United States, and I want both of you to leave with me."

Her mouth dropped open.

"You're leaving?" asked Roberto. "When?"

"As soon as Mr. Morgan can arrange for your political asylum in the United States. The power vacuum that'll be created with Gaddafi's fall will lead to bedlam here in Benghazi, and now we know with certainty it's too dangerous for you to stay here." He paused for a response, but they appeared to be stunned. "Frankly, I'd prefer if you came to Virginia where I could watch out for you and Sofia, but you'll be free to live wherever you want. I'm sure Sofia could work at a hospital of her choosing anywhere in the country."

"That's very kind of you," Roberto said.

He glanced at Sofia. "Sir, to be completely honest, I'm very fond of your daughter, and I couldn't leave her here in this dangerous situation."

Roberto sighed loudly. "But I'm sorry, Stone. I cannot leave Benghazi."

Waverly's hope melted into dismay. "But... Why, sir, if I might ask?"

"The people in this building will take our flat and everything in it the minute I leave. I'll never let that happen."

They lapsed into silence, and Waverly's mind raced a million miles a minute. *Nothing here is ever straightforward. Now what?*

Sofia dabbed away tears with a handkerchief. "I'm sorry. It's just so sudden."

He pursed his lips. "I know, Sofia. It is for me too."

Roberto got up and poured himself another shot of whiskey, then wolfed down the shot. "If you love my daughter, you'll marry her now and take her with you."

"Babbo!" Sofia exclaimed.

"There's no time for civilities," he replied calmly.

"It's okay, Sofia," Waverly said, taking her hand. "I love you and I would ask for your hand this instant, but I promised my son I'd talk it over with him before I married again. That's a pledge I mean to keep."

A wistful smile brightened Sofia's face. "I love you too."

Roberto slumped into a chair, holding his forehead in his hands. *"Pazzesco!"*

"What's that?" Waverly asked Sofia quietly.

"Crazy," Roberto said from beneath his hands. "Can't you call the boy and explain the situation? I'm sure he'll come to love Sofia."

"I'm sure he will. But he's very fragile right now, and I promised to discuss it with him man to man."

Roberto motioned exasperatedly to the heavens and left the room.

Sofia and Waverly sat silently holding hands. Finally, she cleared her throat. "You're a wonderful and honorable man, and I love you. I can't bear the thought of you leaving me. Let me talk to my father and try to convince him it's best for us to go."

"I love you too. I'll come back tomorrow afternoon and help you convince him. I've got to call my ride now, though, because I have important work to do in the morning."

He pulled out his phone. "I'm ready," he said when Hanson answered.

"Okay, we're just down the street. We'll be out front in five."

"Great. Thanks."

He stood, took Sofia's hands and pulled her up from the couch, and kissed her softly on the lips. "I love you."

Her eyes beamed. "I love you too, my darling."

He kissed her on the forehead and led her to the foyer.

"Babbo," she called, "Stone is leaving!"

Roberto appeared from the kitchen. "Stone, please don't misunderstand me. Thank you for thinking of our safety."

"I understand, sir."

"I'll discuss your proposal with Sofia. When will we see you again?"

"He's coming back tomorrow afternoon," she answered.

Roberto opened the door. "Splendid. See you tomorrow."

"Good night." He kissed her on the cheek and stepped into the hall.

Where's Lax?

He set off down the stairs to find the marine.

Sofia set about wiping the coffee table and bar, then took the glasses and plates to the kitchen. When she'd finished, she sat on the couch beside Roberto.

"Sofia, let's settle this now or I won't sleep."

"Yes, *Babbo*?"

He patted her on the knee. "Perhaps we can hire a caretaker to live here with Riza and Malaya while I'm gone."

She threw her arms around his neck. "You're so good to me!"

"And you've always been—"

A knock on the door reverberated through the room. She glanced anxiously at her father, who grabbed his rifle from the gun case and approached the foyer.

"Who is it?" he called out, shouldering his rifle.

"Bert Hanson, Stone's American friend."

Her father opened the door. "Yes?"

"I'm sorry to bother you, sir, but are Waverly and Lax here?"

The hair stood up on the back of Sofia's neck. She leaned past her father. "Stone left ten minutes ago."

Hanson's eyes widened with surprise. "Ten minutes ago?"

She nodded. "At least."

Hanson pulled his pistol from its holster on his belt. "Is there another way out of this building besides these stairs?"

"There's a stairwell in the back that goes down to the alley." Her father shot her a worried look.

"Lock your door—now," Hanson ordered as he slammed the door shut.

She covered her eyes with her hands. "Dear God, let him be safe. Please, please, please."

Ten minutes passed before there was a brisk knock at the door. "It's Hanson."

Her father led the way to the door, holding a rifle.

"What's happened?" Sofia asked.

"Stone and our staffer were kidnapped," Hanson replied dourly.

She cried out and collapsed to her knees.

Her father pulled her up to his side. "Stay calm, Sofia. Maybe he's in one of the shops. Several of them are open until midnight."

Hanson shook his head. "The Berber, Yusuf, saw some men force two hooded men into a van in the alley behind the building."

She gasped. "Oh my God!"

"Roberto, Yusuf says he knows you."

Her father nodded. "He's lived in our alley for years."

"Do you trust him?"

"He's never given me any reason not to."

"He thinks he may have seen one of the men here at the building before, maybe a week or two ago—a muscular young man with a black beard and mustache driving a white van. Does he sound familiar?"

"No. But we keep to ourselves."

Hanson reached into his pants pocket. "Here's my phone number. I offered Yusuf a reward if he sees the kidnappers again or gives you the license plate number of their van. Is there a manager or maintenance man with keys to all the apartments?"

Her father shook his head. "No, each owner keeps his own keys."

"The American soldiers will be here soon. I'll be back later."

The covert team landed the helicopter on top of the building an hour later. Spaceman, holding his AK, was the first one out of the helicopter.

"Did you find Waverly?" he demanded.

"Waverly's been kidnapped," Hanson replied despondently.

"By who?"

"All we know is a group of Arabs."

Damn it all to hell. "I told Fisherman he shouldn't be coming here by himself. I *told* him. What a fucking nightmare. How do you know he's not being held in the building somewhere?"

"Because a man in the alley saw them push him into a van. With Lax."

What an idiot. He rolled his eyes. "And you believed him? How do you know he's not in on it? We need to search this entire building—every apartment, door to door."

Morgan arrived a few minutes later with permission from the NTC to search the building. Spaceman led the operators door to door beginning on the second floor, looking for anyone who'd seen or heard anything. It took them until nearly four in the morning. Surprisingly, only two units didn't answer their knock, and Morgan soon determined those flats belonged to a family living in Cyprus.

The building search was a complete bust.

Spaceman climbed into the helo, collapsed into a seat, and slammed a fist into the seat next to him. *Bam, bam, bam.* "Shit. What a freakin' nightmare. Morgan's right—this is the work of al-Rashid and the February 17 Martyrs' Brigade. I should've shot that fucker when I had the chance."

Fisherman didn't turn around in his seat to answer. "Where do we even start?"

"We start by tripling our efforts to find al-Rashid," he said. "When we find that bastard, we find Waverly."

34

The Devil's Den

The door clanked open and Waverly heard familiar footsteps on water-soaked cement and saw the sudden beam of light that presaged yet another beating. A hand grabbed his hair out of the halo in the darkness and jerked him off the wooden plank where he lay. The light shone straight into his swollen, black and blue eyes, and illuminated dried blood streaks on his bruised and ulcerated face. *They're going to beat me again. Please, God, please, no more.*

"Get up!" bellowed his tormentor.

Waverly rolled onto his stomach, but pain in every muscle and joint in his body paralyzed his attempt to get to his feet. He howled at a kick in the ribs.

"Get up!" Saeeb yelled again.

He struggled to his feet, stooped in the darkness. "What'd you do to Lax?"

"We gutted him," Saeeb snickered. "And you're next if you don't answer my questions. What's your mission in Libya? Tell me, or I'll take you to Qadir."

He cringed at the mention of the sadistic thug who'd tortured him for the last four days. Slaps, punches, whips, prods, electric shocks, near-drowning in waste... He'd endured it all, giving them nothing more than the name they already knew when he arrived.

"How many soldiers are in your unit?" Saeeb bellowed again. "How many CIA operatives are in Libya?"

Waverly closed his eyes against the flashlight.

"Okay, *gawad*, have it your way."

Saeeb shoved him, hands cuffed behind his back, through the door and into the hall, where the overhead lights blinded him. He was herded to a door at the end of the hall. It opened, and another jailer pushed a bloodied Arab out.

The man lifted his bruised and swollen face and locked eyes with Waverly. Waverly flinched. It was Mohammed Zuwaya, al-Rashid's top lieutenant in the February 17 Martyrs' Brigade. Zuwaya grunted when the jailer punched him in the back.

"Keep moving!" the jailer shouted.

"Inside," Saeeb growled.

Waverly stumbled into the room where Qadir, the scrawny interrogator, was standing with his arms crossed. He gave Waverly a gold-toothed grin. "Welcome, *gawad*."

He pulled a wooden stick from a pegboard mounted on the wall, grabbed Waverly's hair, and turned his face. "Open your eyes, Christian."

He did. The other half of the room was clean and well lit, dominated by a stainless-steel autopsy table. The table had been empty every other time he'd been here, but this time, two men with gowns, gloves, and masks stood over a body laid out on the table. One of the men pulled a liver from the open abdomen, put it in a plastic bag, and set it carefully in a Styrofoam box filled with ice.

"We're done," the man said to two attendants behind him. "Take him out and bring in the next."

The attendants grabbed the corpse's arms legs and they carried it through a door in the back of the room. Moments later, they reentered with a struggling prisoner. They forced him onto his back and strapped his arms and legs to the corners of the table.

"No, no, *Allahu akbar!*" the prisoner screamed as one of the gowned men stuck a needle in his arm and started an IV. The prisoner was unconscious within seconds, and the gowned men went to work prepping his eyes to remove his corneas.

Qadir laughed. "That's where you end too, Christian."

"Let's give him the *dulab* today," Saeeb said excitedly.

"Perfect. You'll love this, Christian."

Qadir bent Waverly over and pushed his backside through a worn car tire, folding him in half and forcing his head between his thighs.

"For God's sake!" Waverly screamed. *My spine will be crushed.*

"Okay, let me get the 'for God's sake' stick." Qadir went to the pegboard and pulled down a two-foot board. He smacked against his palm several times before drawing it back over his head and whipping it down with a crack on Waverly's shin.

Everything in his sight went fuzzy and red. *He broke my leg!* He screamed and squirmed to try to dodge the next blow, but Qadir brought the board down on his toes. Waverly shrieked in agony.

"What's your mission here in Libya?" Saeeb demanded.

He closed his eyes. "I don't have a mission," he whispered. "I'm a procurement officer."

"Liar!"

He could smell the garlic on Saeeb's breath.

A foot kicked Waverly's jaw. "Ahh! Please, no! I don't have a mission!"

"What's your real job, Christian?"

He grunted and looked up at Saeeb through swollen eyelids. "I'm not giving you shit."

Crack came the board across the bridge of his nose. Blood spurted from his face.

"You bastard," he whispered.

"Gentlemen," the gowned man across the room called out in Arabic. "I can't concentrate. Can you resume that later?"

"Yes sir," Saeeb replied deferentially. "Sorry, sir."

"And stop hitting him near his eyes. You'll damage his corneas."

His corneas? They'd picked the wrong man in so many ways.

"As you wish, sir. Can I bring you anything? The chef prepared chicken and rice for lunch."

"Just bring me some juice," the gowned man said gruffly.

"Yes sir. Right away, sir." He slugged Waverly in the ear and walked out the door.

Qadir pried Waverly by the arms out of the tire.

He remained doubled over on the floor. *I made it, but I nearly broke. Another minute, and I would have. I can't feel my feet. No matter what, I can't tell them shit. If I give them anything, they'll just want more details that'll put my mission in danger, and then I'll end up on that table. For one lousy cornea.*

Qadir jerked him to his feet and leaned close. "See you later tonight, Christian."

35

Uncertainty

Spaceman reinserted his rifle magazine as Redbeard inched the behemoth armored personnel carrier up the driveway to the Tibesti Hotel.

"I miss this place," Morgan said as he jumped down to the sidewalk. "It's much closer to the shops and restaurants I like to visit. I hardly see my friends anymore."

"You know," Spaceman said, "we still don't know who blew up this hotel."

"And your point is?"

"My point is whoever bombed this hotel may be the same bastard who kidnapped Stone and Lax."

Morgan stopped in front of the entrance. "Let's bring that up with Jalil."

Mustafa Abdul Jalil and General Suleiman Mahmud, the new commander of the National Liberation Army, were waiting for them inside the lobby.

Morgan stepped forward. "Chairman Jalil, General Mahmud, it's a pleasure to see you again."

"The pleasure is ours," Jalil replied courteously. "Mr. Spaceman and Mr. Fisherman, thank you for joining us."

Fisherman shook his hand. "My pleasure, sir."

Spaceman ignored Jalil's greeting. His eyes darted across the reception area. *This would be a perfect spot for an ambush.*

"Right this way, gentlemen," Jalil said. "Mr. Morgan, I believe we'll be meeting in your old conference room."

Morgan's eyebrows shot up. "It's already finished? Maybe I'll move back."

Jalil laughed. "As you say in the States, possession is nine-tenths of the law. In Libya, it's ten-tenths."

Jalil led the way to a sparkling new conference room with a grand chandelier and fine hardwood table. A dozen leather swayback chairs surrounded the table over an enormous Persian rug. The others were totally bamboozled by the effect, Spaceman observed with disgust.

"This is spectacular!" Morgan exclaimed. "Mr. Chairman, are you sure you didn't have someone bomb my office, so you could take over this space?"

"You're welcome to have it back, Mr. Morgan, if you'll pay for the renovations and furniture."

Morgan chuckled ruefully. "Maybe when things calm down a bit."

Spaceman reluctantly took a chair beside the others, next to Jalil at the head of the table.

"Do you have any news about the search for Mr. Waverly?" the chairman asked.

"Nothing," Morgan replied. "We hoped you might have some leads we could follow up."

"Has anyone spotted Abdul-Karim al-Rashid?" Spaceman asked, drumming his thumbs impatiently on the polished tabletop.

"Unfortunately, not," Jalil replied. "We've had four NTC meetings since his disappearance, and neither al-Rashid nor his deputies have been to a single one. General Mahmud ordered his officers to be on the lookout, but there's been absolutely nothing reported."

"I sent out new orders yesterday," General Mahmud added. "The last time anyone reported seeing them was when Zliten fell on August 1. In that battle, the February 17 Martyrs' Brigade coordinated with NLA troops to attack the airport, and several of al-Rashid's fighters were killed. The others haven't been seen since, including al-Rashid himself. Before that battle, I would hear from al-Rashid two or three times a week to ask me for more weapons and ammunition. Since then, I've heard nothing."

"That's very strange," Morgan muttered. "Maybe he's been taken prisoner."

Spaceman stopped twiddling his thumbs. *Or maybe they're hiding him.*

"That possibility crossed my mind," General Mahmud acknowledged. "When the government forces withdrew, most of them retreated to Misrata or further west to Sirte. We know many prisoners were force-marched to the west, since we discovered dozens of dead rebel fighters along those roads."

"Please let us know if you hear anything," Morgan said.

"You have my word," Mahmud replied.

"How's the battle going?" Fisherman asked.

"I'm glad you asked." The general replied and stepped over to a large map of Libya on the wall. "The battle is going very well. With the fall of Tripoli, the largest cities still under Gaddafi's control are this area near Tarhuna, south of Tripoli; Sirte, here on the gulf; and Sabha and its military installations, here in the southern desert. There are also government troops controlling Bani Walid, south of Tarhuna, and Hun, between Sirte and Sabha. My forces took the city of Tarhuna two days ago, and I'm confident we'll take Sabha within a week."

Spaceman slid forward in his chair. *Just as I'd hoped.* "Excellent. When you take Sabha, Gaddafi's escape routes to Algeria will be cut off."

"Exactly," General Mahmud replied with a wry smile. "We've already attacked Sirte from the west, and it's here that we need your help. We've encountered fanatical loyalist opposition near Ghardabiya Airbase here to the south of Sirte, and our forces are bogged down there. We need intensive NATO air strikes to soften up the defenses here west of the airport. Can you help us?"

"We'll make it happen, General," Fisherman said.

"How soon?" Mahmud asked.

"Let's shoot for tomorrow night. I'll let you know if there's a problem with that timeline."

"Thank you, sir. That's all I need for the moment."

Morgan rapped his fingers on the table. "Chairman Jalil, I have a question for you."

"Yes, Mr. Morgan."

"Before he died, General Younes claimed the bombing at this hotel was not the work of anyone from the February 17 Martyrs' Brigade. If not them, who do you think was responsible?"

"I have no clue," Jalil replied curtly. "We've investigated the bombing from every angle without any success whatsoever. It turns out the Knights of Allah weren't involved either. They confessed under torture."

"Do you think whoever bombed this hotel also kidnapped Waverly and Lax?"

Jalil clasped his hands on the table. "Of course, it is possible, but it's pure speculation at this point."

Spaceman narrowed his eyes. Morgan did a good job of waiting the bastard out, but nothing more seemed forthcoming.

"Please make it clear to all the NTC members and their associates that we're searching non-stop for whoever abducted Stone Waverly," Morgan said, "and when we find them, there will be hell to pay."

Jalil stared back at Morgan. "What are you saying, Mr. Morgan?"

Morgan raised his eyebrows. "I'm saying we want Stone Waverly back unharmed. We don't know who took him—at this point, everyone is suspect, especially the men associated with the NTC who orchestrated the murder of General Younes."

"Are you accusing me, Mr. Morgan?" Jalil asked angrily.

"No. But one way or the other, we'll find out who abducted Waverly, and if anyone hurts him, America will not rest until it finds and punishes those responsible."

"Your point is clear, Mr. Morgan. I'll relay your message to my colleagues at the NTC."

Morgan stood, and the others rose with him. "Good afternoon, gentlemen. I'm glad you understand our concerns. We'll be in touch."

T he gentle night breeze dried the sweat on Spaceman's brow as he and Deadeye huddled in the darkness atop a dune with the laser designator, observing the tanks below him.

"Get ready to die," he whispered. *The sooner we waste these guys, the sooner we get to Sirte. I'm certain Gaddafi's there.*

The NATO air strikes on enemy positions surrounding Ghardabiya Airbase near Sirte had begun two days earlier. Those strikes had failed to root out the Gaddafi forces, so the covert operators helicoptered into an area just to the south of the airport and hiked northwest through desert until they stumbled on a company of more than thirty loyalist tanks scattered across a desert lowland.

"Fifteen seconds," Spaceman whispered. He held his breath as time ground to a stop.

In rapid succession, the four closest tanks took direct hits and exploded into fireballs.

"Boom."

"Have them advance on the next tank platoon," Fisherman ordered Puckeater from their position a hundred meters behind Spaceman.

A few moments passed, and three more tanks exploded into fireballs.

Spaceman aimed his laser designator to target another tank buried up to its turret in sand nearly two hundred yards away. "You've got to get closer," he whispered to himself. He crept forward through a ravine and up an embankment to within fifty yards of the tank. He knelt to aim the laser, but a burst of machine-gun fire kicked up the sand in front of him. "Oh, shit!" he yelled as he rolled back down the embankment, got to his feet and ran down the ravine lugging the laser designator past Deadeye. "Run! They spotted me!"

Deadeye fell in behind him and trudged through knee-deep sand toward their designated rendezvous.

The other three operators, reacting to the unexpected burst of machine-gun fire, laid down heavy fire on the enemy fighters' positions and then fell back with Fisherman and the others until they spotted Spaceman and Deadeye running to them. Moving to the southeast, they closed quickly on the helicopter landing site.

"What happened?" Fisherman barked at him as they jogged single file through a narrow, sandy gorge.

Spaceman sucked the grit from his teeth and spit. "The tank commander spotted me."

"Damn it, I told you not to get too close."

"I had to. How else could I paint the second platoon?"

"Don't give me that shit. You can use that laser designator from two or three klicks."

"Not when the tanks are dug into trenches."

"Screw you."

They reached the helicopter a minute later, and the bird lifted off. Fisherman sat seething in the back of the fuselage.

Spaceman kept his head down as the other operators bantered about the near miss. *I did exactly what he asked me to do. Fisherman is out to get me, no doubt about it.*

When the helo set down at the base, Jalal bin Koussa was there to meet them. "Mr. Waverly?" he asked plaintively.

"We didn't find him," Fisherman said glumly. "Sorry."

Jalal bowed his head and fell in next to Spaceman, headed toward the mess tent.

"Spaceman!" Fisherman bellowed. "Meet me at the armory in five mikes."

Spaceman merely waved an arm in acknowledgment.

Spaceman found Fisherman pacing the room when he stepped into the armory with a bottle of water.

"What's up, chief?"

Fisherman got right in his face. "Your drift factor is off the charts, and your lack of discipline is threatening our mission and the lives of your fellow operators."

"I followed your orders to hit the second platoon."

"I ordered you to keep your distance."

Spaceman took a swig of water and wiped his mouth with the back of his hand. "Those fucking tanks were buried in the sand. There's no way in hell I could designate them without getting closer."

Fisherman sighed with frustration. "You've continually pushed the envelope ever since we got here, and it's going to get someone killed. I've a good mind to send you home, even if it leaves us shorthanded."

Spaceman grimaced. "Don't do that, man, not when we're so close to accomplishing what we came here to do. I'll soft-pedal it the rest of the way—you have my word."

Fisherman blinked at him, then shrugged. "This is your last chance. One more screw-up and you're gone. We're going back tomorrow night, but from the southwest, to take out the rest of that tank company. Now get some rest and get ready to do safe work."

Spaceman tossed the bottle away. Safety was the least of his concerns at the moment.

36

Foreboding

Waverly cringed at the sound of the lock opening on his cell door. *Lord Jesus, help me.*

"Mr. Waverly," an unfamiliar voice called out, "I've brought you soup."

Waverly opened his swollen eyes to see a balding, gray-haired man holding an electric lamp and wearing a clean white *thobe* with a black *shemagh* on his head. The man set the lamp down on the plank below Waverly's feet. "Here's a warm cloth to wash your face and hands."

This is some kind of new trick. As reluctant as he was to comply, unbearable hunger drove him to struggle to his side. He slid his feet gingerly off the plank and pushed himself up, took the towel, and wiped his mouth and hands.

"Here," the man said, holding a large spoon to his lips. "Try it."

He looked into the older man's wrinkled eyes. Although he desperately wanted to taste the aromatic broth, he didn't dare.

"Try it. It's chicken soup with thyme. I made it this morning."

He looked down at the floor. *There's probably some drug in it.* Nonetheless, he sucked down a tentative spoonful. It was the most delicious soup he'd ever tasted. "Thank you."

The man refilled the spoon and held it to his mouth. "Go ahead. After what you've been through, you need this."

He swallowed another spoonful. "Who are you?"

"My name is Salef. I'm your new interrogator."

A new interrogator? Oh, damn. What now? "What happened to Saeeb?"

"Same thing that happened to Qadir. Their methods weren't working, so they got sent to the front. They also angered the surgeons. Interrogators are a dime a dozen in Libya, but surgeons are not."

He cocked his head. "You're kidding me."

"No, I'm not, Stone. Can I call you Stone?"

"You can call me whatever you want if you'll give me another bowl of that soup."

"Certainly, I'll get you some more. Would you like a cup of tea?"

"Water would be fine."

"I'll be right back." Salef locked the cell door behind himself and returned a few minutes later with another bowl of soup and a glass of water.

Waverly's swollen, sore hands ached as he grasped the bowl, and he struggled to lift it to his mouth.

"Here, let me help you." Salef took the bowl and held it gently to Waverly's mouth. "Drink slowly, my friend."

"My friend"—here comes the full-court press. He guzzled the soup, and then Salef helped him drink the water.

When he'd drunk his fill, he let out an uneasy sigh. "Thank you. What happens now?"

Salef shrugged. "I need some information, or I'll end up at the front too."

"All I'm willing to give is my name."

Salef chuckled. "I know your name. Come now, you knew I'd expect information. If you want me to help you, you've got to give me something."

"I'm feeling sick to my stomach. Can I lie down again?"

"Of course. Here, let me help you." Salef helped Waverly onto his back.

Waverly took several painful, gasping breaths. *Saeeb must have damaged my kidney when he beat me yesterday. God help me, I can't take any more. I'll have to tell him something unimportant, or they'll beat and starve me again.* "What do you want to know?"

"What's your mission here in Libya?"

He closed his eyes. It was the same question he'd suffered so much to deflect over the past weeks.

"You've got to give me something," Salef whispered. "Were you searching for the special bomb?"

Waverly's mouth gaped open. "I don't know what you're talking about."

"You most certainly do," Salef said. "This is dead serious. Don't play games with me. We know about the special bomb, and we know it's somewhere here in Libya. Tell me exactly what and where it is."

"I don't know."

"Yes, you do."

"No, I don't. I looked for months all over Libya. Nothing."

Salef smiled gently. "Okay, so you admit you searched for the bomb. We'll get back to the location later. Who has this special bomb?"

Waverly began hyperventilating while Salef waited patiently for an answer. *I can't tell him. Nothing but disinformation and lies.*

"I don't know," he finally said.

"Who do you think may have the bomb, and why do you suspect them?"

He groaned and reached ineffectually for his back. "My back hurts so much."

"I suspect that's from the beatings you took. I don't want that or worse to happen to you anymore. Who do you think has the bomb?"

"I don't know, I don't know. Believe me, I wish I did."

"Where do they plan to detonate it?"

They already know there's a bomb. There's no harm in playing along to save my life. "I thought they might try to ship it to the USA or Europe, not detonate it here in Libya. That's all I know. I don't know where it is. I don't know who has it."

"It must be a very big special bomb, a bomb that could cause great damage if it were detonated here in Sirte."

"I think so."

"This is the information I need to satisfy my boss. If I don't get these details, we'll both regret it. I don't want you to end up a donor on the autopsy table like so many others. Do you understand me?"

His eyes closed as he reluctantly nodded his head.

"I'll leave you for now to think about whether you'd like more soup and water or another interrogator like Saeeb. Please consider carefully what I've asked you."

Salef picked up the electric lamp and walked toward the door.

No, no, what else can I give? "How long have I been here?" Waverly called out.

"Almost four weeks."

He caught his breath. "That long? Where is this place?"

"Libya."

"I know, but what city?"

"I'm the interrogator here. If I told you that, they'd kill you."

He swallowed hard. "Okay, are we in the east or west of Libya?"

Salef glanced back outside the cell to make sure no one was listening. "We're in the center. And now that I've given you that, I want you to think about what I need from you. I'll be back in a few hours with dinner."

The door clanked closed behind him, and Waverly was plunged into darkness.

As he lay thinking about what had happened and what he'd told Salef, guilt crept over him, even though he really didn't know who had the backpack bomb or where it was stored. The thirst and hunger pangs would soon return in spades, and the psychological pressure would multiply exponentially. Could he resist this new approach as long as he had the unspeakable beatings and abuse? It was an uncertainty he'd never faced.

He turned a tearful face up into the darkness. *Do Mike and Anne know I'm missing? What's happening with them? How is Sofia holding up now that I've been missing for almost a month? Will I ever see any of them again?*

God give me strength.

37

A Miracle

Somberly adorned in a black gown, Sofia took her father's arm and slowly walked up the weeded cobblestone path to the chapel. Her father, looking dapper in a dark gray gabardine suit, smiled at the priest who watched them from the entrance.

"Good afternoon, Father," he called.

"Good afternoon. I'm Father Amado."

"I'm Roberto Pellegrini, and this is my daughter, Sofia."

"Welcome. Are you visiting Benghazi?"

Her father chuckled. "No, Father, Sofia and I were both born in Libya, and my family has lived in Benghazi for nearly a century. But I'm afraid we've been less than faithful the past few years since my wife died and the church was attacked."

Father Amado smiled munificently "Well, welcome back, and may the Blessed Virgin Mary protect you and yours. Do you live in Benghazi?"

"Our flat is on Omar Al Mukhtar Road, across from Martyrs' Square."

Father Amado took a second look at Sofia's swollen eyes. "Are you in mourning, child?"

Tears threatened yet again.

Her father hugged her to his side. "Sofia's dear American friend was abducted a month ago."

"Oh, dear. We will pray for him. May God bless you and bring you peace, my child. Mass will begin shortly. Please come inside."

Inside the chapel, several dozen worshippers were already scattered across the nave. The congregation was primarily Filipinos and Africans, with a few Pakistanis and Europeans here and there.

As they made their way up the aisle, two young Filipino women waved and called softly. "Sofia, we've been so worried. Are you okay?"

She smiled warmly. "Imelda! Hello. I'm fine, but we've had a family difficulty. I hope to be back soon. *Babbo*, this is Imelda and Julita, my friends from the hospital."

He smiled graciously. "It's a pleasure to finally meet you, ladies. I've heard so much about you."

Sofia glanced at the chancel as the cross-bearer and candle-bearers entered the chapel in their green vestments. "Well," she said awkwardly, "the priest is coming in. I'll see you soon."

They sat by themselves several rows from the altar. The portly European priest greeted the congregation before the Penitential Rite and Opening Prayer. Following the readings from the Bible, he gave a homily appealing for understanding and love among the faithful in the face of increasing strife and intolerance in Libya. He then led the Prayer of the Faithful.

"We pray for those among us who are in pain and suffer."

Her father squeezed Sofia's hand. "Lord, hear our prayer."

"We pray for the families who've lost loved ones in the ongoing war."

"Lord, hear our prayer."

"And we pray for those who have been estranged from you but are in need of thy solace."

"Lord, hear our prayer."

Sofia quietly wept.

Both of them took Holy Communion for the first time in years. A final blessing was given before the priest said, "The Mass has ended. You may now go in peace."

Sofia grasped her father's hand as the other worshippers filed out of the chapel. "*Babbo*, I want to confess."

"As you wish. I'll wait for you here."

She walked out a side door and found the confessional at the end of a short hall. Time seemed to pause as she waited for her turn, then entered and knelt in front of a screen emblazoned with a golden cross.

"Welcome," the priest whispered, whereupon Sofia traced out the sign of the cross across her chest.

"Forgive me, Father," she murmured, "for I have sinned. My last confession was over ten years ago, and these are my sins. First, before today I haven't prayed in over five years, since my mother died. And I've lied many times since then—nothing terrible, but little lies like saying I'm fine when I'm really not."

"It's always better to be truthful in these situations," the priest said.

She sighed. "I know, but I hate to explain why I'm not fine. And then one month ago, a man I love was abducted by a group of Libyans, and I damned all Muslims to hell."

The priest's surprise was palpable even through the mesh. She heard him shift in his seat and clear his throat. "If you ask forgiveness, God will forgive even this."

"This man and I aren't married or even engaged yet, but I love him. The only thing I want to ask God for is a miracle—that Stone will be released unharmed."

This request was met by complete silence from the unseen priest.

"I mean, I know I have no right to ask for anything after I've been away from church for so long, but if God will help this good man, I won't ask for anything else ever again."

Again, her request was met with silence.

"But he might already be dead. I'm sorry." A single sob burst free. "I guess that's everything."

"I'm sure God heard your request," the priest said. "Remember, all things work together for good to them who love God, to them who are the called according to his purpose. For your penance, reflect on the goodness of God and pray five Hail Marys. Now make your Act of Contrition."

She gasped. "Oh gosh, I hope I remember. Ah, my God, I'm sorry for all my sins with all my heart. In choosing to do wrong, I sinned against you, whom I should love above all things. I firmly intend, with the help of your grace, to sin no more and to avoid my sins. Our Savior, Jesus Christ, suffered and died for us. In his name, my God, have mercy."

The priest offered a prayer of absolution.

"Amen," she said.

"God has forgiven your sins. Go in peace, and I will ask all the priests and nuns to pray for this man you love. May God protect and bless him and you."

"Thanks be to God," she whispered. "And thank you, Father."

"Will we see you at Mass next week?"

"Yes, Father. I'll be here every week from now on. Goodbye."

She found her father waiting for her at the end of the hall. She hugged him, and they walked together into a light drizzle falling from a darkened sky.

38

By the Book

Spaceman carried his plate to a table where Fisherman and Deadeye were eating. "Mind if I join you?"

Deadeye pushed a plate of flatbread to the center of the table. "Come on. I was reminiscing about the good old days back in Fort Benning where we did our sniper training."

He smiled. "Georgia—I have fond memories from my time there too. That's where I learned to snipe."

"Did you ever hear of a sniper named Frankie Boy Hurst?"

"Frankie Boy?" He grabbed a piece of bread and stuffed it in his mouth. "I don't think so."

"I was his spotter for nine years, and he was the best I ever saw. He won the sniper award at Fort Benning six years in a row, and it wasn't even close. His name is on that big trophy in the mess hall."

He looked up from his plate. "I never read that trophy, but I remember it. He retired?"

"Nah, he's dead," Deadeye drawled. "He stepped on a mine in Iraq."

Spaceman grunted. "Do you have any more inspirational tales?"

Deadeye chuckled. "Sorry."

"I dated a girl who lived near Benning before I married Ruth," Fisherman said.

"Oh yeah?" Deadeye said. "Was she hot?"

Fisherman grinned. "Aren't all those Georgia peaches hot?"

"I wouldn't know. I never had one."

Spaceman reached for more bread. "None of you dudes ever talk about anything but women and sex."

"What's wrong, little boy, don't you like women?"

"I like 'em fine, but who has the time?"

Fisherman leveled a questioning look at him. "Don't you have a special girl back home?"

He shook his head. "Nope. I had two sisters, and they were enough for me."

"What do you mean, had?" Deadeye asked.

"My oldest sister, Rebecca, died of an overdose seven years ago, and my younger sister is in prison in Tennessee for dealing drugs. That's how they ended up after our parents died when they were just thirteen and ten."

"God, that's awful," Deadeye said. "What the hell happened?"

"They were murdered. I don't wanna discuss it."

"Sorry, let's change the subject," Fisherman interjected. "Spaceman, we all appreciate how you've changed your approach the past few weeks."

So, it was working. "Is it that noticeable?"

"Yeah—and I noted that in your evaluation yesterday. You've become much more of a team player, and all of us appreciate it."

He stared at his plate. "All I've ever wanted was to be a first-rate Snake Eater."

"You are. Keep up the good teamwork."

Jalal bin Koussa stepped out of the mess tent with a teapot and cups. "Tea?"

"Sure," Fisherman said.

"Me too," Deadeye said.

"Mr. Spaceman?"

"No thanks, Jalal," Spaceman replied. He waited until Jalal disappeared back into the tent. "That kid's a fuckin' warrior."

Fisherman nodded. "He's changed a ton since he froze up on that raid when we first got here. Waverly and you had a lot to do with that."

"It's more than that. He's got sniper mentality, great hands, and a keen eye for detail. He's going to be a fine fighter—hell, he already is one. He wants to study engineering when this war is over. Maybe we can help."

"Morgan should be able to put in a word where it counts," Fisherman said. "I'll mention it the next time I see him."

"Thanks. Jalal and I've had many similar life experiences, and I'd like to help him out. In the meantime, I appreciate that you've let him come with us on missions. He flat out saved our butts in Sirte last night. We could've walked right into that ambush if he hadn't sniffed it out by talking to those locals." He picked one last bite of meat from his plate. "What's the plan tonight?"

"I'm not sure until I talk to General Mahmoud. But most of the action is near Sirte, so we'll probably designate some targets there for the NATO fly-boys."

He rolled his eyes. "I wish we could just blow in there tonight, shoot Gaddafi, and end this crap. We know damn well he's in District 2 in Sirte. Whaddaya say we sneak in there tonight, hunt the bastard down, and waste him?"

Fisherman shook his head. "We need to take him alive if we find him. Let the Libyans hang him for all the shit he did to them, like the Iraqis did to Saddam Hussein. These people deserve that."

Spaceman wiped his mouth with a napkin. "Whatever." He stood up and cleared his place. "But I want you to know I'd shoot Gaddafi in the gut if I ever got the chance. I wouldn't take him alive."

Fisherman looked for some sign he was kidding, but there wasn't one. "If you did that, they'd likely try you for murder."

He dropped his trash into the garbage bin.

"Whatever."

39

Clarity

A light snapped on outside the cell. Waverly peered through the darkness, and a frightful sense of foreboding swept over him. *Oh my God, they're coming for me now.*

For over two hours, he'd heard the pleas and screams of men being subjugated in the torture room before they fell quiet, presumably silenced by the intravenous sedative given by the organ harvesters. The air reeked of vomit, feces, and raw meat.

The lock clicked. The hinges screeched, and Salef stepped into his cell carrying a lamp.

"I've brought you bread and soup." He sat on the end of the hard plank Waverly used as his bed. "How are you this morning, my friend?"

He rubbed at his knees, still tender from the beatings. "I was better until the screaming started early this morning."

"The harvesters are hard at work today. This new *naqīb* is ruthlessly efficient, and I have little influence on him. This morning they harvested a leader of the February 17 Martyrs' Brigade."

He sat up. "Abdul-Karim al-Rashid?"

"No, Mohammed Zuwaya. Did you know him?"

"Yes. Al-Rashid's second-in-command."

Salef shifted the *shemagh* on his head and rested his hands on his *thobe*. "I pleaded for them to spare him because he could have been a valuable source of information about the rebel forces and leadership and the special bomb, but the *naqīb* said I'd had long enough with no further progress, and he finally ordered his execution. Truthfully, Zuwaya was evil and nobody will miss him. But your situation is different, and you must help me to help you survive this tribulation— for the sake of Mike, and Anne, and that nurse girlfriend of yours."

Waverly's head jerked up. *You bastard.* "How...?"

Salef smiled. "The CIA aren't the only spies in the world that have ways of getting private information. You should know that better than anyone because you're a CIA spy, aren't you, Stone?"

Waverly stared into Salef's aged eyes. "I'm a procurement officer."

"What were you procuring on your first visit to Libya in 1989 when you met Brother Leader Gaddafi?"

He swallowed, his mouth suddenly dry. "I was procuring oil. Helping with new oil contracts."

Salef smiled. "Do you recall Abdullah al-Senussi?"

Waverly picked at the *shalwar kameez* covering his legs. *This guy knows exactly who I am. I need to play along, see what I can find out about this place and who's in control.* "Gaddafi's intelligence chief?"

"He gave me your file, and he's convinced you aren't really a procurement officer but a CIA operative."

The hair on the back of his neck lifted. "So, I've been imprisoned and tortured by Gaddafi?"

"Yes—and for that, you are most fortunate. As you Americans are so fond of saying, I'm going to be straight with you. The possibilities that you might provide us with information on the special bomb and that we might trade you for safe passage out of Libya for the Brother Leader and his family are the only things that've kept you alive."

Salef paused to let that sink in. "And there's something else you should think carefully about. Your children are now known to those who would have something from you. How safe do you think they are?"

There was no use trying to hide his anger. "You bastard! You'd threaten innocent young children?"

"I'm only the messenger, Mr. Waverly." He turned to make sure nobody was listening to their conversation. "Gaddafi's men are ruthless butchers."

Everything came sharply into focus. His heart pounded with fear for the safety of Mike and Anne. "Can I have some water?"

"Certainly. You think about your children while I get the water." He got up and left the cell, for the first time leaving the door open. He returned a few minutes later with a glass.

Waverly stared listlessly at the glass, parched but unable to drink. "Tell Gaddafi I'll do whatever he wants me to do."

Salef jumped as a commotion erupted behind him down the hall. A blood-curdling scream echoed through the building, followed by muffled pleas and then silence.

Salef set the basket of bread aside as if nothing had happened.

What can I offer? He forced himself to take a sip of water while he thought. "What if I contact my associates in Benghazi and arrange safe passage to Algeria for Gaddafi and his family? If I can arrange that, will Gaddafi guarantee the safety of my children and my safe return to Benghazi?"

Salef smiled. "I am authorized to make this agreement, not only for Gaddafi and his family but also for his colleagues, who will not be safe here once he's gone. I will take you to a special phone that's still connected to Benghazi to make the arrangements. Your conversation will be monitored and recorded."

Salef led Waverly out of his cell and down a crumbling concrete walkway to a stairwell with steps up to a metal storm door. He opened the door, and sunlight flooded Waverly's eyes for the first time in months. Salef steered Waverly across a weeded dirt path to a single-story building, and they entered a small office with a wooden desk and two chairs. An old-fashioned black rotary phone was sitting on the desktop.

Salef lifted the receiver. "We'll call the service line at the old restaurant where your friend Mr. Morgan has his office. I'll dial, and you will ask for him."

"What if he's not there?"

"He's there. Only ten minutes for this call, and you're not to mention your children. Tell him you need to reach an agreement for a caravan of vehicles to pass from the center of Libya to Sabha and from there to Ghat and into Algeria. We'll let them know later where the caravan will begin."

"When?"

"Soon. The exact time will be established in the coming days. You'll call him back tomorrow or the next day at the same time, using the same phone, to confirm a guarantee for safe passage from the NTC and the American government. Then we'll give them two hours' notice of when the caravan will leave and from where, and we will expect them to protect the route we provide. Once Brother Leader Gaddafi and his people are safely into Algeria, we'll take you to Benghazi and release you, with the promise that your children will also be safe."

"What if Algeria doesn't admit them?"

"That's already been arranged. Let me dial." Salef placed the call and handed the phone to Waverly.

There was an answer on the third ring. "Allō."

He glanced at Salef. "This is American citizen Stone Waverly. I must speak to Gus Morgan immediately."

There was a commotion on the other end and loud voices in the background, and more than a minute passed before Morgan came to the phone.

"Stone?" Morgan asked tentatively.

"Gus, it's me."

"Oh, thank God. Are you okay?"

"I'm alive."

"Where are you?"

"I don't know. Listen, I only have a few moments. I must arrange safe passage for Gaddafi and his entourage in a car caravan to Algeria."

"Gaddafi?"

"And his family and friends."

"Where? When?"

"From somewhere in Libya. I'll call with more details in the next two days. The people holding me must have NTC and American guarantees of protection. I'm to call you back at this same time tomorrow or the next day for that guarantee. Then I'll give you two hours' notice of the actual departure. They plan to drive first to Sabha, then to Ghat, and from there into Algeria. I need your assurance that neither the rebels nor their allies will attack them or try to stop them. Once Gaddafi and his people are safely in Algeria, they've promised to set me free and—"

He stopped short at a warning look from Salef. *Oh, my children.*

"I'll make it happen," Morgan said determinedly. "Thank God, Stone. We've hunted for you everywhere."

"Thanks. I knew you'd be searching. Do me a favor?"

"Name it."

"Tell Sofia I love her and tell Jalal bin Koussa we'll play lots of soccer when I get back."

Salef motioned for him to hang up.

"I've got to go. Goodbye." He hung up the phone and took a shaky step backward. The *shalwar kameez* he was wearing was soaked through with perspiration.

"Excellent job, my friend. I'll take you back to your cell."

He wished he had the same level of optimism as his interrogator. *There's no way Morgan can make this arrangement. There's no way the rebels will let Gaddafi go free.*

The cell door swung closed behind him.

No way.

40

Enabling the Beast

Spaceman and Fisherman, fresh from the field and tracking sand on the thick carpet, rushed into the conference room at the US envoy headquarters to join Morgan and Hanson at the table with NTC Chairman Jalil and NLA General Mahmud.

Spaceman slipped into a chair as unobtrusively as possible. *This, I've got to hear.*

"As I was saying, Mr. Chairman, General," Morgan said, "I wouldn't have asked you to come so quickly if it weren't of the utmost importance."

"Yes, yes, you have our attention," Jalil said.

"Stone Waverly called me from captivity this morning."

Jalil nearly choked on his juice. "What? How?"

"He was abducted by Gaddafi's men. His captors allowed him to call me." Morgan recounted every detail of the phone conversation, then pushed his chair back from the table. "That's the situation."

General Mahmud folded his hands in front of him on the table. "How can you be certain it wasn't an imposter?"

"I'm certain it was Waverly, general. We've been friends forever, and I know his voice and mannerisms. The last thing he told me was to tell

Jalal bin Koussa they'd play soccer when he returned. I think he said it to make sure I knew with certainty it was him."

"Where is he?" Mahmud asked.

"He didn't know. We traced the call to the Sirte region."

Chairman Jalil let out a long sigh. "So, Gaddafi has one more trick up his sleeve. What are we going to do now?"

"Mr. Chairman," Spaceman said, "we should do whatever they ask to save Stone Waverly."

"Impossible," Jalil replied dismissively. "I too cherish Stone Waverly and everything he has done to support this revolution, but my people would never accept letting the butcher escape for the life of one man."

I knew he'd say that. This guy's worthless. "General?"

Fisherman shot Spaceman an annoyed look.

General Mahmud folded his arms across his chest and pondered. "With all due respect, Chairman Jalil, I have a different opinion. Gaddafi is finished. Even though we're winning in Sirte and I am more confident every day we'll be victorious there, our forces have taken terrible losses. Two hundred and fifty have been killed and two thousand have been wounded in this month's offensive. The loyalists, including Gaddafi, are surrounded, but if we must fight them street to street and house to house to seal the final victory, thousands more of our fighters will die. Many innocent citizens will die too.

"I say let the bastard go. Save Stone Waverly. When Gaddafi is gone, the war will end. Wherever he ends up, we can pursue charges against him in the International Criminal Court in The Hague for the countless murders and atrocities he's committed."

"He won't get very far," Spaceman said. "That makes a lot of sense."

Fisherman glared at Spaceman. "Will you let me handle this?"

"Whatever you say, chief."

"I guess I'm outnumbered here," Jalil said. "Tell me how you plan to coordinate this escape when every kilometer of road to Algeria is held by our troops. There will be no holding our men back if there's even a hint that Gaddafi is driving by in some sort of caravan."

"We've thought this out, Mr. Chairman," Fisherman said. "We'll make sure the NATO forces, including our air forces, back off as the caravan leaves. General Mahmud will agree to a cease-fire and order his forces to stand down. He'll inform them that an important NTC caravan will be passing through the country, without identifying the occupants. Then—and Spaceman thought of this—we'll make an airdrop to Gaddafi's people with rebel flags. All of the vehicles in the caravan will fly the rebel flag, so the rebel forces won't attack them."

Jalil guffawed. "And you think Gaddafi will agree to fly the rebel flag on his vehicles?"

"He will if he wants to live," Spaceman said pointedly.

"We shall see. He's an obstinate, stubborn man."

General Mahmud tapped his fingers impatiently on the table. "When would this caravan leave?"

"If I get the call from Waverly tomorrow or the next day," Morgan said, "then I'd guess in three to five days—Tuesday, Wednesday, or Thursday—but that's purely speculation."

Mahmud nodded. "In the meantime, I'll have our forces redouble their efforts in Sirte to up the pressure on Gaddafi."

"And perhaps reposition some of your forces away from the highway to Sabha and the highway from Sabha to Ghat," Spaceman added, keeping his gaze on the general so Fisherman couldn't give him another warning look.

"We should meet again after the second call from Mr. Waverly to finalize our plans," Jalil said.

"Synchronization will be critical," Mahmud said.

Jalil stood up. "Let's plan on that. I must go. I'm late to a wedding."

Spaceman scraped his chair back and moved to side of the room. It would take these men several more minutes to move through all their formalities.

Morgan offered his hand. "Mr. Chairman, I owe you an apology for even hinting that you or any other NTC members could have been involved in Waverly's disappearance. I can only explain that the pain in my heart clouded my judgment. Please relay my regrets to all the members of the NTC."

Jalil took his hand. "You're an honorable man, sir, and I accept your apology, but I assure you it's unnecessary. My people and I owe you and your allies a debt we can never repay."

"We'll look forward to a rapid and victorious—"

The door closed behind Spaceman as he strode down the hall. This was no time for pleasantries and posturing. Not when there were objectives to accomplish.

W averly glanced at Salef and then back up the barrel of the pistol held by Gaddafi's burly security chief. *This asshole would love to shoot me right between the eyes.* "Gus, it's me," he croaked into the phone.

"Are you okay, buddy?" Morgan asked.

"Yeah, there was some glitch, but they want to go ahead now."

"We're ready to put the plan in motion. Both the NTC and the NATO forces will guarantee their caravan's safe passage to Algeria."

"Okay, here's their proposal. On Thursday, a caravan of eighty to a hundred vehicles will leave District 2 and drive east on the Coastal Highway. From there, they'll proceed south on one of the southern arteries to the Sirte to Waddan highway. They'll pass through Waddan, where they plan to refuel from a gasoline tanker. From there, they'll proceed to Sawknah and on to Sabha. Finally, they'll drive to the Algerian border station near the Oasis at Ghat. That's where the Algerian authorities will await them."

"What time?"

"I don't know yet. Someone will call this phone two hours before the caravan sets out for Algeria."

"Got it."

"Thanks, Gus. Did you get in touch with Sofia?"

"Of course. She was overcome with joy, and she told me to tell you she loves you too."

"I love her with all my heart. Tell her that."

The security chief grabbed the phone and muffled it against his chest. "Do you think I'm stupid? Quit talking in code, or I'll blow your fucking brains out. Tell them I'll shove my pistol in your mouth and pull the trigger if even one shot is fired on the caravan."

He gave Waverly the phone again.

"… Still there?"

"Yes, sorry. They told me to tell you they'll shoot me on the spot if anyone fires on the caravan."

"We'll do everything we can. Listen, part of our plan is to have all the vehicles in the caravan fly the rebel flag all the way to Algeria."

Waverly cringed and glanced up at the security chief's scowl. "You're kidding."

"Spaceman thought this up. The rebels will be told it's an NTC caravan. I think the plan's just crazy enough to work. The operators will airdrop a supply of antenna flags into the parking lot at Mkmadas Restaurant in District 2 tonight."

"I'll let them know. I must go."

"Good luck, buddy. We're all pulling for you."

"Thanks, Gus. Goodbye."

He handed the receiver to the security chief, suddenly less than hopeful that it would ultimately make a difference. *This is all a sham. They'll never let me go, for fear I'll go after whoever tipped them off about the nuclear backpack bomb.*

Salef led the way back to Waverly's cell—this time, Waverly thought glumly, possibly for good.

41

Cornered

Spaceman inserted the magazine into his pistol and shoved it into the holster on his belt. *I've been waiting for this day for twenty-three years. Twenty-three fucking years.* Then he rubbed his eyes vigorously with his thumbs to make them red, mussed up his hair, and jumped out of the helicopter to the ground.

It took less than sixty seconds before he felt Fisherman's hand on his back. He gave another dry retch for good measure.

"What the hell?" Fisherman said. "What's wrong?"

"I woke up with a migraine," Spaceman grunted. "Everything's spinning, and my vision's full of zigzag lines. I can't even read my watch."

"You're staying here."

"Oh, hell no," he protested and then retched again.

"Get some ibuprofen and sleep it off. Sorry, but we don't have time for this shit." Fisherman turned back to the helo, calling to the pilots. "Let's go."

Spaceman watched him jog back to the helicopter and climb into the fuselage. "Sorry, dude," he whispered, "but I've been waiting for this moment for a very long time."

The helicopter lifted off. Spaceman waited twenty minutes, then radioed the pilot to pass along a very special message. He waited while the pilot relayed the information.

The radio crackled with Fisherman's voice. "Foxtrot 2, this is Foxtrot 1. Do you hear me?"

"Foxtrot 1, I've got you," Spaceman replied. *Ready for your red herring?*

"Where'd you get this alert?"

"General Mahmud's headquarters via the ground line. The backup pilot took the call and relayed it to me."

"And the accident has blocked the whole highway north of Waddan?"

"Affirmative."

"Okay. We'll proceed up there."

"Roger that," Spaceman replied. "I'm feeling much better. I'll head up to cover Sirte in the backup Mi-17 with Jalal bin Koussa."

"You sure you're better?"

"The ibuprofen helped a lot."

"Copy. Glad you're back. Keep us posted. Over and out."

An hour and a half later, the two covert operator helicopters were miles apart, the team headed to Waddan, and Spaceman's approaching Sirte. Spaceman stared down at the monotonous rolling sea far beneath them. Jalal sat nearby, breaking down and meticulously cleaning his AK-47.

Just as they were approaching the beach at Sirte, the copilot leaned out of the cockpit. "Fisherman wants you on the radio."

He scrambled forward and grabbed the headset. "Spaceman here."

"This is Fisherman. We're not finding any accident north of Waddan. The traffic on the highway is flowing normally."

"Mahmud's headquarters called again just a moment ago. The accident was five clicks west of Waddan on the highway to Sawknah."

There was silence for several seconds. "Spaceman, are you fucking with me?"

"That's what Mahmud's people said. I'm just relaying their message."

"Copy. We'll check it out. Are you over Sirte yet?"

"We're just arriving over District 2, but we haven't spotted the caravan yet."

"Keep us posted. Over and out."

Spaceman directed the pilot to weave back and forth across District 2 while he scrutinized the tangle of streets below with binoculars. Finally, on a dead-end residential street a few blocks from Mkmadas Restaurant, he spotted a massive gathering of SUVs, sedans, and technicals with men manning the machine guns in the beds. A horde of people scurried about the vehicles, and a fuel tanker was parked on the street a block away.

"Circle them at high altitude," he yelled to the pilot.

One vehicle caught his eye, a large black sedan with men, women, children, and soldiers gathered five deep around it. It was parked in the driveway of a massive residential compound at the end of the cul-de-sac. He zoomed in and watched a uniformed soldier with an impressive row of medals on his chest place a large box in the back seat. The officer bowed deferentially before hurrying away to a technical, its machine gun glinting in the sun.

"You can run but you can't hide, you bastard," Spaceman whispered. "Jalal, keep an eye on that big black sedan. Don't lose it."

A man in a *thobe* scurried from vehicle to vehicle, mounting flags on each vehicle's antenna. *What a kick in the ass.* He grinned.

The people in the cul-de-sac began to disperse, and a pair of technicals pulled slowly away. One by one, the other vehicles pulled in behind them, and the snaking caravan began to take form. Two-thirds of the assembled SUVs, sedans, and pickup trucks had joined the procession before the large black sedan edged out of the driveway and sped into the growing motorcade.

"No flag," Spaceman muttered.

"What'd you say?" Jalal asked.

"That big black sedan that just joined the back of the line—it doesn't have a rebel flag," he shouted above the engines.

"Spaceman," the copilot yelled from the cockpit. "Fisherman's on the radio."

He handed the binoculars to Jalal and glanced at his watch. It was 0830 hours. "Keep your eye on that black sedan. Do you understand? Don't let it out of your sight."

"Yes, I see it," Jalal said.

"Don't lose it. That's Gaddafi."

Jalal's eyes grew huge and he nodded again.

Spaceman took the pilot's headset. "Spaceman here."

"This is Fisherman. We've flown the highway all the way from Waddan to Sawknah, and there's no accident. The highway is clear. We also flew five klicks to the south of Sawknah, and there's no block there either."

"Copy. I'm not sure what to tell you. I only passed on what I was told."

"Has the caravan left?"

"It's formed, and the lead truck is headed west at high speed on the District 2 Coastal Highway."

"Good. We're headed back to you along the Sirte–Waddan Highway. Keep us posted. Over and out."

Spaceman glanced up front to double-check that the pilot wasn't wearing his backup headset. He wasn't. *Here we go.*

"Oh my God, no!" he shouted.

The pilot twisted around. "What?"

"It's a trick! Stone Waverly was just found dead. Change the radio to the NATO frequency."

The pilot switched frequencies and put on his backup headset.

"Neptune, this is Foxtrot 2, do you hear me?" Spaceman called into the microphone. "Neptune, this is Foxtrot 2, do you hear me?"

"This is Neptune," came the response in French-accented English.

"We've got you loud and clear, Foxtrot 2."

"The American prisoner is dead. It's a trick—I repeat, it's a trick. The caravan is headed west on the Coastal Highway just west of District 2. No, wait—they just turned south at the petrol station. Stop the caravan. I repeat, stop the caravan."

"Copy, Foxtrot 2. We're two mikes out."

Spaceman handed the headset back to the copilot. "Fly over the caravan. When the jets strike, we need to be in position to machine-gun that big black sedan."

The helicopter made a banking turn over a water treatment plant, quickly dropping altitude, and sped north toward the Coastal Highway petrol station. A moment later, the lead vehicle in the caravan exploded in an enormous fireball, followed by explosions behind it near the front of the line. Another fireball erupted at the end of the caravan a few seconds later.

Spaceman grabbed the machine gun. "Swing around!" he yelled. He aimed at the big black sedan and fired a long burst.

Below them, the big sedan careened off the highway and skidded to a stop at the bottom of a sandy ravine. Several men leaped out and ran headlong away from the highway.

The pilot swept past the sedan, and bullets abruptly ripped into their starboard side. Spaceman took aim at a technical, strafing it from front to rear. The gunner dived out of the bed of the pickup, and the truck veered off the road and rolled several times.

The NATO jets roared past again, destroying more technicals and SUVs. The caravan was now scattered haphazardly across the highway and even into the ravine.

"Put us down next to the black sedan!" Spaceman yelled.

A cloud of sand blasted through the open door as they touched down.

He jumped down to the sand with his AK-47. "Come on, Jalal, let's get him!"

42

Belated Revenge

They ran through heavy sand to the shattered black sedan. All the windows on one side were blown out. Spaceman wrenched open the rear passenger door, and a bloody uniformed man tumbled out onto the sand.

He knelt and rolled the man over. "It's not Gaddafi." He got up and poked his AK inside the vehicle. "The car's empty."

"Look!" Jalal shouted, his voice breaking with excitement. "Those footprints lead over that rise."

They sprinted to the top of the rise. A group of Libyan soldiers were almost upon them on the road. Spaceman fired a burst, and the fighters crumpled.

"Come on! Let's follow these tracks."

They hustled through ankle-deep sand as a formation of jets streaked in and launched more missiles at a cluster of SUVs speeding across the desert away from the highway.

The footprints in the sand veered back to the highway and toward a clearing between lines of trees paralleling the highway.

"Look," Spaceman said between ragged breaths, "they're in the culverts." He leveled his AK, Jalal right behind him, and they advanced to the paired cement drainage pipes that coursed beneath the highway.

When they were just twenty meters away, a young man dressed in Arabic attire jumped out from one of the pipes with a rifle. "We surrender! We surrender!" he yelled before abruptly leveling his rifle.

Spaceman cut him down with a burst from his AK. "Come out!" he bellowed. "Come out, or I'll toss in a grenade."

"Okay, we're coming out," a voice echoed from one pipe.

An older civilian man emerged with his hands up. "My master is here. My master is here. Muammar Gaddafi is here, and he's wounded."

"Get him out here now," Spaceman ordered.

An elderly man in a blood-soaked tunic emerged from the pipe with his hands up. His dark hair was mussed around a deep gash on the side of his head.

"What's wrong? What's wrong? What's going on?"

Spaceman grabbed his shirt. "I finally caught you, you piece of shit."

A young man wielding a machine gun sprang from the culvert. Spaceman cut him down with a burst from his rifle. He jerked a hand grenade from his belt, pulled the pin, and tossed it into the cement pipe. A blast was followed by a cloud of acrid-smelling dust that mushroomed from the opening.

The older man pulled a pistol from beneath his shirt. Jalal shot the man in the chest.

"Good shot, buddy," Spaceman said.

He turned back to Gaddafi. "What a pathetic little shit you turned out to be. I should shoot both your knees out and then your elbows, let you feel real pain. I should kick you in the balls before I shoot you in the gut."

Gaddafi bent at the waist, breathing heavily. "What's wrong? What do you want?"

Spaceman stepped behind Gaddafi and patted him down. He pulled a heavily engraved golden pistol from the back of the dictator's *shalwar kameez*. "What's this?"

"You keep it," Gaddafi said with a grimace. "Let me go. What'd I do to you?"

"For starters, you killed the father and brother of my friend here."

Gaddafi looked up the barrel of Jalal's AK-47. "I didn't kill anyone."

"And you fucking murdered my mother and father, Tina and Douglas Brunello."

"That's a lie," Gaddafi said, panting.

"You killed them. You did. I was only seven years old." He was barely whispering.

"You're hallucinating."

"The Clipper Maid of the Seas. Remember that?"

"I don't know what you're talking about."

"The 747 jetliner you blew up over Lockerbie, Scotland. You bastard! You killed my mother and father when you bombed that plane."

Gaddafi's eyes bulged with realization.

"They were flying home for Christmas." Spaceman's voice cracked. "You took my family, my life. I've devoted my whole life to tracking you down, you wretched scum. Pigs like you deserve to die painfully with a bullet in the belly."

He lifted Gaddafi's golden pistol slowly, without breaking eye contact, his finger twitching on the trigger. When the shot rang out, he bit down involuntarily on his lip. He swallowed the bitter tang of blood.

Gaddafi dropped to his knees and fell heavily onto his side, writhing in pain and holding his stomach.

"Does it hurt? Was it worth it, you asshole?" Spaceman wiped his mouth with the back of his hand. "Now you know how all those people you killed and maimed felt. Now you know how their families felt."

Gaddafi lifted his hand. "Spare my life! I'll give you ten million dollars…twenty million!"

Spaceman staggered forward. His entire life felt compressed into the space of this single moment as he pressed the golden pistol to Gaddafi's temple and fired.

Gaddafi took one gasping breath and died.

Spaceman wiped his mouth again roughly and shoved the pistol at Jalal. "Here, tell everyone you killed him. You'll be famous."

Jalal turned the pistol over in his hands and ran his fingers across the engraving. "Thank you, sir."

Spaceman sat down heavily in the sand. Two uniformed rebels were running down the embankment from the highway above. One of them stooped and rolled Gaddafi's body over.

"It's Gaddafi! The butcher is dead! The butcher is dead! The butcher is dead!"

More rebel fighters pounded down the embankment and began to chant and dance around the body.

"Did you kill him?" one of the fighters asked Jalal.

Realization dawned in the young man's eyes.

"Yes," Jalal said, holding up the pistol. "I shot him with his own gun."

The fighter clasped Jalal by the shoulders. "What's your name?"

"Jalal bin Koussa."

"Jalal bin Koussa killed Gaddafi!" the man shouted.

"Jalal bin Koussa! Jalal bin Koussa! Jalal bin Koussa!" the fighters shouted as they danced around Gaddafi's body.

The crowd swelled to more than a hundred rebels all shouting "Allahu Akbar!" and "Jalal bin Koussa!" and firing their guns haphazardly into the air.

Spaceman caught sight of Jalal among the rebel fighters and gave him a thumbs-up.

It was over. It was truly, finally over.

He ducked his head against the swirling sand kicked up by the rotors of Foxtrot 1, the second operator Mi-17 helicopter. Fisherman,

Redbeard, and Deadeye jumped down and sidestepped down the embankment.

Fisherman dragged Spaceman to his feet. "What've you done?"

He pointed to the body on the ground among the revelers. "It's over. Jalal killed Gaddafi."

"You asshole!" Fisherman bellowed. "You killed Stone!"

He drew back and punched Spaceman in the mouth, sending him sprawling.

Deadeye rushed forward and kicked him in the belly. "You worthless piece of shit."

"You're fucking done." Fisherman jerked the AK from his hands.

"Allahu Akbar," he muttered.

Fisherman turned away in disgust. "Get him on the helo."

Deadeye pulled him up the embankment and across the road to the helicopter. "You don't give a shit about Waverly, do you? You just killed a true American hero, and you think you're Superman. You're nothing but a goddamn loser."

He shoved him into the helicopter.

Spaceman stared blankly into the chaos outside as Deadeye secured his wrists with zip ties. He didn't feel like a loser. *Twenty-three long years, and I killed the monster with my own hands.*

He felt like he'd finally won his life back.

43

The White Knight's Return

Waverly stepped out of the car into a throng of revelers. "Thank you, Salef!" he shouted above the din.

Salef smiled and gave him a thumbs up before easing the car away into the crowd.

Waverly turned and pushed past a group of men dancing jubilantly, arm-in-arm in a circle on the corner a hundred meters from the guard shack for the American compound.

"Allahu Akbar!" they shouted repeatedly in unison. A short, bearded man grabbed his arm and tried to pull him into the circle. "Hey, are you English?" the man yelled.

"No, I'm not English," Waverly said, shaking his head. "I've got to go. He pulled away and pushed his way through the multitude along the fence to the guard shack. He pounded on the window.

The young Marine looked up from his computer and reached across the counter. He scanned down from Waverly's unkempt beard and hair to his disheveled *shalwar kameez* before opening the window. "What do you want?"

"I'm Stone Waverly."

"Yeah, okay, what do you want?"

"I'm the missing American operative."

The guard stared at him dubiously. "Let me see your identification."

"I don't have any identification! I just escaped from prison. Listen, call Gus Morgan and tell him I'm here."

"Stay right there." The Marine lifted his phone receiver while keeping an eye on Waverly and the celebrating throng behind him. Suddenly, he slammed down the receiver and stepped outside the guard shack as Hanson ran up behind him from the compound.

"Stone! I can't believe it! You're alive!" Hanson called out as he engulfed Waverly in an embrace. "How did you get here?"

"It's a long story. Where's Morgan?"

"Come on. I'll take you to him." Hanson led him into the compound past gawking aides and guards and took him to Morgan's quarters. "He's sedated. Go on in."

Waverly knocked and pushed the door open.

Morgan sat up in his bed and peered through the darkness. The light in the hall outlined a shadowy figure in a *shalwar kameez* that looked like a specter.

"Who is it?" Morgan queried apprehensively.

"It's me, Stone." *He doesn't believe me.*

Morgan flipped on his light and stared at the man in the doorway. The hair was long and tangled, the beard unkempt, and the face drawn. "Stone!" He jumped up from the bed, rushed across the room, and pulled Waverly into a hug. "You're alive! You're alive! My God, you're really alive!" He held Waverly at arm's length. "What happened to your nose?"

Waverly felt the twisted depression above the tip of his nose. "They beat me." His lips trembled. "But I'm alive."

"And you're here! How'd you get here?"

"My interrogator deserted. He drove me from Sirte. Gus, listen. Mike and Anne are in danger. Gaddafi's agents in the US know who they are and threatened to hurt them if anything happened to him."

Morgan held out his satellite phone. "Call. Call now."

Waverly's stomach churned as he dialed. *My kids may already be dead, and it's all my fault. I should never have left them.*

"Beatrice, this is Mr. Waverly. Beatrice, can you hear me?" He shot an agonized look at Morgan. "She can't hear me!"

"Hang up and call again."

His hands shook as he dialed again. "Can you hear me now? Okay, okay… Yes, I'm fine, but listen carefully. Where are Mike and Anne?" He pushed his hair back from his face. "What time is it there? Okay, listen. Get in the car immediately and pick them up at school.… Don't ask me any questions. Just go pick them up, then drive directly to the Richmond police station on Grace Street. Park right in front, go inside, and tell them to call the FBI. Yes, the FBI. Whatever you do, don't go back to our house.… Marilyn Harrison will meet you at the police station. Wait for her—and her alone. I'll call you back later. Do you understand? … I don't care about the dogs. Go!"

First step accomplished. *That may not be enough. I need to call Marilyn.*

He dialed again, his hands sweaty with perspiration. She picked up on the first ring.

"Marilyn, it's Stone.… I'm fine, but I need your help. Gaddafi's men have made threats against Mike and Anne. Beatrice has gone to pick them up at school and take them to the Richmond main police station. Could you call the FBI and meet them there? … Yes, thank you.… No, I'll be fine, but I have more to do here. I'll call when I can."

He handed the phone to Morgan, but his mind galloped unabated.

"What a relief," Morgan said, shaking his head. "Those bastards threatened to kill your kids?"

"They're safe now. But listen, I've learned something else. The RA-115-2 is in a closet in Atiq Mosque."

Morgan gave him a flat look of disbelief.

"It's been there all along. My interrogator, Salef, told me that Mohammed Zuwaya, al-Rashid's lieutenant, tried to trade the information for his life. He kept calling it 'a special bomb stolen from Russia' and told Salef it's been in a closet in the imam's quarters at the mosque in Freedom Square for five months."

Morgan squinted dubiously. "You mean the square where they cheered us when I first arrived?"

"That very one."

"So, al-Rashid had it from the start?"

"We need the operators to help us go seize it." He held his hand out for the satellite phone again. "Redbeard, this is Stone.… I'm fine, just listen. We need you and all the operators to helicopter to Morgan's headquarters immediately. There's a top-priority mission that must be executed immediately… Damn it! Just get here ASAP."

He hung up.

"What's wrong?" Morgan asked.

"The mechanics are servicing both helicopters. The rotors got sand damage, and it'll be two hours before they can fly. Damn it all."

"We could go with the marine guards."

He shook his head. "Too risky. We need to wait. Listen, the loyalists know about Sofia as well, and her life is in danger too."

"Hanson!" Morgan yelled.

"Yes sir?"

"Get two marine guards into the Toyota Cruiser. We're driving to the Pellegrinis' house in one minute."

"Yes sir!"

Morgan took Waverly by the elbow. "Let's go. I'll call the guards posted at the Pellegrinis' building on the way."

The Toyota Land Cruiser made slow progress, weaving slowly through the hundreds of revelers in the street.

"This is crazy," Hanson complained. "It'll take all night to get through this mob."

"I called Garcia," Morgan said, "but he's not answering. Try calling directly."

Waverly dialed Roberto's number. "Come on, come on," he mumbled frantically as it rang half a dozen times. "Roberto, this is Stone."

"*Oh, Santo Cielo*! Are you okay? Where are you?"

"I'm fine, but I don't have time to explain—just listen to me. You're in grave danger. I need to—"

Waverly stopped at loud pounding in the background.

"Someone knocked on our door," Roberto said.

"Don't answer the door! Get your guns and barricade yourselves in the back bedroom. Is there a phone in that room? Okay, don't open the door for anyone until I call you—not even for the guards. We're on our way there but there's bad traffic. Be strong, my friend."

Waverly turned to the marine guards in the back seat. "Get ready to charge the Pellegrinis' flat as soon as we get there."

"We're always ready, sir," the older guard replied.

The man's calm face looked familiar. "Do I know you?"

"Yes sir, Chad Owens, Delta Force operator, Mosul 2003. Back then, you were Stone Hudson. I got too old for Delta, so here I am guarding these fine diplomats."

Recognition released the knots in his shoulders a notch. "It's a small world. Great to have you."

"This is my partner, Everts."

"Thanks for your help, Everts."

Omar Al Mukhtar Road was teeming with people—Arab and Berber, young and old—shouting, singing, and dancing on the sidewalks and into the street. A young uniformed rebel ran alongside the Toyota Land Cruiser and flashed them a V for victory.

"We're almost there," Hanson called.

Waverly picked up the satellite phone and dialed the Pellegrinis' phone number. "Now it's busy." His stomach churned.

Hanson eased the Toyota Land Cruiser through the festive throng spilling over Omar Al Mukhtar Road and into Martyrs' Square beyond. Finally, he jammed on the brakes. "I can't get any closer."

Waverly grabbed an AK-47 and jumped out, with Owens and Everts right behind him. They shoved through the throng of surprised revelers to the unguarded stairwell door and bounded up to the second floor.

The acrid, sour smell of gunpowder hung heavy in the air.

Waverly eased the stairwell door open and peeked through the crack at the Pellegrinis' open door. *Please, God.* He lowered his rifle barrel and charged across the vestibule.

Garcia lay in a pool of blood just inside the door. Another man in street clothes was slumped motionless beside a rifle just inside the living room.

Owens squatted down to check Garcia. "Dead," he whispered.

Everts creeped across the room and pulled the rifle from the floor. "This guy's dead too."

A rifle burst erupted from the dining room, and bullets pinged across the foyer wall. Waverly fired two short bursts through the open door and charged the kitchen. He kicked the door open and fired again at a figure crouched behind the island. The man cried out, clutched his chest, and tumbled to the floor.

"Don't shoot," another Arab shouted, raising his hands above the island.

"Get down," Waverly yelled. He lunged around the island and bashed the intruder in the forehead with his rifle butt.

"Cover me!" he called to Owens.

In the back hall, he found two more men on the floor outside the bullet-riddled bedroom door.

"Roberto!" he bellowed. "It's Stone Waverly. Don't shoot!"

One of the men feebly raised his hand. "Help me. I can't move my legs. Help me."

Waverly stooped next to the man and plucked away a pistol. "Check him for weapons," he ordered Everts as the marine came up behind him. "Roberto! It's Stone. I'm coming in. Don't shoot!"

He tried the doorknob, but it was locked. He set his rifle against the wall, gathered himself, and crashed against the door. It gave a few inches but slammed against furniture piled against the other side. "Roberto, open the door!"

A jumble of voices issued from the other side, followed by a grating noise.

The door burst open, and Sofia tumbled into Waverly's arms.

He cradled her head to his chest.

"My love," he whispered. "I almost lost you."

"Stone," she murmured against him, "thank God. They tried to kill us!"

"I know, darling. It's over—it's all over."

Roberto stumbled from the bedroom with his rifle. "I had to shoot! That man yelled 'Mukhabarat' and then shot through the door. He hit Malaya in the shoulder."

Waverly hugged Sofia protectively to his chest. "It's okay, Roberto, you did the right thing. I have one more request. Take care of Sofia, and my friend Owens here will take you to Mr. Morgan's headquarters, where you'll be safe."

He kissed her on the forehead. "I'll be back soon, my darling."

He shifted her to Roberto's arms and jogged from the apartment and down the stairs. The Toyota Land Cruiser had made it to the curb but was surrounded by revelers.

One last thing left to do.

44

The Imam's Surprise

Waverly pushed his way through the crowds and knocked on the window of the Toyota Land Cruiser. Morgan lowered the window.

"Gus, bring the satellite phone and come with me. It's urgent."

The retreated back up the stairs into the building. Waverly bounded past the Pellegrinis' landing, his AK gripped in both hands, and continued climbing the stairs.

"Where are we going?" Morgan called after him.

"To the roof. I'll explain when we get there."

He pushed open the door to the dilapidated tar roof, and they were engulfed in the sounds of revelry rising from the street below.

"Give me the satellite phone.… Redbeard, Waverly here. How much longer?" He glanced at Morgan's quizzical expression. "Excellent. We're on the roof of the Pellegrinis' apartment building. Can you pick us up here? … Excellent, see you shortly." He handed the phone back to Morgan. "Listen, when the operators get here, we need to tell them what we're looking for. They need to understand what they're up against."

"We can't do that. That's top-secret, need-to-know information."

"Well, they need to know."

Morgan held out the phone. "Call Langley now and get permission."

"We don't have time. I'm making an executive decision. The director can prosecute me later if he feels the need."

Behind them from the south, the *whop, whop, whop* of helicopter rotors, faint at first, circled the building and then hovered above them before the Mi-17 set down on the roof.

The operators jumped down from the fuselage. Waverly gathered them into a circle.

"You got this from me, not from Morgan," he shouted, glancing over his shoulder at Gus sitting glumly on the low railing at the edge of the building. "A stolen Russian RA-115-2 nuclear backpack bomb was secreted into Libya five months ago. I learned tonight that it's been in the possession of the February 17 Martyrs' Brigade, stored in a closet in the imam's quarters at the Atiq Mosque in Freedom Square. We assume he intends to transport it to the US or another allied country and detonate it. We must take possession of it now."

"This is what you've been searching for with that metal detector, isn't it?" Fisherman asked.

"Yes, although it was actually a radiation detector. I'm sorry, but it was top secret, need to know. To be clear, I have not been authorized to tell you this information, but I'm telling you anyway, and I may get screwed for it later."

He saw nothing but professional focus in their faces, so he continued. "The bomb looks like a big backpack and weighs just over a hundred pounds. It has the yield of two kilotons of TNT."

Redbeard let out a long whistle of dismay. "That could do some damage."

He nodded. "And there's a real danger al-Rashid will explode it straightaway if he knows he's been found out. Are you with me?"

"We're with you!" the operators shouted in unison.

"Then let's do this."

Waverly handed his AK to Deadeye and was a step up the stairs into the helo before realizing Morgan was behind him. "Gus, you don't need to go."

"I want to be there, no matter what. Can you get me a pistol?"

Waverly grinned and wrapped his arm around his friend's shoulders to help him into the fuselage, where Fisherman was already updating the pilot on their new destination.

The helicopter made the short flight to Freedom Square over streets packed with merrymakers waving the red, black, and green flags of the revolution. The pilot banked across the square teeming with people and landed on top of an old municipal building adjacent to the Atiq Mosque.

"Chico and Puckeater," Fisherman yelled, pointing, "you two take those stairs down to the square and approach from the front of the mosque. Cover any attempts to escape into the square. The rest of us will head down that back stairwell and around the outside of the square to the north side where the imam resides. We'll enter there."

The street outside the square was loaded with gleeful revelers dancing and setting off fireworks. The nearest appeared to be stunned by the sudden appearance of armed and goggled soldiers. The covert operators pushed their way along the building and through the mob to the mosque. Rounding the corner of the building, they found a small stone staircase up to a plain wooden door near the ornately carved entrance to the minaret. A sign over the door read IMAM SAYID ESHATI.

Fisherman took the stairs two at a time and pounded on the door. "Open up!" he yelled in Arabic. "In the name of the National Transitional Council, open this door!"

A few seconds passed before a clatter on the other side of the door signaled someone was about to comply.

Waverly took a position beside the door. "Drop any weapons, or we'll shoot!"

The door cracked open and a frail, bespectacled man with a full white beard peered out. "I'm Imam Sayid Eshati. What do you want?"

Fisherman pushed the door open, and five of the Americans pushed inside.

"Where is your closet?" Waverly demanded.

"What closet?" the bewildered imam replied.

"The one where Abdul-Karim al-Rashid stored the bomb."

The old man's eyebrows shot up. "What bomb?"

"It looks like a large backpack with several straps."

The imam's lips made a circle. "Ohhh, he told me it was a tent. I was doing him a favor storing it here because he'd lost his home in the fighting."

Waverly glanced at Morgan and rolled his eyes. "Where did you store it?"

"Right over here." The imam shuffled across his reception room to a closed door and pulled it open.

Fisherman grabbed a flashlight from his belt. The closet was empty except for an umbrella leaning against the wall in the back corner.

The bottom of Waverly's stomach seemed to drop out from under him. "Where is it?"

"Al-Rashid took it two days ago. He bade me farewell, loaded it into the back of a truck, and drove away."

"Oh my God," Waverly muttered, pressing both hands to his eyes. *What do we do now?*

He dropped his hands wearily. "Sir, I hope you had nothing to do with al-Rashid's scheme. That was a big bomb he was storing in your closet, and he aims to kill a lot of people with it."

The imam's mouth dropped open. "I hope you find him before he can do that, Inshallah. I had nothing to do with this. I'm just an old imam."

"I believe you. Did he leave you a phone number?"

"Nothing but a fifty-dinar banknote."

"Did he say where he was going?"

"No, he just said goodbye—but wait a moment," the imam said, poking at his forehead. "I remember the truck driver asking what road he should take to Tobruk. Al-Rashid told him to take the Charruba–Timimi road."

"Was it a pickup truck?" Waverly asked.

The imam shook his head. "A big white truck like they use to deliver furniture."

"What day was that again?"

"Tuesday, right after the Maghrib prayer. I remember because my nephew came over right after that."

"Do you remember anything else they said?"

"I'm sorry, that's all I remember."

Waverly smiled appreciatively. *Okay, I can work with that.* "Thank you, sir. You've been very helpful."

The team crowded out back into the street.

"Tobruk," Waverly said. "That has to mean one of three things. Either they plan to ship it from the port, fly it out of the airport, or drive it into Egypt."

"It'd be suicide to drive into Egypt," Morgan said. "The Egyptians are all over that border."

He nodded. "Agreed. So, it's either the harbor, the airport, or they're relocating it to another hiding spot in Tobruk. Gus, can you call the Tobruk port authority? Get a list of all the commercial and military ships that have left the harbor since last Tuesday or will be leaving during the next week. There can't be that many of them with the war going on."

Morgan nodded. "And I'll call Mahmoud Jibril and get him to grease the skids."

"Redbeard, you call the Tobruk Airport and find out about commercial and private flights over the past two days and next week."

"I remember an email that said the runways had been severely damaged in the fighting and were being repaired," Fisherman said. "If that's the case, there might not have been any flights."

"Let's hope so. It'll take us just short of two hours to fly to Tobruk. Let's get into the air while Gus and Redbeard are checking the port and the airport. If those don't pan out, we can start searching Tobruk for the white truck."

The helicopter flew out across the darkened sea past the coastal city Derna as Redbeard and Morgan worked their satellite phones.

Redbeard got his information first.

"The runways at Tobruk Airport still aren't operational. No flights have left for over five days, and it'll be at least a week before the repairs are completed."

Waverly nodded. "So that's one less route to worry about. Strong work."

Twenty minutes later, Morgan pulled off his earphones and dived into the seat beside Waverly with his notes in hand.

"Two freighters departed Tobruk yesterday. Both were Indian-flagged, medium-size freighters owned by Elektrans Shipping. They were both transporting wool and cattle hides headed for Mumbai. I alerted the US Navy, and two destroyers are closing in on them. They should intercept within four hours."

"Excellent. Do they know what they're looking for?"

"I called Deputy Secretary Steinberg, and he'll alert the navy and the ship captains."

"Perfect. Is that it?"

"No, there's a freighter scheduled to leave for Shanghai tomorrow at 1400 hours. It brought in a shipment of trucks and is leaving Tobruk empty, headed for Malta to take on cargo there."

"Okay, we'll need to check that one out. Anything else?"

"One more: the *Theo B*, an oil tanker that departed the Hariga oil terminal in Tobruk less than an hour ago. It was scheduled to take on six hundred thousand barrels of oil from the newly opened facility. But after taking on less than half that, the captain suddenly ordered the terminal workers to halt further loading and announced an early departure."

Waverly stared into Morgan's bulging eyes. "Did they say why?"

Morgan shook his head, looking energized. "After the port pilot went aboard to direct the tugs, he reported a lot of tension aboard the ship. They even left behind one crew member who'd gone to buy supplies. The ship's newly filed papers say it's headed to North Atlantic Refinery in Newfoundland and Labrador, although their original papers show them headed to Manila."

Waverly frowned. "From the Philippines to Canada?"

"Yeah, a refinery owned by the Korea National Oil Corporation, known for buying oil from whoever's cheapest."

"All that way with less than half a load? Something's not right."

"That's what I thought. The harbormaster gave me their current positon, speed, and direction. That puts them almost exactly due north of our current position, headed northwest at fifteen knots."

"We've got to check them out. Give the pilot that information and tell him to set an intercept course at maximum speed. Ask him for an ETA. Also, see if you can get a blueprint of the tanker."

"Will do." Morgan headed up to the cockpit.

Waverly leaned back and thumped Fisherman on the knee. "Fisherman, tell the team to be prepared to fast-rope onto the deck."

"You got it." He scooted to the back of the fuselage.

Waverly was left in the darkness of the cabin looking out the door at the dark sea below. Exhaustion had set in, and his arms and legs felt shaky.

I can see the report now: "Waverly fell from the helicopter trying to fast-rope onto the deck of the tanker."

45

The RA-115-2

The pilot's got the *Theo B* on radar, ETA eleven mikes. Here's the blueprint of this type of Aframax-class tanker," Redbeard said, showing Waverly and Fisherman his computer screen. "She's 236 meters long and has a normal crew of twenty-five, but they set sail with nineteen."

Fisherman studied the blueprint. "We should fast-rope onto the bow behind this crane and then assault the superstructure through these twin hatches. I think you should stay on the helo."

"No way in hell! I'm the only one who knows how to disarm the backpack bomb."

Fisherman gave him an even look. "Have you ever fast-roped out of a helicopter?"

"It's been a while, but I'll be fine."

"Then let's get ready."

The helicopter streaked across the water toward its target. "One mike," the copilot yelled from the cockpit.

Waverly pulled his night-vision binoculars from their case. "Circle the ship once before putting us down," he shouted.

"Yes sir," the copilot replied.

"She's running dark. No lights at all. Twenty seconds."

The helicopter went into a banking turn, bringing the silhouette of the tanker superstructure into view.

Waverly peered through his binoculars. "There's a man outside on the aft deck holding another man at gunpoint," he said. "Put us down on the bow deck."

The helicopter came to a hover above the deck, and Fisherman threw out two ropes. "Gus, release the ropes when we're all down."

"Sure," Morgan replied. "Good luck!"

Deadeye sat down with his feet dangling out the door and his AK slung over his back.

"Go," Fisherman yelled, the wind whipping his hair beneath his helmet.

Deadeye fast-roped down to the deck with Fisherman right behind him. Waverly went next, in an uneventful, but awkward, descent, and drew his pistol. Puckeater came last. A burst of machine-gun fire erupted when he was halfway down. He dropped to the deck as bullets ricocheted off the crane behind them.

Waverly knelt beside the motionless Puckeater. He pulled his jacket aside, exposing a gaping wound in his neck.

"He's dead."

"You sons of bitches!" Fisherman shouted. "Deadeye, Redbeard, lay down cover fire on the superstructure."

The two operators rose and fired. Tracers flashed off the railings on the upper deck. Fisherman and Waverly dashed up the walkway on the port side as Chico and Checkmate sprinted up the other side. Someone on the upper deck rose to fire, and Deadeye cut him down with a short burst.

Fisherman ducked through the port hatch at the base of superstructure. "Let's head directly to the bridge."

Waverly hoofed up the stairs behind Fisherman. *I'm too damn old for this crap.* He paused to catch his breath on the third landing.

A shot rang out above him. He finished the ascent to find Fisherman standing over a dead Arab as a bridge officer motioned Chico and Checkmate in through the starboard hatch.

"Thank you," the Filipino officer said breathlessly. "They killed Captain Bartley."

"Where are the other terrorists?" Waverly demanded.

"You killed one on the observation deck. The other two ran down the ladder. They may be in one of the staterooms or down in the engine compartment. Be careful—their leader is a savage."

"What's your name?"

"Filipi Martinez. I'm the first mate."

"Mr. Martinez, how many staterooms do you have?"

"Fifteen. Several of my crew are tied up with Captain Bartley's body in the staterooms one deck down."

He glanced out the rear porthole at the helicopter hovering above the stern. "Where did the terrorists stow their luggage?"

"Two decks down, in the tourist staterooms. They paid tourist fares to Manila, then took over the ship and killed the captain when he refused to change our destination to a refinery port in Canada. Then they forced me to do it."

"Chico," Waverly said, "stay here with Captain Martinez and help him set course back to Tobruk. Checkmate, search the captain's quarters while Fisherman and I search the tourist staterooms."

Waverly and Fisherman ducked into the companionway and raced down the ladder to the next landing.

Waverly ducked his head around the bulkhead. The passageway was empty. He'd pushed through the hatch and taken two steps when a rifle barrel poked through the first stateroom hatch and fired a burst.

Fire exploded in his torso, and he went down. Fisherman returned fire and caught the shooter in the abdomen. The man crumpled to the deck outside the door.

"Waverly," Fisherman said. "Are you hit?"

He rolled to a sitting position. "Yeah, it hit my vest but I'm okay."

"Stone Waverly," a gruff voice called from the first stateroom. "Is that you?"

"Al-Rashid?" Waverly yelled. "It's me, all right. You're finished. Come out with your hands up."

"We're all finished. I set the timer on the bomb. I'll have my revenge very quickly."

Waverly looked back at Fisherman as he scrambled to his feet. "Rush him! Now!"

He fired his pistol at the stateroom hatch and burst through into the stateroom.

Where the hell is he? The porthole gaped over the now illuminated main deck below.

Al-Rashid burst from the bathroom and shouldered his rifle. Waverly fired. The shot struck al-Rashid in the chest. His mouth dropped open. He stumbled and garbled something unintelligible before collapsing to the deck.

Waverly kicked the rifle toward the door, stepped over al-Rashid, and knelt beside a ratty-looking, faded green backpack with two large straps stashed in a dusty corner of the stateroom.

The RA-115-2 nuclear backpack bomb.

"How much time?" Fisherman called out from behind him.

"Thirty-seven seconds."

He hit the deck with his legs straddling the bomb. *God, help me remember the sequence.* He wiped his clammy hands on his pants and fished a pair of wire cutters from the breast pocket of his jacket.

23...22...21... He cut the red wire behind the timer and lifted a small access door beside the timer.

13...12...11... He cut a second wire inside.

8...7...6... He unscrewed a wingnut with his fingertips, lifted out the timer itself, and cut one of three wires protruding beneath it.

A buzzer blared from the mechanism.

"Oh, shit!" he cried. *The CIA manual didn't mention anything about a damn buzzer.* He stared helplessly at the timer as it continued: 3... 2...1...

Silence.

He braced himself for a delayed reaction.

Nothing.

"I did it." He rolled backward and clutched al-Rashid's bloody shirt. "Did you hear that, you bastard? I did it. I did it!"

46

Homeward Bound

Waverly leaned against the window of the Toyota Land Cruiser and reached for Sofia's hand. "Are you happy?"

"Very," she replied with a smile, squeezing his hand.

Hanson slowed the armored vehicle to a stop beside one of the Mi-17s, stepped out, and opened the rear door for Waverly, Sofia, and Roberto.

Waverly slid out of his seat first. It was a cloudless sunny day with a soft, warm breeze blowing through the palm trees beside the armory. "What a fabulous day," he called as Morgan jumped down from the helicopter. "The OPS team got the word this morning they're headed home in two weeks. Does that mean you're leaving too?"

"That's the word," Morgan said. "But I'm worried they're pulling us out too early. I'd like us to stay here during the transition."

Waverly nodded as he helped Sofia from the car. "I share your concern, but I've heard the NTC wants all NATO forces out of Libya immediately."

"They may regret that in a few weeks."

Roberto emerged. "So, what's our itinerary, gentleman?"

Morgan beamed, obviously pleased by what he was about to impart. "Good morning, Mr. Pellegrini. This helicopter will fly you to the

French aircraft carrier *Charles de Gaulle* cruising just off the coast. From there, a French jet will fly you to NAS Sigonella in Sicily. Then tomorrow, you'll fly on a big bird to Langley Air Force Base in Virginia."

"That sounds like a great adventure," Roberto replied.

"And hopefully, a calm one," Waverly added.

"Stone hates choppy helicopter flights," Fisherman said with a chuckle.

"You've got that right." He shook the operator's hand. "Thank you for everything. I'll put in a good word when I get back home."

"Thanks. I'm sorry as hell one of our operators put your life in danger."

He patted Fisherman on the shoulder. "All's well that ends well." He glanced back at Redbeard, who was joking with Sofia about how much luggage she was bringing. "So where is Spaceman now?"

"They shipped him out yesterday."

"Is it true?"

Fisherman frowned. "Is what true?"

"That his parents were killed in the Lockerbie bombing?"

Fisherman nodded curtly. "I got confirmation yesterday. He hid it all these years. Apparently, his life goal was to personally avenge their deaths. It's incredible—what are the odds?"

"Probably about the same as winning Powerball. It certainly explains his complete disregard for personal safety on all those operations. Still, I hope they're not too hard on him."

"I recommended a psychiatric evaluation, but they'll probably just fire him. I'm sure he feels like he accomplished his mission."

"Undoubtedly."

Fisherman grinned. "But I still want to know how the hell you managed to get away from Gaddafi's prison in Sirte."

Waverly gathered Sofia under one arm. "Well, after not sleeping all night, I heard huge explosions in the distance and knew immediately that someone had attacked the caravan. Before long, I heard someone going from cell to cell unlocking doors. I was certain I was about to be executed."

"I can't imagine," Fisherman muttered.

"And then, my door opened, and it was my interrogator, Salef. He just said, 'Come with me,' and I followed him through prisoners milling around in the hall outside their cells. He led me outside to a small car, and we pulled out of the parking lot onto a deserted residential street. I was flabbergasted. I finally just asked him where we were going. He said, 'I'm driving you to Benghazi.' And he did."

He looked down and kissed Sofia on the forehead.

"Incredible," Fisherman said. "He drove you all that way to Morgan's compound?"

"Every single mile. What should've been a four- or five-hour drive turned into an eight-hour crawl. Once we got past Ras Lanuf, we ran into spontaneous celebrations in every village and town along the way. The whole time, he talked about the eighteen months he'd spent studying engineering at Purdue."

"He was a Boilermaker?" Fisherman asked with a grin.

"Yeah. He started out as an electrical engineer, but eventually his bosses realized he made a better interrogator. Anyway, he just pulled to the side of the road a block away from Morgan's compound, wished me luck, and drove off into the mob. There were people all around me carrying on and celebrating and trying to get me to join them. Finally, I made it to the guard shack with no ID whatsoever. I told the guard I was Stone Waverly, and he looked at me like I was some crazy-ass homeless person. He just said, 'Yeah, okay, what do you want?'"

Fisherman's eyes bulged. "Who was it?"

He shrugged. "I don't know. I'd never seen him before. But he finally called in when I mentioned Morgan's name, and the next thing I knew, Hanson was at the gate."

Fisherman grinned at Sofia. "Your man is something else—that's a story for the ages. How was your call to Mike and Anne?"

"Awesome. They were so happy when I told them I'd be home soon." Waverly glanced around. "Where's everyone else?"

"They're all with Chico helping the rebels disarm hardcore loyalists in Sirte. They told me to say goodbye, and Deadeye gave me this to give you." He handed him a folded paper.

Waverly unfolded it and found a home address and phone number in Lubbock, Texas. "Give them all my best."

"To you too," Fisherman said. "Safe travels."

They shook hands, and Waverly left Sofia temporarily with Roberto as he approached Morgan conversing with Hanson by the Toyota Land Cruiser. Morgan beamed and spread his arms.

"Thanks for everything," Waverly mumbled from deep within the embrace.

"It won't be the same around here without you."

He patted Morgan on the shoulder. "What's your next assignment?"

"It's unofficial, but Hardy tells me I'm in line to be the first ambassador to the new Libya—that is, if the president agrees and the Senate confirms me."

"Congratulations! They better confirm you, or they'll be hearing from me."

"Thanks, buddy. Best of luck to you and Sofia and the kids."

"My next great mission," he replied with a laugh.

"Something tells me it'll all work out fine."

He patted Morgan on the back one last time. "We expect a visit when you get back to the States. None of this 'I'm too busy' crap."

"You can bank on it."

Just as he was escorting Sofia and Roberto to the helicopter, Jalal bin Koussa came sprinting across the tarmac.

"Mr. Waverly! Mr. Waverly! I was afraid you'd left."

He put out his hand to shake, but Waverly pulled him into a hug. "You've gotten so big!"

"Did you hear?" Jalal asked excitedly. "I shot Muammar Gaddafi."

"It was your duty—but don't ever take pride in killing another man, son, and pray to God he's the last man you must kill. Do you understand?"

"Yes, Mr. Waverly. Inshallah, I want this too. Thank you for changing my life, sir. Without you, I'd still be a servant boy."

Waverly laughed. "I doubt that. Something tells me you will find success in life no matter what obstacles you face."

"Would you still be willing to recommend me for engineering school?"

"Of course." Waverly pulled a pen and a slip of paper from his pocket. "This is my personal email address. Send me a note about who needs the letter and their address. Good luck to you, son." He hugged Jalal one last time and stepped up into the helicopter with Sofia and Roberto.

The Mi-17 lifted off as soon as its passengers got settled, and Waverly waved through the window at Morgan, Jalal, and the others standing together in front of the armory. He watched until they were out of sight.

Sofia leaned against him with her eyes closed. He took her hand. "Are you okay?"

"Yes—but pinch me. I can't believe we're leaving Libya. You're the miracle sent by God to save us, and I love you, my darling, with all my heart. Thank you again for taking *Babbo* too."

He kissed her forehead. "I love you, Sofia, and there was no way in hell I was leaving Libya without you." He grinned. "Even if it means bringing your father along."

She smiled and leaned back onto his shoulder.

The helicopter banked to the north and flew along the desert. After a few minutes, Waverly got a long, final view of Benghazi.

They sped over Benghazi Medical Center and the Tibesti Hotel and skirted Benghazi Harbor.

His mind drifted to al-Rashid and the RA-115-2. *Where had the terrorist been heading? He'd probably intended to divert the ship to New York, every terrorist's dream target, and blow it up at the oil terminal. Or maybe Boston. It didn't matter now—at least until the next backpack bomb disappeared.*

But that's not my problem.

He patted Sofia's knee and kissed her softly again.

The Virginia sunlight dazzled Waverly as he stumbled down the steps from the airplane, shielding his eyes and calling out toward the knot of people gathered below.

"Mike! Anne!" He rushed across the tarmac and swept them both into his embrace. "Dear God, thank you," he whispered, kissing them both on the top of the head.

Beatrice and Marilyn Harrison stood beaming behind them.

"Thank you, Beatrice. And you too, Marilyn."

Harrison smiled. "It's my honor and privilege. You had us all worried for a while there, but I knew you'd accomplish everything you set out to do."

"Did you bring us presents?" Anne asked.

He grinned. "Of course! They're in my luggage. But first, I want to introduce you to our new friends."

Sofia and Roberto had just made it to the bottom of the ramp. Waverly beamed as they approached their little group.

"This is Sofia and Roberto from Benghazi," he said. "They've received political asylum in the United States, and we'll be helping them get settled in Richmond."

"In our house?" Anne asked suspiciously.

"No, honey," Waverly replied, "in their apartment downtown."

Sofia smiled and took Anne's hand. "It's so nice to finally meet you. Your father has told me so much about you. How's your puppy?"

"She's fine. But she's a little pesky sometimes."

"Well, I'm looking forward to meeting her too. Cece, is that her name?"

"Yep—and she's house-trained now."

"That's wonderful." She smiled at Mike and shook his hand. "Mike, it's my pleasure to meet you too. Your father's right, you're a handsome young man. Is Warrior doing fine too?"

"Yes ma'am. She's getting a checkup at the vet this afternoon."

"I understand you are quite a good chess player."

"I won the eighth-grade chess tournament last month."

"Splendid," Sofia replied. "It will be nice to have someone skilled to play with, since your father apparently can't keep up. Let me introduce you to my father, Roberto Pellegrini. He taught me chess."

Mike offered his hand. "It's a pleasure to meet you, Mr. Pellegrini. Welcome to America."

Roberto enthusiastically shook Mike's hand. "Thank you, Mike. It's a pleasure to be here in this great country. I always dreamed of visiting."

An awkward silence fell over the group as Waverly looked around at the faces he loved. *God bless America. This is exactly why I accepted the mission—and why I'll never consider another one.*

What was left to say when you'd just slogged through hell and were standing back in heaven once again?

THE END

ALSO BY STEVEN E. WILSON

Winter in Kandahar

AFGHANISTAN—the name conjures images of rugged mountains, ancient cities, hardened Mujaheddin, a country rife with regional rivalries, and the eternal struggle between Tajik and Pashtun. Afghanistan comes to life in this epic adventure of love, betrayal, and war. Young Tajik Ahmed Jan's heroic journey begins in the Northern Alliance stronghold near Taloqan just a month prior to 9/11. He is swept away by the chaos that soon engulfs the country before a chance discovery propels him to the forefront of the clash between civilizations. Pursued by both the CIA operative Stone Waverly and al-Qaeda, Ahmed Jan struggles to save his people from obliteration and find the true meaning of life in a land where all seems lost.

Ascent From Darkness

A top CIA agent, Stone Waverly, entrusted with a mission to find weapons-grade uranium in the heart of the Islamic world, becomes a real life "007" who sacrifices family for duty to country when he joins U.S. forces and Iraqi peasants alike in a quest to change the face of the Middle East after the overthrow of the Butcher of Baghdad. Masterfully using known facts of the Iraq war, including where weapons of mass destruction may have been hidden and how Saddam Hussein was toppled, Wilson creates a rich fiction which takes you through Syria and Iraq in search of stolen Ukrainian uranium, which, if not found, will almost certainly be used by terrorists. This thriller unfolds like a motion picture, complete with forbidden romance, desperate Special Forces operations, and a never-say-die love of country.

The Ghosts of Anatolia

The Ghosts of Anatolia is an epic tale of three families, one Armenian and two Turkish, inescapably entwined in a saga of tragedy, hope, and reconciliation. Beginning in 1914, at the start of the Great War, confident Ottoman forces suffered a devastating defeat at the hands of the Russians. Pursuing Russian forces drove deep into eastern Anatolia, and the ensuing conflagration, fanned by fear, mistrust, and sedition, engulfed the Ottoman Empire. What happened there is contentiously debated, and to this day remains a festering sore of division. This compelling adventure novel brings these events poignantly to life.

STEVEN E. WILSON, MD was born in Oklahoma City and grew up in Whittier, California and attended California High School. He received a B.A from CSU Fullerton in 1974 and an M.S in molecular biology and biochemistry from the UC Irvine in 1977. He was instructor of biology and chemistry at Rio Hondo College in Whittier from 1977 to 1980. He received his MD from UC San Diego in 1984. He completed his ophthalmology residency at the Mayo Clinic in Rochester, MN in 1988 and was a fellow in cornea and refractive surgery at LSU Eye Center in New Orleans from 1988 to 1990.

Dr. Wilson was assistant/associate professor at UT Southwestern in Dallas from 1990 to 1995. He was professor of cell biology, neurobiology and anatomy and medical director of refractive surgery at the Cleveland Clinic in Cleveland from 1995 to 1998. From 1998 to 2003, he was chair of ophthalmology and Grace E. Hill Endowed Chair in Vision Research at University of Washington in Seattle. Since 2003, he has been professor of ophthalmology and staff refractive and corneal surgeon at the Cleveland Clinic in Cleveland. He was also the cornea and refractive fellowship director there from 2006 to 2017. Dr. Wilson's laboratory is focused on cellular and molecular interactions involved in wound healing and diseases of the cornea, and has been funded by the National Eye Institute of NIH from 1992 to 2021 and supported by several awards from RPB, including the William and Mary Greve International Research Scholar from 1992 to 1994.

Dr. Wilson has authored more than 250 peer-reviewed medical and scientific publications and book chapters. He has received numerous other awards, including a Senior Honor Award from the American Academy of Ophthalmology in 2004, Lans Distinguished Lecturer Award from ISRS-AAO in 2006, ARVO Gold Fellow in 2009, Lifetime Presidential Award from ISRS-AAO in 2009, the Jose Ignacio Barraquer Award from International Congress of Cataract and Refractive Surgery in 2010, and the Richard L. Lindstrom CLAO Award Lecture at ASCRS in 2013.

Dr. Wilson's academic career offers him the opportunity to travel the world, including taking numerous trips to the Middle East and Central Asia over the past 30 years. He wrote his first published novel shortly after the terror attacks of 9/11, although a few chapters of *Winter in Kandahar* were actually written before those events, including Chapter 28 that takes place in Venice—which was the first chapter written when Dr. Wilson visited the city during Carnival that same year. But the nascent novel was re-focused when later that year he landed in Amsterdam on September 11, 2001 shortly before the attackers hit New York and Washington DC. The second Stone Waverly novel, *Ascent from Darkness,* soon followed. *The Ghosts of Anatolia* followed a few years later and could not include Stone Waverly. After receiving dozens of letters and emails asking, "What happened to Stone Waverly?" he decided to write *The Benghazi Affair.* Will this novel really be the end for character Stone Waverly? "Never say never," Dr. Wilson says.